PRAISE FOR AMANDA DOWNUM

"Ethereal, atmospheric, and mysterious."

—Elizabeth Bear, author of *Karen Memory* and *Shoggoths in Bloom*, and winner of the Hugo, Sturgeon, Locus, and Campbell Awards

"Amanda Downum's work is always atmospheric and full of character. These stories range from the melancholic to the downright chilling, and deftly evoke both the truly strange and the very human. I enjoyed them."

—Liz Bourke, reviewer for *Tor.com* and *Locus Magazine*

"Amanda Downum's prose is intoxicating, sensual, layered—both addictive and poisonous, a shot of absinthe with an opium smoke chaser. The stories in *Still So Strange* run the full pleasure/pain gamut of the dark fantastic, offering a bastard cornucopia of gods, monsters and monster-gods, gorgeous terrors etched in salt and blood and gold. It's Clive Barker crossed with Tanith Lee set to a Siouxsie and the Banshees beat, and I loved every second of it."

—Gemma Files, Shirley Jackson Award-winning author of *Experimental Film*

"Amanda Downum's prose is the undertow, gently pulling, promising beautifully cold oblivion in smothering darkness. She makes me shiver and want to lean back and let that pull whisk me away to unimagined places. Downum's not just one of my favorite writers, she's one of the very best dark fantastical writers working today."

—Bracken MacLeod, author of *Come to Dust* and *13 Views of the Suicide Woods*

Still So Strange

ChiZine Publications

Amanda Downum

Still So Strange

Introduction by Orrin Grey

First Edition

Distributed in Canada by
Fitzhenry & Whiteside Limited
195 Allstate Parkway
Markham, Ontario L3R 4T8
Phone: (905) 477-9700
e-mail: bookinfo@fitzhenry.ca

Distributed in the U.S. by
Consortium Book Sales & Distribution
34 Thirteenth Avenue, NE, Suite 101
Minneapolis, MN 55413
Phone: (612) 746-2600
e-mail: sales.orders@cbsd.com

Library and Archives Canada Cataloguing in Publication

Downum, Amanda
[Works. Selections]
Still so strange / Amanda Downum.

Short stories and poems.
Issued also in electronic formats.
ISBN 978-1-77148-439-8 (softcover).--ISBN 978-1-77148-440-4
(EPUB)

I. Title.

PS3604.O99A6 2018 813'.6 C2018-900793-1
C2018-900794-X

CHIZINE PUBLICATIONS
Peterborough, Canada
www.chizinepub.com
info@chizinepub.com

Edited by Halli Villegas
Copyedited and proofread by Leigh Teetzel

Canada Council for the Arts Conseil des arts du Canada

We acknowledge the support of the Canada Council for the Arts which last year invested $20.1 million in writing and publishing throughout Canada.

Published with the generous assistance of the Ontario Arts Council.

Printed in Canada

For the Zoo, for everything.

TABLE OF CONTENTS

"We Are the Weirdos, Mister"

The Stories of Amanda Downum

I wish that I could start this by saying that I remember the very first story I ever read by Amanda Downum, but I'd be lying. It may have been one of the stories in this collection, showing up online for the first time at *Strange Horizons* more than a decade ago; it may have been her novel *The Drowning City*, which had captured my imagination even before I ever sat down to read it; or it may have been something she did for the web-based monster-hunting FBI procedural series *Shadow Unit*. What I know for sure is that ever since I read that first story, whatever it was, I've been waiting for this collection. For some people, novels are the thing, but for me there is nothing more precious than a single-author collection of short stories. Anytime I find a new favorite writer, it's always their collection that I seek out first, their *next* collection that I'm waiting for with bated breath. And from the time I read that first story, whatever it may have been, I've known that Amanda was definitely one of my favorite authors.

In the years since, I've been lucky enough to get to know her a little bit, enough to call her a friend. We bonded over *Subspecies* and Sisters of Mercy references; hung out together at conventions like World Horror and the H.P. Lovecraft Film Festival; explored Portland to seek out the infamous local Witch's Castle, because of course we did.

With all that in hand, it seems like I ought to be well-equipped to introduce you to the stories contained in this, the collection that I've been awaiting for so long, but I can't shake the feeling that it might be better to just get out of your way and let you dive in headlong, let the undertow take you down and down and down, as it does so many of the characters in these tales. After all, if you're already reading this, then chances are you have at least *some* idea of what you're in for, though I can tell you from experience, even if you've read some of these stories elsewhere, nothing can fully prepare you for this book.

It's tempting to call many—maybe most—of the stories in this book "urban fantasy," even the ones that don't take place anywhere near a city, but if they are then they're from a breed of urban fantasy that owes more to Clive Barker and early White Wolf RPGs than to anything you're likely to find shelved under that heading these days.

Whatever you want to call them, ultimately these are some of my favorite kinds of stories: spooky tales that crackle with suppressed energy, feeding off influences that range from Lovecraft and Chambers to fairy tales, Norse mythology, and even the zombie apocalypse, but always performing that rare and wonderful alchemy of transmuting the raw stuff of inspiration into the gold of an original and electric vision.

At the edges of these stories, you can always feel larger worlds unfolding, flexing black wings against the night. Some of these tales share threads with one another, and there's at least one that will feel familiar to those who have read Amanda's excellent novel *Dreams of Shreds and Tatters*. In her own author's note, Amanda calls these stories a "fossil record," "mosaic tiles that don't form the picture they were supposed to." But while they may not form the picture they were originally *intended* to form, the one that we are left with is every bit as vivid and tantalizing as any more fully-fleshed creation could ever be.

In these pages, you'll find tales of cruelty and cunning, of desire and desperation and obsession, and yet, what you will *not* find are dreary stories of drudgery or utter despair, in spite of the many grim tidings within. Amanda sees the beauty that lies in longing with a clarity that few others can match, and as frequently as her protagonists struggle against the beast without—or, perhaps more often, the one within—they are also striving toward some transmutation that is often painful, even brutal, but always breathtaking.

What is it like to be the monster? To be the Other? To be the person standing at the edge of the tide, who can neither be a part of the land nor the sea? What space, after all, could ever really be more liminal than the one in the human (or nearly human) heart? Midian may be where the monsters go, but what of those who can't find a home even among the damned? These are the questions asked in Amanda Downum's short stories, and if there are answers to be had, they are never easy ones.

For anyone who has ever stood at the top of a dark staircase and looked down into the shadows below with as much longing as fear, this is the collection for you. It will remind you of why we're afraid of the dark, and also why we nonetheless venture into it.

I'm going to get out of your way now and let you get started. Whether you're new to Amanda's work or, like me, have been waiting for this collection for years, don't just get your toes wet, dive right in. It's dark down there, and cold, but it's also lovely, and there's light where you wouldn't expect.

Orrin Grey
June 2017

Wrack

Wind keened out of the north as they hauled in the last catch, whipping white froth on wave caps and whistling past the rigging. The sky was green, air tangy with the coming storm; waves slip-slapped against the *Calliope*'s hull. The winch groaned under heavy nets.

Not heavy enough, Jess thought, as the net slopped onto the deck, spraying water and scales. A quarter of what his father had caught on a good day. The off-season would be lean. He glanced away with a frown, rubbing his hands together against the bite of the wind.

"Jesus!" Colin shouted.

Jess turned back to the net, followed his mate's wide-eyed stare to a pale line amid the glistening-dark mass of cod. He took a step closer.

Smooth flesh, marbled blue-green. The curve of a thigh, the angle of a knee. A woman's leg.

"Christ," Jess seconded, crouching beside the net. He knotted his fingers in wet nylon and tugged. Writhing fish slid away from a face smooth as ivory. Dark tendrils of hair clung to her cheeks, tangled with net and fins. Stormlight lent an unreal cast to her skin.

He reached out one scarred hand—

She stirred, wide green eyes opening. Jess's heart jerked and he nearly lost his balance. Then she hissed, baring a mouthful of needle teeth, and he fell hard on his ass. His boots slipped on the wet deck as he scrambled back. Colin cursed and jumped away.

Jess could only stare, his tongue gone numb. The woman stared back, eyes huge, pupils crescent-shaped. She pressed a hand against the net, splaying clawed, webbed fingers.

"Mother of God," Colin muttered, moving behind Jess. He crossed himself, then reached for the knife at his belt. The woman hissed again.

"Put that away," Jess said. He found his balance, crawled closer. The deck pitched—the storm was coming. He showed her his open hands, careful as he might with any wild animal. The net had scraped her arms raw, and the abrasions wept watery blood.

"I'm not going to hurt you," he murmured, reaching for his own knife. Her eyes flickered, but she didn't move. Nylon parted under the blade; there'd be hours of mending later. Fish slithered through the gaps, slapping his hands and boots. When the hole was big enough, he stepped away to give her room.

Her eyes flitted from Jess to Colin and back again as she crawled out of the net, landing on her hands and knees amid flopping cod. No mermaid tail, just lean-muscled legs and wide webbed feet. Her hair clung like sea wrack, scales shining like sequins amid its tangled dark length. Something gleamed in her left hand.

She tried to stand, but her feet tripped her up and her legs gave way. Jess sheathed his knife and knelt beside her. "Are you hurt? Do you need anything?"

It took a second to recognize the low sound she made as laughter. "I need the sea." Jess shivered at her sibilant voice.

"Don't we all?" His calm surprised him, like he cut mermaids out of trawl nets every day. He slipped one arm under her shoulders, the other under her knees, and lifted. He nearly expected her to be spun sugar and fairy wings, but she was real and solid as any woman. He grunted as he stood, and she caught his shoulder.

"We'd get more for her than for any load of fish," Colin said. His face was pale, sickly in the dimming light. He still clutched the hilt of his knife.

The woman stiffened. Jess just stared at the other man until Colin flushed and looked aside.

He carried her to the rail, moving carefully on the tilting deck. The sea roiled, whitecaps rocking the ship, scattering spray against his face. The sky to the northeast was nearly black. Jess paused, hip propped against the rail, and stared at the fairy-tale creature in his arms. "Do you grant wishes?" he asked softly.

She smiled a pretty, close-lipped smile. Her face was a pale diamond amid coils of hair. One wet hand brushed his cheek. "Sometimes."

And she rolled out of his arms and vanished into the waves.

His hand closed around something cold and hard. Gold winked between his fingers—a glittering chain, dark flecks of seaweed caught in the links.

Jess studied it for a moment, then tucked it inside his coat and steered his ship back to shore.

The storm that chased them home lasted two days, keeping boats in the harbor and Jess in his house. More time than he'd spent there in a while; strange to stand so long on solid ground, to lie in a bed without the sea to sway him to sleep.

He lay in the dark as rain lashed the windows and ran the golden chain through his fingers like a rosary. The links didn't warm to his flesh, but stayed cold as the wind outside. His father's stories about sea monsters in the Atlantic no longer seemed quite so outrageous.

He fell asleep to storm-song and dreamed of mermaids.

Jess worried that Colin would go to the papers, despite their agreement not to. Colin went to church instead. A week later he came to collect the last of his pay and told Jess he'd found a job in Providence. They parted amiable enough, but the boy wouldn't meet his eyes as they shook hands in farewell. Jess knew he should find a new mate, but he delayed. He took the *Calliope* out alone, but haddock and tuna were only an excuse.

For weeks he found nothing but fish, and not many of them. His father had suffered under harsh regulations and empty seas, and things hadn't gotten better since Jess inherited the ship.

The sea had always been hard, but at least it had given him one moment of magic.

She came back one evening as the sun melted like butter behind the coast. Jess leaned against the rail, nets long since pulled in, staring at the waves rippling gold and marmalade around him.

He didn't startle as she surfaced along the starboard bow, but his heart beat faster. She floated there for a long moment, hair streaming like ink around her. Dying light gilded her face and the curve of her breasts.

"What are you looking for, fisherman?" she asked at last. Her voice was rough, unused.

He pulled the chain out of his pocket; it gleamed like sunlight against his callused palm. "You left this behind." His voice wasn't any smoother than hers, scoured by wind and salt.

She glided closer. "It's yours. For your . . . chivalry." She smiled. A lovely smile, when he wasn't close enough to see her teeth. "And I hardly deserve it, since I was foolish enough to get caught in your net in the first place."

He ran a hand through salt-stiff curls and tried not to think about the impossibility of this conversation. His tongue felt thick and clumsy and he feared she'd vanish if he spoke again.

"What's your name?" she asked.

"Jesse Finn. Jess."

She watched him for a silent moment. "You can call me Morgan."

"Will I see you again?"

"Do you want to?"

His stomach twisted as he remembered her weight in his arms. Maybe this was what seasickness felt like. "I do."

She slid closer to the hull, until he could see the green depths of her eyes. "Don't be so quick to answer, Jesse Finn. I'm of the sea. I'm always hungry. Whatever you give me, I'll take, and then more."

He swallowed hard. "I'm not afraid of the sea."

She sighed. "You should be." Then she was gone, not even a ripple to mark her passage.

Two weeks later he took the *Calliope* out late, past the shallower waters where he fished for cod, haddock, and hake. He dropped anchor and sat on the deck, watching the stars flicker to life. The wind blew gently against his face. For a few hours he didn't worry about money, or the next catch.

She pulled herself over the rail, skin blazing white, hair a midnight river. A cold, wild thing made of salt and starlight. Jess couldn't move, could barely breathe. She took a halting, uncertain step forward and he rose to meet her.

Her skin was so soft he feared to touch her, but she pushed him down, surging and cresting in his arms, strong as the sea itself. Her teeth scathed both their mouths. He tasted her blood and his—iron and copper and salt sweetness. The cold deck bruised his back, and salt water burned his eyes, but he didn't care. He drowned in her.

Afterward she lay beside him, warm and gentle. Splinters and stray scales poked his bare flesh, but he ignored them. The stars wheeled overhead as they lay together, skin to sticky skin.

"I can't stay with you," she said at last, barely audible over the soft susurrus of the waves.

He ran a hand over her hairless arm, tracing the snake-soft pattern of scales. "I know." The thought of her on dry land, in his tidy little house, was obscene.

"You can't stay with me, either."

His hand paused, then continued its caress. "Why not? This is my home, too."

"This, maybe—" her gesture took in the *Calliope*'s deck, the rigging over their heads "—but not the rest. I can't give you breath with a kiss and take you to my palace below the sea."

He smiled, face half-buried in the seaweed tangle of her hair. "Do you have one? A palace?"

Cool fingers traced the curve of his lips. Salt stung the claw-wounds on his back. "My father does. It's not a place you'd care to visit."

He might have spoken, but she kissed him again, soft and sweet, and stole his voice away.

Three nights he sailed out and met her under the stars. Each time she told him not to stay, each time she was gone in the morning.

On the fourth night her face was grim, and she held back from his embrace.

"I can't meet you anymore." Her tone was cold, but she wouldn't meet his eyes. "My father is unhappy." She glanced toward the choppy black water. "He's . . . jealous."

"I don't care."

"You will." The ice in her voice cracked and she reached out to cup his cheek in one webbed hand. "Please, Jess. You knew how this would end."

He did know. There was no other way. He should simply be grateful for the little time he'd been given.

"Stay close to the shore," she continued. "Catch your fish. Don't look for me again." She stepped into his arms, clumsy on flippered feet. "Let your nets down tonight, and I'll grant you a wish."

"Grant me two." He tilted her face up to his. She let him.

When he hauled in his nets the next morning, they were heavy with fish, rotting wood, and cloth. The fabric split under his touch, and yellow gold gleamed in the light.

For two weeks he did as Morgan asked, trawling close to the shore, keeping his eyes turned away from the broad expanse of the Atlantic. The treasure she had given him was enough that he didn't need to fish again for a long time, but he couldn't keep himself busy on land. He slept on the ship, but even the rhythm of the sea didn't quell his restless, longing dreams.

In the third week his resolve broke. He turned the *Calliope* toward open water.

The storm thundered from the north with barely a gust of warning. The sky turned black as a bruise, and the waves churned into deadly walls of water. The ship was tossed like a toy, tossed and cracked and swallowed down. Before darkness took him, Jess thought he heard Morgan's voice.

He woke battered and half-drowned on the beach, arms locked rigid around a life preserver. The *Calliope*'s wreckage lay scattered on the rocky shore.

When his legs worked again and he stopped vomiting seawater, he staggered home. Home—that little house trapped on a rock. The only home he had now. That night he cried for the first time in years.

But he had his gold, and he didn't starve. Not for food, at least. At night he stood on the cliff and watched the moon rise like yellow silver. He listened for a voice among the churning waves, but it never came.

Three months after the storm, he met Jaime.

She tended bar in a little pub by the docks. Her hair was the color of pirate's gold, her eyes deep and rich as loam. When she smiled at him he could almost forget the sea.

For months she talked and smiled, touched him with freckled, work-callused hands. Then one night she took him home.

His heart broke the first time they made love, but afterward he fell asleep on her soft shoulder. For once he didn't dream. Steady as stone beneath the softness, and she gave as much as she took.

Weeks rolled on and Jaime stayed. When he came home at night after walking the cliffs she didn't ask questions, just held him, warm and safe. Eventually Jess stopped listening to the call of the waves.

If he couldn't tell her everything, at least he could talk to her about how the loss of the *Calliope* ached inside him, how he'd inherited the ship from his father and always meant to pass it on to his own children.

"I can't have children." Her dark eyes were sad. "Does that—"

"It doesn't matter," he said, pulling her close, letting the peppery sunflower scent of her hair fill his nose.

They were married in a little church on the coast, six months after they met. Just maybe, Jess thought, looking into his wife's warm eyes, he could have a life without the sea.

That night a storm howled down, screaming and sobbing, tearing at the house. Jess sat in the dark long after Jaime slept, bitter tears tracking his cheeks. Finally, he walked out into the raging night.

"You knew how this would end," he whispered.

The storm stole his words and carried them away.

A month after their wedding, Jess and Jaime woke in the night to a high frightened wail coming from the front of the house.

Jaime only had eyes for the wriggling, squalling infant on the porch. She scooped the child up, rocking it against her breast and crooning until its crying stilled. Only Jess saw the wide, bloody footprints leading toward the cliff.

A girl, pink and pale, with a crown of wispy curls as bright as Jess's hair had been before sun and wind dulled it. Her blue eyes were very wide, the webbing between her tiny fingers thicker than it might have been, but she seemed a healthy human child.

Jaime cradled the baby as if she'd never let go. She turned knowing eyes on Jess and his heart splintered a little more.

"Call her Morgan," he said, voice rough.

He still dreamed of the sea, when he wasn't up all night helping with the baby. She laughed at thunderstorms, reaching out for the window with chubby hands as if she could catch the lightning. Jaime loved her, and glowed as proudly as any mother; Jess knew how lucky he was.

But he didn't feel lucky, no matter that he loved his wife and daughter. The little house was tidy and warm, but it wasn't his home, however hard he tried to make it so.

He began to walk the cliffs again, but she didn't return. He couldn't lie to himself anymore as he stared at the wild gray sea. His hands were too soft lately, with no nets to mend. He wore the gold chain round his neck; its links never warmed.

One morning he woke early and stood on the cliff watching the sun rise in a blaze of carnelian fire. A storm tonight.

He spent the morning with Jaime and little Morgan. He ran Jaime's golden hair through his fingers and kissed her so often that she looked at him oddly and asked if he was feeling all right. He only kissed her again. Her answering smile was bittersweet.

He gave the chain to his daughter, who cooed and gummed the cold metal happily.

That afternoon, as the sky darkened to tarnished pewter and the wind blew cold and wild along the shore, he went down to the docks and rented a little stern drive. It looked like a child's toy, so tiny, all shiny white fiberglass. The owner cautioned him about the weather, but took his money happily enough.

Waves slapped a warning against the flimsy hull, tossing the little boat until even Jess was hard-pressed to stay on his feet. But he kept going toward the wild verdigris water.

He shrugged off his wet coat, letting the icy wind slice through his flesh. His hands and feet numbed, but the sea spray tasted like wine against his lips.

She came to him on the worsening storm, breaking free of the surging waves. Her hair streamed in the surf, twining around her white arms as she pulled herself onto the deck.

"Go home, fisherman." The wind whipped at her words, tried to drown their voices.

"I am home," he called. He caught her and held her close.

"Go back to your stone and sand, go back to your mortal wife. Go back to our daughter."

"Our daughter is safe. She'll be loved, happy."

She shook her head. Salt water streamed down her face, though her wide, inhuman eyes couldn't cry. "I can never be all yours, Jesse, even if I wanted to."

"But I'm yours, and I don't want to be anything else."

A wave smashed over the prow, knocking them into the wall of the cabin.

"Turn around," she begged. "I'll keep the storm at bay till you reach the harbor."

Water blinded him, filled his mouth, but he clung to her, the only harbor he'd ever need. He knew how fairy tales really ended.

The deck tilted and shook, tossed them off. For a heartbeat he was flying, falling free. Then the water closed over him, frigid and hungry. Morgan was there, arms and witch-wrack hair wrapped around him, holding him fast. Her mouth closed over his, stole his breath.

He drowned in her.

She took him home.

Dogtown

It was closing on midnight when Seth found the gas station, a dirty nameless place on the edge of a dirty little town. The old car shuddered to a stop, needle on E. Traffic was backed up miles from the Texas border, the asphalt artery of I-35 clogged with cars and diesel-belching semis. Maybe construction, or an accident, but he couldn't risk a roadblock. They must have run his prints by now.

Seth pulled up to the pump; he didn't have enough money for this, but stealing another car would be too stupid even for him. He ran a weary hand over his face and got out of the car. Sweltering air filled his lungs, filmed his skin. The blacktop steamed, spitting back the day's heat.

A dog moved by the door, a big oil slick of a beast. It watched him for a moment, long tongue lolling, before giving way. A flickering beer sign washed his hand red as he reached for the door. Seth froze, then shook his head as the illusion vanished. He was tired was all, too tired. There was no blood on his hands anymore.

The door chimed as he walked in and he squinted against the stuttering fluorescent lights, the bright, ugly colors. His eyes burned from want of sleep. Music blared from a stereo behind the counter, all snarling guitars and guttural vocals. Seth winced away from the noise.

"I'm about to close," the girl at the cash register said, her voice tired and bored. A tiny, bird-boned girl, engulfed by her black T-shirt. Dyed-black hair piled up sloppy, a few inches of brown showing at the roots, lips painted dark and glossy as licorice. A sparrow trying to pass as a crow. Metal gleamed in her nose and eyebrow.

"I just need some gas." He pulled a five out of his wallet. Not nearly enough. He glanced around the empty store, tried not to look at the register. "Where am I, anyway?"

"Nowhere," she said, taking his money. "But it's called St. Christopher." Her nails were bitten down, flecked with purple paint.

"Do you know what's going on down the highway?" He tried to keep his voice casual.

"Roadblock." The register clacked shut, and the printer began to stammer out a receipt. "Cops are looking for some psycho killer. They say he's headed this way."

She glanced up just in time to see him flinch. Her eyes widened at whatever she saw in his face.

His vision tunneled.

Her narrow throat convulsed. "I'm only fucking with you. It's just construction—they're always tearing up the road."

Her voice faded under the hum of blood in his ears. Plastic creaked as his scarred hands gripped the edge of the counter.

Calm down. Breathe.

"Jesus . . ." She had one hand under the counter and tension trembled up her skinny arm. "They *are* looking for a psycho, aren't they?" Her nostrils flared as if she could smell the death hanging off him.

"Put the gun down," he said, soft like he was talking to an angry dog. So tiny—her bones would crunch under his hands, brittle and wet. He shuddered, shoulders tensing against the image. The taste of tinfoil filled his mouth.

He was losing it. Too damned tired. Wound too tight.

She shook her head, stepped back. A revolver, too big for her knobby wrists. The steel gleamed cold and harsh.

"That thing's older than you are." He let out a breath and the haze began to clear from the edge of his vision. He wouldn't slip. Not this time.

"It works." Her hands were steady, finger inside the trigger guard, but not squeezing. Not yet.

"Have you ever shot someone?"

Her eyes narrowed, delicate lids smudged with makeup and not enough sleep. "Have you?"

"Yeah. I don't like it."

"Why not?"

"It's too easy. Makes you stupid."

She met his eyes and her nostrils flared again; the silver stud in her nose flashed. The gun lowered, her finger easing off the trigger. "Are the cops really looking for you?"

Seth hesitated, but he never could lie for shit. "Yeah, I think so."

"What'd you do?"

"Killed one, in Oklahoma City."

The music growled in the background as she paused. She didn't point the gun at him, but she didn't put it away, either. "Did he deserve it?"

"I thought so." He chuckled humorlessly; it came out an ugly sound. "He got rough with a girl, thought a badge should get him a free ride."

She studied him, black gumdrop lips twisting. "Did the girl appreciate being rescued?"

He sighed. "No. No, she freaked out, ran off screaming." He shook his head. *Story of my life, right?*

"What's your name?" the girl asked.

"Seth."

"I'm Sephie. You want something to eat?"

Dogs followed them as she led him down the empty main street, the big black hound and half a dozen others. Sephie bared her teeth when one got too close and the dog fell back with a yip.

"Quiet town." Seth's boots scraped softly against ragged asphalt.

"It's dead. Everyone who could get out, got gone years ago."

"Saint Christopher is the saint of travelers." He'd had a little gold medallion once—he wondered where he'd lost it. Probably in the joint, in a lockup somewhere. They all blurred together lately.

Her laugh was dry and humorless. "That doesn't help those of us who're stuck here."

They passed the town square. Broken windows grinned in the lamplight, yellow and jagged-toothed. Boards on windows, chains on doors, a little lawn in the center all gone to brambles. Dust whispered in the wind, the breath of ghosts. Seth's neck prickled.

A dog howled in the distance. Sephie shuddered, and the other dogs whined.

She took him to a narrow diner down the street. The air smelled of grease and burnt coffee and the one tired waitress's cheap perfume, but at least it was cool. Sweat dried on Seth's back, itched against his scalp.

Sephie didn't speak until their food came, and he didn't press her. She looked stretched tight, too—something had her nervous, and it wasn't the killer across the table. Dark eyes flickered toward the window, and the night beyond.

She toyed with her food for a minute, pushing pieces of pancake back and forth through a puddle of syrup. "I need to get out of here."

Seth kept sawing at his steak. It'd been long enough since he ate that he didn't care how tough the meat was. "Where to?" The light burned his eyes, bouncing off the yellow counters and straight into his brain.

"Anywhere you're going. Anywhere but here."

"And you think traveling with a wanted criminal would be the way to go?" The jukebox played, Patsy Cline singing "Walkin' After Midnight." No one was around to eavesdrop, but he still pitched his voice low.

"I need someone who can take care of himself."

"Honey, that sure as hell ain't me, or I wouldn't be here. How do you know I won't kill you, hurt you?"

"You could have done that already." She wiped a drop of syrup off her lip.

He shook his head. "No offense, but that's some damn stupid logic."

Her lips skimmed back in a grin. "And no offense, but I'm not scared of you."

He shook his head again, looked at her twig-fragile wrists and tried not to smile. Maybe he shouldn't judge, though—he'd known some scrawny little fuckers who could kill quick as a snake and twice as cold.

The door chimed and Sephie paled. Seth turned.

Just a bunch of kids, and he almost relaxed, but the waitress startled too, nearly dropping a pot of coffee. A whiff of fear cut through the greasy air.

The kid in front—a rawboned rangy boy maybe Sephie's age—looked at them and grinned like a fox. Sephie was so tense she practically vibrated. Seth's blunt fingers tightened on his knife and fork.

The kid swaggered over to their booth and leaned in, too close, a grin splitting his gaunt stubbled face. He smelled of musk and cigarettes.

"Made a new friend, Sephie?"

"Leave us alone, Caleb."

Her voice was flat and brittle and Seth frowned at the buried fear. He already wanted to rearrange Caleb's smile. Muscles knotted with the effort of holding still. He couldn't keep losing it like this. But she had asked for help.

Caleb reached across the table and snatched a piece of bacon off her plate, crunched it between long teeth. "If you're hungry, babe, I'll find you something better. Something sweeter."

Her eyes narrowed, makeup crinkling at the corners. "Leave us alone." Brittle, but not cracking yet.

Seth gave Caleb a silent three-count before he grabbed the boy's wrist. "The lady asked you nice." He squeezed till bones shifted. Caleb's nails were long as a girl's, thick and hard, and embedded with dark half-moons of grime.

Seth's grip would leave bruises, but Caleb just grinned down at him, all mocking brown eyes and sharp teeth. Then he twisted free, wiry muscles shifting in his forearms.

"I'll be waiting for you, Sephie." He turned and walked out, his friends falling into formation behind him.

Seth flexed his hand, knuckles cracking. "Is that what you're trying to get away from?"

She nodded, looking tiny and lost.

It was a stupid idea. But his life had been a series of stupid ideas for so long, what was one more? He took another bite of his rubbery steak. He'd need someone to keep him awake, anyway.

"Let's get some gas in the car and we can get out of here."

The dogs were gone when they left, silence echoing down the narrow streets. Caleb was nowhere in sight.

"Is he your boyfriend?"

Sephie frowned, stared down at the dust scuffing around her boots. "Once, yeah. Something like that."

"And he hasn't figured out that past tense part yet?"

"Caleb's real good at ignoring things he doesn't like." Moonlight washed her face gray and darkened the circles under her eyes.

"There ain't nobody else who'll help you?"

"There's nobody left. My folks are gone. All the people I used to know either got out of town when they could or fell in with Caleb."

Seth slowed as they neared the square, and he raised a hand, cutting off whatever Sephie was about to say. Shadows shifted amid the briar-choked lawn, more than just trees.

"Will this guy try something," he asked softly, "or is he all mouth?"

"Mister, his mouth is bad enough."

Caleb melted out of the trees, his buddies hanging back in his wake. The swagger was gone now. He moved lithe and quiet. Seth remembered how easily the kid had broken his grip. He wondered if Sephie would really use that gun.

"Were you coming to see me, Sephie?"

"I'm leaving. You can stay here and piss on trees all you want, but I'm not putting up with your shit anymore."

Caleb moved closer, hands loose at his sides, grin harsh and bright. "Sure, babe. And what are you going to do when you get hungry? Did you tell your new friend about that part, or were you going to surprise him?"

Sephie's fists clenched. "Go to hell."

Seth's vision started to narrow, and the metal taste crept into his mouth again. He glanced from side to side, making sure no one was flanking them. Something slunk through the shadows, but it was only a dog. Caleb's friends seemed happy to wait and watch the show. Voices dulled as Seth's heartbeat thudded in his ears.

"Come with me," Caleb said. "If you want to leave so bad, I'll take you. I'll take you anywhere you want to go. I'll take care of you, Sephie. Keep you safe. Make you strong."

"You'd make me a monster."

"Too late for that. I don't see a suit of shining armor on your new friend. Or do you just like him because he smells like blood?" He cocked his head and his eyes gleamed in the sodium glare.

Sephie stepped sideways. "Come on," she said to Seth. "Let's get out of here."

Caleb reached out and caught her arm, so fast Seth could barely follow. "It's not that easy."

It was Seth's turn to smile. "Sure it is." He grabbed the front of Caleb's shirt, hands tingling with adrenaline. "I hate to beat up kids. Get out of here."

Caleb twisted free, fabric tearing. "You should have stayed out of this, old man."

His hand flickered, a pale blur, and Seth's head rocked back. A second later his cheek began to burn, and moisture dripped down his neck. Not a punch—the kid had clawed his face open.

Sephie lunged in, grabbed Caleb's shoulder. "Caleb, don't—"

He shoved her back without looking, sent her sprawling in the street. His friends moved closer, still waiting. "Run," he growled. "I'll give you a head start."

In response, Seth punched him in the face.

Or tried. Caleb was too damn fast. He ducked around the swing, darted in close. Seth glimpsed a mouthful of teeth and jerked back in time to take the bite in the shoulder instead of the neck. It felt like getting bit by a Rottweiler. He grunted as pain ran down his arm like hot grease. He wrapped his good hand around Caleb's neck and squeezed till the kid let go.

It took all his strength to keep Caleb off him. Shadows and yellow light twisted his features into something ugly, blood dripping down his chin, staining those long teeth. He snarled something, but Seth couldn't hear it, couldn't hear anything. Seth kneed him in the balls, punched again and hit this time. Fire in his knuckles—he must have laid his hand open on the kid's teeth.

Thunder shook the air. Caleb dropped back, crouching on the balls of his feet. Seth staggered away, shaking his head against the blood-haze. Adrenaline turned his nerves to razor wire.

The gun gleamed in Sephie's hands and a plume of dust rose off the ground in front of Caleb's friends.

"You think I won't?" The words reached Seth through a long tunnel.

Caleb turned toward her, started to rise. The revolver roared again and he fell back with a shout. But she missed, or didn't mean to kill. Blood dripped down his arm, soaked his shirt shiny in the moonlight, but it was nowhere close to fatal. The air was thick with copper and salt.

The fight had turned them around and now the snarling trio stood between Seth and Sephie and the street leading to the car. Someone must have heard the shots, but the square stayed dark and silent as the last echoes died off.

Sephie backed away, gun trained. Seth moved with her. Blood dripped off his fingers and the haze began to clear. He felt the pain circling, waiting to bite.

They stepped onto the sidewalk, a row of buildings at their back. "There's a key in the outside pocket of my purse," Sephie said, shifting the bag with a twist of her hips. The gun didn't waver. Caleb and his boys watched them from a respectful distance.

Seth found the key, unlocked the padlock and chain on the door behind them. It creaked open into darkness that smelled like mold and sawdust and he followed her inside.

"You stay here?" Seth asked later, sitting in the dark upstairs. No electricity; candlelight gleamed against broken windows. Dogs howled outside and Caleb cursed on the street below.

"We used to hang out here when we were kids. It was like our clubhouse, or something. I got the lock later, when things with Caleb got bad and I wanted a place to hide sometimes."

"I get the feeling there's more to all this than a lousy boyfriend." Seth sat on a broke-backed old couch, his bloody shirt crumpled in his lap, wrapping a half-assed bandage around his shoulder. The bite wasn't bleeding too bad anymore, but it burned, leaking fire through the muscles in his right arm. His cheek hurt worse, the scratches stuck together with a half-dozen Band-Aids.

"A little more than that, yeah." Her eyes reflected the candle flame.

She fell silent for a moment. Seth finished the bandage, rinsed his hands and face with the bottle of water she'd given him, and tugged the torn shirt back on. Movement hurt, but he'd had worse.

"You want to tell me what Caleb was talking about down there? What it was you didn't tell me to begin with? You strung out?"

"No, I'm not a junkie. That'd be too simple." A lighter cracked and sparked, outlining the curve of her cheek. Smoke drifted through the musty air.

"You got another of those?"

She tossed him a pack of Camels and he tapped one out, lit it off the candle guttering beside him, and sucked in a grateful breath. He watched smoke curl and waited for her to speak. It didn't take very long.

"A man came through town a year ago." She turned away from the light, her voice drifting out of the dark. "A wanderer, a magician—a one-man sideshow, we thought. He told us things, Caleb and me and our friends. Secrets. His smile—" Her voice caught. "He took us down to Hell. He showed us the cracks in the world, all the seams people were never meant to see."

A rock thudded off the back wall. Caleb's friends, watching the back of the building while Caleb paced in the street out front. The gunshot didn't seem to have slowed him down much.

"We were just kids. Bored, half-crazy from living here, this town dying all around us. We talked big, all the places we'd go—L.A., New York, New Orleans—but we all knew we'd never get past Lovegrove or Ardmore." She blew out a plume of shimmering smoke. "You ever feel trapped, like you could just chew your leg off if it would get you out?"

Seth shook his head. He must have been that young once, but he couldn't remember it now. "Yeah. I know trapped."

"We were just kids when we followed him down there, into the between-places. He taught us all kinds of tricks. How to steal secrets from the dead. He showed us what gravemeat can do. We ate, and it changed us."

Another pause, another bouncing rock hit the wall. "You think I'm crazy?"

"Eating dead people does seem a little fucking weird, yeah." His mouth pulled to one side; it hurt his face. Tobacco and paper rasped as he took a drag, cherry flickering between his cupped fingers. He started to reach for the little cross he wore before he remembered he'd lost that, too. "But all the prison shrinks think I'm crazy, and I can't argue, so maybe I shouldn't give you too hard a time. Caleb, on the other hand . . ."

Her laugh was harsh. "Yeah. Gravemeat was one thing, but it wasn't long till Caleb wanted something . . . fresher. That was when everything went to hell."

"The dead may not care what happens to them, but I'm rather partial to all my bits and pieces."

She turned toward him, smoke leaking out of her nose. "I'm sorry you got hurt. I was too scared to leave on my own, and I thought maybe . . ."

"You thought maybe the big crazy guy could look after you."

"Something like that, yeah."

"Honey, I can barely look after myself most days." Sweat trickled down his scalp, stinging his cheek and a few other scrapes he'd picked up along the way. "You could just shoot him, you know."

"Yeah." She moved out of the shadows, perched on the crooked arm of the couch. The cigarette trembled in her hands. "I've done a lot of crazy shit, but I've never killed anyone. I thought I loved him once." She ducked her head, brushed a quick hand over her eyes. "God, I'm such a stupid bitch."

After a minute, he reached out with his good hand, patted her shoulder. His palm engulfed her fragile bones.

She tensed for a second, then leaned in a little closer. Her skin was cold, only a little sticky, and he could feel the tension knotting her muscles. He thought maybe he should hug her, or say something, but he wasn't sure how or what. Probably a good thing he'd never had kids, or a woman who stuck around long enough to need comforting.

"Caleb was right, anyway. After we started . . . eating . . . I don't think I can just give it up anymore. Hell, I can't even quit smoking. I don't know what I'll do."

It made his head ache—he'd never been good with complications. Things went crazy, and then he did, and someone usually ended up hurt. You could never count on a junkie for a damn thing, and he wasn't sure if needing to eat people was better or worse than needing horse in that regard.

Sephie ducked her head again, trying not to let him see her cry. Such a tiny little thing. He still needed someone to keep him awake.

"Why don't we worry about that after we get out of here?"

She looked at him, piercings winking in the light. "We?"

Yeah, it was definitely a stupid idea. "I said I'd take you out of here. But if you try to take a bite out of me, I'm leaving your ass on the side of the road."

He picked up the gun off the rickety table. Too big for Sephie, too small for him, like a toy. His hands remembered, palms and fingers molding against steel. He glanced at Sephie. Fucked up, no doubt about that, but no blood on her hands. What was a little more on his?

Caleb still paced outside, his shadow flung this way and that by the street lamps. He glanced up as Seth moved by the window. "Goddamn it, Sephie, come out and talk to me."

Broken windows shivered with the echo of the shot. A sliver of glass slipped free and shattered on the sidewalk. Caleb fell, a dark halo spreading on the ground around him. He twitched, tried to sit up. Seth squeezed the trigger again. The kid stopped moving.

He set the gun down again and scrubbed his hands on his dirty jeans. Sephie stared at him, eyes shining, one hand pressed over her mouth.

"You ready to get out of here?"

After a minute she nodded. "Yeah. I'm ready."

He followed her out into the dark.

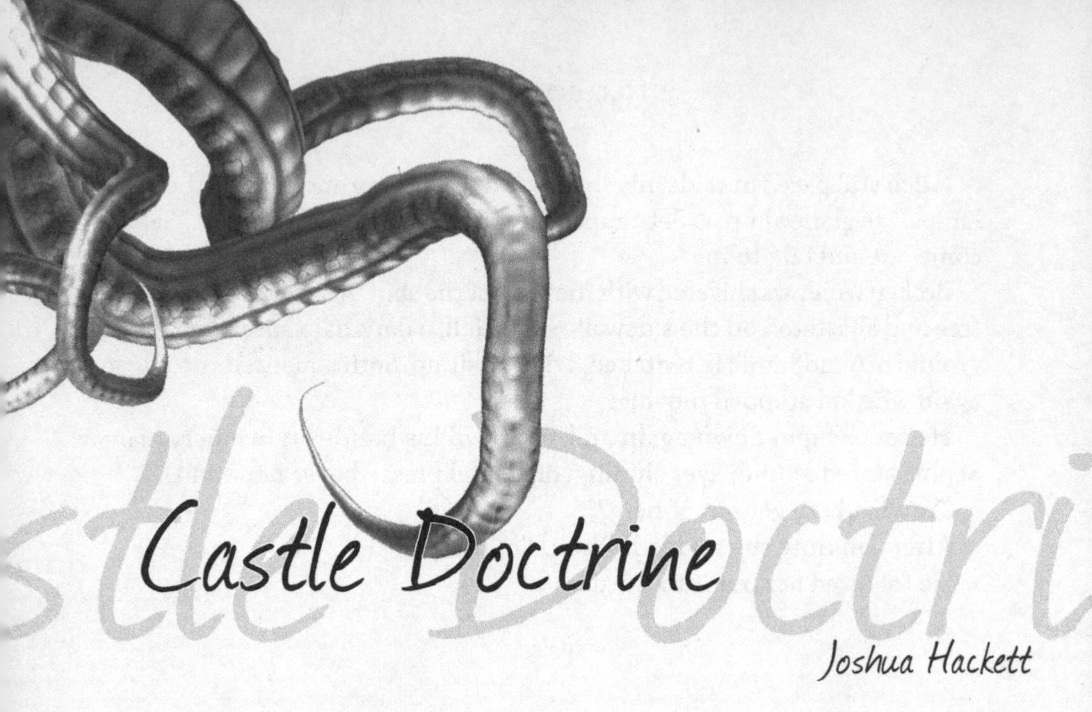

Castle Doctrine

Joshua Hackett

Summer's end
Last wild nights before school
Ugly-minded children knocking over headstones

Castle Doctrine
Applies to occupied graves
But they'd be buried here so we let them go

The Salvation Game

The labyrinth devours light and leaves no bones. Darkness laughs at Lily's flashlight, low chuckles echoing from her every footstep. She trails her left hand along the cold stone wall, searching for any opening.

Keep turning left, the witch said.

Her breath sounds too loud to be her own, some snuffling minotaur stalking her through the dark. The birthmark below her left breast tingles in time with her heartbeat.

Danny is still alive, and close.

Her fingers find a corner and she turns. Grit rasps under her boots; silt coats her hand, itches on her face. The air is too heavy, full of dust that sifted down from rocks cut centuries before she was born. Full of time.

She's deep underground now, the weight of earth and stone pressing close around her, the weight of the cathedral soaring far above her head. Worlds away, those spires and arches, echoing vaults and jeweled Mucha glass. Even farther is the city, and everything real.

Adrenaline roils through her veins. The urge to turn and run is so strong she shakes. But her brother is alive at the center of the maze. She'll find him. She'll bring him out. She has to.

"Are you frightened?"

The woman called Gethsemane lounged against velvet cushions, watching Lily through dancing shadows. Candles burned in bowls of colored glass, their fitful flicker like trapped fireflies.

"Yes." Lily's voice was dry and fragile as dead leaves.

"But you came anyway."

"I don't know where else to go." Lily tried to meet the woman's gaze, but caught only flashes of white skin and black ink. Six months of searching and questioning, six months of dead ends, of people who wouldn't talk to her or had nothing to say. Six months and she ended up here, in this dark room that smelled of poppy spice and anise, of something musky and autumnal. She could only pray that this wasn't another dead end, another waste of time.

"There is nowhere else. Not if you mean to act quickly." Gethsemane leaned forward. Tattoos swirled across the curve of her shaven head, spilled out of her sleeves onto her hands. Shadows limned razor cheekbones, turned her eyes into lightless pools. Lily's skin crawled, but the tingle over her heart held her when she wanted to flee.

"Can you help me?"

"You were clever to get this far, to find me. You've taken risks, put yourself in danger."

She was so tired of playing games. "I need to find my brother. Can you help me?"

"Need is a dangerous thing. I can help you, but what will you do for me?"

Lily swallowed. "Whatever it takes."

"That's a bold promise, and a foolish one. Is your brother really worth so much to you?"

"He's my brother."

The woman cocked a dark eyebrow. "That doesn't entirely answer the question, my dear."

"I have to help him. If I'd—" She stopped, shook her head.

"Go on," Gethsemane said, raising one long white hand. "If . . . ?"

"If I'd found him earlier this wouldn't have happened. I should never have let him run off."

"Ah. So, this is about you. Your guilt."

Her cheeks warmed, but Lily kept her chin up. "My brother is in danger. I need to find him. If you won't help me—"

Gethsemane chuckled. "If I won't help you, then you're quite fucked, aren't you?"

Lily's fingernails bit her palms. "Please."

The postcards started a year after Danny ran away. Montreal, London, Vienna, pictures of cathedrals, of subways, of twisting cobbled alleys, notes written in childhood sibling code. She didn't know how he managed to travel, what he did for money, but the cards said he was all right and she believed him; she would have known if he wasn't.

She dreamed of him: lost dreams, happy dreams, sad and wanting dreams. Dreams of strangers and strange places. Eventually she learned to put them aside, to shove them back in the recesses of her mind where they didn't haunt her during the day. He said he was happy and she told herself that was all that mattered.

She was happy in the home he'd fled, happy with the family who'd taken her in, the first safe and stable home she'd known in years. She was happy—alone in the dark where she could whisper the truth to herself—to have someone looking after her for a change, instead of her constant desperation to keep Danny safe, to keep their mother out of trouble.

She'd failed in that, but it had set her free.

For five years she dealt with that distant echo in the back of her mind. She built a life for herself—family, friends, school, all the simple things she thought she'd never have.

Then the cards stopped and the nightmares started. Dreams of angels and altars, of dark winged things with eyes all full of emptiness and stars. Then her birthmark, their twin-mark, that bruised blue discoloration over both their hearts, began to throb, and Lily knew her brother needed her again.

She followed Gethsemane's directions to Prague, into Old Town, through bitter autumn rain. Icy water soaked her collar, chasing away the jetlag that dragged at her eyes. Somewhere nearby the Orloj chimed the hour.

As Lily neared the Chorea, she knew the witch hadn't lied. Her head echoed with the overlap of someone else's thoughts. After so many years it dizzied her, and she paused on the narrow, cobbled street as the night spun around her in a blur of stinging rain. She heard music, felt the spectral touch of hands on someone else's skin. She felt Danny, and knew he felt her, too.

The miasma of the club enveloped her as she descended the narrow cellar stair, sound and smoke and sweat crawling into her ears and mouth and burning her eyes. Beneath the reek of cigarettes and bodies the air was thick with incense, patchouli and wine, and funeral roses. She worked her dry tongue against the roof of her mouth and swallowed the taste of old pennies. The dance floor sucked her in and she moved with the current, swirling through the tangle of bodies until it spat her out on the other side.

She found Danny lounging in a wide booth against the far wall. Half a stranger now—baby fat melted away, his hair bleached platinum-pale and shorter than he used to wear it—but she knew him. Two girls draped themselves around him; with their wild black hair and matching leopard-skin dresses they looked more like twins that Lily and Danny. All three stared at her with glassy eyes as she approached.

Danny blinked. "I thought I was imagining it. I didn't think you'd really come." His voice was slurred, and he'd picked up a hint of accent.

Seven years like a river between them, dark and wide. Then Danny stood, shook off the clinging girls and stumbled into Lily's arms.

"What are you doing here?"

"I'm here for you." She caught his arms and looked up at his face—farther than she'd had to look up before. She leaned in, enunciating over the throb of the music. "Something bad is going to happen."

He smiled a stranger's smile, wry and amused, so much older than the boy she remembered. "Always looking out for me. Always so serious."

Lily started to reply, but paused. His shirt hung open, revealing a dark mark on his chest. She pushed aside sweat-damp fabric; a tattoo covered his heart, black and yellow ink swirling in queasy streaks, a twisting three-armed spiral eclipsing the birthmark.

"What's this?" She touched the design, scrubbed her fingertips on her pants.

He caught her hand. "It's . . . a long story. I've learned things. Seen things."

Lily frowned. "You sound like Mom."

"It's all real, Lily, everything she used to talk about. Angels and stars and doors. I've seen all of it."

"Mom was crazy." Which didn't make the monsters any less real. Lily had seen enough already to know that.

"She was. She didn't understand—she couldn't deal with it. But I've seen the truth. You wouldn't believe—"

A hand fell on Danny's shoulder and the resonance between them dissolved. A dark-haired man leaned close to his ear. "*Čas vypršel*, Daniel. We should go."

Danny blinked, strobes shining in his glassy eyes. "Yeah, of course. Just a sec."

The man glanced at Lily, then nodded and stepped back. The leopard girls crawled out of the booth and fell in beside him. One of them blew a mocking kiss at Lily—her teeth were filed to points.

"Who are these people, Danny?"

"They're my family." She flinched, and he reached out to stroke her cheek. "You found yours. I had to find mine. I wish you could have come with me, seen the things I have." He leaned down and kissed her forehead, lips cool and dry. "But I'm glad I got to see you again, before—"

"Before what, Danny? What's going on?"

Liquid eyes flickered, glanced away. "I'm leaving. Tomorrow night. I don't think I'm coming back."

Her chest tightened, and she grabbed his hand. "I just found you. Danny, you're in danger."

His smile caught in her throat. "It's not what you think, Lily. It's a good thing. I wish I had time to explain."

The other man shouted over the music, gesturing impatiently. "Daniel!"

"I'm sorry," Danny said, squeezing her hand. "I have to go. It was good to see you."

With that he turned and followed his friends, disappearing into the crowd. Lily followed, but found only writhing strangers and dizzying lights.

"Do you really think you can save him?" the witch asked. Fabric rasped as she leaned back against the cushions.

"I'm the only one who'll even try." Incense filled Lily's head, dizzied her. The air was too thick. "I'm the only one he has."

"What if he doesn't want to be saved?" Lily looked away. Gethsemane laughed, rich as opium.

"Will you help me or not?"

"You're clever, clever and brave. Foolish, too, but time may cure that. I can help you. I can tell you where to find your brother, give you what you'll need to go there and return alive."

"What do you want?"

"Service."

Lily's throat was parched with smoke and dread. "Service. What kind of service?"

"Any kind I ask for." Gethsemane's lips curved. "You'll give me your name, and you'll work for me. Little things, mostly—running errands, fetching and carrying, traveling. Someday I'll ask you to do something you don't want to, something you'll hate, that will make you hate yourself. You'll curse me, and yourself, and your brother. You'll do it anyway. That is the price of my help."

Down and down and down. The walls narrow around her. She can't see, can't breathe. Not enough air, only dust and dark and cold, filling her chest and choking her. Dirt coats her hands and face, tears tracking runnels of slime through the filth.

Her hands bleed from a dozen falls, and her back and breasts are bruised from squeezing through cracks. The flashlight is gone; she's not sure when she lost it. Colors swim through the darkness.

He needs you.

Their mother lost herself in the twists and turns of her own mind, lost herself so deep she could only find her way out with pills and a razor. Danny's found his own labyrinth.

Bile sears her throat, but she chokes it down and keeps moving. She reaches into her shirt, pulls out the amulet the witch gave her, the strange star sigil. For protection, Gethsemane said. Cold and slick against her fingers, something real, a reminder that this isn't all just a nightmare.

If only it was. She would wake up in her own bed and there would be no witch, no bargains, no strange tunnels worming beneath a foreign city.

But this hurts too much to be a dream.

The nightmare was an old one.

Lily climbed the steps to their cheap rented room, dread like ice water in her stomach. She knew what was coming, always knew in the dream, but she could never stop her dream-self, never keep sixteen-year-old Lily from rushing up the creaking stair. Dream-Lily only knew that something was wrong, that Danny was scared and crying.

She'd only been gone a few hours, such a tiny piece of time stolen for herself. They would leave soon, like they always left when the voices in her mother's head got too loud, warning of some danger she could never explain.

It would have been so easy to disappear, to pack a bag and leave when her mother passed out with whatever she was taking to keep the voices quiet that week. But Danny wouldn't leave, and Lily couldn't leave Danny.

She ran up the stairs, heart pounding with Danny's fear, opened the door to find her brother huddled in the corner, rain leaking through a cracked window and puddling on the floor.

No. It had been sunny that day. Bright and warm. The heat made the smell worse.

Dream-Lily turned, saw the bathroom door ajar. She sucked in a breath. In the dream it smelled like roses and incense, instead of blood and shit.

She pushed the door open slowly, hinges squealing, until she saw the first splatter of blood on yellowed linoleum.

Lily woke crying in the darkness of a different city, a different cheap room. Not again. Not again.

Rain rushed through the gutters outside. She huddled on the bed, stared at the darkness beyond the cracked window, and waited for morning.

Light. She doesn't believe it at first, just a trick of her straining eyes, but it doesn't go away. A cold yellow flicker lining the bottom of a door, bright as neon after so much dark. She moves closer, hears a soft susurrus of voices. She wants to feel relief at this break from silent darkness, but it only twists the dread deeper.

The door is metal-bound wood, worn dark and shiny with age and oil. Lily scrubs a hand over her face, wipes dirt and mucus onto her pants. She touches the amulet again, and the knife inside her jacket. A wicked little thing with a curved blade. It severs bindings, the witch said as she pressed the hilt into Lily's hand. Her stomach cramps. She's glad she hasn't eaten today. Fear fills her belly instead. The links of the necklace bite into her palm. She forces her hand to unclench.

The door is locked. Her knock echoes through the wood, reverberates off stone. The voices pause, and footsteps draw close.

"Kdo tam?" a man's voice asks. Lily can barely remember English, let alone Czech, so she knocks again.

The door swings open a few inches and a man's backlit head appears in the gap. The man from the club. His face is shadowed, but she imagines his frown, hears it in his voice. *"Co si přejete?"*

Her mouth is dry. “I’m here for Daniel.”

The door opens wider, spilling light over half his face. Heavy brows draw together. “He is ours now.”

Lily raises her bleeding hand. “I have the prior claim.”

His frown deepens as he stares at her. “I see. Come in, then.”

He stands aside and Lily steps into the sodium-yellow gloom. She clenches her teeth to stop them chattering. Murmurs chase each other around the room as she enters, too low for her to understand.

People stand against the walls of the vaulted room. Lily’s not sure what she expected after Gethsemane’s cautions—robes and chanting maybe, hooded assassins with black knives. But they’re young, ordinary. She could have passed them on the street in a dozen cities and never looked twice. The leopard girls are there, standing beside a stone plinth in the center where Danny lies. They give way as she approaches, wild eyes tracking her.

“You shouldn’t have followed me here,” Danny murmurs as she crouches beside him.

“Please, Danny. I’m sorry I didn’t come sooner. I’m sorry I let you go.”

He wipes away muddy tear tracks on her face. “It’s okay. I found where I needed to be.”

She presses her hand to his chest, trying not to wince as she touches the tattoo. “You belong with your family.”

“This is my family now.” He covers her hand with his. Her scabs split, smearing blood across the ink.

“Come with me, Danny.”

He shakes his head, that bemused little smile curving his lips. “I can’t leave. I’m going tonight, going to the angels.”

“What do you mean?”

“He means,” a new voice cuts in, “that you’ve come too late.” A man steps out of the corner, leather coat flapping around his ankles. He speaks softly but his voice echoes, shivers through the roots of Lily’s teeth. She can’t see his face no matter how she looks. Shadows and light slide off him, want nothing to do with him.

Something glints in his hand: a straight razor. Just like the one her mother used. She tenses, ready to dodge, but he lays the blade on the plinth beside Danny.

“Your brother traveled a long way after you left him, a long way to find us. Tonight, he’ll travel farther still.”

She lets go of Danny’s hands and stands to face the man, but his eyes are full of stars and she can’t meet his gaze. *He left me*, she thinks, but she won’t defend herself to this unnerving stranger. “What have you done to him?”

"We've taken care of him, gave him a family when he had no one else. In return, he's going to help us build a bridge."

His voice rattles in her head like wasps, all pricking feet and buzzing wings, stingers poised. The room spins in a nauseous swirl and she sways.

Her hand closes over the necklace, silver cold and clean against her palm. The insects vanish. The dizziness subsides. Lily sucks in a deep breath, but the man's scent fills her nose and coats her tongue. He smells like altars—dust and bone, frankincense and bitter myrrh. She fights the urge to spit.

"What do you mean, a bridge?"

"A bridge to heaven. A bridge of his blood, of his soul."

She glances at Danny; he's holding the razor, staring at the shining steel. "Put that down." He doesn't listen.

"Daniel didn't tell us his sister was a twin." The man steps forward. "This could make the bridge even stronger." He reaches out with one long hand, then freezes. He looks at the necklace in Lily's hand.

"So. You're already claimed."

The fountain pen warmed in Lily's hand as she stared at the page in front of her. Other names lay in neat lines at the top, but she couldn't read them in the flickering light. She stared at the blank line, the thick paper.

For Danny.

She thought her hand would shake too much to write, but when nib touched paper her trembling stilled. Ink dark as blood, smooth strong lines as she traced the familiar loops and whorls of her name. She paused for an instant at the end and ink feathered through the fibers of the page.

Gethsemane smiled, sharp and cold as a razor. "It's done. Welcome to the family, Lillian."

Lily shivered at the weight of her name on the woman's tongue. "Now tell me how to find my brother."

"Of course." Black eyes held Lily's. "Listen carefully."

"I won't have anything to do with you, and neither will Danny."

The man looks at her with those star-filled eyes and she tries not to flinch. "Daniel has made his own decisions. Your claim is worthless now. But you can still join your brother, join us. I can even protect you from whomever it was you were foolish enough to bargain with."

She turns away, sick from watching him. Danny stares at her with unnerving liquid eyes. "You can stay with us, Lily. Stay with me."

If she'd only argued harder, if she'd only gone with him like he asked. His heartbeat echoes hers and she feels the drug-induced languor that suffuses him. She wants to melt into it, let it wash her clean. She squeezes her left hand shut, spilling pain up her arm. Danny winces.

"Do you really mean it?" Her voice cracks. "Do you choose them?"

His eyes sag shut. He's floating in warmth, warmth that takes the pain out of choices. "I do. I don't need you to save me anymore."

"Daniel." The man's voice shivers through the air. "The stars are setting. We've wasted enough time already."

The watchers move closer, link hands to form a circle. Lily's skin prickles with static. A chant picks up, soft sing-song nonsense syllables that set her head throbbing.

The razor gleams in Danny's hand.

"No!" Lily tries to grab him, but the doorman is there, pinning her arms, holding her back.

Danny gasps as the razor bites, and Lily echoes it. Steel parts skin and meat, finds the vein. He jerks it down, from elbow to wrist; their mother taught them how to do it right. Blood spills black as ink. Lily screams and goes limp in her captor's arms.

Only the ghost of pain, only the flood of warmth. Hot tears slide down Lily's face. Danny raises the blade again, but his hand is slippery and shaking and the second cut is shallow and awkward. It doesn't matter—it'll get the job done.

The doorman lets Lily go and she collapses onto the dirty floor. She can't feel the cold anymore, just the warm wetness, the pulse of life rushing out of her.

"Your arrival is luckier than I would have imagined," the star-eyed man says, standing over her. His voice is nearly lost under the chanting. "The bond between you and your brother will make the bridge more stable. You brother dies, you live, and the way is opened."

The knife in her jacket presses into her chest. Lily knows what to do.

She pushes herself to her knees, draws the blade. The pocket rips with a snarl of leather and nylon.

"What do you think you can do with that?" the man asks.

She rips her shirt open, snapping buttons. Cold prickles her chest as she bares the birthmark. "Sever bindings." She drags the blade across her skin, bisecting the mark. Blood trickles down her ribs, soaks into her pants. Not very deep; deep enough.

A sound like a broken guitar string reverberates in her head. For an instant she's blind and deaf. Senses return, except for one, except for Danny. She staggers to her feet, an echoing empty space inside her where her brother used to be.

Danny's eyes widen as he feels it, too. Blood pools on the stone bench, washes onto the floor. Lily stares at the gaping wounds, but all she can feel is her own abraded skin.

"What did you do?" Danny asks, voice slurring. His eyes are dimming, spine bowing with the effort of sitting up.

"I set myself free." She stumbles toward him and falls to her knees. "Oh, Danny, I'm so sorry." Nothing the witch could ever ask will be so bad. Nothing can make her hate herself more than this.

"S'okay," he mumbles, and his head falls onto her shoulder. "My choice . . ."

"I know." She drives the knife up, through the twisting yellow sign on his heart, through the twin-mark it obscures. He makes a wet choking sound and convulses against her. For once the only pain she feels is her own.

Lily twists the blade and sets him free.

The chorus breaks into screams. She drops Danny's body onto the bloody stone and rises, knife held dripping in front of her. One of the leopard girls collapses writhing to the floor. The other kneels beside her, nose leaking black blood. Lily whirls toward the doorman, but he's on his knees clutching his head. The room shivers. Her other hand grips the amulet as she backs toward the door.

The star-eyed man lets out an inhuman cry. Maybe he'll kill her, and the witch will lose after all. Instead he vanishes in a twist of nothing, a silent thunderclap that shakes the room. She shakes off curses and grasping hands and runs, back into the hungry darkness.

Easier if the labyrinth simply ate her, but it doesn't. She crawls back, bleeding and numb, back to the real world. She crawls back to the witch, who waits with her twisting ink and cold smiles.

Gethsemane touches Lily's cheek, and the gentleness of her fingers is worse than any blow. "Welcome home, Lillian."

The Spiral's Embrace

Joshua Hackett

The spiral's embrace
Deadened sense folding inward
Consumed by the void

Wounded in the Wing

Evening on the ground, deep and violet-gray. Lilah sits on her living room floor, reading by the last dying light while her angel churns restlessly inside her.

Scraps of paper lie scattered around her, a patchwork story in smeared graphite and creased news-clippings. The story of three missing kids: Marla Gray, Jake Frazier, and Thomas Garcia. Only Thomas made the news, the only one with family to notice or care when he vanished. The others were strays, fly-aways, street kids with just their own kind to mark their absence. But that was enough for rumors to reach Lilah.

To reach the angel.

The light dims and her scrawled notes blur beyond reading, but she already knows what happened. Marla disappeared at the end of August, Thomas two weeks later, then Jake two weeks after that. Now it's the middle of October and someone else will disappear soon.

:Tonight,: the angel says.

The house creaks and settles, lonely wood and plaster songs. She misses her grandmother so much it hurts, sharp and thorny in her chest. It wasn't so bad when Bernadette was still alive; the angel was quiet then, nursing old wounds and sleeping most of the time. For a few years it was almost peaceful, once Lilah escaped her mother's worry and the doctors' tests and questions.

But her grandmother died last year, leaving Lilah alone with the angel. The angel and all the monsters.

"I don't want to do this again," she whispers. "Please." She's talking to herself—the angel has no use for her doubts and fears. Lilah still has nightmares about the last time, the stinking carrion thing she tracked down the lightless farm roads outside of town. The smell of meat still makes her queasy sometimes.

She knows better, knows her nightmares are nothing compared to three people missing, three people dead, and who knows how many others before that. The angel doesn't need to remind her that she owes him every one of her nineteen years. She wouldn't be alive at all if he hadn't forced his breath, forced himself, into her stillborn body.

Exhaling the last of her stifling fear, she collects the names of dead children. Lilah is the only one who knows what happened to them, the only one who can give them justice, can keep someone else from vanishing unnoticed.

Who will notice when she disappears?

The prey never sees her coming until it's too late.

Some nights she stoops from the sky, only a whisper of wind through night-soft feathers to warn them, a fall of shadow against the moonlight. Tonight, she hunts more than mice and rabbits. Tonight, the Strix trades feathers for naked skin and walks the humans' bruising concrete streets.

All flickering lights and noise here, miniature thermals as the air gusts warm and cold from open doorways, swirling through the autumn breeze. Sometimes it amuses her to wander into their shops and bars, to see the mad and clever things they create, their endless magpie glitter. She's too hungry for that now.

The night air is cool, but the sidewalk warms her callused bare feet. She walks softly, arms close at her sides. Other spirits, other creatures, hunt this territory, and she isn't vain enough to think herself the most dangerous.

She finds what she wants at a party. Humans crowd loud and raucous as grackles, overflowing from an apartment onto the street below. Sweat and liquor unwind in damp ribbons on the wind. She doesn't brave the press above, but a boy and girl sit by themselves in the shadow of the stairs. Grown by mortal standards, but still with fledgling softness to them. Not mates, she guesses, studying them for a moment, nor siblings, if she can judge human features, but close all the same.

She ruffles ghost-feathers, shaking aside a pang of loneliness. It's been a long time since she saw her sisters, and she's never laid a clutch of her own. Perhaps she should find other prey, one who won't be missed. But she's hungry now. She whispers a suggestion to the wind, sends it drifting toward the humans. A moment later the girl rises and returns to the crowd upstairs, leaving her companion alone.

The Strix closes in.

He looks up as she approaches. He *sees* her, and his eyes widen, murky and translucent as river water. Tension shivers through him, prey-fear, but then their gazes meet, and her spell enfolds him.

A pretty one, fine-boned, dark hair falling in a graceful curve across his face. She smiles. He sets his bottle on the sidewalk and his throat ripples as he swallows. His heart drums; even through the bewitchment, he reacts to her otherness.

Always a pity, to kill the ones with sight. Many of her sisters have tried to keep them as pets, as companions, when the conversation of owls and nightjars palls. That ends badly more often than not. An hour's company might be pleasant, but the Strix finds it safer to kill them before the sun rises. Her kind are solitary.

She isn't cruel—her strikes are swift and clean.

At arm's length from the boy she pauses. Any closer and she loses focus. "What's your name?"

He hesitates, but the compulsion wins. "Gabriel." His pupils dilate. With fear or desire, she cannot tell.

The wind changes and for an instant she senses something. Ghost-feathers flatten against a threat, but she sees only drunken humans, hears nothing except their laughter and throbbing music. The sensation fades and she turns the weight of her stare back to the prey.

"Gabriel." She cocks her head and gives him another smile. "Walk with me?"

Lilah watches from a distance as the creature lures its prey away, not sure if she's relieved or disturbed that it's not like the last one. This one wears the shape of a girl, small and pretty, but the truth shows in its night-shining eyes, in its winged shadow. The boy is too fuddled with glamour and alcohol to notice or care, and he leaves the laughable safety of the crowd.

Lilah's seen him before, remembers his face from the coffee shops and clubs she visits when she needs noise to drown the angel. She doesn't know his name, but maybe that's for the best. Maybe he won't end up with a scrap-paper tombstone.

She gives them a moment's head start, then moves quietly down the stairs. The party goes on behind her, no one notices her leave. If they ever noticed she was there at all. Such careless chaos, doors and windows open to the night, strangers wandering in from the street. More than a hungry monster could resist.

:Careful,: the angel whispers, or as close as his echoing choir-song voice can manage. **:She won't smell you, but her hearing is keen.:**

Lilah pauses in the shadows as the monster and the boy turn onto Lynch Street. "What is she?"

:A wild spirit. A hunter. A killer.: Below that she hears another answer—*an intruder*—and feels a rush like vast mantling wings. The angel is very territorial. His anger burns her, drives her.

Wind tugs at her skirt and hair. She catches the creature's oily-dust scent before it fades beneath the tangled smells of beer and pizza, Chinese food and thrift-store incense. She hopes its lair isn't far; her feet still ache from the long walk from her house. Buses aren't much use when she's hunting.

Footsteps behind her, leaves crunching under heavy boots. Lilah turns to find a girl following her. Short and wiry-lean, hair the color of rust; Lilah recognizes her, vaguely, the way she recognized the boy. She's seen them together. She looks away, but too late.

"You're Lilah, right?"

She nods. The strays know her, come to her for charms and cures and sometimes meals. They think she's a witch, or crazy—neither of which she can argue. They don't know about the angel.

The girl's eyes narrow, colorless in the flickering neon. "I'm looking for my friend Gabriel. He was out here just a minute ago."

Lilah hesitates for a heartbeat. "I saw him." She was never any good at lying. "He went off with a girl."

The girl's square jaw clenches. "Gabe doesn't go off with girls. Not like that."

Lilah shrugs apologetically, starts to turn away.

"Is it true, the things they say about you?"

Some days Lilah wishes she were better at lying. "Most of them."

"Can you help me?" The words sound as if they're dragged out on barbed wire, but the entreaty is real. Not one Lilah can ignore.

"Help you how?"

"Find Gabriel. It's not safe for him to wander off with strangers."

"Can't he take care of himself?"

The girl shook her head angrily. "Not always. He attracts . . . things."

Lilah cocks her head, intrigued even though she's wasting time. "What kind of things?"

"Ghosts." She crosses her arms tight across her chest, as if to ward off disbelief. "Spirits. Like that."

"He didn't leave with a ghost." The girl turns her head, a muscle working in her jaw. Lilah knows she should hurry, but her tongue doesn't stop. "She's something worse." The angel's disapproval scorches her, and she winces. "I'll help him," she says, raising a hand to forestall the girl's anger. "But I need to hurry."

"I'm coming with you."

"That isn't safe."

"Fuck *safe*—he's my friend. I'm not leaving him."

So fierce. What would it be like, to love something—someone—like that? What would it be like to be loved? The angel urges her on, uncaring. It protects humans from the monsters, not from themselves.

"What's your name?" Lilah asks. She might as well know, if she's going to get the girl killed.

"Maddy."

"Come on, then. We don't have much time."

"Can you see in the dark?" the Strix asks, as they stand in the briar-choked darkness behind her nest. The one un-boarded window gapes like a skull's eye. She sometimes shares the abandoned house with a pair of vultures, and oblivious humans who crawl in looking for a place to sleep or fix, but tonight it's empty.

"No," Gabriel says, one foot braced against the drainpipe. "Do you have a light?" Moisture glistens on his face.

"Go on," she says with a smile.

He frowns and shakes his head, but wedges his boot between the rusty pipe and peeling wall and hoists himself over the sill. Dirt and broken glass crunch beneath his boots. An instant later he curses.

"Be careful," he calls, but she's already slipping through the window, heedless of debris. They end up nearly chest to chest in the narrow space. Gabriel lifts a hand to keep them apart, and liquid shines on his pale skin.

"You're bleeding." She catches his hand, tilts the palm up—just a notch of skin missing, likely caught on a nail. He shudders as she kisses away the bead of blood, bitter and salt on her tongue.

She raises her blood-specked lips to his. These clumsy mammal shapes have a few uses. He tastes of fear. So much fear—it's a marvel the weight of it doesn't break her charms. Instead he leans into her kiss, trembling all the while.

"Please," he whispers, the rush of breath ruffling the hair above her ear. Whether he wants her to stop or continue she doesn't know, but she moves away, and he doesn't reach for her.

"Come on." She takes his hand. He follows her into the mold-musty hulk of the house.

"They say this house is haunted," he whispers as they make their way through the darkness. She guides him around broken boards and the gutted bulk of a couch.

"Are you afraid of ghosts?"

"Yes."

"Smart boy." She steps over a fallen light fixture. "Do you think it's haunted?"

He pauses, tugging his hand free. She waits as he cocks his head and listens. "No." His voice is barely a breath. "Not by the dead, anyway."

"What else would haunt a house?"

"Memories. Monsters like you."

She chuckles. "What kind of monster am I?"

"I don't know. I've never seen anything like you before."

She smiles, even though he can't see. "Why are you here, then? Why don't you run, or fight?" Teasing, but curious as well. Her glamour still hangs on him like cobwebs. He doesn't struggle against it.

"I don't know. I've always known something like you would find me eventually, some hungry thing in the dark. I'm tired of waiting for it, of being scared all the time. At least . . . At least you're beautiful."

His voice is so fragile. She feels what must be a pang of conscience. But regret and tenderness will starve a hunter, and she knows her place. "It won't hurt," she says at last, the most she can offer him. "I don't feed on fear."

He sighs, and she takes his hand again, leads him up the stairs.

Away from campus, away from the Friday night crowds and noise, Lynch Street darkens and quiets. Old houses here, some subdivided, others silent and empty. Lawns grow thick and wild, oak and elm leaves curling and drifting across the cracked sidewalks. A small pocket of age, holding out against the renovation that spreads across the city.

Maddy is silent save for the scuff of her boots and creak of her leather jacket, and Lilah's grateful. The angel moves inside her, a pressure in her head, heat in her bones. Some days she's afraid she's too small to hold it all, that its radiance will shatter her.

They don't have to go far to find the creature's lair. Only a few blocks down the street and Lilah stops, a jerky marionette stumble as the angel follows invisible spoor. She looks at the boarded-up face of an old house, two stories with a tall shingle-stripped roof. Paint hangs in curling strips, yellow faded to gray. Vines cover the front porch.

"Here."

"You're kidding. I always heard this place was haunted, but that's just junkies' stories."

Lilah shrugs. "I don't know about ghosts, but this is where your friend went."

"Who is this girl he left with?"

"Something hungry."

Maddy's fists clench at her sides. "What are we waiting for, then?"

"This isn't a game. You could get hurt." It's getting harder and harder to speak, to have any will but the angel's.

"Gabriel is my friend. I'm supposed to watch out for him."

Weeds and briars catch at Lilah's skirt as she circles the house; a thorn traces a line of fire across one ankle. She envies Maddy her leather. She'll have to learn to dress for this. If she survives.

Only one kitchen window isn't boarded up. Her eyes strain against the gloom. Nothing to see or hear, but a ripple along her skin warns of danger. "Do you have a light?" she whispers. Not that quiet will make a difference.

Maddy pulls a Zippo out of her pocket. "Be careful, there's a lot of nails and glass in there."

"You've been inside?" Lilah tucks her skirt up and grabs the drain-pipe.

"A couple years ago. It's full of trash, mostly. Nobody squats there for very long. I didn't think it was very spooky, but that was before I met Gabriel. I notice that stuff now."

Lilah runs a hand along the inside of the windowsill searching for nails. She's never asked the angel if he can cure tetanus. As she hoists herself up, something screams and bursts from a tree-top, loud rustle of leaves and wings. Lilah loses her balance, barely catches herself from falling headfirst into the house.

Maddy starts, then laughs shakily. "Just a bird."

"I think that was the alarm." Lilah jumps down, wincing as a rock gouges through the thin sole of her shoe. "We should hurry."

Gabriel's heartbeat echoes in her ears as the Strix leads him into the shadows on the second floor, pulls him down onto a shabby mattress. He can't see the bloodstains on it. His pulse throbs under her hands. She imagines the hot arterial rush, the taste of flesh and rich organ meats. For now, though, the other hunger is stronger. She kisses him softly, no teeth or talons, and runs her fingers through his hair.

"Do you ever get lonely," she asks, stroking his cheek, "packed so tightly in your houses and cities?"

"All the time." He touches her gently, fingers tentative over her collar bone, down her shoulder. "I used to think I'd go crazy with it. It's been better lately, since I met Maddy." His voice catches on the name and the spell on him ripples. A weak point in her glamour.

"It's always hard for ones like you, isn't it?" She traces a fingertip over his eyelids and he shudders. "You humans cast your will on the world so carelessly, and so few of you can see the real world at all."

"What about you?" he asks. "Do you get lonely?"

"Sometimes. There aren't many of my kind. We're between things, too wild to ever live with men, but drawn to them as well."

"Is that our fault? Did we cast our will on you, too?"

"I don't know. I am as I've always been, and my mother was the same. If our foremothers were different, I never heard of it."

"I wish I'd met someone like you before," he says softly. "Another spirit, I mean. Maybe I wouldn't have been so afraid. You're still going to kill me, aren't you?"

She sighs. "If not you, then someone else—that's what I am. Would you choose another in your place, if I let you live?"

"I couldn't do that. But I don't want to die." Wonder in his voice, like it's a revelation. She's seen many humans who thought they wanted death, until they found it. She has no answer for him, and pulls his face to hers again.

She pauses mid-kiss at the sound of footsteps in the grass. An instant later a nightjar shrieks a shrill *meep meep meep* in warning. Intruders. Not just mortals, either. Shadow-wings flare against the threat; she might walk softly outside, but this is her place.

"Wait here," she tells Gabriel, tightening her web of spells.

Lilah's bravado is no match for the dark that fills the house like tar, and neither is Maddy's trembling lighter flame. By its glow, the floor glitters with broken glass and aluminum cans. Shadows flow across the walls, pooling in doorways and corners; graffiti writhes, incomprehensible and arcane. Boards creak beneath their feet. Lilah shudders at the thought the dark and musty spaces lurking under the house.

"Where are the stairs?" she asks. Her voice is deeper, hollow—soon only the angel will speak.

Maddy stares at her, eyes wide. "By the front door. This way."

Another corner turned, another room gaping in front of them, reeking of urine, rats, and mildew. Lilah rubs her nose, stifles a sneeze. Still not as bad as last time.

Something capers across the wall. Maddy starts; the flame sways and gutters. "What the fuck is that?"

Lilah tenses, but the angel doesn't stir. "A trick," she decides after a minute, praying she's right. "An illusion. She knows we're here."

The ceiling creaks over their heads.

"Gabriel," Maddy whispers.

They ignore the crawling shadow puppets. Lilah wants to run, but holes gape in the floor, and she'll be no use at all if she breaks her leg. As they enter the front hall, the light falls over something perched on the banister.

Maddy curses; Lilah gasps as the angel surges beneath her skin. The Zippo dies. She jumps to the side, arm thrown up to ward off a strike, and screams as something cold and cruel bites her heel.

The flame returns a second later. The staircase is empty.

"Sorry," Maddy says, "I burned myself. Was that a trick, too?"

"No." Lilah balances on her good foot and reaches for the other. A curving shard of glass pierces her rubber sole. She gasps as she pulls it free; blood pulses hot and wet into her shoe.

"Are you okay?" Maddy asks, moving the flame closer.

"It's nothing." She tosses the bloody glass aside, limps on the ball of her foot. "Come on, she's waiting for us."

The lighter fails again at the top of the stairs, but the glare of streetlamps and glow of the half-moon replace it. A balcony lies open to the night, doors missing from their hinges. A humid breeze spills over the broken rail.

Standing in the empty doorway is the monster. She still wears a girl's skin, but her wings cast a wide shadow across the floor. The angel mantles at the sight of her. Lilah bites her lip against another scream.

"Where's the boy?" she asks. The words throb through her fragile vocal cords. "Where's Gabriel?"

The creature cocks her head, fixes Lilah with one shining eye. "An angel? Is that what's inside you?"

Before Lilah can answer, Maddy charges the winged girl. Lilah shouts a warning, but the monster simply bats her aside, sends her rolling into a wall.

:Stay down!:

Maddy crouches against the wall and doesn't move.

"I won't let you kill anyone else," Lilah tells the bird-girl.

"Do you stop owls from hunting rabbits? Do you save mice from cats?"

"People aren't rabbits."

"No. You make so much more noise." Her eyes flash as she steps closer. "What are you doing hiding in a mortal child, angel?" The word is mocking and ugly.

"Helping me stop you."

The monster laughs sharply. "He's using you. I've met their kind before." Her voice softens. "Do you need help to cast him out?"

:No!: Lilah isn't sure if that's her word or his, but then he claims her voice entirely. **:She is mine.:**

The monster screeches like a harpy. "Coward. Child, whatever he's told you is lies. The poet had it all wrong—a caged robin doesn't set heaven in a rage. Angels aren't free, and they envy anything that is."

"You're lying." Before she can say anything else, the angel's fire spills out of her. Great burning wings unfold around her, and flames flicker hot and sharp along her hands. A falcon's cry rips from her throat. The monster shrieks in response.

The harpy strikes, neither bird nor woman but something in between, curving talons and furious wings, feathers banded gray and dark. Beautiful and terrible. They meet in a storm of wings and flame. Lilah chokes on the stench of burning feathers.

She waits for the pain, for the rending claws. Instead the creature rips free of the angel's fiery embrace, wheels in a shower of blood and charred feathers and flies for the balcony. The angel cries out, a terrible shrill of pain and fury. For an instant Lilah thinks he'll pull her along in pursuit, send her tumbling over the railing to the weed-choked ground below.

He stops, brilliant pinions beating the air, and retreats, pulling back inside of her in a scalding rush. Tears well in her stinging eyes; her skin tingles like sunburn.

Not all the fire vanishes; flames lick the walls, scorching the tattered wallpaper. By the orange glow she sees Maddy and Gabriel leaning on each other in a doorway, staring at her. Tears glisten on Gabriel's cheeks and his shirt is half-unbuttoned, but he looks unhurt.

"Are you all right?" Lilah rasps, stumbling to her feet. The angel curls inside her, whether wounded or quiescent with victory she can't tell.

For a moment they just stare, and her chest tightens. What do they see? An angel, another monster, a crazy girl? No one will understand. She's not sure she understands herself.

Maddy takes a hesitant step forward. "Are you okay?"

"Yeah." She tries to sound brave and unconcerned, and then yelps as she puts her weight on her injured foot; blood squelches in her shoe. The flames spread toward the ceiling, raining sparks onto the splintered floor. "We should go."

She turns to the stairs and nearly loses her balance. Maddy's hand closes on her arm, holds her steady.

"Thank you," the girl says, the words nearly lost in the crackle of the fire.

Lilah smiles, soft and shaky, and leads them down the stairs.

The Strix pauses on a rooftop at the end of the street to wrap herself in owl-skin and nurse her wounds. Her breast is blistered and bloody, her wings burned. Fluid leaks from her left eye, the membrane scorched. Char flakes from her remiges as she settles her wings, and it's all she can do not to scream in pain.

Half-blind, she watches the humans stumble out of the burning building. Already she can see the bonds forming between them, prey huddling together to ward off the hunters and the night. The angel will cage them with bars of fear and need, and they'll thank him for it. Her pride stings nearly as badly as her blisters. At least the angel won't soon forget her talons.

Gabriel glances back as they walk away. Too far to see her, but her chest aches all the same; too much time amongst men has left her muddled and foolish. He'll be happier with his own kind, with his own monsters. Her kind are solitary.

Fire laps out of her ruined nest and she turns away from the blinding glare. Human voices rise in panic. Soon their sirens will begin to wail. She needs to find a new place to lair, to rest, away from their noise and lifeless concrete. She needs wild places to heal her, to cleanse her heart of useless wants. Mice and rabbits will keep her fed.

She spares one last glance for the humans, still clinging together as they disappear into their brick and concrete warren. The night air stings her wounded wings as she takes to the air, following the setting moon toward the horizon.

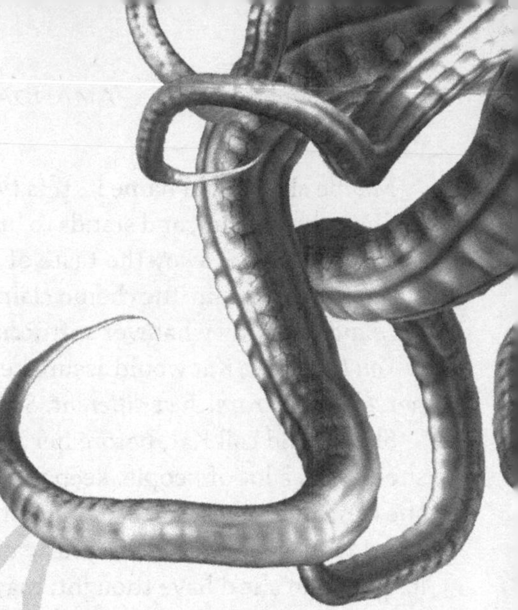

Flotsam

Three long days in Connemara, and on that third summer-short night Rebecca Killian admits a truth to herself.

She came home to die.

If anyone asked where her home was, she'd say New York, of course New York, her loft and the gallery. Or maybe the apartment in Berlin where she goes to rest and refuel every so often. She floats—floated—all over, but those are places she always drifts back to.

Like she's drifted back to Ireland now.

That night, whiskey still warm in her blood, she opens the window in her rented cottage to let in the smell of summer and the sea. It washes over her, fills her lungs, and she cries.

The first tears since the diagnosis, leaking hot and silent down her cheeks, cool by the time they drip off her chin. When the last drop is shed, she closes the window, wipes the salt and snot off her face, and goes to sleep.

The dying is a secret. As far as the rest of the world is concerned she's here on vacation, a change of scenery to get her out of a funk.

So, Rebecca staggers out of bed at a reasonable hour, stumbles to the bathroom and runs the water to cover the sound of her vomiting. Like morning sickness. She laughs between bouts of retching. She never thought her womb would grow anything, but it turns out to be fecund after all. It won't stop growing now, never mind that uterus and ovaries are gone, lost to the second round of surgery.

Maybe she should name it, this twisting tumor child.

She spits, flushes, and stands to brush her teeth. A stranger's face watches her as she scrubs away the taste of whiskey and bile, all gaunt angles and silver-streaked hair. The chemo claimed her long auburn curls, and the cancer's melted away whatever softness she ever had.

You look good, Kat would assure her whenever Rebecca stopped to stare at herself in mirrors. *Just different. Striking.*

She should call Kat, before her agent starts to worry—worry more. She should call a lot of people, keep up the ruse, sneak in a few goodbyes while she can. She makes a list while she showers, names and faces hanging in her mind while she closes her eyes against soap and stinging spray. The list is longer than she'd have thought; maybe she'll start tomorrow.

Siobhan's making breakfast, or at least coffee, still in boxers and tank top, hair sleep-tousled. Something so familiar about the sight, though Rebecca's only known the girl a week. Her stomach takes a little sideways step.

She's not here to have a last fling, she reminds herself as she takes the proffered cup, even if the girl is pretty. Very pretty, a sylph-punk girl, supple tree-limb grace beneath the big boots and chrome and purple-tipped hair. *She's too young, anyway*. Though that never stopped Rebecca before.

The summer apprenticeship was something Kat talked her into a year ago, just before they found the first tumor. She could have cancelled, but now she's glad she didn't, glad to have some company this last summer.

Siobhan leans against the counter, pouring milk into her mug. She looks far too fresh and cheerful for someone who drank just as much as Rebecca did the night before. "Henry said he saw a girl in the bog. A faerie girl."

"Oh?" A quick glance for permission as she reaches across the table for Siobhan's cigarettes. She quit five years ago, for all the good that did her—might as well enjoy them now.

"Red hair and white skin, like a fae thing, dressed in white." She grins. "And she just disappeared into the mist."

Smoke trails out of Rebecca's nostrils as she arches an eyebrow. "When was this?" She takes a sip of steaming coffee.

"Last night, he says. He brought the groceries by just now, when you were in the shower." Siobhan's shirt catches on her nipple rings as she sits, and Rebecca tries not to notice.

"We should find her," Siobhan says, still smiling. "Maybe she'll pose for us."

"Maybe." Rebecca smiles back, but her stomach's sour again. Hundreds of red-haired girls in Ireland, no doubt, hundreds of children who think they see faeries. She drags deep on the cigarette, trying to settle her stomach. No reason to think it's her girl, her faerie.

No reason to think Aoife waited for her.

Siobhan vanishes into her bedroom-cum-studio that afternoon, and Rebecca does the same. Canvases stacked in the corner, a block of wood, a bagged slab of clay—she stares at all of them for several moments before pulling out the little velvet pouch tucked into the bottom of her suitcase.

She sits on the bed, holding the bag in one hand, caressing the nap of the cloth with her thumb. Stones click and clatter inside. She unties the drawstring and pours them onto the rumpled bedspread.

Beads tumble free in a glittering stream, glass and green gems. Jade and jasper, striped malachite and shimmer-soft labradorite fire. Set in gold wire links now, but not yet connected. She collected them all over the world, one by one, every time something reminded her of the brilliant changeable green of Aoife's eyes.

She's never sold one of these necklaces, only given them as gifts. This was the first she ever started, maybe the last she'll ever finish.

Rebecca finds her pliers and shears. Her hands are still her own, at least, unchanged by disease—lean and callused, long-fingered, short-nailed. Muscles and tendons ripple as she twists the links together, motions so familiar she hardly has to think of them.

She's always been proud of her hands; they've never betrayed her.

That evening Rebecca and Siobhan walk along the beach, as the sun bleeds into the sea and the moon rises over the rounded peaks of the Twelve Bens. Insects chirp and buzz in the salt-damp shadows. Siobhan unlaces her stompy boots to wade in the shallows. Rebecca smiles to herself—for the first time in months it's not even bittersweet.

"Swim with me," Siobhan calls, silhouetted against the violet and vermilion sky.

Rebecca turns her head, hopes the girl can't see her smile crumble and fall away. "I don't swim." Her toes clench in dry white sand—not even powdered quartz, but shells ground fine and white by the waves. Like she's not standing on land at all. She fights the urge to step backwards.

Siobhan makes a disappointed noise and splashes farther out, but soon she trudges back, jeans wet to the thighs, and walks beside Rebecca the rest of the way.

They walk in comfortable silence till the last glimmer of twilight is gone. The stars burn white against the forever-stretch of sky. By the light of the sickle moon she makes out a dark shape against the shore ahead, the outline of a house.

She pauses, hands clenching in her pockets. Whether she's afraid of what was or what might be, she can't say, but she can't face that house tonight.

"Let's go back," she says, voice as careless as she can make it. "I'm too old to be hiking around in the dark."

Siobhan snorts, and her eyes and piercings gleam silver. The skeptical noise would be flattering, if Rebecca's stomach weren't so cold. They turn back toward the cottage.

The next day Siobhan locks herself away with a painting again. The girl is good—a pity there's not more time to tutor her.

Rebecca fusses with sketches for a while, but eventually the sunlight on the water and wind in the grass pull her out of the cottage. The necklace gleams on the nightstand, and she slips it into her pocket. She runs the stones through her fingers like prayer beads as she walks the two miles to Roundstone.

She worries for a moment that someone might recognize her, but that's foolish. More than twenty years since she's been here, and she barely recognizes herself these days. She wanders in and out of shops, picking up shiny trinkets and putting them down again before finally buying a pack of cigarettes and a postcard to send Kat. The shopkeepers are two old women, gray and creased, one slightly more stooped than the other.

Rebecca counts out unfamiliar Euros and drops them into the old woman's wizened hand. "I used to know someone named Dowan," she says, too casual.

For once she's glad her accent's gone flat as a Yank's. Rebecca pretends not to notice the woman blanch. "She said her family came from around here. Do you know the name?"

The older woman mutters under her breath.

"What was that?"

"There was a family by that name 'round here once," the old woman admits, lips pursing. She slides the change across the counter. "Your friend is better off far away from them. They weren't good folk. Anyway, they left Connemara, years ago. We've not seen sign of them since, and good riddance."

The older woman mutters something else. Rebecca lets it go, smiles, says good day, and leaves the shop.

But she heard. *They went back to the sea*, the crone said.

She doesn't go back to the cottage right away. Instead she gathers her courage and keeps walking, down the curving road they followed last night. Too bright a day for fear, for twisting night-dread. Dog's Bay glitters brilliant blue-green, stretching out beneath the vault of sky to meet the deeper wilder Atlantic. Gulls' cries echo down the shore, cormorant grunts and the kittiwake's shrill *kittee-waa-aake*. She can pretend it's just a walk in the sun, until she reaches the abandoned house.

More than abandoned, she can see now—roof fallen in, the walls cracked and gutted by fire. Grass grows tall inside the skeleton, vines digging into chinks between the stones.

All gone. Aoife and her family. Her hulking brothers and taciturn father. The Fomorians driven back to the sea. What happened to Aoife's mother, with her nervous eyes and fluttering hands—did she go into the water, too, or did something else befall her? Maybe she fled the ocean, the way Rebecca's father did. Maybe she had better luck in that.

Rebecca pulls out the necklace, lets it dangle from her fingers, scattering light against the stones. The little bronze frog sways back and forth amid the shining green. Aoife loved frogs. She caught them in the bog, stroking their slimy backs and playing with their toes. She kissed each one before she set them free—even convinced Rebecca to try it once. They never found a prince, or a princess.

They had each other, and didn't mind.

No reason to think Aoife would have waited for her.

She hangs the necklace from a broken stone, where it gleams like absinthe tears. "I did come back," she whispers to empty house.

She dreams that night, dreams of her last show. The gallery all light and noise, voices like bird-chatter as the guests drift about in sleek black, from sculpture to sculpture, painting to painting. Kat moves among them, beaming, chatting up a critic from some magazine or another.

Almost a pleasant memory, but her mother stands next to her, watching Rebecca with pearl-clouded eyes. Dead eyes.

"You always were a morbid child," she says, staring at a sculpture. One of the sea-change series, a sea horse curled inside the shell-white curve of a plaster pelvis. "Did I ever tell you about your father?"

Then she's gone, and Rebecca knows as much about her father as she's ever going to. She turns away, looking for Kat, when a rank brine-stench fills her nose.

Aoife stands in the corner. Aoife and her family.

Scaled things, spined, wide mouths filled with rows and rows of teeth. Aoife's father stands behind her. His hands on her shoulders are webbed and clawed.

"It's time to come home," Aoife says. Her voice is a frog's croak, the roar of the tide.

Rebecca wakes in shadows and moonlight, sick sweat sticking the sheets to her flesh. She stumbles to the bathroom just in time to retch.

Dying or not, she still has things to do, things to think about besides memories and dreams. She spends the morning with Siobhan, going over the girl's work. She hasn't played teacher very often, but it's oddly enjoyable.

She studies the canvas from across the room, drags on a Silk Cut and exhales toward the open window. A winterscape, cool and gray in the slanting summer light, the dark line of a tree, and a girl's red hat stark against shades of pale. Footprints dot the wide white space in the foreground, not quite where the girl's should be. There's something eerie and haunting in that disconnect.

Siobhan watches her silently, her perfect stillness a fidget all its own. White paint smudges her nose, and Rebecca fights the urge to wipe it away. She can imagine the feel of the girl's freckled cheek against her palm.

Just the whiskey talking, she tells herself, the shots she spiked her coffee with to take the edge off the pain, to dull the barbed wire wrapped around her hipbones. That might make a nice piece, if she can remember it.

"The lines of the tree could be smoother," she finally says, letting out another jet of smoke. "It's pulling the eye the wrong direction."

Siobhan studies the painting, frowns, and nods. "Yeah."

"Other than that, it's damn good."

"Really?"

"I'll never coddle you, sweetie. You've got a great eye, and you're young enough yet to not sweat the technique. Give me a set like this and I'll give you a show."

Siobhan's grin shines brighter than all her silver and chrome.

They stay up late talking and drinking. Siobhan recounts school exploits and Rebecca makes her travels sound more interesting than they really were. Eventually, Siobhan starts to wilt and staggers off to bed. Rebecca's glad she's not as drunk as she could be; the invitation in the girl's eyes is clear as brushstrokes.

When she's safely alone again she uncaps the bottle, and pours a healthy shot. Just enough to kill the pain, to kill the dreams.

As she raises the glass she hears the song.

So faint at first she thinks it's just the wind or the waves, just an ocean susurrus. It spools over the casement, creeps beneath the door, a haunting siren's aria. Only a moment and it's gone, but too late for Rebecca to pretend she never heard, to pretend she imagined it. A shipwreck song.

She sets the glass down and goes to dash herself against the rocks.

Across the sloping lawn, grass slippery beneath her bare feet. Down the rocky bank to the beach, to the ribbon of shell-sand shining white under the moon. On the distant curve of the bay she sees a paler glimmer.

She wants to run but fears breaking the spell, scaring away the waiting shape. One step after another, till she knows it's not an illusion, till her eyes tell her what her heart knows.

Aoife.

She's changed. Rebecca knew she would be, spent years wondering and dreading and marveling how she might. How many paintings has she done, how many sculptures, imaging all the ways Aoife could have changed?

The reality is less, and more.

Red hair and white skin, like a fae thing. Like the girl Rebecca remembers.

Her hair is a coppery tangle, snarled with seaweed. Skin like moonlight, like nacre: luminous, iridescent. As she moves closer, Rebecca can see the shimmer of scales, the mud and mildew streaking the white dress. The smell of moss and brine fills her nose.

Aoife's eyes are wider than before, pupils misshapen, but that summer-green fire is still Aoife. The necklace gleams against her throat, mermaid's treasure.

She holds out one long white hand. Rebecca takes it, barely a heartbeat's hesitation at those curving claws. Their fingers can't entwine, not with the veiny webbing between Aoife's grown so thick, but they clasp, cold on warm, smooth on callused.

"You came back." Rebecca brushes a cautious hand against Aoife's cheek. Hair coils around her fingers, too thick, clinging. She pulls back, fighting a shudder.

"I waited," Aoife says. Rebecca glimpses the needle teeth behind her wide mouth. Her voice is a sibilant whisper, like wind in leaves, like waves on sand.

The Dowan family. The Daoine Domhain. The people of the deep.

But still Rebecca's oldest friend, her first love, her cousin. She takes Aoife in her arms, holds her close, and breathes in the smell of the ocean.

"I knew you'd come back," Aoife whispers. "You couldn't stay away forever."

Rebecca laughs, half a sob. "I'm dying." She guides Aoife's hand down to her belly. "Cancer."

Fingers splay, claws pressing through cloth. Breath hisses between sharp teeth. "It's eating you alive."

"It's in the bones now. Soon it will spread to my spine. There's nothing anyone can do anymore."

"Come with me." Rebecca shivers as Aoife's hand slides lower. "The sea can cure you. Nothing is hungrier than she is."

"Cure me." Her voice cracks, mouth gone dry. "You mean change me. I'd be like you."

"You'd be with me. Forever." She cups Rebecca's face in her hands. "I'll never be sick. I'll never die. But it's lonely, sometimes. I still remember a woman's heart."

Rebecca's heart cracks like glass. "I said no, Aoife. I walked away, remember. What makes you think the sea would take me after all this time?"

"I can intercede. I'll go to the deep places and beg for you. Mother Hydra will listen."

"Aoife—"

Cold fingers brush her lips, silencing her doubts. "You've had your life on land. There's no need for you to die a mammal's death."

Her mouth closes on Rebecca's, cold probing tongue and razor teeth. Her kiss tastes like a shipwreck. Wide webbed hands slide under Rebecca's shirt, leaving trails of damp. Twenty years, but her body still remembers Aoife's touch, no matter how she's changed. Her hands clutch wet fabric, searching for buttons on the white dress.

Aoife's hair clings to Rebecca's face and shoulders, anemone tendrils trapping her as they sink to the sandy, salt-slick grass, washing up against the beach like so much flotsam.

The moon has set when Rebecca stumbles back to the cottage, the stars blinded by a swath of clouds. No one to see as she staggers tingling and half-numb across the beach. Her heart won't slow its mad rhythm; every throb of her pulse burns in the bloody scratches Aoife left on her back and thighs.

Her whiskey still sits on the table, gleaming in the warm glow of the kitchen. She drains it, and then another, but as she falls into bed her mouth still tastes of the sea.

She dreams of Aoife, again and again. Rebecca follows her through the water as it changes from clear to blue to black, until light and color are only memories. The only illumination is the phosphorescent glow of Aoife's skin, a lure to draw the unwary.

Down and down and down, into the cathedral of the abyss, to an altar-throne where things older than gods hold court. Rebecca wants to look away as Aoife prostrates herself before their bloody scarlet gaze, as she gives herself to the writhing teeth-and-tentacle embrace of the Hydra.

But she cannot blink, cannot turn aside.

Even waking can't banish those images. She doesn't dare profane them with paint and canvas.

Then the dreams stop, and she knows Aoife's paid whatever price they asked of her.

For the rest of the week she can't work, can't concentrate. She's short with Siobhan, or doesn't speak at all; she has no answer for the hurt in the girl's eyes.

Live in pain perhaps another three months, or live forever. It doesn't seem much of a choice.

She could have chosen it twenty years ago, when Aoife first started to hear the call of the waves. Rebecca heard it, too, but feared the change, feared the *other*. She fled Ireland, fled Aoife, and channeled all that siren song into her art. She's never regretted her life, for all the dark hours of the night when she's wondered *what if*.

But now . . .

Rebecca stands on the beach, toes in the sand, watching the moon hang pale and swollen over the water, its light painting a silver road along the waves. The tide swells in response; she can feel it in her blood, calling her out, calling her down.

She thought Aoife would be here, but the bay is empty. This road she'll have to start on alone.

She doesn't realize she's moving until the sand changes under her feet, from dry and soft to sodden and clinging. She strips off her shirt and underwear, leaves them like driftwood on the shore.

Water swirls around her legs, sliding cold between her thighs. Sand slips under her feet, sucked away with every lapping wave. Deeper and deeper. The sea rises over her hips, her waist, reaching higher. The silver road stretches before her.

She can keep walking forever, into the endless blue wine.

Rebecca opens her mouth, tongue heavy with salt. Maybe she means to call Aoife's name, or just take a last breath, but a shout echoes behind her and she turns, clumsy, waves tugging at her legs. She slips and goes under, rocks and sand scraping her knees as water closes over her head. It burns her nostrils, chokes her.

Hands close on her arms and pull her up. Siobhan's wiry arms around her, dragging her onto the beach.

"Don't you bloody leave me," the girl mutters. "Not like this." They collapse on damp sand and Rebecca coughs and sputters as Siobhan slaps her back.

"I wasn't—" But she can't explain that she wasn't trying to die, that wasn't the point at all, and then Siobhan is kissing her, stealing her words away.

Nothing like cold mermaid kisses—Siobhan is warm and sweet, smoke and honeysuckle, muscles strong and lithe under smooth skin. Light spills from the hall, limns the planes and curves of her body.

Rebecca lays her palm over the girl's belly, feeling the rhythm of blood and breath, studying the line and contrast. Siobhan takes her hand, twining their fingers together.

"Don't leave me," she whispers, "not tonight."

"Not tonight." Rebecca lowers her head to Siobhan's breast, tugs the silver ring until she moans; they don't speak again.

But morning comes, and the conversation they can't avoid. Rebecca explains the cancer, the diagnosis—four months, if she's lucky.

"Oh." Siobhan's blue-gray eyes widen. "Oh, god. I thought . . ."

"You thought I was just a drunk?" She chuckles wryly as the girl blushes.

"I'm sorry about last night. I didn't know you were in so much pain. It wasn't my place to interfere."

"No, don't be sorry." She lights a cigarette, looking anywhere but those stricken eyes. "I never should have thought of leaving you with no explanation—it was a shitty thing to try."

"What are you going to do?"

"I don't know."

She thinks of all the paintings back in the loft, all the pieces she's started and abandoned in the last six months. Not much of a swansong. The cigarette burns in her hand, orange ember consuming paper and tobacco. Can webbed hands hold a brush?

"I don't know."

Another day with Siobhan, talking about paintings. Rebecca could give her a show—easy to imagine those haunting pictures hanging in her gallery. Easy to imagine the girl sprawled on the wide bed in her loft, purple-tipped hair rasping against the pillows. Kat would like her.

They don't talk about choices, about the future. That night Siobhan makes love like she's already lost, like Rebecca is a ghost in her arms. A tear splashes Rebecca's lips, a tiny ocean against her tongue.

Eventually Siobhan's breathing slows, deepens, and her arm around Rebecca relaxes. She doesn't stir when a pillow replaces her lover.

The tide is pulling out, leaving dark swathes of seaweed limp on the sand. This time Aoife waits on the beach, waves breaking around her ankles. She's shed the white dress, along with any pretense of humanity. A creature of salt and bone, of razor spines and scales and writhing anemone hair. Rebecca meets her glowing eyes and it's all she can do not to fall to her knees on the sand.

Siren, sea goddess—Aoife could take her, drown her and eat her and give her skeleton to the hungry sea, and Rebecca would never regret it.

But she doesn't. Instead she steps forward, hand outstretched, and Rebecca sees the familiar in the *other* again. The necklace sparkles on her cousin's white breast.

"Please—" Her voice is fainter. Gill-slits flutter around her collarbones, below her ribs.

Live three months in pain, or live forever with the woman she loves. How can such a choice be so hard to make?

"Even the sea won't wait forever," Aoife says. "Come with me."

Before Rebecca can answer, those luminescent green eyes flicker over her shoulder, toward the cottage. She glances back, sees a slender shape silhouetted in the open doorway. Then the door closes.

Rebecca moves forward, takes Aoife's hand, kisses her cold salty lips. "I'm sorry." She steps back, toward dry ground.

"But you'll die! Pain and death and rot—what kind of end is that?"

"I've never been as brave as you."

"Don't leave me again." The tide draws back and Aoife slides with it.

Third chance. Last chance. Rebecca bites her lip until copper washes over her tongue.

"I'm sorry. I love you. I always will."

She turns away from Aoife, away from the hungry sea, and walks up the hill to the cottage. The wind dries her tears.

Siobhan sits at the kitchen table, pouring the last of the whiskey with a trembling hand. She startles as Rebecca walks in, and drops of amber liquid spill. The empty bottle clacks against wood.

Rebecca wipes salt off her cheeks and tries to smile. "Have you ever been to New York?"

It won't take me back

Joshua Hackett

It won't take me back
Face plunged into brackish waves
The gulf of my tears

Ghostlight

Fog rolls over the bayou, smoke and mirrors. Night coming on, and the marmalade sky drips thick and sticky through the trees. Memory crouches in the crook of a black willow, five trunks cupped around her like a giant's hand. Black willow for divination—if she listens close to the sighing branches, sometimes she hears things.

Today the tree says something's coming.

But she's watched the crossroads for hours and nothing's come. The tree just repeats itself, the rustle nearly lost beneath whining insects and deep bullfrog calls. Samaritana says trees are no good with time, leastways not people-time. If a tree tells you something, it might have happened a hundred years ago, or might not happen for another hundred. Memory understands; time was strange for her, when she slept in the deep mud-dark of the swamp. She dreamed things there, before the witch pulled her out, like nothing she ever saw when she was alive, nor anything she's seen since.

The light dies, purple shadows sliding across the water as night drags out of the trees. Something slithers through the weeds, bigger than a frog or snake. Memory stands, brushing off her dress though it never takes a stain. Whatever's coming, it's not worth sitting in the swamp all night.

She pauses at the crossroads, staring down the road that leads away, leads out. Memory's never been down that direction, but the witch tells stories about cities that burn with lights, about cars and crowds and things she can't even imagine, like a carnival that never stops. She daydreams about following that weed-choked path, till she finds the roads made of tar and asphalt, black and pebbled like a snake's skin, roads that lead to the carnival towns.

She knows she never will. What's out there for a dead girl?

"Good evening, Memory."

Her hands clench in her skirt as she turns. Stupid to hang around the crossroads at nightfall—she can hear Samaritana's chiding voice, and the nearly forgotten echo of her mother's.

A man stands in the gloom beneath the willow, his hat pulled low over his eyes. Memory doesn't relax, even though she knows him; familiar isn't always safe around here.

"Hi." Don't talk to things if you don't have to, the witch says, but don't be rude. It's never smart to be rude.

He smiles, and she forces herself to relax. Maître Carrefour, the witch calls him, but Memory always thinks of him as the Alligator Man. His skin creases black and leather-shiny around his obsidian eyes, and he smiles so slow and wide. The witch says he doesn't have much use for dead girls, and not to worry about him, but Memory can't meet his eyes without breaking out in goose pimples.

"What are you doing out here by yourself, Miss Memory?" His voice is like the secret places in the swamp.

"The tree said something's coming. Did it mean you?"

He smiles, sharp and ivory. "Trees don't pay much attention to me. But someone is on his way. He'll be here tonight, I think. Why don't you run home and tell Samaritana that she'll have company."

"Are you coming, too?"

His smile stretches. "I'll be along. I'm going to wait for our guest, and make sure he doesn't get lost. You should hurry—the swamp's no place for children after dark."

"I figured that out already, thanks." She probably shouldn't sass him that way, but he only laughs. Memory turns and runs down the packed-dirt path, away from the crossroads and the Alligator Man's smile.

She keeps to the skin-roads, threading a careful path through the muck and tangled cattails. The badlands are faster, but more dangerous. When solid ground ends she paddles the rest of the way in a leaky old canoe. The oar breaks the green skin of the swamp, scatters ripples across the water below. The fog glows silver where moonlight leaks through cypress branches and trailing moss. Seeing in the dark is one of the few nice things about being dead.

A leathery head surfaces near the boat, nose-tip and gleaming eyes. Memory waves, and it sinks again. Alligators don't care about dead girls, but other things come out at night, things that won't care if she's alive or not when they get hungry.

Thimble Island rises out of the tattered fog. Once there was a town here—or at least a collection of houses—older than Memory, but it didn't last as long. Now it's just ruins, all rotted boards and rusty nails, caved in and sagging, home to nothing but snakes and palmetto bugs and bad memories. Only the witch's house still stands, warped and tired but holding on. Sometimes Memory wonders if Samaritana made a charm for the house, too, a spell to call it back from wherever buildings go when they die and dream.

She moors the boat to a stump on the shore, wondering how the Alligator Man and his guest will find their way across the bayou. He should have thought of that before he sent her running errands.

Samaritana is cooking dinner when Memory hurries up the back steps. The kitchen smells of catfish and wood smoke. The windows are thrown open to catch the sluggish breeze. The witch turns as the tattered screen door opens, her face etched in lamplight, hawk-nose and cheekbones and coal-dark eyes. Her skin glistens golden-brown like polished juniper. A tignon holds back her wild curls.

"You're out late." Muscles ripple in Samaritana's arm as she flips the fish on a cast iron skillet.

"I met the man at the crossroads."

She frowns, carving deep lines around her mouth. "What does the old devil want now?"

"He's coming here. He's bringing company."

"Well. We'd better set another place for dinner, then."

Memory feels someone coming before she hears footsteps, that cold, shivery, crawling-bugs feeling she gets when the witch works her magic. Samaritana wipes her hands on a rag and straightens her shirt, mouth set tight like she's expecting trouble.

Boots thump on the steps, a man appears at the edge of the light, fuzzy through the screen door. "Good evening, ma'am," he says when Samaritana opens the door. His voice is smoke and gravel. "I was told you'd be expecting me."

"I heard I'd have company. Nobody told me what to expect. We don't get many visitors out here."

"I'm looking for something. You might be able to help me find it. May I come in?"

Samaritana reluctantly steps aside, and the man crosses the threshold. He wipes his muddy boots on the mat and takes off his battered hat. His face is battered, too, deeply seamed, his hair the color of rust and ashes.

"You're in time for supper," she says, nodding toward the table.

"Thank you, ma'am. It's been a long walk."

Memory knows she's staring, but she can't stop. The only other person who's set foot in the house since she's lived there is Judah Barton, who brings them coffee, spices, and kerosene once a month. He trades for charms sometimes, or just a meal and an hour's conversation. He's a little crazy, but Samaritana trusts him, and Memory does, too. This stranger doesn't look especially crazy, or especially trustworthy.

His mismatched gray eyes catch hers before she can look away. He knows—she's sure he knows. Through her artificial skin, past the memory of her flesh, he can see the truth of her, the cobwebs and secrets where a little girl's heart should be.

Samaritana steps between them, not quite touching the man's arm as she leads him toward the table. "Since you've come all this way, why don't we eat first? Then you can tell me what it is you want my help with." She forks fish and rice onto a plate and sets it before him. "What's your name?"

"John Grey."

Samaritana chuckles as she reaches for the pitcher. "I'll bet it is. Well, M'sieu Gris, I'm afraid the tea's gone warm, and I'm all out of ice."

They eat quietly. The witch and the stranger eat, at least. Memory pushes bits and pieces around her plate and pretends to drink, breathing in the spices and herbs. Afterward she helps Samaritana clear the table and boil water for coffee while the stranger rolls a cigarette.

"So, M'sieu Gris," the witch says as she sets out the cups, "what is it that you're looking for?"

"A monster."

Samaritana pauses for a heartbeat, cup half raised. Steam twines around her face as she takes a sip. "Monsters."

Memory wraps her hands around her cup even though it can't warm her. The swamp is home to lots of monsters. Some they avoid and ward away, but some of them Samaritana protects. She wonders if she'll be helping dig a grave before breakfast.

John Grey shakes his head. "Just one monster. He hasn't been here long, I think. He swam in from the Gulf. A crafty old snake, but there aren't many places big enough to hide him."

Memory frowns. She's never heard of any snakes around, besides the usual water moccasins and hognoses. She can tell though from the tilt of Samaritana's chin, that she knows what he means.

"What do you want with him?"

"To ask him a question. That's all."

They stare at each other, the witch and the stranger. Memory's frown deepens. So easily she's shut out, like when her mother and father started talking, or her mother and grandma. Samaritana doesn't usually make her feel like a little kid.

After a minute Samaritana looks away. "Memory, do you mind sleeping in my room tonight, so M'sieu Gris can have a bed?"

She knows a dismissal when she hears one, bites her tongue as she nods. She pours her untouched coffee back in the pot, and retreats down the dark creaking hall.

Samaritana comes in hours later. Memory lies still on the edge of the big bed, staring at the shadowed ceiling as the witch slips into her nightgown. The mattress creaks as she slides under the soft-worn sheet, and the heat of her leaks through the cloth.

"Are you going to help him?" Memory whispers.

"I don't know yet."

"Why didn't you tell me about the snake?"

"He's dangerous," the witch says eventually. "Hungry. I didn't want you getting hurt."

Too late for that. But that's not Samaritana's fault, and she doesn't say it. She doesn't say *I can take care of myself*, either. They both know that's not true.

She doesn't say anything at all. The witch's breathing deepens and slows. Memory stares into the dark, and lets herself fade.

In the morning, Memory helps Samaritana wash her hair on the back steps, holding the bucket while the witch works soap into her tight black curls. Water drips down her shoulders, spots her hitched-up skirt; her damp chemise clings to her breasts. She's the most beautiful woman Memory's ever seen, though it feels like betraying her mother to think such a thing. She used to wish she'd grow up half as beautiful, before she realized she'll never grow up at all.

Samaritana leans over as Memory pours the water slow and careful through her hair. Charms rattle around the witch's neck, beads and amulets and mojo bags, and she holds them out of the way. One of them is Memory's, bone, hair, and a scrap of rotted cloth wrapped up in silk, the spell that makes her solid and real again, even if it can't bring her back to life.

As she sets the bucket down, Memory finds John Grey watching them, a cigarette smoldering in his hand. The witch raises her head. Beads of water glisten against her cheek, tangle in her eyelashes. She smiles slowly. Memory's stomach feels too small, heavy with things she can't understand. She understands enough though, that Samaritana's words are no surprise.

"*Mon chou*, would you mind going out for a while? Maybe bring me back some blackberries?"

She nods, throat tight, and takes the empty bucket as she bolts down the steps. She doesn't look back to watch the witch lead the stranger inside.

She's still picking blackberries as the sun climbs toward noon. Thorns prick her hands, but the holes close right back up. She sucks the sour juice off her fingers before the stains fade.

Grey's magic prickles over her skin before she hears his boots in the grass. She sighs in relief; the bucket's almost full, and she's bored with the thicket. He stops beside her, stooping to scoop up a handful of berries. Insects drone through the heavy air. Neither of them speak for a time.

"How did you die, Memory?" he finally asks.

"I don't think that's any of your business." Her father would have slapped her mouth for that tone, but Grey just chuckles.

"No, it probably isn't." He eats another berry; the juice stains his teeth. "But you see, I know a trick. If I see a corpse hanging from the gallows, I can call his spirit back to speak with me. That trick works just as well with dead girls. So why don't you tell me a story?"

She glares at him, and he stares back with his spooky eyes. She doesn't think he's joking.

"I went out after dark," she says after a minute, scuffing the toe of her boot into the mossy dirt. She's only told the story out loud once before, but she hears it over and over in her head every day. "I knew better—all sorts of hungry things are out at night. But this one . . . He came to my window to tell me stories, about all the shining cities outside the swamp. I should have told my mother, she would have chased him off. She was a witch, near as good as Samaritana. But I liked his stories, full of things I'd never seen, never would see in the swamp. He said he could show me all sorts of wonders, and have me safe in bed by morning.

"I knew better, I really did, but the stories were so beautiful I forgot. One night I slipped outside after my parents were asleep."

She trails off with a shrug. It could have ended there, even if it hadn't. But Grey isn't buying it.

"And then?"

A compulsion in the words, a pressure like a stone under her tongue. She scowls and looks away. "The monster was there, waiting for me." The memory comes, never far away—that thing in the dark, night-shining eyes and sharp white teeth. "Before he could eat me up, my mother came out. She got between me and the monster. I ran inside, yelling for my father to get the shotgun. But it was too late. By the time he got there my mother was all torn up. We tried, me and my father and my grandmother. We tried, but she didn't make it to dawn."

"That is a distressing tale," Grey says after a minute's silence. "But I only count one death so far."

She digs her toe deeper into the mud; water begins to pool in the hole. "We buried my mother in the swamp a day later. Wrapped her up, weighed her down, and sank her into the deep places. My grandmother drew hex-marks on her shroud to keep the fish and gators away. That should have been my job, but I hadn't learned enough. Everyone knew what happened, knew that it was my fault. Nobody said anything, but my father couldn't even look at me. And my grandma . . . Her eyes were so mad and sad and disappointed. I couldn't stand to go home after the funeral, couldn't bear to have her look at me that way again. I ran away. Still wearing my best dress." Her fingers clenched in the white eyelet lace of her skirts.

"The last thing I remembered I was crying and running. Then it was dark, and then Samaritana was pulling me up again. I drowned, I guess. No monsters, no gators, just a stupid little girl who wandered too far from the path."

She can't cry anymore, but she scrubs a hand across her face anyway. Tilting her chin, Memory turns back to Grey. "You happy now?"

His face creases thoughtfully. "Thank you, Memory."

No pity, no you-poor-thing. It's worse than if he made a fuss. Memory turns and runs. He doesn't call her back.

Halfway to the house, she remembers the bucket. She almost leaves it, but pride wins. She moves quietly through the brush—maybe Grey will have gone.

As she slinks closer to the thicket, she hears voices. Grey and the Alligator Man. She ducks into a bramble cluster and listens, ignoring the thorns that scratch her arms and catch at her hair. At least she doesn't need to breathe.

"I've told her for years that she should leave the swamp," says the Alligator Man, his back to her, "but she doesn't listen to me." He takes a berry, licks the juice off his fingers. "You, though—I think you might convince her."

Grey pulls out his pouch and rolls a cigarette. "Why would I do anything that you want me to?"

"Because we want the same things—some of them, at least—and I'm more than willing to help you."

"Your help I can do without."

The dark man laughs. "Have you convinced yourself of that, tree-hanger? You wouldn't be here without me, to say nothing of all the other times."

"All I've found here is a witch and a dead girl. The world is full of those."

Memory bristles, forces herself to stay still. Grey exhales a mouthful of smoke, and for an instant their eyes meet through the cloud.

"The witch will take you to the snake." If the Alligator Man knows she's there, he gives no sign. "She's almost decided that already. If the snake knows what you need, his answer will have a price. You'll need the payment."

"You mean the girl."

Memory's fingers close around a bramble cane, and she remembers what it feels like to be sick to her stomach.

The Alligator Man shrugs. "She's already dead—it would be a kindness, really. A kindness to her, a meal for the beast, one less fetter holding

Samaritana to this rotting corpse of an existence. You may need a witch before this is over."

She hates them both right then, a hate so strong and sweet that for a minute she feels alive again.

Grey drops the end of his cigarette and crushes it beneath his boot. "I may. We'll see what the snake has to say."

He starts toward the house, and the Alligator Man vanishes. Memory crouches in the brush for a long while after, hands clenched to still their shaking, while midges whine and gnats cloud over the pail of blackberries.

Samaritana's in the kitchen, sweeping the floor and humming softly when Memory drags the berries inside. Grey's nowhere to be seen. She can't feel him either.

"Are you going to help him?" she asks Samaritana as she hoists the bucket onto the table.

The broom's rhythm falters. "I think so." The witch looks at Memory and her eyebrows rise. "Do you think I shouldn't?"

A serious question, not just humoring a child. Memory aches where her heart should be. "They want to use you, Grey and the dark man."

She chuckles "Of course they do." Her humor dies, and she leans the broom against the wall. "Honey, the world is full of people who want to use you, one way or another. That devil Carrefour is worse than most. He's tangled me too well."

"Does that mean you'll let him? Let them?" Memory sits, boot heels scuffing against the chair-rung.

Samaritana sighs, and the creases around her eyes deepen. Memory forgets that she's so much older than she looks. "That's what happens, sometimes, even with people who mean well. You use them, and they use you. The trick is not to hurt anyone more than you have to and not to let them hurt you. When I decided to come out here, I didn't think I could manage that anymore."

"And now?"

"Now I'm not sure. The world always catches up eventually. Maybe I should stop hiding." She smiles a crooked smile. "It's not all bad out there. It's time you saw someplace besides the swamp."

Memory nods and doesn't speak. She should tell her the rest, about the snake and his price, but she can't. She knows the truth: there's nothing out there for a dead girl.

She sleeps in her own bed that night. It smells like a stranger, and even after she flips the pillows and throws off the blanket she still can't rest. Everything's changing all around her, ever since Grey set foot in the house. Everything seemed stagnant when she was alive, and she hated it. Now she's the unchanging thing, and this creeping difference fills her with dread.

She could run away, take her chances in the swamp.

That scares her, too, but she can't stop the thought. Her body feels like a stranger as she rises and opens the window.

The breeze laps slow and heavy over the sill, rustling the leaves outside. Webs of moonlight and shadow ripple across the ground. Marshlights flicker in the distance, a sickly blue-green glow to lead careless travelers astray. They were ghosts, her mother told her, their skeletons long buried in the silt. She never asked Samaritana if that was true. Was she a corpse candle once? One more tiny light not realizing it was already snuffed?

She can run again. She can't drown this time, doesn't have to worry about gators and swamp cats. She can sleep in the cool dark mud with the frogs, and listen to their froggy dreams.

But Samaritana wants to leave, and Memory can help her do it. She doesn't think she could stand to disappoint the witch the way she disappointed her family. Maybe the Alligator Man is right, maybe it's a kindness. Samaritana can always find another girl, living or dead.

She stands at the window for a while, listening to the frogs. Does it hurt to die when you're already dead? The frogs don't know. Finally, she goes back to bed and fades into the dark.

Samaritana and Grey make their plans over breakfast the next morning. At dusk they'll row into the deep swamp to find his snake. Between-times for between-creatures, the witch says.

Memory helps with the chores, sweeping and dishes and pulling weeds in the garden. It should be different, her last day here—her last day—but it's the same as any other. She wants to ask Samaritana for another story. There are so many things she's never asked, and now she'll never know them.

So many things she never asked her mother, either. Time always seemed like it would stretch on and on forever. Now it's snipped short.

Grey finds Memory as afternoon shadows begin to crawl away from the house and out from under trees. Samaritana threw them both out so she could work on a charm.

He cracks a match against his thumbnail. "You know what's going to happen." Not really a question, so she doesn't bother to answer.

"Do you do this a lot?" she asks instead. "Feed girls to monsters?"

"Only when I have to." Smoke curls from his nose, writhes around his face. "A willing sacrifice is a powerful thing. Thank you."

"I'm not doing it for you."

"I know."

She wishes she could be angry again, feel that rush of hate, but it's faded into the cobwebbed spaces in her head. "What happened to your eye?"

He touches the scars on his left eyelid, scratches his stubbled cheek. "A willing sacrifice."

"Do you ever miss it?"

"It aches sometimes," he admits. "But the prize was worth the loss."

"What is it you want the snake to tell you?"

"I'm looking for an old friend. I've been looking for a long time. I think—I hope—that the snake knows where to find him."

"What if your friend is dead?"

He shrugs. "I'll deal with that if I must. But I don't think he is. We're hard to kill."

Bitterns coo in the gathering dusk as they push off from the landing. Beyond the trees the sky is streaked orange and gray. Samaritana doesn't argue when Memory climbs in the boat. She realizes the witch knows what's going to happen. That hurts, a tight ugly knot in her stomach, but she won't back down now. It'll be over soon.

Grey rows while Samaritana gives directions from the prow. Memory crouches in the stern, watching the water. Her pale reflection stares back.

She's never been so far out on the bayou before, even the few times her father took her fishing. Not even when they buried her mother.

They're not alone out here; she feels eyes all around. Grey does, too, and his hands tighten on the oars. Samaritana touches his shoulder, shakes her head—these are her monsters.

The last of the honey-colored light begins to die as they reach a clearing amid the tangled trees and cypress knees. The oars still, and their last ripples scatter and fade across the mossy water.

Grey stands up, moving carefully. The boat creaks, and a thread of water winds across the worn wood, puddling against the edge of Memory's boot. The quiet stretches. Nothing happens for so long that she thinks they've come to the wrong place. Then something moves.

A gator, Memory thinks as the surface swells and parts, but it keeps rising and she realizes it's a monster's head. Only its head, longer than a tall man. Water sluices off its ridged skull, glistens on scales the size of her hand. Its eyes are burning slits. Not a snake, or a gator. A dragon.

A forked purple tongue flicks between jagged teeth, and its yellow eyes widen. "Is that you, One-Eye?" His voice echoes between her ears, inside her chest.

"It is."

The dragon rises higher, ribbons of moss dripping from his curving neck. His wake rocks the little boat. "I thought the wolf made an end of you, though there were always rumors. Have you come to let me finish the job?"

"Not today, old worm." He spreads his empty hands, but Memory feels the magic crawling through him. Samaritana tingles with it, too, her eyes narrow as she studies the dragon. "Today I only have a question."

"My answers have a price. Have you brought me something?"

"You killed my son, worm. Why should I owe you anything but a spear?"

"I did, didn't I? But that was so long ago, I can't even remember what he tasted like. You've woken me, and I'm hungry now. So, ask me or fight me, but I'll have a meal from you either way." He glances at Memory, and her nails dig into her knees. His teeth are much bigger than her last monster's.

Grey's hand curls at his side, relaxes again. "I'm looking for the jackal."

The dragon blinks lazily, and his head sways closer to the boat. "I haven't seen him since I last saw you. But," he adds grudgingly, "others of my kin have. He's gone below, into the city of the dead. My father's armies besiege the walls."

"Why aren't you with them?"

"War is boring. I prefer water and sunlight and fat fish."

"How can I reach the city?"

"That's three questions, old crow. I can't answer that one—you'll have to find your own way." He moves closer, till the water dripping from his jaws splatters the boat. "You have your answer. I'd like my meal now, please."

Grey's eyes tighten. For one wild second Memory thinks he'll refuse. But he nods, and her hope dies. The monster waits, watching them with one heavy-lidded burning eye.

Memory stands up, and Grey inches aside to let her pass. Samaritana turns to face her, unhappy lines carved across her face.

"I'm sorry we have to say good-bye this way," the witch says softly, laying her hands on Memory's shoulders.

"It's all right. It was just a—" She pauses, groping for the right word. "A respite, wasn't it? I'm already dead."

"Maybe so. But I'm glad I found you, Memory." Samaritana kisses her forehead, lips warm on unreal skin. Memory thinks her dust-and-cobweb heart will break to pieces. The witch sorts through her charms, pulls one off and ties it around Memory's neck. It hums against her chest, throbbing gently like a pulse. The dragon makes an impatient sort of noise.

"Do you remember what I told you, about people and the world?"

Memory nods, one hand clutching her charm.

"You keep that in mind, and I think you'll do all right."

Something's wrong. She can't find her voice.

"What are you doing?" Grey asks. The boat shudders as he shifts his weight.

It rocks harder as the Alligator Man appears beside him. Memory startles, and it's a miracle they don't capsize. The monster's head swings around to watch; she wonders if he'll settle for just one meal if the boat turns over.

"Samaritana, what are you thinking?" the Alligator Man asks.

The witch stands, one hand still warm on Memory's shoulder. "You know exactly what I'm thinking, old devil." Her smile is fierce and bright in the gloom. "It's about time I rid myself of you."

"Don't," both men say with the same breath.

Samaritana laughs and turns to Grey. "I've bought you your answers, M'sieu Gris. You look after my child."

She holds his gaze for a long moment until he nods.

"Don't," says Memory, the word forced clumsy past her teeth. "I said I would." She wants to run, to throw herself off the boat and be done with it, but her feet won't move. "I don't want anyone else to die for me."

"Oh, *mignon*. A mother won't begrudge her child her life. You deserve more than you've had. I'm sorry I can't give you more than this." She turns away, stands at the prow of the boat. "Come on, old snake. Let's finish this."

The Alligator Man reaches for her, but the dragon is faster. The boat rocks with the absence of her weight. Memory screams once, and it's over.

A few bubbles rise, then the bayou settles. The dark man vanishes with a snarl.

Memory sits down hard on the wooden bench, her hands clutching the charm. Everything's spinning. She wants the world to shake with her grief, wants the sky to rage and thunder. But there's only the breeze sighing in the trees, the drone of insects, and the frogs' slow sad songs.

Grey stands still for a minute, staring at the water. After a while he sits and takes up the oars, and rows them back to Thimble Island. A bird calls in the dark. The swamp goes on the way it always has. The world goes on, and Memory still can't cry.

And In the Living Rock, Still She Sings

In a cavern beneath the skin of the world,
She sings.

Songs of sunlight, wind and waves,
The things she gave up,
Traded for rocks and bones
And the ghosts of children.

Traded for him.

Her voice stills; the serpent stirs.
Green as apples, green as poison,
Child of Nidhogg, the root-gnawer.
Beautiful and terrible, it ripples across the stone.

He closes his eyes.

Bound by chains, by weight of the mountain,
Bound by the bones of children.
Only choices bind her, but they weigh as heavy.

What do they say of her,
The chain-makers, the child-slayers,
Do they call her loyal?
Do they call her a fool?

When he wooed her, they lay by the water's edge,
And the wind heard all their whispered promises.
She knew he was a liar always,
Clever hands and wicked smiles.

She has learned to lie beneath the mountain.

Let them think her weak,
Those who know nothing of waiting.
She reads the weft and warp of fate,
Sees the strands upon the spindle.
The wind-age is coming, the wolf-age,
The time of breaking chains.
Twilight is coming soon.

She will teach them what she has learned of poison.

Shadow of the Valley

Into the shadow of the valley of an underpass I track my prey. His stink trails through the rank city night, a subtle-sweet decay. Beneath the meat, Heaven.

I grip my sword hilt, palm slippery. Sweat crawls beneath my jacket; my stomach roils.

Broken glass crunches beneath my boots. He shrugs aside his cocoon of dirty cardboard, rises on jerky marionette limbs. Doesn't attack, doesn't speak, just watches me with a face too young for those sad eyes. A hospital bracelet hangs around one knobby wrist. He raises a hand in greeting.

Easier if he scourged me with curses and righteous wrath.

His eyes shine brighter, mask slipping. He knows me, knows what I do. My threats and entreaties die unspoken, no match for that calm strength.

"I'm sorry." I draw my sword, needle-shard of ice and darkness.

He steps forward and spreads his arms.

Ofanim. The Wheels. The Many-eyed Ones.

He sheds his mortal guise like grimy clothes. A rush of heat and wild kaleidoscope flames, radiant sunrise against sin-black night. The underpass blazes like a cathedral.

So beautiful, my brother. His symphony swells inside me, light and motion and glorious purpose.

I have purpose, too. The sword weighs in my hand.

For all his brilliant fury, he is at peace. The love and sadness in his eyes outshine his fire.

Half-blind with tears, I strike and miss, strike again. He catches my wrist, pulls me close. No anger in him, only love. Gently he holds me, stronger than my fragile flesh. Tenderly he wipes away my tears, that I may see him. Inexorably he meets my eyes.

He shows me paradise, the glory he left to be a soldier in this war. Glory he carries still. He offers it to me. If I lay down my sword, lay down my bloody purpose, my master's vendetta. Set aside my burdens and follow him.

Home.

My sword falls from numb fingers. The ofan enfolds me in his dizzying electric embrace. We rise together, weightless, the heart of an atom amid incandescent wheels.

I love him.

I hold his gaze, drink down the wonders he offers. My hand slips inside my jacket.

His song resonates in my bones. It will shatter me. Peace, an end to suffering, respite from this war. I give him what he promises.

My dagger slides between his ribs, into his borrowed heart. Ensorcelled steel binds angelic aether to rough clay, transubstantiates him till he is as mortal as I am. I twist the blade; his blood bathes my hands.

We sink to the broken, bitter earth. Glass bites my knees as I cradle him. My tears splash his face. His eyes, brimming with love, slowly dim.

I hold him close until he's gone, an empty shell in my arms. My flesh unscathed—he's wounded me like no other. The night reeks of carrion and bitter tears.

We have fallen so far. I have farther still to go.

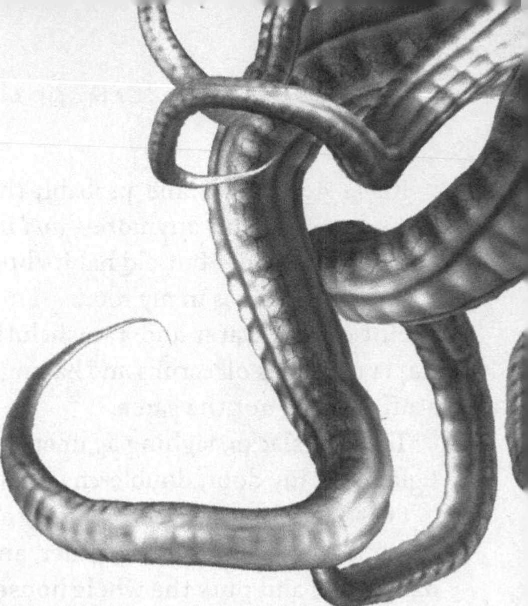

Red

In the dream I'm in a garden. In the dream I'm not alone. A girl stands beside me, a girl with eyes red as poison apples. She takes my hand, and her skin is cold.

"We have to go north."

I wake with the taste of storms in my mouth and screams echoing down the hall. Slow and dream-sticky, and for a second I don't know where I am, but I'm on my feet with my gun in my hand before my eyes are all the way open.

A second later I sigh, rubbing crust out of my eyelashes left-handed; only Amber and her nightmares. I was dreaming, too, but it's already crumbling like sandcastles. Even familiar screams shouldn't be ignored, though, so I ease the door open, glancing both ways before I slip down the hall.

Amber's awake when I get there, sobbing and gasping while Kayla pats her back and murmurs soothing nonsense. Kay gives me a nod and I lower the gun. The metal is cool and heavy against my thigh.

"You okay?" I ask, still froggy from sleep.

Amber nods, scrubbing away tears. Her hair stands in tousled cockatiel-spikes, the bright red of Kool-Aid faded now to dirty pink. "Yeah, sorry. It's just—" She waves a hand at the barred and shuttered window, at the rushing rain beyond.

"Yeah."

"Everyone okay?" Dave calls from down the hall. He's shy about the girls' rooms.

"All clear," I yell back.

Kayla lights a candle and I squint at Amber's creepy Kit-Kat clock—nearly eleven in the morning. Early for me, but I doubt I'll get back to sleep, or find the dream again if I do.

"Get some more rest," I tell Amber. "I'll do your detail today."

Kayla gives me a smile, probably thinking of my good karma. She doesn't call herself Wiccan anymore—*and it harm none* didn't last long after the end of the world—but old habits linger.

I wash and dress in my room—I miss running water most of all, I think. A pint of cold water and a washcloth don't measure up to a real shower. Kayla makes us oil scrubs and baking soda shampoo and all kinds of hippie stuff, but it's not the same.

The rain slacks, sighing against the window. The storm is almost gone. I glance at my door, double-check the flimsy hook. Just a quick look . . .

I ease the shutters open, wincing at every tiny squeak. The others would never let me live this down either, and not in a teasing way. It's stupid and dangerous and puts the whole house at risk. But I have to see.

Crooked bars behind the shutter, glass cracked and streaked behind them. And beyond them all, the storm.

The sky is the color of the space behind my eyes, red-black and shot through with distant lightning. Scarlet streaks the windowpane. The end of the world is beautiful.

Distant thunder growls and its voice is the voice of my dream. *North*, it says. I shudder as images surface: a garden blooming with poison-red flowers, unfurling their creepers in the twilight; a girl with eyes the color of poppies. *North*.

My hands shake as I close the window tight. We forgive each other all manner of quirks to live like we do, but the others won't forgive this. My secret, the taste of red rain on my lips. I tasted the rain and I'm still alive—still human, still sane—but I feel the storms coming now, and the monsters that sprout like mushrooms in their wake. Kayla thinks I'm psychic, and I let her. They'd kill me or turn me out if they knew.

I've lost two families already to the apocalypse rain. I can't bring myself to give up this one.

Amber was on clean-up crew today, so I help Seb sweep and do dishes. There's extra scrubbing—tomorrow we're hosting a gang-meet. We check in with each other whenever we can, but every three months one gang hosts the others for a formal get-together. I get a quiet nagging fear before every meet. I know the others do, too: What if this time someone doesn't come?

Seb is probably disappointed about the schedule switch, but he doesn't say anything. He doesn't say anything ever, as far as I can tell. He's certainly never said he has a crush on Amber, but my intuition still works, even if the water and electricity don't. He's the youngest of us, still just a kid when the first storm came six years ago—now he's callused and hard-eyed, the fastest of all us on the draw. You'd never know he's only fifteen.

Not even two years younger than me, but some days I feel a hundred years old.

Kayla comes down by the time we're finished, and I make coffee and we sit in the gloomy kitchen waiting for the red storm to blow out and the next to blow in. It always rains after, a real rain. We don't know why—new weather patterns, or maybe the world is trying to clean out the contagion. We don't know much of anything, except to adapt or die.

After a long quiet, Kayla nudges my foot under the table. I look up, realizing I've been staring into the dregs of my coffee for ten minutes or so. "What's up, kiddo?"

"I had the dream again," I say, though I didn't mean to.

"North?"

I nod and sip cold coffee to keep my mouth busy. I've told her about the thunder, but not the garden. And not the red-eyed girl—that part is new.

"It comes with every storm, doesn't it?"

If Kayla weren't smart and perceptive, she never would have held the Orphans together this long. Still, sometimes I wish she were a little less smart. "Pretty much, yeah."

"What do you think it means?"

"I don't know. But it feels important. It wants me to answer." I give her a crooked grin. "That's probably a bad idea, though."

It's Kayla's turn to frown at her mug. A familiar clatter and bang drifts from outside—Nik and Geoff setting up the catchment. The clean rain is here.

"Probably. We'll talk about it later. After the meeting."

After the rain stops and the boys give the all-clear on the weather, I suit up and do the rounds. It's been quiet lately, and it's starting to bug me. Not the itch in my blood that means something's really wrong, but a vague distrust. Nothing moves outside, but my hand stays near my gun as I circle the grounds.

Home is a castle. A little castle on a hill in the middle of downtown Austin. A military school back in the 1800s. I don't know what happened to it after that—it was closed and boarded up when we moved in. It's not as defensible as Los Calaveras' headquarters, or as gorgeous as the Spooks', but it's got a great view.

The last rainclouds snag and tatter against the skyscrapers. Glass spires and ziggurats fade into the haze, their grimy windows reflecting the light in streaks and flashes, crackle-finished. Below them, a baby forest grows. Nature moves fast now that the world's fallen apart.

Too fast, sometimes. The trees are pressing against the fence again and we pruned a week ago. Lately the plants have started to change, too, strange new flowers and fungi sprouting in the shade. Kayla doesn't like the look of them. She's kept a close eye on the greenhouse since we saw the first one, but so far we haven't been menaced by bloodthirsty tomatoes or savage zucchini.

Ivy twines through the fence, leaves and spiraling tendrils softening the lines of the wire. I rip it away with gloved hands, trying not to think about the garden in my dreams. The original fence couldn't have kept out a lazy dog, let alone zombies, but we put up chain link and razor wire. Geoff and Dave talk about building a real brick-and-mortar wall, but I like being able to see what's lurking on the other side.

Halfway through my circuit I get a shiver, the nasty kind, but it fades too quick to figure out where it came from. I can't see anything moving in the brush, except a couple of squirrels that don't seem any more vicious than usual. The gates are all locked, the tripwires un-sprung. I'm less scared of shamblers than of other people, really. We have a sturdy truce with the Spooks and Los Calaveras, but you never know. Things were ugliest during the gang wars, when you couldn't trust anything that moved, living or dead. It calmed down after the Kings and Hammers got slaughtered, but I worry. We're still human, and even a good apocalypse can't cure humanity of stupidity. I won't feel humans coming.

I check in with Dave after my rounds. He's the last of the Hammers, the only one who didn't go down to monsters or other gangs. He's really not so bad, now that he doesn't call himself Thor. It took a while, but losing enough fights with Geoff eventually knocked the racist bullshit out of his head. We don't even flinch at his swastika tattoo anymore—it's just another scar. We're all orphans here.

After lunch I take my knitting and sketchpad up to the tower. I'm halfway through a scarf that I think will be Amber's birthday present, if I finish it in time. My grandmother taught me to knit, another world ago. Besides my middle name, it's all I have left of her. Twelve inches of pointy steel are nice to have around, too. The sketching is just for me, the last part of me from before the rain, when I was a daughter and a granddaughter, a sister and a girlfriend, a student and an artist. All the things I lost when I became a survivor, an Orphan.

Underneath the chilly gray November sky, I can almost make believe the world is still alive. Except for the silence. No more traffic, no more humming wires, no more distant voices. Not even screams and gunshots lately. Just the wind and the last of the rain dripping from the gutters, the soft scrape of my pencil on scavenged cold-press paper.

The shiver comes back, a prickling below my skin. I glance up from my drawing and scan the yard, one hand drifting toward my gun. Nothing inside the perimeter, or on the road. There. On the slope below the house, amid crumbling cement terraces and rusting rebar, the skeletons of stillborn condos, something moves.

A girl.

She stands there, watching me through the fence. Her stance hits me first. It's not the dazed sway or wary crouch of the shamblers. She stands hip-shot, one thumb tucked into a pocket of her tattered jeans. Like a living person. I raise my hand, lips parting to call, when the rest sinks in: her sickly gray pallor, the ugly wound stretching across her left shoulder, blood streaking her face. My hand falls.

She cocks her head and waves back.

I stand there for a minute, gaping. I swear she grins at me. I've never seen a zombie move like that, and it's too bright out for the nastier things. But the rain evolves. All we can do is try to keep up.

Footsteps rattle the stairs and before I can second-guess myself I shake my head at her, make a shooing gesture. I don't trust Seb or Dave not to shoot first and think later. But it's only Nik. By the time he climbs up, the girl is gone.

I have a new secret.

Nik isn't even wearing his gun. I should bitch at him, but I'm too busy trying not to look nervous. It must not work, because he says, "Sorry, did I scare you?"

"It's the quiet. It gets to me after a while."

He nods. "Do you mind?" he asks, pausing with one foot still on the stairs.

"No, come on up." I pull my yarn bag out of his way, sneaking a glance at the hill to make sure the girl is gone.

Nik is a year older than me. He should have started college this year. Tall and skinny, with a beaky nose and dark hair that's always flopping in his face. He liked gaming once, movies, computers, rock climbing. The sort of boy I would have been friends with. The sort of boy I might have dated. It hurts to hang out with him sometimes. We all get that pain; it's called *before*.

We stand in silence, leaning against the crenellations and watching the clouds tatter and drift away. I wait for the awkward moment to come. Nik's been trying, in his quiet way, to put the moves on me. Don't get me wrong—he's cute, and I'm tempted. A lot tempted. I can't even remember my last kiss. But so much could go wrong, besides any of the usual relationship messes.

Michelle was six months pregnant when she got caught in a storm. She died slow and screaming for five days before Kayla shot her. Nobody talks about it, but we can't forget. Even if a baby didn't kill me from the inside out, who knows what the lingering traces of rain in my blood would do?

I turn to collect my sketchpad. My drawing stares up at me—a forest, rough and smudged, thick graphite shadows between the trees and flowering vines that dangle from the branches like spiders.

I flip the sketchbook closed and gather my stuff.

"Audra—" Nik looks so sad. I know we can't put the conversation off any longer. "Did I do something? You keep avoiding me. . . ." His hair falls over his long-lashed dark eyes and I want to tuck it back.

"I'm sorry. You haven't done anything. It's not you—" Nik grimaces, and I can't finish the sentence. Some lines don't get any less lame even after the world ends. "It's everything." That's still horrible, but it's true.

"Yeah." He smiles, wry and understanding. I wonder if maybe I'm being an idiot. "It's not like either of us could move out if we had a bad breakup."

"I'm sorry." I lean in to kiss his cheek, my bag held between us like a shield. The smell of his hair nearly undoes my very limited virtue.

"It's okay." He touches my arm awkwardly. "I'll see you around, anyway."

We laugh, but it's strained. My eyes are blurring by the time I get back inside; I blame hormones.

I'm restless all day, picking up a dozen projects and setting them down again. Finally, I put my leathers on again and take another walk around the perimeter. What I'd really like is to walk outside, down Castle Hill, through the broken streets, a different view to clear my head. But outside is too dangerous alone.

I feel a shiver at the northeast corner. To the north lies an overgrown driveway and the broken remnants of a house, nearly consumed by trees and brambles. East faces downtown, and the slabs of broken, weed-choked cement below the fence. I can't see anything but a few birds moving in the trees. I glance back, but I'm alone in the yard; the turret is empty.

Leaves crunch, a single deliberate footstep. I spin, hand dropping to my gun.

The girl. She stands at the bottom of the terraced wall, watching me through the fence. When I recoil, she shows me her empty hands, slow and careful like I was the one who might bite.

She's my age. Was my age. Dressed in dirty jeans and a tank top, thick black hair pulled back in a braid. Her skin must have been a warm golden-brown once, a shade or two darker than mine; now it's cold and sallow. The wound I saw this morning is still there, a nasty gash on her shoulder, skin flapping to expose raw flesh. No blood or infection, just dark pink meat and pale marbled fat. Her eyes are wide under thick arching brows.

Her eyes are red. Not clouded zombie eyes, but clear and bright, carmine and carnelian.

My breath catches. "I saw you—"

She raises her eyebrows, living movement on a dead face. "This morning, yeah." Her voice is soft and raspy, but human. I notice her draw breath to speak; she wasn't breathing before.

"No. I saw you in a dream."

She smiles, flashing white teeth. "That's romantic, but we're taking things a little fast, don't you think? I don't even know your name."

My face goes hot. Zombies don't smile like that. They don't tease. Even the other things, the ones that prowl outside camps at night, crying and wailing like lost children—even they don't *flirt*.

"You're different," I whisper, mostly to myself.

Her smile widens; her eyeteeth are thick and sharp. "You haven't shot me yet, so maybe you're different, too."

"What are you?" I flush again, hotter this time. I've shot dozens of monsters, but that was just rude. "I'm sorry. I mean—"

The dead girl laughs at me. "I'm Natalie." She presses one palm against the fence.

"Audra." I squat down so we're closer, but don't touch her hand. I may be going crazy, but I'm not stupid. "What are you doing out there?"

"The same thing you're doing in there: surviving."

"Are you . . . hungry?"

"All the time." Her smile twists and falls away. "But I don't eat what you eat anymore."

I was afraid she'd say that. "You're hurt." Which sounds stupid, considering she's dead, but that cut makes my skin crawl to look at.

"This?" She pokes at the skin flap and I cringe. "It doesn't hurt, really. Sort of itches. I have to keep the bugs out, though."

"I should go," I say, my mouth dry. "Don't— Don't talk to any of the others. They might not—"

"Care that I'm different?"

"I'm sorry."

She shrugs. "Not your fault. Thanks for not shooting me."

"I— You're welcome." This isn't the strangest conversation I've had since the world ended, but it's close.

Natalie takes a step back, then pauses. "You said you dreamed of me. North?"

My mouth falls open, but before I can answer someone calls my name. I turn to see Geoff halfway across the yard. When I look back Natalie is gone.

"What is it?" Geoff asks as I hurry to meet him. Trying not to act like I'm hurrying.

"A cat. He looked healthy, but he ran away."

Geoff nods sympathetically. His shirt is soaked, and stray soapsuds cling in the dark cloud of his hair. "Sorry, Aud. You know we can't have pets."

"I know. I just miss my old cat."

He pats my shoulder. "Yeah. Get your laundry, kiddo. We don't want to stink for our guests."

I don't look back as we go inside. I don't open my window. But when I dream that night, I dream of red eyes.

The others arrive before noon the next day. I stand on the turret with Nik and Amber to watch them ride in, waving the blue flag that means all clear.

It's hard to look tough riding bicycles, but Las Calaveras manage in their chains and painted jackets. The Spooks pedal up the hill behind them, dressed all in black, as usual. We laugh about the colors sometimes, but I have to admit they look pretty impressive.

The Calaveras sent six people this time, the Spooks five, putting the temporary population of the castle at eighteen. Nearly ten percent of the city's current population. Math didn't use to depress me this much.

Gang-meet means presents. Our guests bring cookies, tamales in an insulated bag, two bottles of wine, a bag of yarn, two 10-packs of AA batteries, and a fancy set of knives. We give them fresh vegetables, a jacket too big for any of us, a fountain pen with an extra nib and a bottle of ink, a pair of blankets that Kayla and I knitted, and a zombie teddy bear still in the original box. Maybe that shouldn't be funny, but I think it's pretty cute. Cat, the head Spook, coos at it like it was a baby and hugs Kayla. We've run out of so many things, but Cat never seems to run out of eyeliner or hair dye. There's lots of hugging and "You look good!" and manly handshakes between the guys.

Usually we draw straws to see who attends the meeting and who keeps watch, but today is different. Marisela, the Calaveras' leader, asks all the girls to join them while the guys wait outside. Geoff frowns and Nik raises his eyebrows, but no one argues with her—she makes the tamales. I sit in the back next to Amber, trying not to feel like I have "fraternized with the enemy" written across my forehead.

"Lupe had her baby," Marisela tells us, after we've settled in the kitchen and coffee and cookies have been shared. "A boy. She named him Carlos, after his father." Carlos Senior died six months ago, so the congratulations are a little sad. Marisela waits through them like a proud grandmother. She's not even forty, but her brown face is seamed, her hair already gray.

"That brings us to my main concern," she continues. "I've discussed it a little with Cat, but it affects everyone. We need children, or we'll never rebuild."

I shiver, despite the body heat filling the kitchen; beside me, Amber does, too. She wouldn't say that if she'd seen Michelle. Or maybe she would. Marisela's seen her share of terrible things. She had a daughter, *before*. The worst part is, she's right.

"We'd need more resources for children," Kayla says. "Better security."

Marisela nods. "My people are already working on it, for Carlos. Children will make these things happen. It's too easy to put it off, to say *maybe next year*. Then a dozen next years pass and half of us are dead. If we want to survive here, to build, it has to happen."

Kayla doesn't answer for a minute. Her shoulders sag. "I've tried. Me and Geoff, I mean. For the past six months. I know that's not very long, but . . . I have tried."

I lean back, frowning; Amber starts beside me. Nice to know I'm not the only Orphan with secrets.

Marisela nods, her dark eyes creasing with sympathy. "Give it time. It's not only your burden." She looks around the room. I try not to duck when her gaze touches me.

"It shouldn't be anyone's burden," Kayla says, catching that glance. "I want a baby. Amber doesn't, and Audra is too young."

Amber's never talked about children one way or another, but I know what Kayla really means. The nightmares, the panic attacks, the way Amber shuts down when the storms get bad—she's the most fragile of all of us that way. I doubt a baby would help. Especially after Michelle.

"I don't want a baby either," Cat says, picking at her nail polish. "Never did. But Mari's right—we have to do it, or Austin will be empty in twenty years." She nods to one of her companions, a skinny girl not much older than I am. "Angel is willing to try."

Marisela looks back to me. I want to crawl through the wall. "How old are you, Audra?"

A stray cookie crumb scrapes down my throat. "Seventeen next month."

"Young, but not too young to think about it."

Kayla frowns. "You can't make—"

"Of course not. But I can ask. And you can think about it. Which leads me to my other idea. We should consider an exchange of members. One or two people, for several months at a time. To learn new skills, meet new people."

Meet new people we might want to have babies with. I have a dozen excuses to say no: I'm too young; there's no one I like that much; I'm terrified of the idea. But the real reason—the red seed inside me—I can never share that.

"We'll think about it," Kayla says. "Any other news?"

Cat sits up straight. "We've seen a couple of scavengers creeping around downtown. The human kind. We've tried talking, but they run. I don't know if they're crazy or dangerous or just scared, but keep your eyes open."

"I have a question," I say, before the meeting ends and turns into socializing and dinner. All eyes turn to me and my cheeks scald. "I— Some of you know that I . . . feel things, right?" The last word comes out a squeak. I may be effectively proving that I'm too young for anything. Marisela and Cat nod. Kayla frowns, but gestures for me to go on. I take a deep breath, forcing the rest out in a rush.

"I've been having dreams lately. The same dream. I hear a voice telling me to go north. I wondered if anyone else ever has that dream."

Silence fills the kitchen, broken by the scuff of shoes and rasp of cloth.

"Tia Soledad has dreams like that," Marisela says at last. Soledad is the Calaveras matriarch; a *curandera*, they say. I've only met her once, but I'm willing to believe she's a witch. "She says she dreams of a garden, a place of death." She crosses herself, though she's a Catholic the way Kayla used to be a Wiccan. "It makes her afraid." She catches my eye. "Even if it didn't, 'north' is too vague to go looking."

The others nod, and I can't argue. I can't argue that in my dream, the garden isn't a place of death, only of different life. A place of change. The way I'm changed. Maybe the way Natalie is, too. I can't say any of that, so I shut up and help get ready for dinner.

The Spooks and Calaveras spend the night, which is weird but nice. Weird to have strangers in the castle, people we don't know and trust like our own kin. Nice to hear laughter and new voices, to see a dozen people camped out downstairs like a grade school sleepover. Cat brought hot chocolate; the miniature marshmallows have fossilized, but no one complains.

The warm fuzzies last until Marisela finds me in the kitchen, rinsing out the cups. Her company should be reassuring. She's strong and smart, with a brusque competence that reminds me of my mother. But after the meeting, I would rather face a zombie.

"I scared you today. I'm sorry."

"It's not you." The line doesn't sound any better than when I said it to Nik. I set the last cup in the draining board and start wiping down the silverware.

Marisela laughs. She's had twenty extra years to hear lame excuses. "I'd like you to come back with me. Not to get knocked up," she adds as I fumble a handful of forks. "Just to visit for a while. Tia Soledad would like to hear about your dreams."

And I want to know about hers. If I dream of the garden because I'm tainted, does that mean Soledad is too? Or is there another cause? I don't know how I'd ask her without giving up my secret, but I'm almost willing to try.

"I'd have to ask Kayla."

"I talked to Kayla already." I duck my head so she can't see my face. Of course she did. "She says it's your decision. I'd send someone to replace you, of course, so the Orphans wouldn't suffer."

The Orphans are the smallest group, barely enough of us to keep ourselves safe and fed after Michelle died, and Jamie before her. But we like it here, together. Marisela's exchange student program is a good idea, but I'm afraid it will lead to the Orphans finding new families.

"Thank you for the invitation," I say, risking a glance at her face. If she has any ulterior motives, I can't read them in her dark eyes. "Let me think about it."

"Of course."

Dawn is a peach and periwinkle glow behind the jagged lines of downtown when I leave my room. Dreams ache in the pit of my stomach. Not the thunder dreams, but nightmares about Nik and Michelle and red-eyed babies. I shove my first-aid kit under my jacket, guilt like a hot hand on the back of my neck.

Kayla has the morning watch, which is good and bad. She doesn't need explanations when I tell her I want to go for a walk alone.

"You've been restless for a while, haven't you?" she says. That's the bad part. "Before yesterday."

I hadn't thought about it, but she's right. The answer is obvious: ever since the dreams started.

"You want to go north."

I shrug, shoulders hunched to hide the bulge under my jacket. "I know it's stupid, but yeah. What if this is real? What if it's important?"

"I don't know. I guess you have to decide what's most important to you."

"Marisela thinks that Tia Soledad could help me understand the dreams."

"Maybe she can. Do you want to go?"

"No," I say, as honest as it gets. "But if you want me to . . ."

"I don't want. But it might be a good idea. It would make Marisela happy, and you would learn things. I don't want things to get bad between the gangs again."

No one would survive another war.

"Let me think about it. Let me go for a walk. Outside. I'll be careful."

"All right. But don't go far, okay?"

"I won't."

Natalie is waiting for me in the same spot, crouching below the wall where no one in the castle could see.

"Hi," she says. In the soft dawn light, her smile looks like a living girl's.

I try to smile back, but it feels crooked and wrong. "If I come out of the fence, are you going to eat me?"

"No eating. I promise." She traces an X over her left breast. "Cross my heart and hope to be pecked apart by buzzards."

"Are you alone?"

Her smile fades. "Completely." Loneliness on a dead girl's face is the saddest thing I've ever seen.

I unlock the padlocked lesser gate, holding the chain carefully so the links don't rattle. My skin crawls at the sudden vulnerability, but I don't feel anything but the familiar itch of Natalie.

She keeps her distance as I creep down the slope, trying not to scare me. Maybe she's scared, too.

I duck low to keep out of sight of the castle, crossing the wide expanse of graffiti-scarred cement till we're behind a broken wall.

"Sit down." I point to a chunk of concrete. "I'm going to fix your shoulder."

"What?"

"It's driving me crazy. You're not afraid of needles, are you?"

That makes her laugh, and she sits. She laughs again when I rinse the cut with hydrogen peroxide, but I remember what she said about bugs. Nothing's hiding in the wound now, thank god.

The guilt is back, stronger than ever. I wouldn't feel bad about giving her food, but medical supplies we might never replace.

"Tell me about the dreams," I say as I thread the needle. Her skin is the same temperature as the air, dry and firm. She doesn't smell dead, which is a nice surprise. A little like dry leaves, but mostly like nothing at all.

"They started in the spring." She sits very still. As she pauses, I hear the pop as the tip pierces skin. She watches as thread slides through meat.

"Does that hurt?"

"It feels weird. Like forcing an earring through a closed hole." Her hands twitch in her lap, as if she wants to gesture when she talks. "They come with the storms. The dreams, I mean. I was finally getting used to . . . you know. Then they started. First the thunder told me to go north. Then I saw the garden."

"Did you—" I concentrate very carefully on holding torn skin closed. "Did you see me?"

"Not at first. Not until I got close. I came from San Marcos."

"On foot?"

Her shoulder shakes with her laugh. I wait till she stops to keep sewing. "A zombie riding a bike would be a little ridiculous, don't you think? Besides, I don't get tired anymore. Only—"

Hungry. I'm glad she doesn't say it. Her face is only inches from mine, inches from my throat and other soft bits. Adrenaline rushes through me, and my hands tingle on the needle. Natalie turns her head away. I appreciate that, too.

I tug the last stitch and tie off the thread. They're not quite even, but it's a lot better than looking at raw meat.

Natalie stretches, testing the thread. "That feels better. Thanks." Her eyes meet mine and she leans in.

I freeze. My life doesn't flash before my eyes, but I do have a long second to think *ohgodnostupididiotnottheface*. Then she kisses me.

Her lips are cool and dry. She tastes like storms. Her fingers brush my cheek, soft as a moth's wing.

My pulse beats hard in my mouth when she pulls away; my stomach is floaty and too small.

She raises a hand, lowers it again. The sun has cleared the broken towers and pale gold rinses her face. Her eyes, at least, are alive; wide pupils contract at the touch of light. "I didn't mean to do that," she whispers.

"I—" I lick my lips. I'm not sorry, and that probably means I'm crazy. "It's all right."

We stare at each other in the rising dawn. I don't know what to say, and for a moment it doesn't matter. Then Natalie's nostrils flare and her eyes move, tracking behind me, and the moment is gone. Footsteps scrape on broken stone.

I spin, clumsy and slow, waiting for the thunder of a gun. It doesn't come.

Nik stands on the terraced hill, one hand on his gun, the other sagging under the weight of a pack. It's my pack, and that confuses me more than anything else. Then it clicks: he brought my bag because he heard I was leaving. Kayla and Marisela must have thought I'd made up my mind.

Natalie growls, sharp teeth flashing. Nik's gun clears his hip.

"No!" I twist in front of her. It's not the stupidest thing I've done today. "Don't. Nik, please. She's different."

"Audra?" His voice is tiny and confused, but he doesn't shoot.

"It's all right. I'm not—" Not infected. But that's not true. "She didn't hurt me," I say instead. "She won't hurt you."

"What's going on? Kayla said you might be leaving."

"She was right." I have made up my mind now, and the rush of knowing dizzies me. "But I'm not going with the Calaveras." Behind me, Natalie makes a small surprised sound. I can't go back to the Orphans now. Nik might keep my secret, but I can't ask him to. I can't stay with the Orphans, and I can't go with Marisela.

"Where?" he asks. He lowers the gun, but doesn't put it away.

I glance at Natalie. She nods, her hand brushing mine.

"North. Tell Kayla I went north. I need to know what's there. I— I'll come back if I can."

He nods, his face slack and sad. My bag drops to the ground with a thump. He twitches as I get close.

"Thank you." Kissing him goodbye seems like a bad idea. Instead I brush my hand against his shoulder.

"They'll come looking soon," he says, taking a step backward.

I shoulder my pack. Natalie's hand is cool and dry in mine as we start down the hill.

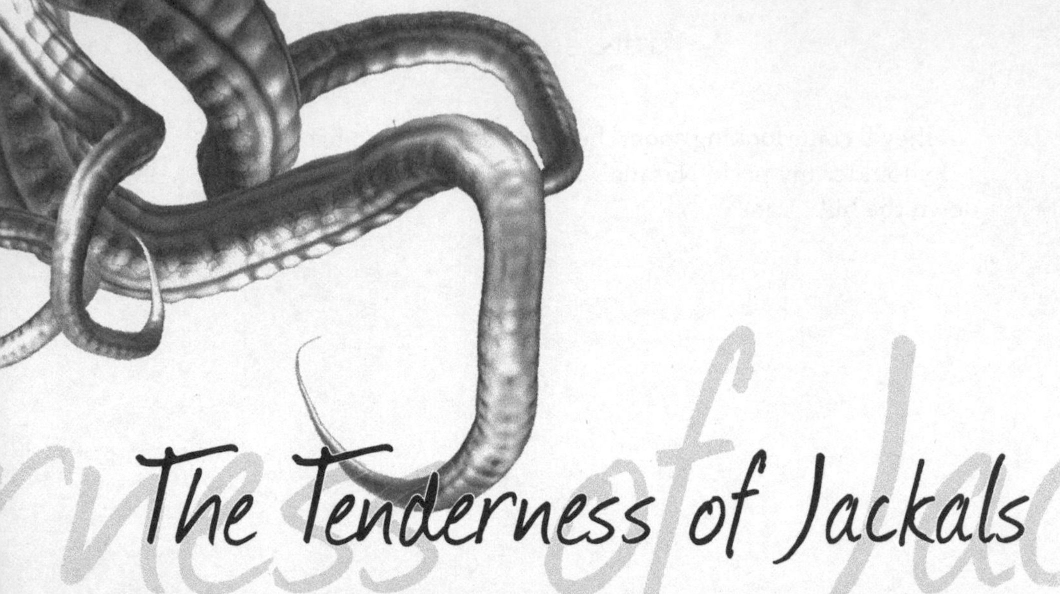

The Tenderness of Jackals

The train chases the setting sun, but can't catch it. Not even the high-speed line can catch the sun, and the InterCity-Express slides into the Hannover Hauptbahnhof as purple dusk gives way to charcoal. In the hum and whine of its wheels, Gabriel hears the wolves.

Soon, they whisper.

He drags on his cigarette, watching the sinuous white-and-red curve of the train vanish behind the station. Eyes flash in the darkness, nearly lost in the neon and glitter of the Promenade shops. Smoke curls from his nose, twists a sharp-jawed head toward him before it unravels on the breeze. *Hungry*, it growls.

He waits a moment longer; reluctant, if not defiant. Savoring the smoke and the night, air that doesn't reek of the tunnels—musk and meat and thickening tension, the ghouls snapping as often as they spoke and the changelings cowering out of their way. Everyone knowing the wolves were waiting and no one wanting to answer the call. Until finally Gabriel, newcomer, interloper that he is, couldn't stand it anymore and went above to face them.

Thinking about it is enough to ruin the taste of his cigarette. He crushes the butt underfoot and goes inside, accompanied by ghostly wolves. It's easier to acquiesce. Everyone does, they tell him.

Too bright inside, new glass and metal guts dressed in old stone skin—glowing screens and signs, light gleaming on the tiles, restaurants, and expensive shops. He watches the train disgorge its Berlin passengers. Footsteps and hushed voices echo through the vaulted room, eerily muted. Commuters and students, tourists, a pair of gray-coated Bundeswehr officers. Nothing that looks like prey.

The tightness in his chest eases. Maybe not this train. Maybe it won't be tonight. Maybe he won't be the one to feed the wolves after all.

Then he sees the boy.

He might almost be a uni student, or at least pass for one. Fashionably threadbare jeans and T-shirt, a sweatshirt tied around his waist despite the heat, a backpack stiff with paint and patches hanging off one thin shoulder. Dark hair falls over his eyes, but can't hide the sleepless shadows under them. He glances around, shoulders hunched, hands tight on the straps of his bag. Too far away for Gabriel to smell his nervous sweat, but he imagines the scent of it clearly.

So do the wolves.

One of the soldiers moves past the boy with the barest brush of sleeves; the boy shudders. Gabriel shivers too—for an instant the light is wrong, twisting and dimming. The station darkens, shrinks. The soldier glances down, his face scarred, his uniform stained and decades out of date.

Then it's gone and the soldier walks on, neat and pressed once more. The boy's face pales. It's always easier for the walls to slip here, in the between-places. Too bad he can't understand the warning.

Their gazes meet, hold for an instant before the boy looks away. Gabriel steps back, wraps himself in shadow and watches the boy glance at the ticket counter before turning toward the exit. The wolves breathe hot and hungry on his neck.

The strays, the runaways, the lonely and the lost—these have always been their prey.

The killings started in 1918, when the war had left Germany broken and starving, left more children with nowhere to go. At least twenty-four young men and boys lured away from the train station with promises of jobs or food or a place to sleep, or even just a cigarette and a soft word. Gabriel knows the taste of that desperation; it's how he first found the ghouls.

At least twenty-four people murdered here in six years, probably more. Such a small number, really, not even a dent in the population. Not like the genocide Gabriel's grandparents escaped in 1915, or the holocaust that swept Europe with the next war, or even the civil war that Gabriel survived. Insignificant, as atrocities go. But it was enough to birth the wolves.

Gabriel wonders how many more people have been killed in Hannover since they came. Killed by people like him.

He follows the boy outside, away from the wicked lights. The last colors of dusk have faded and the night closes around him, warm and heavy, full of the rush of fountains and the hum and purr of traffic, footsteps, and voices. The wolves follow, full of hunger and approbation. So much easier to give them what they want—what they insist he wants, too. He knows the hunger, doesn't he? The desire for the chase, to feel skin part and blood flow, the taste of hot meat. Gravemeat can never truly sate.

His nails carve crescents of pain in his palms. *You're nothing,* he tells them. *Nothing but ghosts and echoes. Specters to be laid to rest.*

Their toothy laughter echoes in his head. Maybe, but they're not wrong.

The prey—the boy, he corrects himself savagely—pauses beneath the statue of Ernst August, sinking heel to haunch and leaning against the plinth. His movements are jerky with fatigue. As soon as he thinks no one's watching his expression flattens. He tugs a pack of cigarettes out of his pocket, shakes out nothing but a few flakes of tobacco. He crumples the box with a soft curse.

Gabriel's cue. The wolves urge him on, intangible noses nudging his back. They've seen this play acted out a hundred times. They know the lines.

He steps out of the gloom of the betweens and his shadow falls over the boy's face. He holds out his own pack. *"Willst du eine Kippe?"*

The boy startles, then tenses. His wary thoughts are easy to read—he should say no, get back to the laughable safety of other people. Sensible prey-thoughts.

Instead he pulls a smile on like an ill-fitting mask and nods. Humans are rarely sensible enough. *"Danke."*

Gabriel raises an eyebrow at his accent. His lighter cracks and orange flame dances over the boy's face. Childhood softness still clings to him, despite his lanky limbs and thin cheeks. His skin has a smoothness that won't survive a razor. The flame catches flecks of gold in his hazel eyes as he leans in and drags deep. A pretty boy—the wolves approve. Gabriel lights a cigarette of his own and flips the lighter shut, letting the dark lap over them again.

"American?" Smoke leaks out of his mouth around the word—innocent coils, this time.

The boy nods. Salt-sweat and unwashed hair, the cloying chemical tang of cheap soap, and under it all the metallic richness of flesh and blood. He pushes himself up, still leaning against the concrete pedestal and trying to look nonchalant.

"What are you doing in Hannover?" He tries to quash his curiosity—whatever the boy's story is, he doesn't need to know it.

"Just passing through." His voice is dull—not shy or sullen, but uncaring. Going through the motions.

Gabriel watches the Promenade. People ebb and swirl heedlessly around them, blind to the sharp-toothed specters. Sweat prickles his back, and hair sticks and itches on his neck. The wolves are quiet. They don't care about the particulars of the hunt, only the red and messy end.

"What's your name?" he asks. He doesn't need to know that either, but anything's better than *boy*, or *prey*.

"Alec. You?"

He pauses, thinks of a lie. But what's the point? "I'm Gabriel."

Alec studies his cigarette. "You're not German, either."

Gabriel smiles. "No. Armenian, by way of Beirut."

"What are you doing in Hannover?"

"Talking to you." He grimaces as soon as the words leave his mouth.

Alec smirks, the most expression he's shown yet. "That's a lousy line."

"It is. Sorry. But really, I don't know anymore."

Liar, mock the wolves, their eyes glinting.

The boy smiles slowly, a better fit than the last one. "That sounds like a line, too." Engaging now, like this is familiar. Gabriel nearly shakes his head; a stranger trying to pick up teenagers shouldn't be reassuring.

He might be a monster, but he's not that kind. Tires squeal on the street and he hears the wolves' laughter. *Whatever gets you through the night*.

"How old are you?" he asks. It's expected.

"Eighteen." Not even trying to sound convincing.

Gabriel drags on his cigarette. "Does that ever fool anyone?"

Alec shrugs. "No, but it makes them feel better. If I said sixteen, would you walk away?"

"No," he says after a moment.

The boy lifts his eyebrows, but his stomach growls before he can reply. He blushes, his cynical façade crumbling till he's just a kid again.

"Come on," Gabriel says, crushing the cigarette under his heel. "There's a kebab stand down the street. I'll buy."

Alec hesitates, another flash of wariness. Instincts trying to save his life. But they're too far into the game now, or he just doesn't care. He nods, and follows Gabriel away from the train station.

The wolves stalk silently behind them.

Selim is working the *imbiss* tonight. He nods at Gabriel as they approach, glances at Alec and asks a silent question with one eyebrow. The boy's stomach rumbles again at the smell of meat and garlic and cumin.

Gabriel shakes his head—*not one of us*. Selim frowns as he realizes what's happening; he's seen the wolves himself. He hands Alec his *döner*—made with safe meat, not what the ghouls eat—and takes Gabriel's money, his face creasing into an unhappy glower.

"What's his problem?" Alec asks softly as they leave.

Gabriel fights a frown of his own. "He doesn't approve." Selim was a changeling like him, taken as a child instead of born to the tunnels. Maybe it's easier for the ones who never had a human life. He hasn't asked.

Gabriel watches with amusement as the sandwich disappears with the speed only the starving and adolescent can manage. When it's gone, Alec crumples the wrapper and licks tzatziki off his fingers.

"Thanks." Honest gratitude, no coyness, and Gabriel can't meet his eyes. But everywhere else he looks he sees the wolves. He swallows hungry spit, thinks of turning around. But gravemeat won't sate this hunger.

They walk through the dark streets, away from the crowds. The noise of traffic fades as they follow the Altstadt's narrow cobbled streets. Shops are closing, people heading for home. Alec shifts his bag from shoulder to shoulder occasionally, but doesn't complain. By the time they reach the river, though, he's growing restless. So are the wolves.

"Do you have a room somewhere?" he asks. "Somewhere we could go?"

"No. Should I?"

Alec frowns and shrugs. "I guess not." There are always alleys for this kind of thing, after all, whether it's prostitution or murder. Not affected nonchalance, Gabriel decides—the boy really doesn't care. He wishes he could wonder what could crush someone so young that way, but he knows all too well.

They cross the river and turn at the Leine Palace, its long pale façade facing the water and the greenway on the other side. The building is dark and quiet, streetlamps shedding pools of yellow over grass and trees and empty benches. Traffic flows on the other side of the park, but Gabriel isn't worried about being interrupted. People know when to look away.

He stops at the little bridge leading to the palace's glass doors. The metal railing is still warm; the river ripples below. Stairs descend to the water, but he can't see how to reach them from here. The bittersweet scent of water and wet rock fills his nostrils. It's a cleaner river than some—fish still live in it; the whisper of death is only his imagination.

Alec stands beside him, propping his elbows on the stone. "Looks like a nice place to dump a body," he says with a crooked smile.

Gabriel's lips pull back. "Twenty-four of them, actually." He chuckles as Alec starts. "Not me."

"No, I mean—" The boy laughs, a breathless nervous rush. "I was only joking."

"I wasn't. Hannover had a serial killer once. Fritz Haarmann—do you know the story?"

"No." Hair flops over his eyes as he shakes his head. "I never went in for true crime stuff."

"He killed a lot of people. When he was done with the bodies, he dumped them in the river."

Alec makes a face, stares down at the water in disgust and fascination. "What do you mean," he asks a second later, "when he was done with them?"

"He sold the meat on the black market. That was the rumor, anyway."

"God. Why do people read about stuff like that?"

"They think monsters are interesting." His mouth twists wryly as he remembers his own horror and fascination when he realized the shapes prowling the bombed ruins of his neighborhood at night weren't soldiers or thieves, weren't anything human. Easy to admire their teeth and claws and strength when he was weak and helpless. Easy to want to join them, when he was alone and starving. But he's still alone, still starving.

"You don't need to kill twenty-four people to be a monster."

"No." Gabriel picks at a rust spot, trying to ignore the breath of wolves. "It's much easier than that."

Something in his voice makes Alec look up, Adam's apple bobbing in the slender softness of his throat. The prey part of his brain sees what the thinking part tries not to—Gabriel's night-shining eyes, the length of his teeth and thickness of his nails. At last, a real reaction—fear threads acrid through his scent. His pupils dilate. No doubt his hands are tingling as his heart pumps faster, as the atavistic survival instinct screams at him to *run run run*.

He'll run, and Gabriel will give chase, ghost-wolves beside him, and the night will wash red and none of them will be hungry anymore. For a while.

Alec's bag slips off his shoulder, thumps against the cobbles. His narrow chest hitches with breath, the sound loud and ragged in Gabriel's ears. He can hear the boy's heart now, and his vision tunnels. Hunger makes his teeth ache.

But the boy doesn't run. His hand clenches white-knuckled around his backpack strap—an awkward sort of weapon, and he doesn't swing it.

"What are you?"

Gabriel lets out a breath he hadn't realized he'd drawn, and the red fades from his vision. The wolves whine and growl.

"I'm a monster. A *ghul*—an eater of the dead. I'm a killer, too." Alec stares at his face; Gabriel can feel himself changing. Nothing drastic, but the bridge is enough of a between-place to allow it. His teeth sharpen, crowding in his still-human jaw. Nails curve into claws and his vision brightens.

"And that's why you picked me up? To kill me. To eat me?"

He nods slowly.

"Well." The boy shakes his hair back, trying for that cynical affectation again. "At least you're not just another asshole john."

"This isn't a joke."

"No." Alec reaches out to touch Gabriel's face, traces a fingertip down his temple and the length of his jaw. Stubble rasps against his nail; Gabriel feels it in the roots of his teeth. "I can see that."

Wonder in his voice, or something like it, and while his fear hasn't faded, neither has it worsened. Gabriel catches his hand, feels the boy's pulse fast and strong against his fingers. Like looking into the past, into a mirror. The wolves whine, confused and annoyed.

Footsteps echo on the sidewalk. A woman walks along the river, a pocket-sized dog straining against its leash ahead of her. The Pomeranian growls as it passes the bridge, yips and dances. The woman looks up, hurries her pace when she sees Alec and Gabriel, tugging the dog away. The streetlight shows her moue of distaste.

"Schlampe," Alec says, loud enough to carry. The woman stiffens, but keeps walking, disappearing into the shadows of the park. Gabriel's lip curls, but the wolves ignore the interlopers. Easier prey, perhaps, but not to their taste.

Gabriel realizes he's still holding the boy's hand. He lets go, scrubs his palm on his pants. "Go. Follow her. Get on a train and get out of the city. You'll be safe."

"Safe?" Alec laughs, hard and sharp. "You're kidding, right?"

"Better than dead."

"I'm not sure about that." He lifts his chin. Adolescent defiance, but something deeper and uglier beneath it. "You think I don't know what happens to kids like me? You think I don't know about monsters?" He jerks his sleeve up, baring the edge of one thin shoulder, round blistered burn scars and a purple-green bruise. His fear is gone now, buried in rising anger.

Gabriel takes a step backward and the railing gouges his back. "It's easy to think you want to die when you're young. Trust me, you don't."

"Really?" His face flattens again, and it's all Gabriel can do to meet his eyes.

"I don't want to hurt you." It comes out a growl and they both flinch. "They do."

He points past the bridge, to the wolves lurking at the edge of the lamplight. Alec frowns at the shadows. "What—" He stops, mouth sagging open. Eyes gleam back at them, red and gold and copper-green. "What are they?"

"They're ghosts, but not of men. Enough death and pain in one place start to wear patterns. They're the ghosts of acts, of madness and hunger and murder."

"And they want . . . more?"

"What I told you before, about human meat sold on the black market? It was more than a rumor. But Haarmann and Grans weren't selling it to the people of Hannover. They were selling it to ghouls. To my people.

"We're monsters, but not killers. We try, at least. They knew where that meat was coming from, but they chose not to ask, to look the other way. More people, more children, kept dying, and the wolves wormed their way into their hearts." He shakes his head. "All our hearts. Maybe they've been there all along."

Alec looks at him, darkness hiding his face. "And you?"

"I killed someone, a long way from here. He called himself a soldier, but he wasn't much older than you, young and foolish. I didn't plan on it, didn't mean to, but I killed him and ate him. It's the law—no fresh meat. Once you break it, once you taste fresh blood, you want more. I ran, came here to hide, but the wolves were waiting for me."

"Now they have you," Alec whispers, "and me."

Gabriel nods. The wolves wait, mockery silenced.

"Go ahead." Alec moves closer, meets his eyes. "I mean it. I'm going to die anyway, right? I'd rather you killed me than somebody else." Gabriel tries to turn away, but the boy grabs his shoulder. "Please! I can't keep doing this. I'm so fucking *tired*."

"Then find another way. You don't want this."

"Fuck you." He jerks away with a snarl. "Don't you fucking tell me what I want." He reaches into his pocket and pulls out a butterfly knife.

Gabriel tenses. The wolves tense. He feels them quivering, mouths watering.

The knife flips open, light running along the blade. Gabriel waits for the attack, but instead Alec brings the edge down against the inside of his forearm. Blood wells, floods the night with red and copper.

"What are you—"

"This is what you want, isn't it? What they want?" He gestures toward the wolves, flinging drops of blood onto the sidewalk. The shadows seethe, their hunger a burning weight in Gabriel's head, his own hunger a weight in his stomach.

He clenches his fists, claws digging into his palms. "Don't."

"What, do I need to run?" Alec's lip curls. "There's always a game, isn't there. Fine, I can run if that's what it takes." He raises his bleeding arm toward Gabriel. "Catch me."

He bolts for the park. The wolves bay, so loudly Gabriel thinks his ears will burst. The night washes red and roaring and his vision locks on the boy's slender back. Muscles bunch and coil and before he can stop himself he's giving chase. Wind in his face, his pulse nearly drowning the rasp of denim, the crunch of grass under Alec's boots.

The boy makes it halfway across the greenway before Gabriel catches him with a tackle that knocks the air from both their lungs. They fall in a tangle of elbows and knees, the roots of a tree hard beneath them.

He wants this, the wolves chorus. *Give him what he wants. You'll be kinder than the others. Go for the throat.*

Alec curses, struggles. The knife traces a line of heat across Gabriel's arm before he knocks it away. The boy's hand knots in his hair as his teeth graze skin, and he can't tell if it's an attack or an encouragement. Soft flesh parts, sweat and blood slicking his lips, salt and seaweed. He growls at the taste of it and the wolves howl their victory, drowning Alec's sobs.

His jaw aches as he stops, trembling with the need to bite. One hand gouges the dirt, the other tugging the boy's head back. Alec's chest heaves against his, breath wet and ragged. Tears run down his cheeks, drip down his neck to smear the blood.

"No," Gabriel breathes, though the effort dizzies him. "I'm not this kind of monster." He pushes himself off, disentangling his legs. He shakes his head, inhales the scent of crushed grass and earth along with salt and blood and fear.

Alec sobs, curling on the ground, one hand touching his bleeding throat. "It figures," he chokes. "Of all the monsters I meet, you're not monster enough."

"I'm a ghoul, not a killer. A jackal, not a wolf." He crouches beside the boy, hands between his knees. Adrenaline tingles in his cheeks and fingers, pushing back the hunger, clearing his head. "We haunt graveyards, eat corpses. We skulk in the shadows and the seams of the world, in the between-places. We steal children and raise them in the dark."

Alec sits up with a wince, smearing dirt on his face as he wipes at the tears and snot. At the last, he glances up, eyes puffy and wet.

"That's what I am," Gabriel says, not sure if he's telling the boy or himself. "I won't kill you. But—" He hesitates at the thought. But it's all he can offer. "I can steal you. You may not thank me when you see what it means," he warns, as the boy's eyes widen. "You'll never escape it, once you know. Hunger and darkness and dead things. That's what I can give you." Not here, not the Hannover warrens with their miasma of guilt and yearning, but there's a whole world to see. He started over once—maybe he can do it again. Maybe Alec can do it, too.

The hope on Alec's face is terrible, hope and fear and longing. A second's doubt, and then he pulls his mask of unconcern on again. "Why didn't you say so?" He stands awkwardly, favoring his wounded arm.

Gabriel finds the fallen knife, closes it and hands it back. The wolves watch from the darkness, whining and slinking.

There will be more. They always come, the killers and their prey. You won't stop us. You can't atone so easily.

"But I won't be your killer," he whispers to the dark. "And he won't be your prey." It's not enough, but it's something.

It's a life.

Family of Bones

Joshua Hackett

Our war
With them
Is never-ending
But that is not who we are

Our desire
For flesh
Is never filled
But that is not who we are

Our visage
Twisted echo
Is never welcome
But that is not who we are

Grave-tenders
Hunger-tamers
Family of bones
We are

The Garden, the Moon, the Wall

The ghosts follow Sephie to work again that day.

They stand outside the windows of the bookstore, staring in with empty eyes—more of them now than a few days ago. She tries to ignore them. At least they never come inside.

Most of them, anyway.

The light dims as she's shelving books, and Sephie turns to find her ex-boyfriend grinning down at her, pink filming his long ivory teeth. He tilts his head, shows her the still-wet ruin a bullet made of the left side of his skull. Her hands tingle with shock as the smell of his blood coats her tongue—copper sweetness, and beneath that the familiar salt-musk of his skin.

A wink and he's gone. The air smells like books and dust and air freshener again. Sephie wobbles. The stack of books in her arms teeters and falls, hardbacks and trades thumping and thwapping one by one, echoing in the afternoon quiet.

The third time this week. Cursing, she crouches to pick up the books, and pauses as she reads the nearest title.

Lycanthropy: An Encyclopedia

Caleb always was a smart-ass; she shouldn't expect that to change because he's dead.

"Are you okay?" Anna calls from across the store.

No, she thinks. *Not even a little.*

The sky darkens as they close the shop, October nearly over and autumn chewing the days shorter and shorter. Purple eases into charcoal, and the grinning jack-o-lantern moon rises over the jagged Dallas skyline.

The moon doesn't bother her, never mind Caleb and his lousy jokes.

Sephie lights a cigarette as Anna sets the alarm and locks the back door. Her hands shake, the itch in her veins more than nicotine can ease.

"You want to get some coffee?" Anna asks, pocketing her keys and pulling out her own cigarettes. Her nails are orange and black to match her Halloween hair. Her lighter rasps, and the smell of cloves drifts through the air.

Sephie swallows, tongue sticking to the roof of her mouth. The shakes are coming on for real. "That'd be nice, but I need to run some errands. Maybe some other time." She likes the bookstore better than any of the other jobs she's had, and doesn't want to get fired because someone thinks she's a junkie.

It's not like she can tell them the truth.

"Sure," Anna says, waving as she turns toward her car. "See you tomorrow."

"Yeah. 'Night." Sephie ducks down the alley toward the street, trying not to think about Anna's bemused little smile.

Tonight will be bad—she hears it in the roar of traffic, sees it in the halos bleeding off the street lamps. Cold sweat greases her scalp and neck; she can't wait another day.

Hunching her shoulders, she slides into the ebb and flow of downtown streets.

For a few blocks everything's okay. The night hums with traffic and voices, the cacophony of city noises. The air tastes of exhaust and asphalt, the sewer-stench of the Trinity fading now that summer's passed. She catches a whiff of decay, of meat, and saliva pools on her tongue. But it's only a dead dog, not what she needs.

Then it happens, that sideways lurch, and she's alone on the sidewalk. No more neon and shining glass, no more noise. Dusty brick and stone instead, grime-blind windows and the moon grinning overhead.

And the ghosts.

She's learned not to stop, not to listen to their whispers. Keep walking, eyes on the sidewalk—don't look at those pale faces peering out of the shadows, bruised and bloody or just empty, eyes burning with an aching need.

She knows the feeling, all too well, but she can't help them. She can barely help herself.

Her nose wrinkles against the smell of this place. The city stinks, but at least it's a living stench. This is dry bones and dust, old tombs.

The wind that sighs from alley-mouths is worse: sulfur and ammonia, sickness and pain. It aches when it touches her, makes her eyes water. Her footfalls echo as she lengthens her stride. It will pass. It always does. She has to keep moving, out of the between-places.

But she's a between-thing now, and she may never leave this place behind.

A breeze eddies past her, and Sephie stumbles to a halt. Rose gardens and evergreen, the smell of evenings as summer melts into autumn. The smell of her dreams.

The fragrance leaks from under the door of a narrow shop. She reaches for the knob with a trembling hand.

Her stomach cramps. Already the braver ghosts are moving toward her, murmuring, pleading.

She turns and runs, and doesn't stop until the world slips back to normal.

Bobet & Cask Funeral Services is long closed, but a light burns in the back. Sephie crouches in the shelter of a hedge, holly pricking her back as she finishes her last cigarette and tries to slow her breathing. Her legs cramp from exercise, but that's nothing to the pain in her gut. She drags her fingers through the curling cowlicked mess of her hair.

Peter waits by the back door, even though she's early. Hands in his pockets, shoulders hunched, eyes flitting back and forth like a cartoon spy.

"You should start smoking," she says, moving out of the dark. "It'd look more natural."

He jerks and presses his back to the door. The smell of his fear cuts through the muggy night. Sephie's stomach growls.

"I—" He stammers and tries again. "Come inside."

He always invites her in; he's read too many books. She follows him through the corridor, down the stairs to the morgue.

The air smells of chemicals and death. Her sweat gels in the cold, sticking her shirt to her back. A body lies on a metal table. Peter glances at her, blue eyes narrowing, like he thinks she'll start gnawing on an arm.

She's not sure what would happen if he weren't here.

He opens a refrigerator, takes out a lidded plastic bowl. "It's heart, liver, some other things. . . . A car crash, so I could take a little more than usual."

"This guy?" She nods toward the corpse in his funeral suit, wrinkled face coated in makeup that can't simulate living color, no matter how skillfully it's applied.

"No, he had a heart attack. The accident was a few days ago."

Sephie smiles, close-lipped. "Thank you." She tugs a roll of bills out of her pocket, trades it for the container. He tried to give the money back, once, but she makes him keep it. She's afraid he'll ask for something else if she doesn't.

He stands there watching her, gangly and awkward, while her fingers tighten on the plastic and she swallows hungry spit. Finally he ducks his head and retreats. "I'll be outside if you need me."

When his footsteps recede, Sephie sinks onto the cold tile floor and opens the container. Thin slices of organs—pomegranate heart and pinkish-brown liver—slivers and cubes of fat-marbled flesh. Once he gave her an eyeball, but it was salty and bitter, too gross even for her.

She saves the heart for last, chews it slowly, sucking bloody juice out of the muscle. Shudders ride her, and she closes her eyes against a flood of scattered images and sensations. She doesn't want to know about the person whose heart this was.

"This is what you left me for?"

She opens her eyes to find Caleb crouching in front of her, long hands dangling between his knees. Blood and brains drip onto the floor, vanishing when they hit the tile.

"Leave me alone!" Her voice cracks. The empty bowl falls from her hand and rolls in a lazy spiral.

"Tell me this is what you want. Tell me you don't miss me."

She closes her eyes, pulls her knees tight against her chest.

"Tell me you wouldn't rather eat that boy of yours. He might like it."

A hand touches her knee. Sephie gasps, but it's only Peter. "Are you all right?"

Caleb's vanished again.

She stares up at Peter—she feels his pulse through her jeans, hears the nervous rhythm of his heart. He wants her. He's afraid of her. He smells like food.

Caleb knows her too well, damn him. She's had more than one daydream about fucking Peter on a cold steel embalming table. Some of those fantasies end with her tearing the poor boy's throat out. The smell of warm flesh fills her nose.

She pulls away, crab-crawls across the floor and stumbles to her feet. Peter gapes; she's getting faster.

"I'm fine." She nibbles a drop of coagulated blood from under her nail and straightens her blouse. "I need to go."

Peter frowns. She can see him searching for the nerve to ask her to stay. He's like the ghosts, needing, wanting. Whether he wants a girlfriend or a pet monster, she's not sure, but she can't offer him either.

"Thank you," she says again, cutting him off. "I'll be back next month, okay?"

He nods, shoulders sagging. "Yeah. I'll see you then."

Sephie flees up the stairs, into the dark, and hurries for home.

The apartment is empty. Seth's gone a lot lately, looking for work—jobs that pay cash and don't run background checks. Sometimes, like this week, it's out-of-town work, leaving her alone. Hard enough to sleep most nights, even with his steady snoring drifting down the hall. When it's her and the echoing silence, it's nearly impossible.

The ghosts never come too close when he's here. This week she's seen a few lingering near the stairs. Even if they don't find her, the dreams always do.

She slips one of Seth's cassettes into the old tape deck by her mattress. Sephie teases him about his music, sad bluesy stuff a few generations before her time, but some of it's pretty. Billie Holiday's husky-soft voice chases away the silence, wraps around her like a blanket.

Her gun is a hard lump under the pillow; she always sleeps with it when she's alone.

Tell me this is what you want.

She thought she was rid of Caleb six months ago, when she left him sprawled in a cooling pool of blood on a dusty Oklahoma street. Not that she could even do that herself—she had to find someone else to pull the trigger for her.

His words echo in her head. Is this what she wants? The cramped apartment, the string of lousy jobs. Gravemeat and ghosts. Seth is gone half the time, and she doesn't dare make other friends, not even something as simple as getting coffee with Anna.

She's wanted lots of things over the years—travel, excitement, glamorous jobs that turned out to be too little glamour and too much work. But the one thing she's always wanted, as long as she can remember, is to not be afraid anymore.

"I've done a great job of that, haven't I?" she whispers to her pillow, to the gun beneath it.

The tape clicks over to the B-side before she drifts off. Lady Day's voice follows her into the dark.

She dreams of the wall again. A wall in a dark forest, stones pitted and pocked with age, veined with moss and ivy. Too high and sheer to climb, so she follows it on and on, searching for a door. Her fingers bruise the green, filling the air with its musty-damp scent, and sap clings sticky as blood on her skin. Eyes gleam in the shadows around her.

The werewolves.

Tall spindly beasts, long-armed and stilt-legged, tongues lolling amid bone-needle fangs. They never approach, never touch her, only stare and follow, muttering and laughing to themselves, singing to the swollen orange moon.

Maybe there's no door, no opening, and she'll circle the wall forever. But Sephie's smelled the wind from the other side, a wind that smells like forests and gardens, like heaven. Roses and evergreen, ripe peaches and fresh bright blood.

She knows, with the certainty of dreams, that the garden is a place for her. An Eden for ghouls and monsters, where the trees pump blood instead of sap and hearts grow ripe and beating on the vine. A place where she'll never have to eat cold meat, never have to kill. Where she won't be afraid.

It's enough to keep her walking the wall, night after night, ignoring the werewolves' snuffling laughter.

She doesn't find the door tonight. Instead the dream splinters and she falls through the cracks, back onto her sagging mattress. The bedroom ceiling stares her down while Billie Holiday sings about the moonlight.

Something woke her, but she's not sure what, until the mattress creaks and a warm weight settles over her. Familiar scratch of stubble, the taste of Caleb's skin.

He shouldn't be here, but his hands are sliding under her shirt, callused fingers kneading her ribs, and her body still remembers him, remembers when she didn't spend the nights trembling and alone. She arches against him as his tongue traces the line of her throat; her fingers tangle in his wet hair.

"Tell me you don't miss me." His breath tickles her sternum as his fingers slip beneath the elastic of her underwear. She bites her lip and doesn't answer.

His hair trails over her stomach, leaving warm wet streaks behind. "I would have taken care of you." He tugs her underwear over her hips and her breath hitches. "I still need you, Sephie." His tongue slides below her navel, followed by the pressure of teeth.

"Caleb—" She shrieks as he bites. Light flashes in the window and she sees her blood on his mouth, his blood smeared over her breasts and belly and hands, his eyes gleaming amber in the glare.

She wakes with a gasp. She's alone again, with the music and the soft sounds of traffic beyond the window, and only sweat slicks her skin.

Sephie can't sleep again that night. When dawn creeps through the blinds she's aching and groggy. She wants to call in sick, but she gave Peter the last of her cash and the electricity bill is due soon, so she drags herself into the shower when the alarm shrieks.

She searches the foggy mirror for changes, like she does every time she eats. Maybe her teeth are a hint longer, a little sharper. Her nails have thickened, so strong now she can't chew them like she used to and has to worry at her cuticles instead.

She thinks of Caleb's bloody grin, the dark half-circles under his nails. She's not like him, no matter what she's becoming.

Not yet, at least.

Another day of ignoring ghosts, of dodging Anna's questions and invitations. She aches with tension and fatigue by the time she gets home.

Caleb waits for her, bleeding on her dumpster-rescue couch. Sephie pauses on the threshold, nearly turns and runs. But she's too tired, and running hasn't worked so far. She locks the door behind her.

"What do you want?"

"Your help." It's not what she expected. He's too serious; it looks strange on him.

"My help? Maybe you should have asked for that before you started stalking me. Anyway, you're dead."

His eyes fix on her. "Whose fault is that?"

"You should have let me walk away." But it's hard to stay angry with a dead boy. Arguing with Caleb is familiar, almost domestic, better than being alone.

"You weren't walking—you were running. You wanted me to be strong. You wanted me to be scary. And then you couldn't handle it."

She closes her eyes. "I wanted to feel safe."

"If I could have given you that, I would have." She feels him in front of her, though she never heard him move. His hand cups her cheek, cool and rough, his touch lighter than it ever was. If she pushes, she might pass right through him.

"How did you find me, anyway?"

"I can feel you, everywhere I go. We're still all tangled up together."

"I'm trying to cut myself loose." She reaches up, not quite touching his bloody face. "I am sorry, though, about how things ended."

"Then help me. I can't stay here, Sephie, even for you. It's getting harder and harder. It hurts. But the badlands are worse."

Despite everything, in spite of the blood, the too-sharp teeth and gleaming eyes, he's still Caleb. Still the boy she fell in love with. She was always a little afraid of him, but it was a safer fear than others.

"What can I do?"

"You've seen it—the garden, the wall. I need to go there. I need to get inside."

"I can't find the way in. It's only a dream." But she remembers the door downtown, the smell of roses and summer.

They just have to get there, past the waiting dead, through the empty places. The thought makes her sick.

But if it weren't for her, for her fear, Caleb wouldn't be dead. Wouldn't need her now.

"Come on." She touches his cold hand. "I think I know the way."

The moon watches them as they cross the city's dark reflection, spilling light the color of rust. In the distance something howls, like no dog Sephie's ever heard. The dead follow in their wake, nearly a dozen of them now, watching with hungry eyes.

"Have you talked to them?" Sephie asks, trying not to glance back at their silent shadows.

"No. I think they're scared of me." He pauses. "We're scared of each other."

The shop is still there—she was afraid it would vanish, that she imagined it to begin with. This time she sees the sign: *The Dream Merchant*. As Caleb tries the door, she turns to face the ghosts.

"What do you want?" Her throat is dry as dust.

Caleb catches her arm. "Sephie, don't—"

"We want out of here," the nearest answers. A woman, her ashen face mottled and sunken, hair like cobwebs tangling over her shoulders.

"I don't know what to do. I don't know how to help you."

"Take us with you." She nods toward the shop. "Whatever's in there, it can't be worse than this place."

"It's locked," Caleb says, slamming his hand against a pane; it doesn't even rattle. "I can't break it."

Sephie touches the door. It feels real enough, peeling paint and dry wood, cold dirty glass. She can't see through the windows. Before she can think too long, she punches the glass. She gasps as it shatters, and pain spills hot up her arm.

The blood that wells across her knuckles is real. The smell fills the air, bright and rich against so much nothing. The ghosts sigh like wind in the grass, and sway forward. Caleb's nostrils flare, and Sephie pulls her hand away.

Careful of the glass, she slides her good hand through the broken window, fumbling till she finds the lock. The door opens inward with a rattle of bells. She listens for an alarm, but hears nothing.

The howl echoes again, closer now.

"Come on." Caleb steers her through the door, but Sephie calls back to the ghosts.

"Follow us if you want to, but I don't know where we're going."

One by one they trickle over the threshold, into the darkness of the shop. Sephie shuts the door behind them, and turns the lock. Blood drips from her fingers.

Caleb grabs her arm. "There it is."

She sniffs and catches the smell again, somewhere across the room.

"What exactly are you looking for?"

Sephie spins, heart leaping in her chest, as a light blossoms on the stairs. Her eyes water at the sudden brightness, and she raises a hand against the glare.

"Who are you?" Sephie asks. The light is wrong, milk-blue and cold, obscuring the man who holds it.

He chuckles dryly. "I'm the owner of the building you've broken into, the floor you're bleeding on. I'll ask again—what is it that you want?"

"We're looking for the garden."

The glow dims enough for her to catch his puzzled frown. His black hair is tousled, shirt hanging open, and stubble darkens his jaw. "The—Ah." His eyes flicker toward the other side of the room. "I see. Who are you, young lady? The Pied Piper? The dead are much more of a nuisance than rats."

All the ghosts huddle behind her, even Caleb, shielding their eyes from the pale lantern.

"Please." The word catches in her throat. "I'm sorry about the window. But I have to take them to the garden."

"I run a business, not an underground railroad for the dead. Such services aren't free."

"I don't have any money. But I can get some—"

He studies her for a moment, his eyes veiled. "I'm sure you can. What surety will you give me, if I let you pass tonight?"

She opens her mouth, closes it again. "What do you want?"

"I'll have your name, as a down payment."

"No," Caleb whispers.

"It's Sephie."

"No, my dear. Your whole name. I'll know if you lie."

"Don't," Caleb says, louder. He moves toward the stairs. "Leave her alone."

The man raises the lantern higher. The light blazes, and Caleb falls back with a groan. "The name, if you please. Or I can send your friends back to the ground where they belong."

"Sephronia Anne Matthews."

"Excellent. Very well, Sephronia." She winces at the sound of her name in his mouth. "You and your friends may go down."

He descends the rest of the stairs and the wraiths flinch from glare as he passes. He unlocks a door in the far wall; it looks like a closet, but when it opens a quiver runs through Sephie's bones. His cold light can't touch the blackness inside. One of the ghosts moans.

"This is it?" But she can smell it, warm and sweet as summer.

"That is the way."

She glances at the man. "We can come back this way?"

"You can. We still have your debt to settle."

"What now?" Caleb murmurs.

"We go down." The steadiness of her voice amazes her. Her good hand gropes for Caleb's as they step into the dark.

His grip tightens painfully on hers, and she remembers the last time they went below, the trip into the darkness that started all of this. The gravemeat, the secrets of the dead. When they first became monsters, between-things.

But this road doesn't smell like death.

The ghosts make no sound behind them; Sephie doesn't look back.

She brushes her wounded hand against the wall, leaving a trail of blood—better than breadcrumbs. It feels like cement at first, cold and rough, but the texture changes, becomes sleeker, slicker, ridged and curving.

She doesn't know how long they walk, or how far. Step after step, one foot after another. The dark mutes sound, erases time.

Eventually the wall falls away and the smothering sensation eases. A moment later the stairs give way to a gentle slope; earth and rocks skitter beneath her boots. The air warms, and a humid breeze carries the smell of green things. The dead whisper among themselves. Sephie's hand is falling asleep in Caleb's, but she doesn't let go.

The gloom changes ahead, lessens. The mouth of a cave—they're almost out.

Something moves, something with rasping breath and scraping claws. Three pairs of eyes burn against the darkness.

"What's this now?" A guttural voice. Nothing that comes from a human mouth.

"Little feet trip-trapping down our stairs," another whispers. "Is that you, merchant?"

"No, sisters. It's the little dreamer." The third voice is a woman's, deep and rich.

"Ahh, so it is. I knew she'd find the way eventually."

"She brought her friends."

"What do you want, little ghoul?"

Sephie tries to moisten her tongue. "We want to find the garden."

"Well, that's easy, isn't it sisters?"

"All you do is follow the path."

"But you must pay the toll, to leave the cavern."

"Yes. Passage is not free."

"Not again." Sephie tugs her hand free of Caleb's, flexes tingling fingers. "What do *you* want?"

Even as her eyes adjust, she can't make out the speakers. Only vague shapes and glowing eyes, gold and silver and poison green. They smell like fur, like musk, blood and autumn leaves.

One of them laughs, a chuffing animal noise. "Come closer, child."

Caleb tries to hold her back, but she shakes off his grip and steps forward. Shadows lap over her, thicker and cooler than the air, and she shivers. Something crumbles beneath her foot, dry and hollow; she doesn't look down.

"What's the price?" She searches her pockets. Coins on the eyes of the dead, but she can't remember where she read that.

"Not that," says one of the women—or whatever they are—as change rattles in Sephie's pocket. "We have no use for money."

"And I doubt you have enough for everyone you've brought."

The sisters move closer, surrounding her. Hot breath tickles the back of her neck.

"Orpheus sang his way in," says the shadow on her left, the green-eyed, with the dry sibilance of a serpent. "Do you have a song for us?"

Sephie shakes her head. Even if she could carry a tune, her voice is caught in her throat and she can't remember the words to any song she knows.

"She's bleeding," the golden-eyed beast purrs.

Sephie flexes her right hand; crusted blood cracks on her skin.

"She is." The silver eyes lean in. "Living blood. It's been a long time since we've tasted that."

She holds up her hand. "Is this enough? Will this pay our way?"

The green-eyed sister hisses. "Ghoul blood is cold and dusty. I want something sweeter. Perhaps . . ." Something cool and scaly touches Sephie's cheek and she fights a flinch. "A young girl's tears. Yes."

"Sephie—" Caleb's voice drifts through the dark.

"Be silent, little ghost. This is her bargain to make."

Long clawed fingers catch her right hand, pull it down. Hot breath stings the cuts. She clenches her fist, reopening the wounds. The pain of tearing scabs makes her gasp, makes her eyes water.

"Blood and tears, fine. Take them."

Serpents writhe against her face, tongues flickering toward her eyes.

"If we all may name a price," the silver-eyed woman says, "then I want a kiss."

Sephie closes her eyes. Moisture beads on her lashes, and the snakes lick it away. The beast's tongue laps her hand, hot and rough, rasping against the cuts. "Fine," she whispers. "Just do it."

A cold, lifeless hand tilts her chin up. The woman's mouth closes on hers. Silk-dry lips, icy tongue, teeth like icicles. She tries to breathe, but the kiss steals the air from her lungs, steals the heat from her veins.

We can take it all, the woman's voice whispers deep in the whorls of her brain. *All your pain, all your fear. Even your debt. We can take everything, and you'll be free.*

She's truly crying now, crying and bleeding and gasping for air. Snakes in her eyes, teeth piercing her hand, and that tongue in her mouth, leeching her dry.

What does that leave for me?

Nothing. You'll have nothing, be nothing, want nothing. Nothing will ever hurt you again.

She can't answer, can't feel her limbs or her tongue. Caleb is shouting somewhere far away, calling her name. She can't answer, because she's falling into the dark.

But the dark doesn't want her, spits her out again, and she wakes with a gasp. Cold, so cold—she can't stop shivering. Caleb holds her; he's warmer than she is.

"What happened?" she whispers.

"They're gone. I thought you were, too."

She sits up, rubs her stinging eyes. Her right hand is shredded, like she was mauled by a dog, but none of the wounds are bleeding. Her chest aches and it's hard to get enough breath.

"Where are the ghosts?" she asks, glancing around the empty cavern.

"They went on, into the forest."

Carefully she stands, leaning on Caleb. He feels more solid now, more real. Or maybe she's less.

"Come on. Let's find the garden."

A path leads into the trees, like the sisters promised. Birds and insects sing in the darkness, and animals move through the underbrush. The peach-golden moon is high overhead, shedding light through the canopy.

The trail takes them straight to the garden wall. This time, the gate is easy to find. Curling iron, the bars wrapped thick with vines and flowers. One side stands open—the werewolves are waiting for them.

This time, Sephie isn't afraid.

"Hello, children," one beast says. After the guardians in the cave, its deep voice is welcoming, kind. "We wondered when you would find the way."

The wind drifts past them, flutters Sephie's hair. The fragrance of the garden eases some of the aching cold inside her.

She turns to Caleb. His color is better. As she watches, his constant dripping blood slows, dries. An instant later the wound is healed, leaving nothing but tangled dark curls.

Her wounds are still there.

"Come with me," he says, stroking her hair. "Stay with me. We'll be all right here."

She leans against him, hears the whisper of a heartbeat in his chest. So tired. Not scared anymore—now she's just numb. It would be so nice to rest.

Caleb bends down and she lifts her head for a kiss, a kiss to warm her frozen lips, to ease the memory of the cave. It could be like this here, like it was before things went so wrong.

Will Seth wonder what happened to her? Will Anna? Will they worry? She won't be hungry here, won't owe anything to anyone.

Nothing.

"I'll take care of you," Caleb whispers, his stubble scratching her lips.

She stiffens, turns her head aside. "You never could do that."

"I tried to be what you wanted. . . ."

"I never should have asked." She pulls away, runs her fingers over his cheek. "I'm sorry."

"What's up there for you? What's worth going back to?"

"I don't know. But it's something. It's my life."

"Sephie—"

"Goodbye, Caleb."

She tilts her head toward the gate, and the waiting monsters. "Go on."

He takes a hesitant step toward the garden. She waves once in farewell, then turns away. She doesn't look back.

The cavern is empty. No one challenges her as she climbs the black and winding stair.

Halfway up, her hand starts to hurt again, and then to bleed. Not long after, she begins to cry. When she reaches the top of the steps, her chest burns, and all her weary muscles ache. But she's not afraid.

As Sephie opens the door, the weight of her debt settles heavy on her shoulders. She pauses on the threshold, breathes in the garden again. Then she steps into the light and noise and stink of the world.

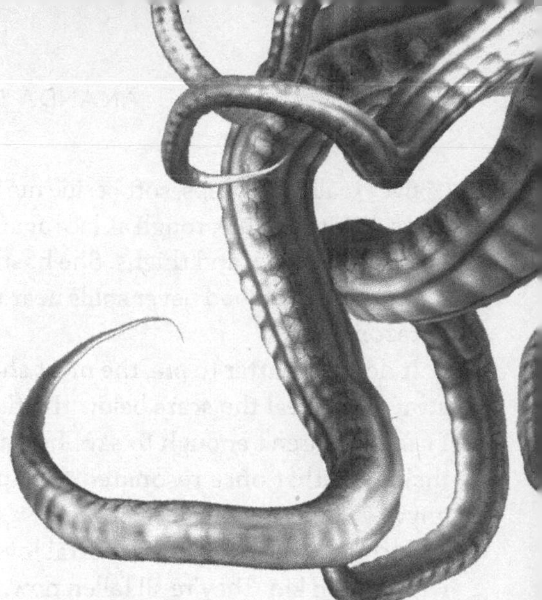

Catch

I jump, knowing she will catch me.

For one perfect instant I'm flying, muscles stretching supple as I roll in midair. Luna's strong white hands clasp mine and the shock of our impact ripples through me. We swing down.

Gravity always wins.

The world drowns in wind and surf: the ocean-murmur of the crowd, the roar of blood in my ears, whistling air. For an instant Luna's painted face is close to mine, the only clarity in the swirl of light and color. The net waits below us like a spider's hungry web; it won't catch us today.

My palms slap the trapeze bar and I twist into a handstand. The crowd cheers, and I remember how it feels to fly.

But gravity wins and the show ends. Luna and I retire to our trailer, sweaty and warm with a pleasant exertion-ache. I wash and stretch before muscles cool and stiffen, watching Luna in the mirror as she wipes away her makeup.

She paints her face with night: black and navy, cerulean and indigo, hints of amethyst. Her armor. She can't face the crowds without it.

Makeup vanishes, inch by inch, baring pale soft skin until only the violet circles beneath her eyes remain. She switches off the lamps before peeling off her leotard; she can't bear the light on her naked flesh. Her skin is all the radiance I need. Her pulse thrums with the lingering high of the show. My heart speeds in response as she falls into my arms.

Eventually she sleeps, soft beside me in the darkness, and I trace her tangled scars. White on pale, rough as lace against the delicate skin of her wrists, her breasts, her belly, and thighs. She hasn't cut herself since we became lovers, makes sure her blood never spills near me, but I see the wistful way she looks at razors.

It doesn't matter to me, the meat she despises so, but I can't take the pain away, can't heal the scars below the flesh. The scattered moments of solace I can offer aren't enough to save her, aren't enough to ease the empty place inside me that once resonated with purpose, with my Word. I take them anyway. *She* is my purpose now.

Such a fragile thing, this mortal love, so unlike the fierce exultation I felt with my old kin. They're all fallen now, scattered, and sometimes this fearful love is better than wandering alone.

It can't last. She's dying, faster than most.

It can't last, but some nights I can pretend.

Time washes past like a river, and day by day I'm buried beneath its sediment.

The next night we fly again, the moves familiar now as breathing. Maybe more so.

Tonight, something's wrong. A smell in the air, nearly lost beneath salt and sugar and grease: something dark, sharp and sour. Familiar. Luna frowns as I nearly miss a mark. I can only shake my head.

I open my eyes as I swing toward her, glancing down at the blur of the crowd. Something watches me, a dark shape at the edge of the stands, eyes like nettles on my skin.

Luna stretches toward me—

I fumble, a second too late. Skin brushes skin, then I'm falling, tumbling down to the hungry net. The crowd gasps like a wave.

I land on my back, teeth closing on my tongue as I bounce. Nylon burns my wrist; a nail rips as I clutch the weave. Luna hangs from her knees above me, one hand pressed to her mouth in shock. I've never fallen before, not like this.

The clowns come tumbling out, mocking me in pantomime. I roll off the net, waving to show I'm not hurt, even though my knee twinges as I land. Jack the Ringmaster hurries to cue the next act, and fire-eaters chase the clowns away to clear the ring while Luna climbs down to meet me.

The watcher has vanished.

"What happened?" she asks in the trailer, as I slump on the bed with an ice pack melting on my knee. My torn fingernail throbs, and I pity the creatures trapped in this ridiculous flesh.

"Nothing. Just clumsy."

"Bullshit." She straddles a chair. She must be distracted for such an unladylike move. "I saw your face, Sol. You were scared. You're never scared."

You scare me. "I thought I saw someone, in the crowd. Someone I knew a long time ago." As much truth as I dare.

"Who?"

"No one you ever want to meet. Please," I say as she opens her mouth, "leave it. For now, anyway."

She frowns, the colors on her face twisting like clouds. "For now. Will you be all right if I go help the tumblers?"

"I'll be fine."

When she's gone I toss the icepack aside and heal myself with a thought. The absence of pain laps over me like cool water.

I want to tell her, have always wanted to, since her tears first summoned me back to the world of flesh. I've walked among men enough to know better—they want miracles, and I have none to give. Even when I was whole, even with my kin around me like a choir, I couldn't have given Luna what she needs.

Though I'm reduced and alone, my enemies are still strong. *Please, let me have been wrong. Let them not have found me*. I don't know what I pray to. I don't know what might be left to hear me.

The circus is closed the next day. I hoped to take Luna into town, or down to the beach. Instead she's sullen and withdrawn all day, snapping if I get too close. Throughout the camp people groan and mutter; doors slam, curses bounce between the walls. Dogs whine and pace, or lie listless in the dust outside their trailers.

Wind whistles off the ocean, fluttering pennons and rattling tents. On the air I catch the scent again, tangy and sweet, like mint and lime and lavender, but too sharp, too sour. They've come for me.

The carnival grounds lie beside a short cliff that spills into dunes and beach grass, down to the gray, churning sea. Such places call us: liminal spaces, betweens. The borders between earth and sea, sea and sky. Clouds roll past, gray and heavy, scattered patches of blue appearing and disappearing again. I could vanish into that blue.

Not today. I breathe deep, and whisper a name as I exhale. "Nangaithya." The word unravels on the breeze.

Beside me, laughter. "No one's called me that in a long time."

I nearly stumble as I turn, one hand raising to ward her away. So easily she throws me off balance—it wasn't always that way.

She perches on the warped guardrail, bare feet dangling. Young and pale, this shape, one I've never seen before. Fashionably gaunt, cut-offs hanging low on bony hips, ribs like sticks of a fan below her bikini top. Pin-feather stubble covers her scalp, and one long green-dyed lock drifts in front of her eyes. I might pass her on the street and not look twice, except for those eyes. Green as absinthe, green as an old bruise.

Her gaze chafes. The sea breeze smells of death and rot. I shake my head, fight off her miasma. She laughs again. Piercings flash in her ears, her eyebrows, nose, and lips.

"I've missed you, sister." The endearment like a razor blade on her tongue. "What do you call yourself now?"

"Soleil." Names are no more to us than the flesh we shrug on and off. Nothing that can bind. "And you?"

"Hunter. Easier on modern tongues."

"Are you hunting me, now? Where are the others?"

"I'm alone." She shrugs, acromion and clavicle stark beneath thin flesh, and slides off the fence. "Even they don't find me easy company. And I wasn't hunting you. Your lover led me here."

My spine stiffens "What does Luna have to do with this?"

"He's mine. I'm inside him."

"Leave her alone."

"Oh, sister." She moves closer and my skin crawls. Metal gleams along the curve of one eyebrow—not hoops or studs, but razor-tipped fishhooks. Light shatters on their barbs. "*She* will always be mine, as long as she's trapped in that sad broken flesh. My name is written in the folds of her brain."

"Not if I can help it."

"What will you do?" She tugs absently at one of the hooks as she speaks, until a crimson thread trickles around her eye and drips off her cheek. "Smother her with your affection, blind her to the truth?"

I step forward. "I'll protect her from you."

Her face softens. "You've fallen so far, haven't you? We are as we were meant to be, all of us. We *are* humanity, the flaws that give it luster. You'd keep them placid as cattle, lifeless and dull."

"I just want them to be happy!"

"It doesn't work that way. It never has." She reaches up, strokes my face, sharp-nailed and soft. "We don't have to be enemies. You don't have to live like this. Come with me. We can heal you, give you a new purpose. Or even peace, if that's what you want."

Her touch resonates through me. Beneath all the differences, we're the same. Purpose. Peace. I could stop living this lie, this false and futile life.

"No." I strike her hand away. "I have a purpose. I may be broken, but I can still fight."

Her eyes sag shut. When they open again all the softness has fled. "As you wish. You always were the ones who wanted war." Her grin bares sharpened teeth. "A pity we're so much better at it."

Weakened, but not helpless. Power answers my call, flaring around me like invisible wings. I reach deep inside, find the fractured sound of my Word, and armor myself in it, driving back the fear and doubt she wields.

"Sol?"

Luna stands behind us, eyes wide in the pallor of her face. The wind tugs at her hair and scarf. She should be my strength, but I sense her fear and my armor cracks and fissures.

Hunter smiles, slow and sharp. "You see? He feels me—he'll always come when I call."

The words are soft, but Luna's hand flies to her throat, clutching her scarf tighter against the telltale bulge.

Hunter leaves. No dramatics, no lightning or flame, just turns and walks away, down the slope toward the sea. She leaves bloody footprints on the grass, and her sweet and sour scent unwinding on the breeze.

I can't hide my fear from Luna. I can lie, unlike some of my kin—truth and solace aren't always easy bedmates—but I don't like to. Instead I distract her with kisses, take her in my arms, and wrap her love around me. I whisper spell-songs in her ear until she sleeps.

This urge terrifies me, sickens me—to take comfort instead of to give it, to shelter in something so much frailer. How long has it been since I was whole?

She smells of sandalwood and smoky vetiver, and the faint masculine sharpness that the black-market hormones can't entirely drown. A scent I've known for three years, comforting and familiar as the sea, but no matter how deeply I breathe her in, Hunter's scent lingers.

Envy, unhappiness, discontentment. My sister's Word seems such a little thing, but she's one of the most dangerous of us all.

Eventually Luna's breath deepens into a faint rattling snore. I shrug off rumpled sheets and dress.

The night tastes safe. The camp sleeps, exhausted after Hunter's restless unhappiness, but a lamp still burns in the witch's trailer.

Madame Zoya has been with us for a month, a temporary replacement while the usual fortune-teller is away. She reads palms and cards, assisted by her silent daughter Illyana. Not a charming woman, but her prophecies ring true. I avoid her as much as I can.

The door opens before my knuckles land. Illyana gestures me inside without a word. The air is fragrant with garlic and rosemary. Under that, darker notes, like stale incense and dead roses. Her lip is cracked and swollen from a blow, inexpertly hidden with makeup; she can't be more than fifteen, and already her eyes are hard.

Zoya drapes herself in scarves and rattling beads, rings heavy on her bony hands. An amber pendant rests against her chest, an insect frozen in its heart. Jack says familiar clichés comfort the audience, but I doubt Zoya is putting on much of an act. I wouldn't take an apple from her.

The old woman studies me. "I wondered when you would stop hiding from me," she says at last, a smile thinning her lips. "Did you think I would catch you in a bottle?"

"I'm no djinn. And I didn't think you'd be foolish enough to try."

"Prideful angel." Her eyes glitter amid rice-paper folds of skin. Flesh hangs loose off her fragile bones. "What do you want?"

I glance away from her face, and time's slow decay. A crystal ball sits on her table beside a plate of half-eaten toast. Not glass, like she uses with clients, or even quartz, but a dark purple stone, swirled like a night sky. "Can you scry for me?"

"I could." She steps back, deeper into the cramped trailer. "But I don't need crystals or cards to see the danger around you. I don't want to see it. Mankind doesn't need your battles. You'll only bring grief on all of us if you stay here, like you did today."

We did it for you. My throat closes against the words. *We fought and fell for you.* But I'm too proud to trade recriminations with this shriveled witch. Too proud and too desperate.

"Then don't help me. But help Luna. She's in danger."

"Her worst danger is herself, and I can't help that."

"There must be a way—"

"A miracle is what you want. You won't find one here."

"No." Bitterness scalds my throat. "I can see that."

I turn away before she can answer, Illyana moving in my wake. Her pain catches me when I would storm off—the throb of the fresh blow and duller, deeper grief beneath it. I'm not yet so fallen that I can ignore her hurt.

My hand brushes hers as I step down, a touch of comfort, a brief surcease of pain. So little compared to what I could once do, but her eyes widen as a spark passes between us. The door shuts softly behind me.

Luna tosses in her sleep, nightmare-restless. I sit beside the bed all night, watching a candle melt into a puddle of wax. Too like a deathbed vigil for my taste, but I can't rest, can't leave her alone.

Through the narrow window the sky pales to charcoal, swirled violet and green-gold with distant city lights. What can I do? Even if I had a miracle for Luna, what would I do afterward? Save humanity one soul at a time? I choke on a laugh. No wonder so many of my brothers and sisters fell, or sold themselves in service to older, deeper powers.

The metal stair creaks and I spin, hand clenching for a weapon that isn't there. I ease the door open, catch a flicker of movement the in the shadows, retreating toward Zoya's trailer. On the step below me flutters a folded note, pinned beneath a stone.

Adrenaline tingles in my hands as I retrieve it.

The Blue Fairy, it reads in slanting script, and underneath that, an address.

I learn that the address is a downtown club—not the Blue Fairy, but the Threshold. It might be a trap, a trick, a false hope, but I need to know. Jack gives us the night off—I don't dare leave Luna alone. It's been long enough since we went out that the novelty distracts her from questions.

We're both quiet on the drive into town; the borrowed car growls, and the tape deck clicks and chatters in the silence between songs.

"You know you can tell me if something's wrong," she says softly. "It's not like much is going to shock me."

I turn away. The window reflects my rueful smile. "I know. I will. Just . . . not yet."

She nods, hands shifting on the wheel, and falls silent as the city lights burn brighter ahead.

"I've been here before," Luna says as we reach the club. "It used to be called the Cenobium." Surprise in her voice, and something else. She doesn't talk much about the time she spent in the city, but I've seen the scars. The ones she gave herself, and those she didn't.

"Do you want to go somewhere else?"

"No," she says at last. "It was a long time ago."

The bouncer gives me a curious once-over as he checks my ID. I nearly laugh. Luna wraps her throat in scarves and shining chains, covers her face with her hair, but I'm the one people wonder about: my height, my narrow hips and chest, the length of my hands. No one ever doubts that the delicate woman on my arm is more, or less, than she seems.

The interior is shaped like a church. The DJ stands ensconced in the chancel and the nave has become a writhing dance floor, apses budding on either side. Music fills the vaulted room, the bass shivering behind my sternum. Strobes flash red and cobalt blue. The air tastes of sweat and liquor, the haze of the fog machine. In one of the side rooms a man is strapped to a rack and flogged. Barely hard enough to leave welts, let alone do real damage, but Luna stiffens and looks away.

I lead Luna into the throng of dancers, moving close to her while I scan the room. Hints of magic, human and otherwise, but nothing strong, nothing I can trace. After a few songs I leave Luna on the dance floor and shoulder through the press to the bar.

"I'm looking for the Blue Fairy," I say as the bartender mixes the drinks.

She rolls her eyes, but nods. "Downstairs," she mouths over the thump of the music, and gestures toward a hallway past the DJ's dais.

I drain my tequila sunrise to wash away the taste of smoke and salt, and press the second plastic cup into Luna's hand. "I'll be right back," I shout in her ear, nodding toward the restrooms.

The hall leads to a narrow curving stair; I pass a nearly coital couple and open the door at the bottom of the steps. I half expect a challenge, but no one pays any attention as I slip inside.

Music still throbs in the room below, but no one dances. Shadowed booths line the walls, colored lamps dripping from chains. The center of the room sinks into a small amphitheater, lit by a brilliant white surgical lamp. A man slumps facedown over a tattooing chair, baring his back to the woman behind him. A few people lean against the rail, watching her work, but most mind their own business.

A tattooist, I think at first. Then I smell the blood. A scalpel flashes in her hand; another gleams on a tray beside her, next to forceps and piles of gauze.

A tall woman, lean and dark. The light shines blue on the curve of her shaven head, lines the sharp edges of her jaw and cheekbones. She glances up as I approach the stairs, pearl-black eyes meeting mine.

Her stare takes my breath. Instead of a woman I face seething darkness and a thousand burning eyes. The vision vanishes as quickly as it came. She smiles, slow and amused. Not human, but who or what she is I don't know.

I should flee, but she tilts her head in invitation. I step into the pit.

"Would you like to watch?" Her voice is deep and rich. "I'm nearly finished." The blue on her skin isn't just the light—loops and whorls of iridescent ink shimmer as she moves. The man doesn't so much as glance at me.

I don't trust myself to speak, so I lean against the rail and watch her work.

The man's back is a mess of blood and raw flesh, from his left shoulder to the base of his spine. A dragon emerges from the meat, slender and sinuous. The woman raises the scalpel and traces another curve, perhaps a quarter of an inch thick; a line of red trickles down. Delicately, she teases the top corner of skin up with the blade, then tugs at it with forceps. The man shudders as flesh peels away. The wound glistens, white-marbled, then fills with blood. The woman wipes the drips carefully and drops the bloody gauze into a metal bin. The strip of flesh follows.

The taste of pain floods my mouth; my fingers tingle. But he wants this and it's not my place to take it from him. My shoulders tense as she makes the next cut.

Only a few more pieces to form the dragon's claws and scales. The man's eyes are glazed by the time the woman cleans his back and sends him on his way.

She collects her tools and turns to me, peeling off blood-streaked gloves. "What can I do for you?" she asks, that knowing smile on her mouth.

"They call you the Blue Fairy?"

"A silly name, isn't it?"

"Someone sent me to you."

One eyebrow raises. "Do you want to be cut? You have beautiful skin."

"No." My cheeks sting and she laughs.

"A pity. I've never had an angel under my knife before."

"It's not for me. I need a miracle, not a knife."

Her forehead sparkles as it furrows. "What kind of miracle?"

It feels like a betrayal to share Luna's secrets, but I explain as best I can about the body she hates so, the depression, the drugs, the disease that's slowly killing her, the doctors who've turned her away.

She shakes her head when I'm finished. "Do you have any idea what you're asking, angel?"

"I've tried to help her." The words catch in my throat. "But I'm not enough."

"Not enough." She laughs again, short and sharp. "In a perfect world—well, in a perfect world I suppose she'd have been born a woman. In a less perfect world, she'd have a supportive family, friends, doctors, and therapy and medication for the depression. In this world she has none of those. She's been used and broken a dozen times over. You thought you could undo so much damage by yourself?"

Her smile stretches when I don't answer, flashing white teeth. "Silly little angel. Such a human sort of hubris."

"Can you help her or not?"

"I can, but I'll need your assistance."

"Whatever she needs."

The woman cocks her head. "If you want me to help, first you'll need to get her back."

"What?" Understanding sickens me before she answers the question.

"She's not upstairs anymore. Whoever she left with isn't human."

It's been so long since I flew. I wish I could enjoy it now.

The city sprawls below me, a twisting web of lights, and the blackness of the sea beyond. Thermals buffet me, swelling under my wings. The trapeze can never match this.

My eyes water from the wind and smog. I fly blind. I don't need to see to find Luna; her presence—her pain—reels me in. I lost more time than I realized with the Blue Fairy.

Hunter isn't trying to hide. I follow the echo of Luna's heart to a seedy motel near the beach. A neon palm tree flickers beside the office, fronds writhing in the dark. Hunter's scent leads me to a room at the end of the row; the door isn't locked.

The room smells of mildew and sex, Hunter's skin and Luna's. Sharp, metallic blood. Someone gasps as the door swings open. A second later a lamp clicks on.

Luna sits on the bed, naked and bleeding. Red drips down her arms and stomach, feathers across white sheets. A dozen tiny cuts, and the razor cradled in her hand. Her eyes are wide and drowning-dark.

"Why didn't you tell me?" She clutches the sheet around her. It still hurts every time she hides from me.

"I'm sorry." The words are so useless. Everything I do is useless.

Hunter steps out of the bathroom, all pale skin and metal, wings like tattered midnight. "Do you see now? You can't stop me. You can't save him. You should have taken mercy when I offered it."

"There's no mercy in you."

"Razors are always merciful. Ask Mark."

Luna winces at the name she's tried so hard to erase. Her pain spreads inside me like a fracture.

If there's nothing left, at least I can die fighting.

With a falcon shriek I lunge at Hunter. She laughs and spreads her wings.

Flesh falls away. We fight as fire and rage, shadow and scorn. No need for fists or swords, only talon-tipped thoughts, knife-edged purpose. Once our battles scorched the sky, shook the world from heaven to the deeps and all the places between.

This is no battle, it's a massacre. She's whole, stronger than ever. I have no chance.

I fall, shattered. Her teeth and claws close around me. One bite, one mouthful. I won't even make a meal to her. It will all be over. Peace.

No, she whispers, vibrating through all my broken places. *No mercy, sister. Not now. Live, and learn, and suffer*.

She spits me out, back into the world of men, back into my cage of meat.

I wake with my head on Luna's lap, her tears on my skin. Her face is bloody from Hunter's fishhook kisses.

"I never wanted you to save me," she whispers. "I only wanted you to understand. You can't be everything to me. I can't be everything to you."

Truth, not solace.

Her blood stains my hands as she helps me rise. Her words fall like prophecy. "You can't fix me."

"No." No strength for me in this truth. But still hope. "But what if someone else can?"

"Sol—"

"No." I catch her hands and hold them tight. "I mean it. What if someone could make you what you want to be? Would you take it? Would you let me give you that?"

Her shoulders slump, collarbones flaring. Bruised and bloody and tired, such a fragile thing in my arms. So much stronger than I am. "I've heard so many promises."

"No promises, but a chance. Come with me. Please."

It's worth almost everything, that flight with Luna in my arms. Her heart races when we land, eyes shining with a wonder I haven't seen in so long. Some hurt deep inside me eases.

The club is nearly closed. The bouncer tries to stop us, but a word of command sends him stumbling back. My wings enfold us; even weakened and invisible people give us room.

The dark woman waits for us below, all her blades shining and clean. "I wasn't sure you'd make it back," she says with a smile.

Luna gives me an uncertain glance. "Sol?"

"She can help you. Can't you?"

"I think I can." She smiles at Luna. "So you're the one who wants to be a real girl."

Luna nods, trembling against my arm.

"You know I don't work for free." Black eyes meet mine, and she cocks an eyebrow.

"I'll pay, whatever you want."

Her smile is as reassuring as a shark's. The woman beckons Luna forward, and after a second she obeys, descending the steps and moving into the circle of light.

"Strip," the Blue Fairy says. "Let me see what I'm working with."

Luna flinches, but she does it. Her hands stop trembling by the time she's unlaced the second boot. Cloth puddles around her feet. Lifting her chin, she kicks it aside and steps forward.

The Blue Fairy circles her, nodding to herself. "You'll do." She traces a fingertip under Luna's left breast. "Silicone, or saline?"

"Saline."

"Good. I'll take care of those in minute. But first—" She crooks a finger at me. "This is where you come in."

"What do you need from me?"

"Power. A change like this needs fuel. Take off your shirt."

My nipples tighten in the chill as I obey.

"Now show me your wings."

Hunter left me weak, and the flight back to the club drained me further still, but I obey, transubstantiating aether into flesh and feathers. They shine copper and gold as I unfurl them. Luna makes a wondering noise deep in her throat.

The woman points me toward the chair and I straddle it, vinyl padding cold against my chest as I lean forward. My pulse nearly chokes me.

"Do you understand what I'm going to do?" the woman asks softly, crouching beside me.

"You're going to use me to change Luna."

"That's right." She strokes my wing and I shudder. "You realize that when I'm done, this will be gone."

"I know." The admission hurts less than I imagined. I'm broken anyway, fallen. Better to end it like this. Peace at last, and one final moment of purpose.

She picks up the scalpel. "This is what you want?"

"Do it."

The incision hurts just as much as I thought it would. I bite my lip, taste blood. More blood wells beneath the blade, rolls lazily down my back. My wings dissolve to shining light. I struggle to keep that from fading, too. I don't have the strength to call them back.

The scalpel traces one line of pain the length of my shoulder blade, then another. "The wedge makes it easier to remove the skin," she explains, resting one hand on my back to steady herself. "Leaves a better scar."

I can't feel the forceps grip the tattered flesh, but I feel it when she pulls. Luna gasps with me; she sounds so far away. Not just meat and blood, but a piece of me. The wings are only ephemera, an image man has cast on us, or a vanity we indulge. The sacrifice is real.

Consciousness slips as she makes the next incision, but I hold on. I have to make sure Luna is all right. Then I can rest.

It's over. I feel untethered, as though I might float away or fall to pieces. The Fairy wipes blood off the small of my back, fingers lingering in a caress.

"All right," she says. "Now the real work."

A ball of light glows on her palm, the remnants of my wings. She moves her hand and the sphere remains, hovering at her command. I reach for it tentatively, but it doesn't answer. My back burns.

She picks up a clean blade and turns to Luna. "I need to take those implants out. You may want to hold onto something."

Luna blanches but leans back against the railing, hands white-knuckled around the metal.

"I'll reopen the inframammary incision," the woman says, tracing the faint white line beneath Luna's breast, "cut through the scar tissue."

"You need gloves. My blood—"

The woman laughs. "Don't worry about that. Just brace yourself."

Luna nods once.

She screams as the blade bites, but she doesn't move. A rivulet of blood traces the line of her rib cage, then another. The woman slides her fingers into Luna's breast, and Luna whimpers as a blood-streaked white bubble slips out of the wound. The woman tosses it aside and opens the other scar.

When it's done, Luna slumps against the rail, sobbing softly, her chest bloody and sunken. She has an erection.

The Blue Fairy lays the scalpel on the tray, wipes the gore off her hands. "This is it. This change won't be undone."

"Do it." Pain roughens Luna's voice.

I stumble off the chair, hugging myself against the chill. My eyes water as the movement stretches the wounds. Gravity drags at me, and I ache to let go of the flesh, the pain.

"Not yet," the dark woman says. "I'm not finished."

The price.

She takes the ball of light, cradles it between her long hands, and advances on Luna. "This will hurt."

She pushes the light into Luna's chest.

Tears blind me. Luna screams, and it's all I can do not to run to her, not to crawl. The roar of my pulse drowns her cries, drowns everything. I sink through the pain into the dark below.

I wake on cold cement, stiff and aching. Scabs crack as I sit up, lines of fire carved into my shoulders. Luna crouches beside me, still streaked with blood, but the skin beneath is whole. Changed.

She touches her face, her throat, her breasts. One hand slides hesitantly between her legs, and she makes a soft sound. "It worked," she whispers. Even her voice is changed. "Sol, it worked."

She crawls to me, takes me in her arms. Her face is a mask of joy and wonder. I wait to feel it inside of me, wait for her happiness to ease my pain.

It doesn't.

I can't feel it at all. Her skin, her hair, her lips on mine and her blood drying under my hands, but I can't feel her heart. I feel mine in every cut and scrape.

The Blue Fairy is gone.

Luna helps me up. Her shoulders are narrower now, hips broader. Her scars are gone. I've never seen her so radiant.

I stumble as I stand, gravity harsher than ever. I try to heal my swollen lip but nothing happens. The place inside me, where there was once my Word, or the remnants of it, is empty. Nothing but meat.

"What's wrong?" Luna frowns as she touches my cheek.

"I'm—" The word sticks in my throat. "I'm human."

I can't fly.

"Oh." I can't meet her eyes, can't stand the pity there.

We scavenge up our clothes. She helps me ease my shirt over my ruined back, leads me up the stairs. The more she moves in her new flesh, the more graceful and assured she grows. She doesn't need me anymore.

I've fallen so far. I don't know how to catch myself.

Blue Valentine

John Valentine drove into Dallas with twilight at his back. Early February darkness ahead. The lead-bellied sky threatened to crush the city, and only the neon spikes of downtown held it at bay. He nursed the dregs of his coffee—cold and sour now, but all that kept his eyes from closing. Thirteen hours on the road from Atlanta with only the tape deck for company, his rusty tenor singing along to keep himself focused.

I got a letter this morning, how do you reckon it read?

It said hurry, hurry, the girl you love is dead.

A message on his answering machine, actually, a red light blinking to greet him when he'd staggered home in the dead hours of morning. The girl he'd loved once had left it.

Val, it's Chloe. Charlie's dead, Val. Come and see me.

Same old Chloe—she never could just ask for anything, always suggesting or telling or commanding. But her voice was so rough, so tired, and very nearly scared. He'd never heard Chloe James scared in all the years he'd known her. It was enough to make him pack a bag and start driving, the rising sun chasing him down I-20.

Chloe's directions led to a hotel, not her house. A nice hotel, but that was no surprise; Charlie had been rotten with money for years. Val parked in the tall building's shade and heaved himself out of the cab, his back twinging after sitting so long. The wind smelled of exhaust and concrete, dirty and gray. The cold ached in his bad knee, in the scars on his shoulder. Light bounced off polished marble and wood in the lobby, stabbed cut-glass knives through his eyes.

He braced himself as he knocked on Chloe's door. Six years since he'd seen her. At the wedding. The door opened and there she was, stepping into his arms, his name on her lips. He pressed his face against her hair, breathed in her smoky patchouli-spice scent.

She pulled away and led him into the room. She wore the six years well—they suited her better than widow's weeds. Delicate lines traced her dark eyes, framed her mouth. She tucked a stray curl back into her chignon, and Val felt even grubbier. He always felt that way around her.

"Are you all right?" he asked, looking closer. She was good with makeup, but her eyes were shadowed, cheeks thinner than they should be.

"I'm holding up." She tilted her chin, daring him to argue. Same old Chloe. "You look tired."

"Long drive. I haven't slept yet."

Her face softened. "Thanks for coming, Val. I didn't know who else to call."

"Not Zach?"

"No," she said, "not Zach." She turned, poured a glass of liquor from a bottle on the table. Her hand trembled, amber liquid splashing loud. The smell of sweet almonds filled the air.

Val lowered himself onto the couch, frame creaking under him. A mistake—too comfortable, and sleep waited for him the second he dropped his guard.

She poured another glass and handed it to him. He didn't drink much anymore, and Amaretto was never his favorite, but he sipped the cloying sweetness. Warmth lined his throat, blossomed in his stomach. "What happened, Chlo?"

She sat on the edge of the bed, glass cradled in her long brown hands. "He shot himself. A week ago."

Val forced a breath through the tightness in his chest. "That's not how I'd have guessed he'd go." He took a gulp of liquor. Another and the glass was empty.

Chloe smiled bitterly. "Me neither. I spent a lot of nights sitting up, wondering if he was dead in a ditch somewhere, but I never thought it would happen like that."

The room blurred around the edges and Val's eyelids sagged. He resurfaced a moment later to Chloe's hand warm on his shoulder, her frowning face close to his. He yawned till his jaw cracked. "Sorry, Chlo. I don't mean to pass out on you."

"If you don't, I'll just have to tell you everything again tomorrow." Her frown smoothed, and she brushed his stubbled cheek. "I'll sleep better with you here."

He was asleep before he could answer.

He dreamt of Charlie and Zach, the three of them lounging in the old Blackwater Bar that burned down years ago. Charlie laughed at some joke of Zach's, and Chloe swayed on the dance floor, her red dress glowing in the dim lights.

Good old times, except Charlie's curls glistened with gore, and blood dripped down the side of his face and splattered the scarred wood of the bar. Then it wasn't the Blackwater, but the Red Door in Memphis. The air stank of smoke and blood, and bodies sprawled across the floor.

"Good times, huh Val?" Charlie's voice came out thick and sticky.

"Why'd you do it, Charlie? What happened?"

"You'll see, won't you? You always see." Charlie laughed a wet corpse laugh and Zach joined in. Their laughter chased him out of the dream.

Val woke to dawn edging the curtains and the heater growling loud in the quiet room. He rubbed his face, the texture of the couch fabric embedded in his skin. Chloe sprawled on the bed, still wearing her black dress, hair trailing across the sheets in wild midnight coils. The nearly empty bottle of Amaretto sat on the nightstand, beside a full ashtray.

He didn't love her anymore. Not really. It didn't make the memories ache any less. She didn't stir as he tucked the blanket over her. He grabbed the key card off the table and headed down to his truck.

The sky paled to the color of pigeon wings, darkness lingering in the valleys between skyscrapers. As Val pulled his bag out of the front seat, he felt eyes on his back. He tensed, riding out a shudder, and glanced over his shoulder. Someone stood in the shade of the alley's mouth.

Sunlight spilled further across the ground. The figure and the creeping feeling vanished. When he'd decided neither was coming back, Val reached under the seat, reassuring himself that the box with his shotgun was where it was supposed to be.

Chloe stirred as he came out the bathroom. His shirt hung open, and her sleepy eyes widened when she saw his shoulder and the mess of scar tissue there—a souvenir from his last trip to Memphis. Val turned away to do up the buttons.

"What did that?" She reached for her cigarettes.

"Something nasty."

Her lighter rasped, and she sucked in a deep breath. Smoke leaked out of her nose in lazy curls. "They're true, aren't they? All the crazy things Charlie used to talk about."

Val sighed. "They're true."

"Shit." She rose, straightening her dress with careless grace. "There's something you should see." She tossed her suitcase on the bed and flipped it open, pulled out a piece of paper in a clear plastic cover.

"What is it?"

"Charlie's suicide note."

"Why don't the police have that?"

"I never showed it to them." She shoved the note into his hand, plastic crackling. He turned it over slowly. A white sheet of paper with Charlie's familiar scrawl on one side, a fat envelope tucked into the sleeve behind it.

After a moment Val let his eyes focus on the words.

If you find this, baby, I'm sorry. I'm sure it ain't pretty, but believe me it could have been worse.

Call Val. I got some bad people after me, and I'd rather the bullet than what they'll do. I hope to hell they'll leave you in peace, but call Val anyway. He'll look after you. Give him this envelope—there's nothing in there you want to see. I know you haven't thought much of me lately, but it's still more than I deserve.

Sorry to keep running out on you, baby.

Charlie

Val drew a deep breath and looked at Chloe; she dragged on her cigarette. "Did you open the envelope?"

"Of course I did."

"Why didn't you give it to the cops?"

"Read it—you'll see."

Plastic fluttered softly; his hands were shaking. He sank onto the couch and slid the envelope into his hand. It was full of newspaper clippings, and another letter in Charlie's handwriting. The beginning of a headache pulsed behind one eye. Whatever was written there, he didn't want to know.

Val unfolded the paper and began to read.

An hour later Val sipped an overpriced coffee as Chloe drove to the house. The caffeine helped the pain in his head; he wished it could help against the voices.

I've done some bad things, Val, but I swear I didn't know about this. He called in a favor, and I couldn't say no. I didn't think it would be so bad.

Same old Charlie. *The Devil asked you for a favor, and you didn't think it would be so bad?* But Charlie didn't answer.

Just like Memphis, only this time it had been Charlie leading the sheep to the killing floor.

"Are you still teaching?" he asked Chloe, when the silence in the car was thick enough to choke on.

"Yes. At SMU." She glanced at him from the corner of her eye. "You didn't think I'd trust Charlie to take care of me, did you? Twentieth Century Literature, and a section of Modern Drama. But I haven't gone in since . . ."

"What happened? You found him, right?"

Her knuckles blanched on the steering wheel as she drew a breath. "He'd been at the casino in Shreveport all week—he wasn't supposed to be home for few more days." She shook his head. "I was more resigned than anything when I found his car in the drive. We fought nearly as often as we spoke, lately."

They turned a corner, and the houses around them became larger, richer, lawns too green for the ass-end of winter. Val kept his eyes off her face, watched webs of branch-shadows ripple across the windshield.

"Something bothered me as soon as I went inside. I couldn't figure it out then, but it was the silence. Charlie always had the TV on, or music playing. He could never stand quiet for long.

"I found him in his study." She paused for a moment, the engine's purr loud in the stillness. Leather creaked as Val shifted his weight. "I thought he was passed out at first. Then I saw the blood, and the gun."

Chloe tapped the brakes a little too hard and turned into a driveway, past an iron fence thick with bougainvillea, and parked beneath of a winter-bare elm. A black Jag was parked in front of them. Gravel crunched as they walked toward the house—a sprawling two-storied building, red brick and white columns. A pretty house, tasteful. Scraps of crime scene tape fluttered around the door.

When the last chirp of the alarm died, silence echoed around them. Val shut the door against the wind, but the house was still as cold as the day outside.

"I haven't been back," Chloe said, wincing as her words bounced of the foyer's high ceiling. "Not since the detectives finished looking around."

"What did they say?"

"They can't find any proof it wasn't a suicide. Charlie was drunk, the gun was his. Some people at the casino said he'd been upset before he left."

"But?"

"One of the detectives thinks I'm hiding something." She gave him a crooked smile. "I can't imagine why. He asked a lot of questions about Charlie's affairs, and mine. My lawyer bullied him off."

She tilted her chin toward the curving staircase. "His study is the last door on the right. If you want to see."

Val straightened his shoulders and started up the steps. Chloe trailed behind, silent as the dead. That was a bad simile, of course; it had been a long time since the dead were quiet around him.

The door stood open, a chill draft gusting down the hall. Curtains fluttered and wind keened softly through the jagged shards of a windowpane.

"What happened to the window?"

"Charlie threw a paperweight through it, I think. They found it on the lawn outside."

A heavy cherry wood desk stood against the closest wall, a leather swivel chair beside it. The only other furniture was a pair of tall bookshelves and an expensive stereo. Val glanced at the stack of CDs and frowned as he saw Zach Marlowe's face grinning back at him. The latest Black Dog album. He had them all himself, of course. Whatever else you could say about Zach, the boy knew how to play guitar. Val turned back to the desk, circling the chair to get a better view.

Blood splattered the wall, a red-brown spray with thicker, grayer clumps. More stained the floor, dark and stiff on the cream-colored carpet. A few rusty trails streaked the chair leather. Even with the draft, the stench lingered.

"They said I could call someone, a clean-up crew, but I haven't been able to do it yet." Chloe folded her arms tightly under her breasts, her mouth pinched at the corners. "What did Charlie think you could do?"

Val sighed. "See. He thought I could see." He sat in the bloody chair.

His eyes sagged shut. For a moment he heard the harsh edge of Chloe's breath, the whistle of wind and the thud of his heart in his ears. Then with a lurch, it fell away.

The pen shakes in his hand as he signs the note with clumsy strokes. Ink bleeds and feathers across the paper. Whiskey numbs his tongue, burns in the pit of his stomach, but can't chase the adrenaline-chill from his fingers.

Something scrapes the window and he spins. A pale grinning face peers in, tapping its nails against the glass. He curses, grabs a marble paperweight off the desk, and flings it. The window shatters and wind howls in, fluttering papers. The face vanishes, but laughter echoes on the draft.

Palms sweaty, he lays the pen across the letter and envelope to hold them down and fumbles for the revolver. Blue steel gleams oily in the lamplight, heavy in his hand.

The barrel slides cool and slick between his lips, rattling against his teeth as he trembles. The taste of oil and metal floods his tongue and the front sight gouges the roof of his mouth; he fights not to gag. His finger settles across the trigger.

Someone laughs again, closer now.

His finger convulses.

"Val!"

His eyes opened to Chloe crouched in front of him, her nails gouging half-moons of pain in his hand. Val shuddered as his own clammy flesh settled over him again. He scrubbed a hand over his face and touched the back of his head gingerly, half-expecting to find wet blood and brains.

"Val, what happened?" Chloe tilted his face till he met her eyes. "You turned white and started shaking."

He blinked, trying to clear his head of Charlie's last seconds. "I saw. I saw what Charlie saw."

Later—how much later he wasn't sure—he drifted in the red-tinged dark behind his eyes, an ice-pack sweating cold through his hair and spotting the hotel couch with damp. Hollow laughter echoed in his head, glass shattering and the click of the trigger. His mouth still tasted like gun oil.

The door shut softly, but he winced at the sound. He heard Chloe moving through the room, then a rattle of ice and the snap and hiss of a can opening.

"Here, drink."

Moving still hurt, but he propped himself up and took the fizzing glass of Coke. Cold and syrupy sweet, it washed the taste of pain and metal off his tongue.

"Thanks."

Chloe sat on the bed, a darker shape in the curtained gloom. "Is it always like this? When you . . . see?"

"If somebody died, yeah."

"Have you always been this way? You never said anything."

"No, not since after the Blackwater burned. Didn't Charlie tell you?"

"Charlie told me a lot of crazy things." She paused. "He said the three of you went down to the crossroads."

"That's right. We gave the bar a wake, got falling-down drunk and staggered out to the nearest crossroads. Charlie was joking with Zach, saying he ought to call the Devil to teach him to play guitar. Zach said he could already play as good as Robert Johnson and the Devil would have to offer him something else. Then they got to talking about what it would take for them to make a deal."

"What did they want?"

"Nothing fancy. Zach wanted to be a rock star. Charlie wanted money and women."

She was silent for a moment. "What did you want?"

"I said . . . I was drunk and depressed, and I said all I wanted was to see something. Something to make me believe."

She leaned forward, hair slithering over her shoulders. "What happened then?"

"At first, nothing. We stumbled home, passed out, nursed our hangovers the next day, and went on with our lives. We talked about finding a gig, but never did. Then one night some friends of Zach's asked him to fill in for their guitarist at a show up in Chicago. There was a scout in the audience. Not long after that, Charlie got his first break. Then you came back to visit, and you and him . . . got together."

"Are you saying Charlie and I ended up together because he made a deal with the Devil?"

Val shrugged, sipped at melting ice. "I don't know. I just know what happened."

She chuckled. "I wish I could blame some of the things I did back then on infernal powers, I surely do. But I believe in free will."

"So do I. It's always worse that way."

"Val—"

A knock at the door made Val's head reverberate, and he winced. Chloe started, then rose to answer it, switching on a lamp as she passed.

"Chloe." A man's voice, low and smooth. Familiar. Val nearly dropped his glass.

"Marcus." She fell back a step.

"I wanted to see how you were doing." The man stepped into the room and Val stood so fast his bad knee twinged.

The man she called Marcus froze for a beat, eyes wary behind tinted glasses. He hadn't changed in three years, except to grow out his snuff-colored hair and pull it back in sleek cornrows.

"I'm sorry," he said, "I didn't realize you had company."

"John is an old friend of Charlie's," she said. "John, this is Marcus Nash, one of Charlie's business partners."

Nash grinned, bright as piano ivory. "Oh, Val and I know each other. We go back a while."

Val met the man's pale gaze through amber lenses. The taste of old blood filled his mouth. His scars throbbed.

"I thought you might have got out of Memphis." He fought to keep his fists from clenching. This wasn't the place for a fight.

"Of course I did. I thought we'd see each other again. But now's not the time to reminisce." Nash turned back to Chloe. "I'm glad you're not alone right now. You should stop by the bar, if you're up to it. Everyone wants to see you. And—" he paused delicately "—I hate to mention it, but there are a few business decisions we need to make."

"I'll stop by," Chloe promised, with a smile that didn't reach her eyes.

Nash turned, cast a last backward glance at Val. "You come, too, Val. Friends from Memphis are in town, and we've got so much catching up to do."

Chloe bolted the door behind him.

"What did he mean?" she asked as the gray day faded into the dead color of dusk. "About Memphis."

"I got tangled up in something ugly." Val touched his scarred shoulder. "It's where I got this."

"Nash was part of that?"

"He called himself Monroe there—Nathan Monroe—but yeah. It was the same kind of thing that's going on here."

They both glanced at the envelope on the table, full of news-clippings from Texas and Louisiana papers. Missing persons, from Shreveport, Bossier City, Dallas.

I've seen what happens to the people who disappear.

When Charlie fucked up, he didn't do it by half measures.

"I knew Charlie was mixed up in something," Chloe said. "I thought maybe it was drugs. But this . . . Murders. Monsters. Ever since he died, I've felt people watching me. Following me. I thought I was going crazy."

She stared at the book of matches on the nightstand. "I should have burned it. The letter, the pictures, all of it. I still could. Sell the bar to Marcus and get the hell out of here."

"You can, if that's what you want."

"What are you going to do?"

"Settle up with Nash, or whatever his name really is."

"That's it? You'll just walk in there and what—fight him? Shoot him?"

"Chloe— I see all these horrible things. Not just the things people don't want to see, but the ones they can't. If I don't try to stop them, who else will?"

"You have killed people, haven't you?"

"Yes."

"Does that make you better than people like Marcus?"

"No." He shook his head and sighed. "No, it makes me just as bad as them."

She was quiet for a minute. "I'm still not sure you and Charlie weren't both crazy. But I'll help you." She cocked an eyebrow as he opened his mouth. "You're not leaving me behind."

There'd be no arguing with that stubborn tilt of her jaw. "All right. What did Charlie name the bar?"

She smiled wistfully. "The Blackwater."

Saturday night Deep Ellum was thick with cars and people, bright with gold and chrome and sequins. Music drifted through a dozen doors, rap and pop and techno. Robert Johnson and Bessie Smith played here once, when clubs like the Harlem and the Palace were still around. But if they'd left any ghosts behind, they weren't the kind Val could see.

When you go down to Deep Ellum, keep your money in your shoes

Women in Deep Ellum got them Deep Ellum blues.

It wasn't his money Val was worried about; his sawed-off twelve-gauge gouged his side under his coat.

The reincarnation of the Blackwater sat at the end of Elm Street, where the noise and neon dimmed. An unassuming building—black bricks and a simple red sign, windows painted blind—but a line of people stretched from the front door.

They parked in the back, in a staff-only slot, and Chloe headed for the service door. She and Val both startled as someone called her name.

An orange spark flared in the shadows, then vanished as a man crushed out his cigarette. Tall and broad and dark-skinned, camouflaged in the darkness. The front of his T-shirt read BOUNCER.

"Chloe," the man said again, stepping forward and offering a hand. "It's good to see you again. I'm real sorry about Charlie. We all are." His hand enveloped hers.

"Thank you," she said with perfect grace. "I need to see Mr. Nash. Is he here tonight?"

The man nodded, frowning. "He's down in the office. Chloe—Dr. James—" He held her hand too long, and she let him. "You're not planning to sell the place, are you?"

She pulled free gently. "I don't know, Ty. I don't know what I'm going to do."

Ty nodded, still frowning, and stepped back to let her pass. Val watched the space between them; Chloe wouldn't have to stay lonely for long.

"Hey." The man's hand landed on Val's arm as he tried to follow, and he tensed. So damn close—but the bouncer was staring at his face, not the bulge under his coat. "You're John Valentine."

"Yeah, that's me."

"Wow. I knew you and Charlie went back, but I never thought I'd meet you. I heard some of your old tapes—you were ace. You don't play no more?"

"Nah." His mouth twisted. "I guess I just don't feel it anymore." The lie burned like bile.

"That's a damn shame. But enjoy the show tonight."

"Yeah. Thanks."

Inside a band was setting up, and people claimed tables and lined up at the bar. As Val followed Chloe toward the stairs, sweat prickled under his arms. This would be Memphis all over again.

Eyes followed them, glittering in the dim light. A woman grinned, flashing teeth that belonged in a Doberman's mouth. No one else noticed; they never did, until it was too late.

Background noise died as they stepped into the office. Nash looked up from account books; his glasses were gone. Without them his eyes gleamed pale and nearly colorless in the fluorescent light. Eerie, but only human.

The Judas goats were worse.

Nash looked Val over and smiled. "What are you going to do? Shoot me?"

"Shouldn't I?"

"You could. You might even kill me. Then my friends upstairs will call the police. What would you say, Val? Would you tell them about Memphis, about the Red Door? Would you tell them about the monsters?" He chuckled. "Just because you play vigilante doesn't mean we have to follow your rules."

"What about Chloe?"

"Whether Ms. James is your accomplice or an innocent bystander is up to her."

Chloe lifted her chin. "That's Dr. James, thank you. I suppose this is where you ask me to sign papers for you."

"Unless you'd rather keep Charlie's share and work with us. You're a hell of a lot more sensible than he was."

"I don't think your business is anything I want a part of."

"Val told you all about us, did he?"

"You kill people? All those people who disappeared around your casinos?"

"Not me personally—not usually." He shrugged. "Supply and demand.

I'm just making a living. I don't even hold a grudge about Memphis," he said to Val. "These things happen. Not everyone feels the same way, of course. Unless you plan on playing vigilante tonight, I think you and Dr. James should leave."

Val nodded slowly, teeth clenched. "I'll be seeing you."

Nash grinned. "I'll be waiting."

As Val turned the doorknob, it swung in against his hand. A woman stood in the doorway, the woman from upstairs. In the better light, he recognized her.

"Ellie."

"Hello, Val." She smiled. Chloe gasped.

Ellie reached up, slid her hand under his coat and traced the scars on his shoulder. Her chill soaked through his shirt. "I see you kept my souvenir." She'd dyed her hair auburn; it drifted around her face in an autumn curtain.

"I didn't think you made it out."

"Barely. My sister wasn't so lucky." Her fingers tightened, strong as rebar.

"Ellie." Nash's voice was low, cautious, like he was talking to an angry dog. "They were just leaving."

"Of course they were." She leaned in, pressed her cold dry lips against his cheek. Val's balls tried to crawl up his throat. "You run along now, sweetie." She winked at Chloe, stepped back enough to let them pass, but not enough that Val could avoid brushing against her. Her eyes flashed copper-green like a cat's as she moved from light to shadow.

The wind chilled Val sweat-soaked shirt as they stepped outside. His heart throbbed in his throat and he smelled his own fear-stink. Chloe walked sure as ever, but her hands were balled in her coat pockets.

"What is she?" Chloe asked, locking the door as soon as they were in the car.

"A monster. A killer."

"Jesus." The car jerked out of the parking space and she swore again, easing off the gas. "We can keep driving," she said as they left the noise and crowds behind. "There's nothing here I can't live without."

It was the closest he'd heard her come to admitting she was scared. It was also the best idea he'd heard in a long time.

"I can't. I can't leave them here like this. But you should go. You got someone you could visit?"

"And leave you to get killed? I just lost my husband, Val—don't make me lose a friend, too."

They stopped arguing by the time Chloe snapped her suitcase shut. Val was amazed how close he'd come to winning.

"You hurry up and take care of this." She shrugged into her coat, draped a scarf around her shoulders. "I'm not much good at waiting."

His mouth twisted. "I remember."

Her expression softened. "I know how you felt, Val. Sometimes I think—"

"Don't. It was a long time ago. You don't owe me anything."

She nodded, picked up her suitcase. "You call me soon." She pressed her lips against his cheek as she left the room.

Val sighed, ran a hand over his face. Time to finish this, to get the hell back home.

Chloe's car was gone by the time he reached the parking lot. Neon stained the clouds green and orange; behind the false light he felt the edge of dawn, still an hour or two away. He needed a place to rest before he went back to the club.

"This better be the last time I have to clean up your mess, Charlie," he muttered to the dark. Charlie didn't answer.

Val fished his keys out of his pocket as headlights cut around the corner. He fumbled the ring, caught it, and slid the key home as the car slowed and someone leapt out. His hand brushed the shotgun just as she hit him, slamming him into the side of the truck and twisting his arm behind his back.

"My sister was everything to me," Ellie whispered, pressing against his back. The words ruffled the hair above his ear, cold as the night air. "Do you know what it's like to lose everything?"

"No."

"You will." She slammed his head against the side of the truck, and the world shattered into red and black.

Val woke in the dark, sprawled on a bed that smelled like Chloe's perfume, his memory evaporated like spilled liquor. Then he tried to move and the pain brought it all back. His mouth tasted like dirty pennies.

A lamp clicked and the space behind his eyes washed from to black to red-orange.

"Chloe?"

"What are you doing, Val?"

He opened his eyes to see a man leaning over him, a mournful look on his dark face. A handsome face, and familiar, one he'd only seen in photographs. For an instant he thought he was staring at a ghost.

The man laughed, and Val knew better. "I'm afraid not." He took off his hat, ran a long-fingered hand over close-cropped hair. "He was a good boy. A fast learner. A shame, him dying young and hard like that. You'll die hard, too, Val, if you keep this up."

Val touched his head cautiously—a tender knot swelling on one side, the other scratched and blood-sticky. He pulled a chunk of asphalt out of his hair and winced as his vision blurred again.

"What do you want?"

"You were in a bad spot. I thought maybe you could use my help."

Val wanted to spit, but his head hurt too much to try. He didn't mean to speak again, but the words scraped out of his throat anyway. "Where's Chloe?"

The man wearing Robert Johnson's face whistled a familiar tune, sang a few lines under his breath.

"Once I had a sweetheart, she meant the world to me.

She went down to Deep Ellum, now she ain't what she used to be."

He straightened his jacket. "You know, Val, all you have to do is ask and I'll help you. Have I done anything but give you what you asked for?"

"Go to hell."

"Have it your way. Don't worry, though, the cavalry is on its way."

Val was alone again, the heater growling softly in the quiet. He might have imagined the whole thing, but the light was still on.

He tried to stand, but nausea drove him back to the bed. He drifted for a while, till a knock at the door dragged him out.

He made it across the room without vomiting or falling, though it was close. He fumbled the door open, half-expecting another punch in the face. But it was only the bouncer, Ty.

"Where's Chloe?" Then he blinked. "What the hell happened to you?"

Val chuckled, and regretted it. "Somebody hit me upside the head." He staggered as he stepped back, and only Ty's arm kept him from falling. The man grunted as Val's weight hit him.

Ty eased him onto the couch and ran his fingers over the lump on Val's head, tilted his face toward the light and studied his eyes. "I think you've got a concussion."

"I suspect I do. What are you doing here?"

"Looking for Dr. James. She's not answering her phone, and the hotel said she went out last night and never came back. What are you doing here?"

"Seemed like a good place to pass out. You checking up on Chloe now?"

Ty pulled a leather case out of his pocket and flipped it open. The badge gleamed, slick and shiny. "FBI. Charlie Cole and his partners were under investigation for money laundering, among other things."

Val started to laugh, but it hurt too much. "Is Chloe under investigation, too?"

"Dallas PD thinks she was involved in her husband's death." His dark eyes searched Val's face. "Was she?"

"No." Val remembered not to shake his head just in time. "She didn't have anything to do with it."

"Good."

His laugh was short and bitter. "You're in love with her, too, aren't you?"

Ty's eyes flickered away. "Where is she?"

"Maybe the club. Nash wants her to sign it over to him."

"Is that who hit you?"

"His people, yeah."

The other man's jaw tightened. "I thought so. You need a hospital."

"Not yet. Take me with you." He caught Ty's arm. "Just let me see that Chloe's okay, and then I'll call the ambulance myself. What time is it?"

Ty glanced at his watch. "Quarter till five. The club's not open yet."

Almost night. "We should hurry then. Before too many people show up."

"You mean civilians like you? All right, let's go."

Two cars were parked behind the Blackwater, neither of them Chloe's. Ty pressed a button on his cell phone before he unlocked the back door. "Backup's coming."

Gun in hand, he slipped inside. Half an hour till sunset.

They found Chloe sprawled across Nash's desk, wicked midnight hair tangled around her head, face ashen in the warm pool of lamplight. Her throat was a red ruin, gnawed to the bone. Not enough blood left to puddle.

Ty made a choked noise, but Val looked away. The scene was meant to distract him.

Sure enough, someone moved across the room. Val threw himself to the side as a muzzle-flash burst orange and gold. Ty cursed, and another shot cracked. The smell of blood filled the room.

Val lunged and tackled Nash. The man grunted as they hit the ground. Ty's bullet had caught Nash in the shoulder and blood soaked hot through both their shirts.

"Damn it," Nash muttered as Val caught his wrist and slammed his gun hand against the floor. "I told her this was stupid."

"It surely was." Val grabbed the gun and pushed himself to his knees.

"She's not dead. Chloe, I mean. Not for much longer, anyway. Not unless you hurry."

"Either way, you won't see it." He pulled the trigger, and Nash's head burst into a crimson halo across scuffed green carpet.

"You okay?" Val said, turning back to Ty. Adrenaline drove back the pain in his head, drew everything sharp-edged.

The younger man slumped against the wall, cell phone in his good hand. He pressed a button and the screen flashed, then tucked the phone away and grabbed his left arm. Blood soaked down his sleeve. "I will be. What did he say about Chloe?"

"Nothing," Val said after a heartbeat. "Just being ugly." He glanced at the second door behind the desk. "Sit tight while I check the other room."

Ty nodded, still staring at Chloe. Val checked the clip in Nash's gun. The door was locked, but he found the key in the dead man's pocket. The door opened into bitter-smelling darkness. He closed it behind him, groping for a light switch.

Ellie lay on a bed against the wall, a sheet wrapped around her shoulders and her bare legs drawn toward her chest. Just like a normal girl, until you noticed she wasn't breathing.

She stirred at the light, made a soft noise in the back of her throat and tugged the sheet over her face. "Marcus? What time is it?"

Val's hand shook, slippery on the gun. Easy when they came at you snarling, all flashing eyes and teeth. She was just a girl—

He forced himself to think of the scars on his shoulder, of Chloe's bloodless face.

"Marcus?" Ellie propped herself up, blinking sleepily. Her eyes widened.

The first bullet ruined her pretty face. She fell back writhing while her blood—Chloe's blood—soaked the sheets.

The next shot took out her throat and a chunk of spine. One more in the head and she stopped twitching. It was always easier with the shotgun. He tugged the sheet over the mess of her skull, watched the stains leak through white cloth. The smell of rot bloomed.

Val nearly made it to a trashcan before he threw up.

As he laid his hand on the doorknob, he knew something was wrong. He brought the gun up as he stepped out—

Chloe knelt beside Ty, her hands slick with blood. She turned, eyes flashing; red dripped from her chin, soaked her dress dark and shiny.

"I—" She scrubbed a hand over her mouth, but it only smeared the mess. "I could smell it—"

Ty's gun lay by his side. He hadn't even though to use it on her.

Val's hand clenched, finger trembling against the trigger guard. Three shots and it would be over.

She stared at the gun. "Val—"

He didn't love her anymore. He didn't.

"Go upstairs," he said after a moment. His voice was raw and ugly. "Bring me anything that'll burn, and matches. And clean yourself up."

Her eyes narrowed at the order—some things would never change—but she rose. Already she moved differently, smoother, sleeker.

Val found more locked doors in the basement, but didn't bother looking for the keys. He could smell them inside, Ellie's friends—maybe fifteen minutes left before they woke. The cops would be here soon.

Chloe helped him soak everything in whiskey and rum and lighter fluid. She only paused for a second when she looked down at Ty. Flames licked blue and gold across the carpet, the desk, the bodies; more caught the piles of rags and boxes Val had stacked outside the locked doors. Chloe hissed softly as the fire rose and he flinched from the sound.

He flinched from her cold hands, too, but she didn't let go as they climbed the stairs, held him steady as his feet dragged and vision darkened. Outside the sky hung dull and heavy, clouds hiding any last scraps of sunlight. Chloe's eyes flashed gold as they stepped into the sodium glare of the parking lot.

"What are you going to do?" she asked.

"Go home. You should get out of here, too, in case the fire doesn't finish everyone off."

She nodded, watching him like she wanted to speak. But she didn't. Still Chloe, no matter what else she was now.

"I can't stay with you, Chloe. I'm sorry. You'll be all right." Hell, she'd likely thrive.

She leaned in, pressed her cold lips against the corner of his mouth. "Maybe I'll see you again."

Pain threatened to leak out his eyes, and he squeezed them shut. "I hope not."

"Goodbye, Val."

He opened his eyes in time to see the shadows close around her. Sirens wailed nearby. He stared after Chloe for a few seconds, then started for Elm Street as night fell down.

Out of Gas

Joshua Hackett

Cross-country travel
A road trip
Turns into a chase scene

Too far from home
Headlights flash, doors lock
I cry for help

but

There are no werewolves
In Shreveport

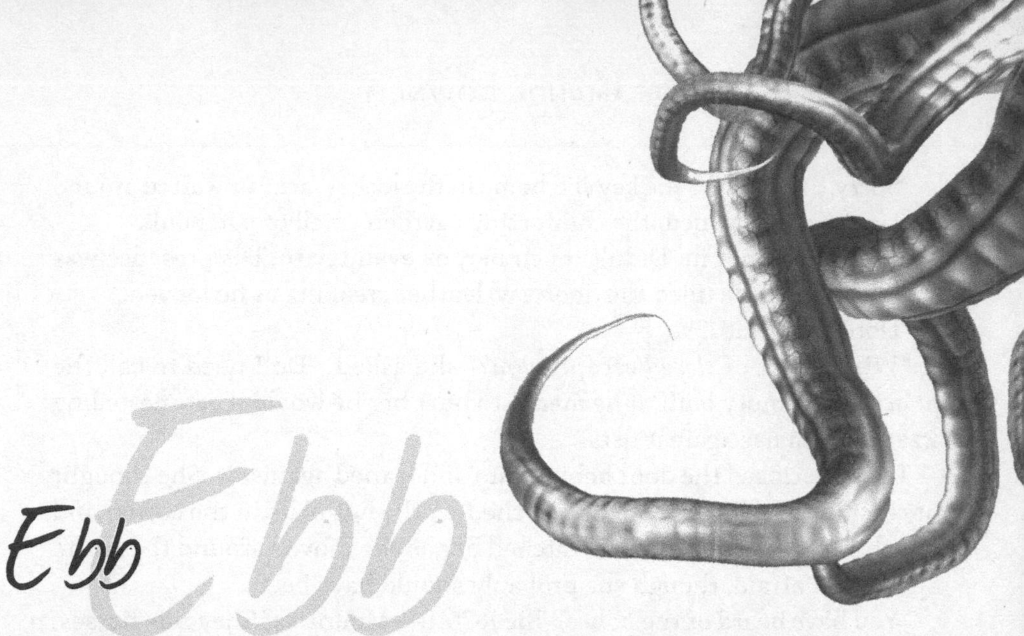

Ebb

The motorcycle waited outside Celia's apartment, a sleek machine-beast brooding by the curb, engine popping and clicking in the cold. So out of place among the cheap and sensible cars along the street. She heard her name in its weary ticks, read it in the smooth lines of black and chrome.

They'd found her.

She'd known it would happen eventually, but the sudden reality shook her. No warnings, no portents. Some psychic she was. The wind whipped at her hair and skirt as she stood frozen on the sidewalk, keys biting her palm as her fists clenched. She should turn and walk away.

But Micah would never ride that beast of a bike; no one in her family would. So who had found her, and why?

Curiosity won—curiosity and the ache in her back. Relaxing her grip on her keys, she went inside.

The hallway was dark as ever, fragrant with kimchi and spices from the Korean grocery next door. Bass rattled through the walls from the apartment above her little shop; she listened for a message in the *thump thumpa thump*, but didn't hear one. Besides the message to leave another complaint with the management.

He waited in the shadows by her door, a tall leather-clad shape, helmet tucked under one arm. Celia kept moving, finding her key on the ring by touch, trying to keep her hands from shaking. The air was heavy with intention, but intention as to what she couldn't say.

"Madame Celia?" A deep rough voice, like whiskey and gargled razor-blades. Just a hint of teasing as he nodded his bald head toward the sign. The moons and stars and hand-painted zodiac signs were due a little mockery.

"Sorry, I'm closed." The key slid home in the lock. Warm air wafted around her as the door opened, the comforting earthen smell of patchouli.

He followed her in. Didn't touch her, or even try to. His presence was threat enough. He filled the doorway, leather creaking as he moved.

"Don't be afraid."

"Which part of *closed* escapes you?" she asked. "Do I need to call the police?" An empty bluff; if he meant to hurt her he would. Fortune-telling wasn't much use against fists.

The man closed the door behind him and leaned against it. She thought of reaching for the phone, but switched on the hot plate in the corner and put the kettle on instead. He watched her as she moved around the room. She wasn't afraid, though she probably should have been.

"You have heard of the police? The RCMP—Mounties? They ride horses, fight crime, protect young women from hooligans." She pressed her tongue between her teeth to stop babbling.

A smile rearranged his weathered, sun-bronzed face. "What did the doctor say?"

The first real fear constricted her chest. She started to cross her arms, forced them back to her sides. "She says I need more iron—borderline anemia. Thanks for the concern."

"Boy or girl?"

"I didn't ask."

"I thought you were psychic."

She smiled, too sharp, and fought to keep the tension from her shoulders and voice. "If you come back during business hours, I'll be happy to tell your fortune." She blinked, looked at him *otherwise*. His aura seethed with dark angry flames. Tight spirals of red and black swirled up his arms—more violence than she'd ever seen in one person. Harnessed, contained.

"Did my family send you?" She couldn't imagine her mother hiring goons. Micah would have come himself. But she'd been wrong about them before, hadn't she?

"No, but they're looking for you. They're close."

She recognized the truth in the words. "Then what do you want?"

"If your family is after something, Ms. Waite, it's my job to make sure they don't get it."

"If I wanted them to have me, I wouldn't be here, would I?" The kettle began to whistle, but she ignored it.

"If you really mean to hide from them, you'll have to do better than this." He reached for the doorknob, then paused. "If you want to get away, I can help you."

"And if I don't?"

He shrugged and opened the door. The darkening of his aura was all the answer she needed.

She lay in the bathtub that night, enclosed in its slick porcelain shell. Water buoyed her, caressed her. Bland, chlorinated water, chemical-safe, no hint of swamp or sea. Nothing that might change her.

She was changing already. She pressed one hand against her stomach and felt the pull of amniotic tides.

The dreams were bad, the first two months—she couldn't tell portent from fear. Dreams of sirens and sea monsters and slippery scale-cold bodies. Once she dreamed she was heavy with fish eggs, a womb full of glistening roe. That was when she cracked and made an appointment at the clinic.

But the doctor found only one heartbeat, healthy and normal. With that her fear eased, and the vision came easily. A daughter, with Celia's cracked-peridot eyes and Micah's dark hair and almond-bronze skin. No fins, no scales.

What will you do? the doctor had asked when she saw the doubt on Celia's face.

I don't know, she'd answered.

Whatever you choose, decide soon.

Her mother wanted this baby. Celia knew she shouldn't keep it. Knew she couldn't give her up.

"What will you be?" she asked. Water pressed against her ears, distorted the words. "What do they want you to be?"

Celia never met her father. A Gilman, her mother told her, an ugly frog of a man. She called Celia her little tadpole. Never very fondly.

The Waites, Esther always told her daughter, were not fish, not frogs. They were sorcerers, magi, not backwater freaks who couldn't decide which direction on the evolutionary ladder they wanted to go. Celia had met a few Marshes and Gilmans, and was glad she took after her mother's side.

Not enough for Esther, though. Never enough. She frowned at her daughter's wide swamp-colored eyes, looked down her aquiline nose and told Celia to stand straighter, lose weight. She berated Celia's wild talents and dreams, cursed her inability to master ritual and summoning.

But we're your family, Esther would say between chidings. *We love you. No one but family will ever really love you.*

She dreamed of Micah. Not a portent or vision, just old sorrow, bitter joy. She'd dreamed of Micah a lot in the last three months.

Laughing, bright-eyed Micah Fischer, who'd proved her mother wrong, proved that someone could love her. She'd smiled to herself at his name, at the sea-storm colors of his aura, but she'd never looked too deep. He really loved her, and that was enough.

It might have still been enough, even after the phone calls she wasn't meant to hear, the dark flashes of avoidance. Even after she suspected the truth, that her mother had arranged everything, arranged the love of Celia's life as coldly as Esther had arranged to lie down with a frog who did not become a prince. It might have been enough.

Until she woke one morning and knew with blood and bone that she was pregnant, knew that it was her mother's design.

Then the nightmares started. Then she ran.

She fumbled through the next day's appointments, telling lonely widows and neurotic housewives what they wanted to hear. More truth than she intended slipped into her readings, and the cards whispered sly asides. By the time her last customer left, Celia's hands shook so badly she could barely shuffle the deck.

She glanced past her gauzy curtains and hanging beads toward the street. It seemed empty, but she felt the presence waiting there. Her back and her breasts ached again. All she wanted was to lie down.

Instead she wrapped herself in coat and scarf and braved the biting December afternoon. The wind slipped its fingers up her skirt, lifted the curls off the back of her neck. The sky hung low and leaden, threatening rain.

Her eyes passed over him once, twice, but on the third look she saw through the glamours wrapped around man and bike. He sat, one leg balancing the massive machine, and watched. Or she guessed that he watched; the helmet's visor hid his face.

She approached, chin raised, and stopped within arm's reach of him. "What's your name?"

For a moment she stared at her own dark reflection in his helmet. The he raised the visor with a black-gloved hand. "Etienne."

"If you're going to stalk me, don't you think you should at least buy me dinner first?"

That earned her a smile. Good—she wanted him smiling, not threatening. If the two were any different.

"What's your pleasure, then?"

Her own smile was sharp and teasing. "Sushi."

"Why did you warn me?" Celia stirred more wasabi and soy sauce with one chopstick. "Why not just . . ." She shrugged.

"I don't like to just . . ." He returned the gesture, eyes glinting. The chopsticks were tiny and graceful in his broad blunt hand as he picked up another California roll. A tattoo crawled down his left arm, poking its head out of his sleeve; a snake, maybe, or a dragon. "And," he said after he swallowed, "I thought you might really want to get away from them. But I couldn't be sure."

"No." She sipped bitter green tea and watched plates of sushi float past the counter on tiny boats. "I might just be trying to get attention, after all. Trying to prove something."

"You could disappear. That would prove something."

"Disappear. Is it that simple?"

He shrugged again. "It could be."

"Why do you care?"

"It's my job." His face was impossible to read, but she caught the swirl of emotion out of one *otherwise* eye. Old guilt, old regret. Celia pushed a slice of ginger around her plate and chewed the inside of her lip.

"Are you going to keep the baby?" he asked later when he walked her to her shop door like a dutiful date. She still couldn't summon up fear in his presence, for all he unnerved her. He might kill her, but he couldn't really hurt her—not like her family could.

"I shouldn't, should I?" She touched her stomach—not showing yet, though the waist of her skirt was snugger than usual. She let him see the doubt in that gesture, the desire. Lure them in with breadcrumbs of emotion; her mother taught her that.

"Even if she's . . . normal, I still don't know what I'd do with a child. My mother didn't set the best example." Truth, all of it. The truth was always more dangerous.

"She?"

One corner of her mouth curled. "I am psychic." She hesitated. "What does my mother want with my baby?"

"I don't know. But she went to a lot of trouble to make sure this baby happened."

"People do that, don't they? Want children. Try for children."

An ugly frog of a man. Like lying down with a toad. But I wanted a child. Always that distant look in Esther's eyes when she said it. She'd wanted a child, but not the one she'd had. *But we love you.* Maybe she only wanted a real daughter, not some pale fat frog of a girl.

But Celia knew her mother never *only* wanted anything, not without a tangled skein of reasons and plans and prices.

She dreamed of sunlight on the water, of columned cities in the deep and a haunting choral swell of siren-song. She dreamed of stormy seas, of waves lashing cruel and wild.

This is hers, not mine. All this is hers.

What could she be to this child?

She woke with tears like sea-salt on her tongue, and no answers.

It rained the next day, cold and sharp. Celia eventually took pity on her stalker and invited him in for tea. His glamour might fool the eye, but not the weather; water glistened on oiled leather, soaked the neck of his shirt where helmet and collar didn't seal.

As he shrugged out of his jacket she thought she saw steam rising off his skin. Fire and rock, whatever else he might be, not someone to be easily turned. But maybe she could wear him down.

"Do you do this often?" She passed him a towel and their hands brushed. For a heartbeat she felt heat like a volcano's breath, smelled smoke and ash and hot metal. The smell of destruction. She jerked her hand back.

"Too often," he said, drying himself as best he could.

Goosebumps crawled her arms. "Why?"

"Mission from God." He said it with a smile and a shrug, but he wasn't lying. "I help people who need it."

"You hurt people, too." The bloody streaks twining his hands told that story eloquently enough.

"Only when they need it."

Silence stretched, broken only by their breath and the patter of rain. "Are you going to hurt me?"

"I don't want to."

She turned to pour the tea, spooned milk and honey into his. A whiff of clove and cinnamon and dark anise drifted through the air. "Why do you care about any of this? About me and my baby." Heat soaked her hands through the worn mismatched cups. She held them tight to still her trembling.

"Your family is dangerous. I can't let another child suffer for their schemes."

A bit late for that, isn't it? "What do you mean, another?"

He glanced away, his colors clouding. "There was another girl, once. Another Waite. I tried to help her, but it was too late. She was already tangled too tight in her father's webs, and I couldn't cut her loose."

"What happened to her?"

"Her father used her up. She died in a madhouse."

Celia set her cup aside untasted. "You think that will happen to my daughter?"

His eyes were dark beneath heavy brows. "I think something worse might happen to her. Ephraim used his daughter because she was convenient, but

Esther doesn't do anything without a reason. I don't know what she wants her grandchild to do, but it won't be good."

"You think she'll be dangerous? Just because she's my daughter?"

"Maybe not for who she is, or even what, but if your mother has anything to do with it . . ." He lifted broad bloody hands in a shrug.

Celia sipped her tea, but all she tasted was bitterness.

She dreamed of her daughter. A laughing infant, a confection of brown sugar and almond milk in her arms. A laughing child, running down a beach, curls bouncing wild in the sun.

Running away, toward the foaming waves.

She will never be all mine.

Celia woke at dawn and knew Micah was coming, felt the connection between them reeling him in. The smell of his skin lingered like a ghost. She rose and dressed in the dark. The need to see him filled her chest, sharp and heavy, but she couldn't stand the thought of being cornered. She needed air, space—somewhere she could escape again if she had to.

She waited in Stanley Park as the sun rose behind the clouds. Rain rippled over the water, trickled down her face. Through the shifting haze, she stared at the statue of a girl sitting on a rock, gazing at the sea. Only a girl in a wetsuit, but she could have been a mermaid, some lonely ocean child.

"Is that what you'll be?" she whispered, one hand on her stomach. "A mermaid, a siren? Will your feet bleed on dry land?"

She felt Micah approach, felt him like a wave. He came alone, and that eased some of her twisting fear. She turned to watch him and the bottom fell out of her stomach.

No frog prince, Micah. Tall and lean, sleek-muscled shoulders buried under sweater and coat. His hair curled in the rain, clung to his cheeks and brow. She wanted to touch him, to know he was real. She stood her ground.

"Celia—" Her name caught in his throat. She met his dark eyes and her own throat closed. "Cel, you scared the hell out of me."

There had never been anyone before him. Not when she could see every lie, every denial, the murky shades of ulterior motives. She'd never met anyone else who could win past her sight, past all her insecurities and neuroses.

"Tell me the truth. About us."

He sighed, shoulders slumping. "They asked me—the family asked me—to find you, to meet you. That was all. Your mother said she thought we'd be good together. So I met you, and she was right."

"What if we hadn't worked? What then?"

"I don't know. No one ever talked about that." He pushed his hair off his forehead with a long-fingered hand. "It wasn't some dark conspiracy, Cel. It was just a suggestion. And I'm glad I listened."

"It never mattered to you that it was all arranged?"

"Why should it? I love you."

Every word of it true, every word a weight in her chest. "What about our baby?"

His eyes widened. "It's true? When?"

"Sometime in June, most likely. If everything is normal."

He walked toward her, reached for her, and the distance between them vanished too fast. She stiffened in his arms, gasped, then relaxed against him with a sob. The scent of wet wool filled her nose as she pressed her face against his chest. Beneath that she could smell the salt-sweet of his skin.

He held her, stroked her hair, whispered her name as the rain misted around them. Just a boy and a girl, and their baby. All she'd ever wanted. A family. Love.

She let Micah lead her away from the shore, his arm around her safe and warm. She felt eyes on her back as she walked.

They lay on her bed, skin to skin. Micah's hair still smelled like rain. He pressed his hand to her stomach and made a low wondering noise.

"What should we name her?"

Celia smiled, nestled her cheek against the curve of his neck. "I don't know yet." Even as she said it a name rang in her mind like a chime. A name heavy with implication. She shoved it down, pushed it away.

"My mother wants the baby."

"Of course she does. Why shouldn't she want a grandchild?"

"She wants *this* baby, Micah. That's why she wanted us together."

He wrapped his arms around her. "Don't be so paranoid. This isn't some plot, some breeding program. Your mother just wants you to be happy. I know she doesn't show it sometimes, but she loves you."

He believed it.

Was that it? Was she just paranoid? A neurotic mess of a girl, too screwed up to let herself be happy.

"Come home with me," Micah murmured against her ear. "Everything will be all right. Or—" He tensed. "Or run away with me. We don't have to go home, we can go anywhere. Just us." He caressed her stomach. "Just us. Celia, marry me."

Her breath caught, then rushed out on a sigh. Tears prickled her sinuses. "Micah—" She kissed him until they were both too breathless to speak.

She dreamed of a dragon, a kraken, vast and ancient, sleeping in the lightless depths, buried beneath eons of silt. A nest of ancient bones crumbled around him. Sometimes the kraken's sleep grew troubled and he tossed, wings flexing, tentacled face turning. The seabed shook and cracked. New wounds split the skin of the earth.

She saw her daughter grown, standing by the frothing sea. Spray glistened on slender limbs, soaked wild dark curls. The woman raised her face to the thunder-dark sky and sang. Whether she meant to sing the beast to sleep or rouse it, Celia didn't know.

This is what she is meant to do.

Micah still slept when night came, his face smooth and peaceful. Celia slipped out of his warm embrace. She didn't know how she'd slept alone so long, didn't know how she'd even lived before she met him. Her heart was cold as glass.

Etienne waited outside the shop, leather blending with the darkness. They stood in silence for a while.

"He wants me to run away with him."

"That's good."

Her smile hurt. "No, it's not. Micah is . . . He's the kindest person I've ever known. He doesn't believe my mother would ever hurt anyone, let alone her family. He'd forget, or just not care. We'd run away and in three weeks he'd call to tell her how we're doing, to let her know everything's okay."

Etienne watched her for a moment. "You could get rid of the baby."

The fear, the nightmares. The laughing eyes in her dreams. "I can't."

She waited for threats, but none came. He wouldn't hurt her. He'd let her walk away. But she couldn't do that either—she'd need help when the baby came.

Celia let out a breath, watched it stream away in the wind. "Come with me."

Red and black rippled with relief. "Yes. Do you want to say goodbye?"

The glass in her chest broke into a thousand glittering shards. "No."

He nodded and led her toward the motorcycle. She kept her eyes on the back of his jacket. If she turned she would crumble to salt.

The wind sighed cold and damp around them as he lifted her onto the bike. The engine growled to life, rumbling through her bones. "What are you going to name her?"

Her arms closed around his waist. She smiled into the dark, bittersweet. "Andromeda."

Snakebit

The horses were restless.

Sounds of snorts and hooves tangled through Lanie's nightmares, familiar dreams of smoke and screaming. She woke with a start. Beside her Merle stirred and swore.

"Between you kicking and them carrying on it's a wonder I ever sleep." He always woke up cranky. It usually made her laugh, but now her hands tingled with nerves.

"I'd better go check on them," she said, peeling back the sheets.

He propped himself up on one elbow. "You sure?"

"Go back to sleep." The breeze from the open window dried her skin as she groped for a pair of jeans and shoved her feet into the nearest boots. Merle was snoring again by the time she was dressed.

She took the flashlight from the nightstand—and after a second's hesitation, the pistol from the drawer. If something was out there spooking the horses she'd be better off with the shotgun, but the fit of the revolver against her palm was comforting.

She crept down the stairs, careful of the creaking middle step. Darla was a light sleeper—she took after Lanie that way. Mackenzie slept deep as her father and woke just as crabby. The back door needed oiling, but Lanie knew where to lean on it to stop the hinge from squealing.

The November night was cool and sticky. Wind keened soft around the eaves, setting the chimes clashing and teasing goosebumps along her arms and breasts. Past the glare of the barn light, stars drifted against the black velvet sky. Plains and fields rolled to the horizon, the boundary between earth and sky marked by distant turbines, white as bones in the glow of the waning moon. Nothing seemed out of place, but the back of her neck still prickled.

Gravel scraped under her boots and she winced, even though it would be better to let an animal know she was coming. Coyotes still haunted the plains.

A horse snorted and kicked the stall while she juggled gun, flashlight, and keys. Probably Susie—Diego was the calm one. A cat bolted as Lanie opened the door, eyes flashing in the dark. The pungent smell of horse and hay and packed earth washed over her; usually a comfort, but now the nightmares were fresh in her mind. Too easy to remember smoke and blood, the screams of frightened horses.

They'd had seven horses when the old barn burned. Five survived the fire. Since Roy Baxter died and Lanie and Merle moved into the house, they'd sold most of the horses and land. She hated it every time, but it was true they didn't have time or money to look after so many animals. She'd put her foot down for the last two, though—the girls needed to learn to ride.

Susie snorted again. "What is it, Susie Q?" Lanie asked softly. She balanced the flashlight on the stall railing and reached out to stroke the mare's velvety nose. Lips moved across her palm, hot and damp and searching. "Sorry, darlin'. I didn't think to bring you anything."

The horses' insistent nuzzling calmed her nerves. After a minute she switched off the flashlight and stood in the darkness scratching their heads. She tucked the gun into the waistband of her jeans so she could use both hands. "What if it was just you and me?" she whispered. "Where would we go?"

But there was nowhere to go, and she knew it. Too many fences for horses to run free anymore, and nothing for her but this house where she grew up. This new barn that reminded her of the old one. This life she'd cobbled together from the rags and bones of her childhood.

I always knew, her father said one night after Cody ran off. Drunk off his ass, like he had been for weeks. *It's in our blood. We're all snakebit, all of us. You might as well get used to it, 'cause you'll never be happy.*

She'd believed that for years, through Cody's disappearance, through the terrible night in the barn years later, through the ugly years after high school when she tried everything she could find to kill the unhappiness and nearly died of it. Then Merle came, and Mackenzie, and she'd told herself her father was wrong. Just a bitter old drunk, and she could do better.

Diego leaned across the door of his stall, nosing her shoulder until she gave him more attention. Her hand slid down the coarse sleekness of his neck and she itched to get a saddle, to ride and ride and not think of anything but the wind and the rhythm of the horse.

But she'd regret it in the morning, and the girls had to be up for school.

If horses were wishes, went a song. If horses were wishes, she'd used up most of hers. Better to save the last for when she really needed them. She gave Susie and Diego a last ear-scratch and retrieved the flashlight. She should salvage a few hours of rest.

Something moved at the corner of her eye when she stepped outside. She spun, the gun scraping the small of her back as she yanked it free. The flashlight beam cut through the darkness, but found nothing except the side of the stable and the fence behind. The night-darkened wall bled crimson in the light.

Heart racing, Lanie circled the barn twice, searched inside before locking the door. The horses were calm now, but her hands shook as she fitted the shackle into the padlock. Silly horses, silly woman, all of them jumping at shadows. She tried to convince herself of that as she walked back to the house.

Darla waited at the top of the stairs, scraps of light clinging to her white nightgown and blonde curls. Lanie shoved the gun behind her back before her daughter could see it.

"What's wrong?" Darla asked.

"Nothing, sweetie. The horses were restless, is all. I calmed them down.

"I dreamed I saw a ghost."

"No ghosts here, pumpkin." Lanie climbed the stairs, careful of the creaking step even though she wouldn't wake anyone else. "Just horses and little girls who should go back to bed." She ran a hand over Darla's hair—still baby-fine, fair as Merle was as a boy, until his hair darkened to ash blond. Mackenzie's had deepened to chestnut. Neither of them inherited their mother's mess of black curls.

"Would the horses see a ghost?" Darla said as Lanie steered her down the hall.

"I don't know. You can ask them tomorrow after school." The gun gouged her back when she bent to kiss her daughter's head. She breathed in the warm smell of Darla's hair. "Good night, pumpkin."

"Night, Mama."

Merle barely stirred as Lanie slid back under the covers. The horses stayed quiet. Her hand rose to the crook of her neck and left shoulder, fingers brushing long-healed scars. She'd told Merle a dog bit her, years ago when the marks were still obvious.

Ghosts weren't what she was afraid of at all.

On Wednesdays she met Naomi at The Wrecking Ball for drinks and pool. Naomi was the last of her old friends. The last tie to her wild youth. The rest had all died or run off or swung hard the other way, found rehab and Jesus and burned old bridges.

The air was heavy with smoke and spilled beer. From the next room came the clatter of pool tables and off-key karaoke. Lanie nursed her drink and half listened to Naomi's flirting and law office gossip—all names redacted, but the town was too small for that to make one bit of difference.

"You're not listening to a word I'm saying, are you?"

Lanie looked up from picking the label off her sweating bottle of Corona and realized she couldn't remember the last ten minutes of the one-sided conversation. "Sorry. I didn't sleep much last night. The horses were fussing."

Naomi made a sympathetic noise and picked a cherry out of the melting ice at the bottom of her glass. "How are Merle and the girls?"

"Sounder sleepers than I am. Merle's helping Mackenzie make a diorama for a book report tonight."

Naomi tilted her head with a laugh, strawberry blonde curls breaking across her shoulders. "Oh, honey. Your family is adorable, but it all sounds so damn domestic."

Lanie shrugged and grimaced. "Lucky for the girls Merle's better at that kind of thing than I am. I'd probably just raise them in the barn with the horses."

She drained the last lukewarm mouthful of beer. It tasted like bitter water and lime and she wondered if she should switch to whiskey or call it an early night. She was still wondering when the stranger walked in.

A small man, skinny and not tall, a faded black coat flapping around his hips. She couldn't see his face, but something about the way he moved stirred long-buried memories. Her breath caught. There'd been a pack of them. . . . But when the door chimed again it was only Bobby Franklin from the diner down the road, and whichever waitress he'd taken up with this week.

The stranger scanned the room and Lanie felt a prickling chill as his eyes moved over her. His hair was fine and straight, the color of dead leaves, drifting around a pale, seamed face. Shadows pooled beneath deep-set eyes and lined the hollows of his cheeks. The crowd drew aside for him without seeming to notice.

"Not your type, is he?" Naomi asked, kicking Lanie's ankle under the table.

Lanie tried to answer, but her tongue had gone numb and the man was already moving toward them.

"Good evening," he said. His voice was low and rasping. He stood as far back as he could without shouting, hands clasped, slight and unassuming.

Lanie's heart still sped, pulse climbing in her throat. Beads of moisture shone in his hair, dappled the shoulders of his coat. "I hope I'm not interrupting."

Naomi leaned toward him though he was nothing like her type, either. Her eyes glinted with sharp-edged humor as she glanced at Lanie. "I was just boring my friend to tears. We could use some interrupting."

His cheek creased. His eyes glittered like glass. "I'm glad I could help, then. I'm Jonah. Jonah Crow."

Naomi's smile flashed. "That sounds like a preacher's name. And you look like one in that coat."

This smile was slow and anything but godly. "Not me, but my daddy was once. It rubs off."

Naomi laughed and Lanie wanted to slap her, to scream at her that he was dangerous, nothing to flirt with. But her mouth was a desert and her hands were frozen white-knuckled on the edge of the table.

"Well, Jonah, I'm Naomi, and my bored friend here is Lanie. Would you care to join us? You look like a man who could use a drink." One nail tapped the side of her empty glass suggestively.

"I am, but that's not why I'm here." His cold eyes settled on Lanie. "It is Lanie Baxter, isn't it?"

She stiffened, heat rising in her cheeks. "It's Goss now."

He glanced at her left hand and nodded. "I've come about your brother, Ms. Goss."

A brittle silence settled around their table. Naomi stood, her stool tottering, and pasted on a smile.

"Looks like a pool table opened up. I think I'll win a few bucks off Luke Anderson. Nice to meet you, Mr. Crow."

Jonah cocked his head in a silent question. When Lanie didn't answer he settled on the empty stool, propping his elbows on the table. Lanie stared at his pale eyes, then wondered if she shouldn't. He looked away first.

She should be terrified. She should be angry. But she recognized the electric current that rose in her as anticipation. How long had it been since she'd felt that?

"You came to the house last night." The words fell into the stillness between songs.

"I did. I would have talked to you then, but . . ." Narrow shoulders rose in a shrug. "I thought you might feel more comfortable in public."

She very nearly laughed. "You spooked the horses."

"Not me. There was a coyote prowling around."

"Was?" Anger stirred now, but Jonah shook his head with a chuckle.

"Nothing like that. I'm fond of animals."

"You only hurt people?"

"That's right. But I'm not here to hurt you, Lanie. Just to talk."

Her name in his mouth made her shudder. "What about Cody?"

If he'd had a hat, she imagined he would have taken it off. Instead he dragged a hand through his hair. It was warning enough.

"He's dead. I'm sorry."

She could have said: *He died nineteen years ago*. She didn't. "How?"

"If you'll forgive me saying so, he was young and stupid and thought nothing could touch him. He was wrong."

Cody would have been thirty-six this year. Not exactly young. But he'd been seventeen when he vanished, and that was how she'd remember him.

"Merry went with him," Jonah added.

That drew her up. Merry. Meredith. Cody had told her the name one night before he disappeared, a big dumb smile all across his face. *I met a girl, Lanie*. She remembered the pale shape in the shadows beneath his window, the slender figure behind him in the doorway of a narrow dark house in Abilene. A beautiful white face with sad eyes. Sad, hungry eyes.

"You were there, weren't you? In Abilene?" She hadn't seen any other faces that night, none that she could remember when she was awake. Only eyes shining in the darkness, voices whispering too low to make out.

"I was. It was a brave thing you did, following him there. Stupid as hell, but brave."

She hadn't felt brave at the time, only scared, furious with Cody for running off, leaving her and their father alone. Running off just like their mother had when Lanie was three.

"Why are you telling me this?"

"Because I thought you'd like to know. That you deserve to know. And that you've seen enough to understand."

"I've seen too damned much and I don't understand any of it."

"He cared about you."

She laughed harshly, before forcing her voice low. The last thing this town needed was more gossip about her family. "He cared so much he tried to kill me?"

"Ah." Jonah swallowed. The rings of his larynx pressed against the thin skin of his throat. "So that's what happened. I hope you can forgive him, whatever he did. It's hard to go home. Hell, it's hard to be here now, talking to you. It's worse when you're young. Worse when it's someone you knew."

How long has it been since you were young? But she didn't say that either. "Where are your friends?"

"Gone."

"Gone?"

Another shrug. "Some like Cody. Some just wandered off. It's rough sometimes, living like we do."

"How do you live, exactly?"

He turned Naomi's empty glass between his hands, pulled his fingers away slick with condensation. "The same way you do, I imagine. But . . . messier."

Her scar throbbed. Jonah's nostrils flared as if he could scent her nerves. He probably could.

"I should go." Her stool skipped on the tacky floor as she pushed back. "I— Thank you for telling me."

Jonah's hand closed on her elbow to steady her as she stood. His chill soaked through her sleeve and she felt the strength in his fingers despite his gentle touch. He smelled of rain and autumn, clean and cold through the layered scents of sweat and smoke and spilled beer. He smelled like nothing at all.

"I'll walk you out," he said. She didn't try to stop him.

The rain had stopped, but clouds slid low across the sky, snagging against the distant silhouettes of grain elevators. Lamps glazed wet asphalt with marigold light. Lanie drew a deep breath, tasting rain on concrete. By the time they reached her truck she'd gathered enough courage to ask her question.

"Was Cody happy with you?"

Jonah was quiet for a long time. Lanie's breath misted in the damp air; his didn't. "He loved Merry," he said at last. "Or wanted her enough that he couldn't tell the difference. He was young and cocky and selfish—that made it easier. It was that cockiness that drew her in the first place. But time doesn't always temper us the way it does . . . people like you. Cody kept on like that, wild and reckless, not growing out of it."

Lanie thought of how she'd been just out of school. Scared and aching, willing to hurt herself or anyone else just to feel something different for a while. Sometimes, when the highs were high enough, she'd wanted to stay that way forever. But it could never last.

"What about you?" he asked. "Are you happy?"

"I have a family. I love them." Which wasn't more of an answer than he'd given her, but it was all she had. Jonah nodded. From his silence she thought maybe he understood.

"Take care," he said at last, stepping back to let her open the door.

"What will you do?"

He paused, half turned, and light lined the bones of his face. "I'll pass through soon. But your friend was right—I could use a drink."

She watched through the rain-beaded windshield as he walked back toward the bar, drifting like a wraith across the pitted asphalt. Her hands ached on the steering wheel. She shouldn't let him go. She should warn someone.

Instead she put the truck in gear and drove toward the dark country roads that led to home.

Merle and the girls had gone to bed by the time Lanie got home. A light burned in the kitchen, illuminating the diorama on the table. A black horse ran along a paper beach while a faceless human figure stood against the cardboard background, watching him go.

She should check on the girls and go to bed, curl up against Merle and cry herself to sleep. Let go of the misery she'd carried for nineteen years. Cody and her father were dead, but she wasn't, and she had the chance for happiness that had escaped the rest of her family.

Had her mother been happy, wherever she'd run to?

She took the bottle of whiskey down from the cabinet and poured herself a double. The glass warmed between her hands as she sat at the table, staring at the paper horse. *Pour it out*, she told herself. She knew better than to drink in this mood.

"I missed you, Sis."

Nothing would ever drown her brother's voice, but she threw back the whiskey anyway. One shot, then another, till her head grew heavy and tears dripped down her cheeks.

"Cody?" Hay crackles underfoot as she steps into the barn. Horses snort and stamp. The kerosene lantern sways in her hand, casting shadows from wall to wall.

You were dreaming, she tells herself. But restlessness dragged her from bed, and in the darkness below her window she'd glimpsed a familiar shape slipping inside the barn.

"Lanie."

She jumps at his voice and the lantern flame gutters. There, at the edge of the light, stands her brother. He hasn't changed a day in three years. Tall and lanky, skinny arms corded with muscle. So pale, though, and his eyes—they glisten by lantern light. She can't look away.

He moves like a shadow, but his arms are solid and strong around her. He holds her tight, her face pressed against the worn cotton of his shirt. He's cold, though, and his chest is too quiet against her ear, too still.

"Look at you," he whispers, before she can follow that thought to its conclusion. "You grew up." His breath stirs her hair. Her head fits under his chin now.

"You left me!" She slaps his shoulder. "You ran away like Mom!"

"Hush, Lanie." He tightens his arms around her, gentle but much too strong. "You knew I couldn't stay here. You shouldn't, either. You'll end up like the old man, bitter and miserable."

She tugs free and he lets her go. She sets the lantern on a beam, scrubbing away tears. The horses' eyes shine liquid in the shadows, flashing as they toss their heads.

"I'd be a lot less miserable if you'd stayed." She means to sound angry, but her voice cracks.

"I'm here now."

"But you're not staying."

"No." He closes in, backing her up against a hay bale. He touches her cheek with one cold hand—he used to pinch her cheeks to piss her off, but this is nothing like that. Her heart races, pulse fluttering against his touch. His eyes flash copper-red like an animal's and she remembers the dark house in Abilene.

"What happened to you?"

"It only hurts for a minute," he murmurs, hand sliding down to brush her hair back from her neck. Panic closes her throat. She's trapped against hay and wooden beams and his hold is cold and hard as rebar.

"Cody—"

His mouth presses against her neck and something sharp and electric moves under her skin. Then comes the pressure of teeth, a sudden stab and hot red pain. She tries to scream but all that comes out is a breathless gasp. Lanie writhes, but can't break free. Struggling makes the pain worse; moisture leaks down her shoulder, cooling as it soaks into her shirt.

The pain eases in heartbeats, replaced with warmth and dizziness. One hand clenches in Cody's shirt to hold herself steady. To hold him closer.

A horse whinnies and kicks the stall. The clatter snaps her out of the soft, melting lassitude. *No*, she tells herself. "No."

The sound is barely a word. Cody doesn't hear or doesn't care, but it's enough to rally her fading strength. She struggles again, groping behind her for the lantern. Her fingers hook on hot metal but it tumbles from her grip. Glass shatters. A horse screams.

Cody jerks away and Lanie slumps against the hay. Firelight shines in his eyes, gleams crimson against his bloody mouth.

"Lanie—" He stumbles back as smoke drifts through the air. "Lanie, I didn't mean . . ."

Someone yells outside. Lanie's eyelids droop and by the time she pries them open again Cody's gone. Static fills her ears like the crackle of burning hay. Someone shouts her name. Smoke fills her mouth when she tries to speak, dragging her down into warm, red darkness.

"Lanie!"

A man's voice. She woke slow and muddled, pain lancing through her neck. One hand flew to her shoulder, but found only scars. She'd fallen asleep at the kitchen table and the pain was the ache of a bad angle. The smoke was nothing but whiskey, sour in her mouth.

"Dammit, Lanie."

She opened her eyes to see Merle pulling the half-empty bottle out of her numb hand. Pins and needles rushed through that whole arm as she tried to sit up.

"I guess I'm taking the girls to school, then," he muttered.

"Mom, are you sick?" Mackenzie asked, watching from the doorway with wide eyes.

"Your mother is drunk, is all," Merle said. "But don't repeat that at school, please. Or tell your sister." He leaned toward the stairwell. "Darla! Hurry it up, pumpkin!"

Lanie dragged a hand through her tangled hair. Her chair scraped against the floor as she stood. She staggered on her way to the sink and Merle's dark eyes narrowed.

"Christ. I thought you promised not to drink like this anymore. And not around the kids."

"It's Cody." His name scraped out of her throat. "He's— A friend of his found me last night to give me the news."

"Oh." His broad shoulders sagged, and the anger drained away. "Oh, shit, sweetheart." He reached out and pulled her into his arms, callused fingers snagging on tangles as he stroked her hair. "I'm sorry, baby."

She took a deep breath, steadying herself with the smell of his shampoo and aftershave, the steady throb of his pulse. "I'll be okay," she said. "It was just a shock."

"Of course. Stay home today. Get some rest. Drink some water."

"Yeah." Her smile felt crooked and strange. Merle looked as though he wanted to say something else, but she turned away to kiss the girls. "Hurry up, kiddos. You don't want to be late."

Lanie spent the morning on the rocking chair on the front porch. The chair her father had carved for her mother when she was pregnant with Cody. When the sun balanced at the top of the sky and the shadows were short and sharp, her phone rang. Lanie looked at Naomi's number on the screen and a knot of tension she hadn't named loosened an inch or two.

"You sound rough for someone who only had one beer last night," Naomi said when Lanie answered.

"I might have had more than that when I got home."

Naomi made a sympathetic noise, then paused. "Your friend Jonah bought me a drink last night. Or three."

Lanie's hand tightened on the phone. "He's not my friend."

Naomi laughed. "He should be. But since Merle would hardly appreciate that, I'll keep him for myself."

Her breath rushed out. "He was one of Cody's friends. The ones he ran off with. They're bad news, Naomi."

"Hell, sweetie, so were we once."

We never killed anyone, she nearly said. It was true, but only for dumb luck or the grace of God—she knew which one she believed in more.

"But he said he came to tell you about Cody," Naomi went on. "It wasn't anything good, was it?"

"No."

Naomi sighed. "Oh, sweetheart. I'm so sorry. Do you need to talk?"

"I will, most likely. But . . . not right now."

"Of course. You call me as soon as you do, though."

Lanie nodded, for all the good that did. Naomi knew her well enough to understand her silences. She meant to say something reassuring and hang up, but when she drew a breath something else came out.

"Naomi, if anything ever happened to me, you'd look after Merle and the girls, wouldn't you?"

Voices rose and fell in the background while Naomi hesitated. "I would."

"Good. We'll talk later." As she lowered the phone, she wondered why the words were cold and bitter as a lie in her mouth.

After that she couldn't sit still any longer, never mind her unhappy stomach and the angry spike between her eyes. Instead she tugged her boots on and scraped her hair back and went into work. The noise and bustle of the warehouse didn't help her nerves or her head, but she could answer phones and type in orders no matter how hungover she was. The guys in the back noticed the set of her shoulders and left her in peace. She kept at it till the day faded in a slate and salmon wash across the west and the last of her coworkers forced her to leave so they could lock up.

Jonah waited for her by her truck, leaning against her tailgate motionless as a scarecrow. The breeze tugged at the hem of his coat, lifted strands of his hair.

Lanie sighed. All last night's adrenaline was spent. "Why are you still here?" It sounded ruder than she'd meant it to. She wondered if that should bother her or not.

"I'm not sure." Jonah straightened, and his shoulders shook in a silent laugh. "Hell, that's a lie. Can't you guess, Lanie? I'm lonely."

She didn't need to guess. She could feel that black empty space inside him. Like looking into a mirror in a dark room. "So you're talking to me?"

"I don't have to pretend around you."

She didn't know what to say to that. She settled for, "If you want to talk, get in. I'm too old to hang out in parking lots all night."

That drew a low, rusty chuckle from him. "Some things we're never too old for." He opened the passenger door and slipped in.

Maybe if her mother had stuck around Lanie would know better than to pick up strange men at night. Her father hadn't bothered with that lesson, just skipped to the part about where to kick anyone who gave her trouble and how to throw an uppercut. Her father fucked up a lot of things, but she didn't think that was one of them.

They drove in silence, away from the glare and traffic. If not for the reflection of the dashboard lights in Jonah's eyes, she might have been alone.

"You've done pretty well for yourself," he said at last. A little upward lilt at the end, not quite a question.

"I guess I have." Most days she didn't feel like she'd done anything at all, except let Merle take care of her. But even that had been an effort at first.

"Your girls are beautiful."

That cut through her detachment. She rounded on him, lip curling, and the truck veered and shuddered. Jonah raised a placating hand. "It's not a threat," he said. "I had daughters once, too. A long time ago."

Hands white-knuckled on the wheel, she forced her eyes back to the road. "What happened?" She wasn't sure she wanted to know, but the question slipped out all the same.

"I went away. Looking for work. I told them I'd come back. I *meant* to go back. But . . ."

"You never saw them again?"

"Once. Years after. I didn't let them see me. It's easier that way."

An ugly noise like a stillborn laugh crawled out of her throat. "Easier. I don't know what would have been easier. If Cody had never come back, or if he'd finished what he started." What would that have meant, though? Her dead body crumpled in the hay for their father to find in the morning, or one more pale, hungry girl drifting through the night? She'd been drifting ever since, anyway.

"Nothing about living is easy," Jonah said, so soft the hum of engine and tires nearly covered the words. "But even now I think it's better than the alternative."

Lanie shifted gears as they came to a tilting, bullet-scarred stop sign. She felt the cool touch of his hand on hers a second after he pulled away.

"This'll be my stop. Goodnight, Lanie."

Then she was alone, headlights cutting through an empty crossroad.

The call came the next day at work as the sky began to bleed violet and marigold. "Lanie." Merle's voice crackled over a bad connection. No, she realized an instant later: his voice was cracking. "Lanie, come home."

Her throat squeezed tight. "The girls—"

"They're fine. They're fine, I promise. It's—" He took a hitching breath. "It's Diego. It was colic, we think. We found him. By the time the vet got here . . . I'm sorry, sweetheart. Please come home. Darla's taking it hard."

"I'm on my way." She hung up before the last syllable left her lips.

Dr. Leicht's truck was outside the barn when Lanie pulled up. The trailer door stood open a few inches, and she was grateful as any coward that it was too dark to see inside. Merle and Mackenzie stood by the barn door. Merle's eyes were bloodshot, his shirt dark with sweat and dirt. Mackenzie hugged herself like her skinny arms were all that held her together. Lanie went down on her knees beside her. The girl submitted to her mother's embrace, but stayed stiff and shivering.

Merle folded his arms around both of them, burying his face in the crook of Lanie's neck. She flinched as his breath moved hot across her scar.

"Where's Darla?" she asked, unclenching her hands from Mackenzie's shirt.

"In with Susie."

She followed the sound of Darla's breathing to Susie's stall. The girl crouched beside the railing, folded up on herself like Mackenzie. But when Lanie opened her arms Darla fell into her with a fresh sob. She tried to speak, but all that came out was a hiccupping "Mama."

"I know, baby. I know."

They knelt there until Darla's sobbing slowed and she slumped bonelessly in Lanie's lap. Lanie picked hay out of her daughter's dusty hair while Susie stamped and snorted in confusion and concern. She was dimly aware of the sound of voices outside, the slam of the trailer door and the cough of an engine starting, but the warm darkness of the barn enveloped them, separating them from the rest of the world.

"Now Susie will be all alone," Darla said at last, scrubbing her face with her shirt collar.

"No, she won't, sweetheart. She has you and Kenzie."

Darla's swollen eyes narrowed at the absence there. The promise Lanie couldn't make. But all she said was, "That's not the same."

"Maybe not, but it's still a lot." And it was. So why did she feel so damn empty?

Lanie lay with Darla that night, inhaling the scent of strawberry shampoo and that sweet, unfinished child-smell. Breath and blood moved beneath her daughter's bird-light bones. *Stay here*, she thought. *This is real*. But rest wouldn't come for her even after everyone else settled into miserable, exhausted sleep. She finally crept onto the porch to listen to the night.

His boots were silent on the gravel. He stopped at the foot of the steps as if he needed an invitation to come closer. Lanie went to him instead.

The boards creaked under her weight. All the gravity that didn't touch him tugged at her, dragging her down, chaining her to this house, to this life. If horses were wishes, she only had one left.

"I'm sorry," Jonah said, soft as the wind.

They stood together for a while, staring past each other.

"I have to go," he said at last. "Or I might do something stupid." It could have been a threat, but mostly it was sad and lonely. "I'm glad I got to see you again, Lanie. I'm sorry it couldn't have been . . . different."

"Do you ever show up anywhere with good news?"

His shoulders lifted once. "No, probably not. So hopefully I won't see you again."

He turned, and the wind lifted his hair to eclipse his narrow profile. One step, then another, and he would be gone. She would be alone, bound to this life she'd chosen, that she'd let grow around her stone by stone.

"Wait," she whispered.

Jonah paused, unmoving.

You have a life, she told herself. *You have a family*. So had her mother. So had Cody. It hadn't held them, in the end.

She reached for his hand. His skin was cold through and she felt the starkness of tendon and bone. Fragile as a bird, like something she could shatter. He didn't move.

"Tell me to stay," she said. "Tell me I have a life here. Tell me how lucky I am."

His eyes glinted deep in shadowed sockets. "I don't have to tell you that, Lanie."

"Then tell me you don't want me to come with you."

"I can't tell you that, either." His fingers curled slowly around hers. "I don't have to pretend with you, remember."

She didn't look back at the house she'd grown up in. The house that held everything she'd loved for the past ten years. The things that held her up but couldn't fill her. She didn't need to look back.

The night opened wide and empty in front of her.

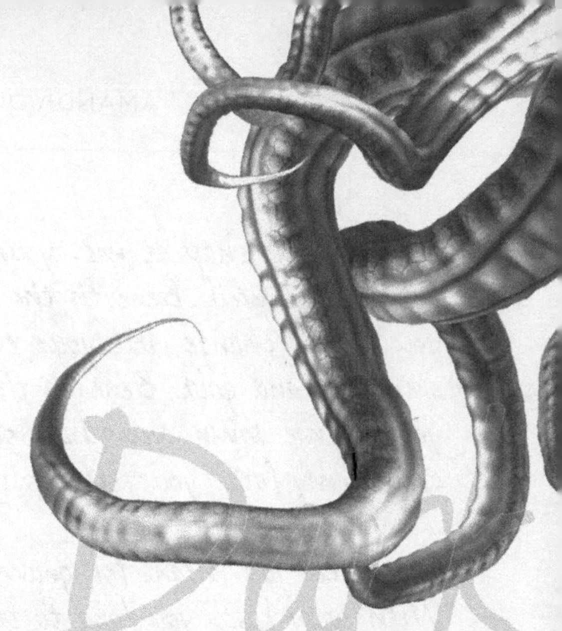

In the Dark

"Can you see in the dark?"
you ask, and in your eyes
a flash of gold. The cold moon
rises, grinning white as bone,
sharp as your smile, as your bite.
Shadows stretch between the trees.

I walk with you among the trees,
our shadows eaten by the dark,
shoulders hunched to winter's bite.
Night-birds watch with wary eyes.
Branches shine as pale as bone,
stark against the grinning moon.

Sometimes, you say, beneath the moon
your people gather amid the trees,
to feast on blood and flesh and bone.
I'd never see them in the dark,
only a flash of crimson eyes
before I felt their breath, their bite.

Playfully you snap at me; your bite
I know too well. Beneath the moon
you do not change, but your eyes
shine red and gold. Beneath the trees
you lay me down, your hair so dark
around my face, your skin as white as bone.

Your teeth are meant for gnawing bone
With every kiss, you long to bite.
You know I can't see through the dark.
You know I'm lost without the moon.
I'm lost within this maze of trees,
In the blood-gold glimmer of your eyes.

The truth is written in your eyes,
clear as tooth marks on a bone—
we won't always be alone among the trees.
You'll tire of this playful bite.
We'll have company besides the moon.
Still I follow you into the dark.

I wait to see their eyes, to feel the bite
That opens to the bone, red and white beneath the moon.
You'll leave me in the dark among the trees.

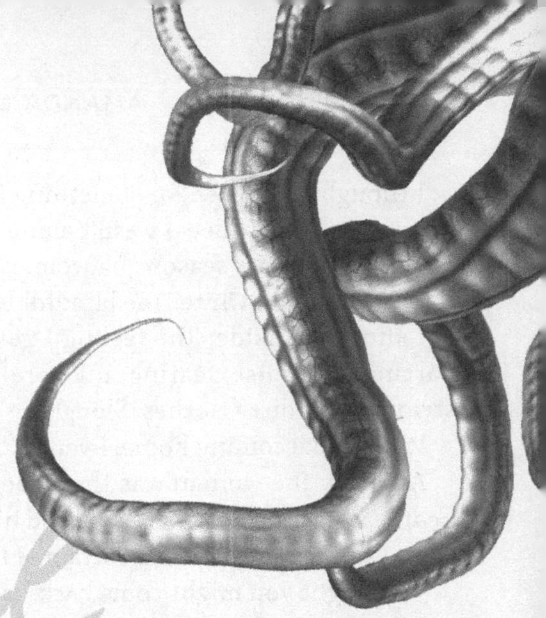

Saudade

Last night I dreamt I went to Carcosa again.

I'm glad you're enjoying this.

I couldn't resist. But it's true.

You must have dreamt of it before now.

Of course I have. Months of nightmares. Hands and teeth and laughter. Running blind, lost, alone. But those were just fear and memories. Last night was different.

Tell me.

I stood outside the gate. On a narrow stone causeway that once led over the water. It was shattered, like someone had taken a sledgehammer to it.

Not too far from the truth. It was destroyed centuries ago, when the lands of dream stood together against the Yellow King, and broke the bridges and sealed the roads. But that's another story. Go on.

The water was black as ink, the clouds the color of bruises. Like before. It smelled the same, sweet and sharp and stinging. The fog held everything close. All I could hear was the wind and waves, like my own heartbeat.

The gate stood open, unguarded, tangled all over with vines. I suppose Carcosa doesn't care about keeping things out. The desolation weighed on me. I thought that I ought to be afraid, but all I felt was melancholy. I wanted to cry.

I don't know how long I stood there. There was nowhere to go but in. The vines swayed, pale creepers latched tight to stone and iron. I didn't want them to touch me, but I kept moving closer and closer. I wondered if the city would look the same. Empty buildings, deserted streets.

Carcosa changes its skin as soon as the viewer looks away.

But not its heart.

No. Not its heart.

I thought that then, or something like it. Maybe I said it out loud. And as soon as I did I knew I wasn't alone.

"Carcosa has its seasons," a woman said, "like anything."

The woman in white. The blindfolded woman.

I shivered inside. The feeling I get when I wake into a dream. A veil parting, or a mist clearing, if I were being poetic, but really it feels like stripping off dirty clothes. Sloughing dead skin.

It feels like coming home. Even in Carcosa.

Anyway. The woman was there, behind me on the quay. Her face was nearly as pale as her robe. She stood like a statue, but something made me think she was tired. I wasn't afraid of her, but I knew I probably should be.

"I thought you might come back," she said. "I've been watching."

I flinched at the sound of wings, but it was only a bird. A raven circled once over our heads and settled on the gate. It avoided the vines, too. It watched me with one black eye. I had the feeling I should have known its name.

"How?" I asked. "How did I get here, I mean?"

"You left part of yourself, last time. Just a little piece, but it builds a bridge. The more you visit, the easier it will become to return."

I knew she was right. I could remember a bargain. But I couldn't remember what it was I'd lost.

"I don't want to visit."

"It isn't always terrible, you know." She smiled then, just a little. Her lips were pale and dry. For the first time I wondered if there was a real person under her blindfold. If there ever had been. "All right," she admitted, "it's supposed to be terrible. But it's not always like your last visit."

"You nearly killed me and my friend. You tried to bind him. Your sister raped and tortured him. You expect us to forget that? To forgive it?"

"She has done worse to me. I have done worse to her. We aren't always as we are now."

"What do you mean?"

"Now she is my sister. She has been my daughter, my mother, my lover, rival, and ally. We have been many things to each other throughout the years. Everything changes here eventually. Sometimes she is cruel, sometimes I am. Carcosa is rarely a place for kindness."

"You're not really selling me on the vacation package."

"Carcosa is due for a change. The king is stagnating, and trapping us with him. My sister's cruelty amuses him, so she remains cruel. He calls me his seer, so I remain blind. He makes his little bargains with mortals and then forgets them. He broods on ancient grudges. We play out the same scenes over and over. You and your friend are the only new thing that has happened in Carcosa since I've worn this skin."

"What do you want from me?"

"Your help."

"I nearly died here! My friend nearly died. Other people did die. We aren't meant to be here. Your sister and your king tried to use us as a bridge to the waking world."

"It was an ambitious plan. They came far closer to succeeding than I would have credited. But that isn't my goal. Spilling our troubles into other lands won't solve them."

"Carcosa is not a dream I can control. I can't change things here."

"I'm not entirely convinced of that. Your friend took a piece of Carcosa with him. Something older than the King."

She glanced at the water, or turned her head that way. I remembered drowning there. Remembered the thing waiting below.

"It's with him still, isn't it? The power hasn't consumed him?"

"That's none of your business."

"I could make it mine. I might be able to help him." Two stains began to spread across her blindfold. Dark and red, soaking through the cloth.

"We've had all the gifts from Carcosa we need, thank you. If you want a revolution, then good luck. We won't be your playthings again."

Part of me was fighting the dream by then, trying to wake up. But—

But?

I was curious. How could I not be?

She held up her hand and the raven came to her. Her blindfold was saturated. Red began to drip down her cheeks. I thought it was blood at first, but it smelled like wine. The bird sidled up her arm to rest on her shoulder, and rubbed its beak against her hood.

"Your friend is not the only person to find Carcosa. You know that. Even his escape isn't complete. The lost and the seeking will always make their way here, but you could change the welcome they receive."

Then it was over. I was awake.

"Manderley may be ours no longer, but Carcosa is forever. Isn't it?"

Elizabeth Drake leaned back in her chair. Sunlight washed the hotel's patio, glittering on glasses and silverware, blazing off the sea beyond. Waves flashed like facets on a sapphire. The light stopped inches from their table, blocked by the roof's shade. The tile floor was cool beneath her bare feet. Soon the sun would crest the rooftop and chase away the shadows.

Still dreaming. Not Monte Carlo, but a resort in Mexico where she'd spent spring break with her aunt when she was fifteen. Her companion across the table was neither Evelyn Drake nor Maxim de Winter.

He called himself Seker, and Sebastian Sands, and likely a thousand other names as well. He was as dangerous as any inhabitant of Carcosa. She couldn't trust him. But she smiled to see him now.

He smiled back. In the shade his dark skin was nearly purple. He wore a linen suit, the jacket slung over the back of his chair. A carafe of ice water sweated onto the white tablecloth. Mimosas fizzed gently in crystal flutes. They were alone on the patio. The only sound was the distant rush of the sea.

"Nothing is truly forever," Seker said. "But as humans measure time, Carcosa may as well be eternal. It will stand long after every living memory of yours is dust." He lifted his glass in a sardonic toast. "So what will you do?"

"Was she telling the truth?"

"I don't know. About many things, certainly. About her intentions? You'll have to judge that for yourself. Are you going to help her?"

"How could I?"

"That seems disingenuous, for someone who invaded Carcosa once already and stole a prize from the King. Despite every warning, every consequence, every chance to fail."

"I had help."

He raised an eyebrow. "You wouldn't now?"

"It was for Blake. I could never have done that for myself."

"This wouldn't be for you either, would it?"

Liz shot him a sharp glance. "You tried to stop me the first time."

"I tried to discourage you. Look how much use that was."

She picked up her mimosa. It smelled wrong somehow. Or maybe she still didn't like mimosas any more than she had when she was fifteen. She set it down again untasted.

"I could never ask Blake to go back."

"No. That's something he would have to choose for himself."

Liz stared, as if she would find any answers in the polished mask he wore. "You want me to do this."

"I watch humanity waste its potential every day. Dreamers. Artists. Scientists. Scholars. There is a cosmos of knowledge and experience to be had, and people turn away from it. Pretend it doesn't exist, or find reasons why they can never reach it. I have heard every excuse that can be offered.

"Whether or not the two of you ever return to Carcosa is immaterial. But you have both been given rare opportunities. I would be disappointed if you chose not to make something of them."

"You call what happened to us an opportunity?"

"What happened to you was monstrous. Both in the way humans reckon suffering, and by being a portent or a warning. Blake involved himself with things he didn't understand, and was harmed and changed. Now he has the choice to either hide from those consequences, or transform himself. On his own terms."

"And me?"

"You are a true dreamer. A rare enough gift. Rarer still, you have some slight understanding of what that means. You could create wonders. Instead you drift through two worlds, little more than a ghost in either, shackled by your own fears."

She flinched, and pulled her hand away from her glass before she could knock it over. As if that mattered in a dream.

Seker's voice softened, which only made it worse. "Am I telling you anything you don't already tell yourself?"

She closed her eyes against the truth. When she opened them again the sun and sea were gone, replaced by a cold room washed gray by shadows. Unreal. Unfamiliar, for a moment. But this was home. Her house, at least. The drafty colonial she, Alex, and Blake had shared for the better part of a year. Nearly four in the morning. The other side of the bed was empty and cold. She had thought Alex might keep less nocturnal hours when he finished defending his thesis, but nothing had changed.

She wriggled free of the nest of blankets, wincing at the chill. The radiator ticked softly in the stillness. Outside the bedroom window, ice-rimed oaks creaked in the breeze. Somewhere nearby a snowplow growled.

Some nights, when she woke alone in the dark, the panic took her, convinced her that Blake and Alex were gone. Dead or missing or simply moved away, leaving her behind. Tonight, though, the fear was quieter, more insidious.

Lights burned downstairs. Liz crossed the room slowly, navigating the places that made the old floors squeal and groan. If she kept her weight toward the wall, she could descend the stairs without raising an alarm.

Little more than a ghost.

Alex sat in his study, shoulders hunched like a vulture over the book open on his desk. Lank dishwater hair drifted across his face. His lips moved soundlessly as he read. He didn't look up when she paused in the doorway. She didn't speak.

Blake, at least, was asleep. Sprawled on the couch with a lamp burning. He must have come home from work not long ago. He'd stripped off all his winter layers, but still had on the button-down shirt he wore to tend bar. A sketchbook lay open on the floor beside him, the page blank.

Should she wake him? Drag Alex into the room as well and tell them about her dreams. They had promised, in the wake of Carcosa, to keep fewer secrets. But Alex would only worry about things he couldn't change, and Blake had salvaged some fragile peace in the past few months. She couldn't take that from him, not yet.

Soon.

For now, she was awake, and might as well stay that way. There was bread dough waiting in the refrigerator. She could turn on the lights and warm up the kitchen, pretend she wasn't a ghost in her own house. Pretend the three of them might go on like this, that it was enough for any of them.

"We can never go back again," she whispered to the hallway, "that much is certain."

The past and the future were both too near. Where, then, was left to go?

Hiding in the dream

Joshua Hackett

Hiding in the dream
World outside, beyond grey fade
Hiding in the dream

Aconite & Rue

One gibbous-mooned night, winter waning but still holding fast, the wild things gathered in the Forest to dance.

Elle didn't dance, didn't brave the kaleidoscope of light and noise—strobes and pounding drums, snarling voices, air thick with sweat, perfume, and a dozen kinds of magic. Instead she lurked in a shadowy corner. Those that wanted her would find her.

She smelled the heady scent of faerie a heartbeat before three Sluagh appeared, melting out of the darkness with liquid grace. They huddled together, shivering despite the heat of the club. Elle reached into her skirt pockets, produced three tiny cloth pouches, one for each. Hands stretched toward her, white blossoms unfurling in the gloom, and the charms vanished into their shabby clothes; they sighed as one.

"Thank you," whispered the leader, soft as wind under a door. His hand was steadier already as he pressed money into Elle's palm. Real money, not faerie gold. They knew better.

She nodded. The Sluagh bobbed their heads and vanished. A little less pain for them now, as they walked the tangled city streets, the maze of glass and steel with its scabby concrete skin and cold iron bones, veins full of dragon-fire and dragon-greed.

She needed the money, might as well do business while she was here, but she'd rather be home with her books and her plants, her potions and spells and quiet. But Rowan had wanted to go out, and Elle followed. She tucked the money away, walked to the railing overlooking the sunken dance floor to find her sister.

Rowan swayed among the crowd, red dress glowing under the scattered lights, scarlet ribbons shining in her long cinnamon hair. So at home among the wild things. She raised her head, glanced unerringly at Elle, and her eyes flashed copper-green as she grinned. *Come and dance*, her smile said. Elle smiled back and shook her head. She'd be tired enough tomorrow as it was. Rowan rolled her eyes and spun away, arms raising as she writhed to the beat.

Elle tilted her watch toward the erratic light. Late, the witching hour come and gone, time for this witch to head for bed. She had to go out tomorrow, and Rowan had to stay in, and they'd both need their rest.

She felt someone watching her, a breath of displaced air, and turned to see a man beside her. Patchwork leather coat, beads plaited in his long black hair, a whisper of magic fine as mist. She cocked her head expectantly—someone else looking for charms.

"Dance with me?" he asked instead, his voice nearly lost beneath the music.

She blinked, cheeks flushing. She couldn't remember the last time someone besides Rowan had asked her to dance. Through the haze of smoke and sweat, she smelled the clean musk of his skin.

Only a dance. But she'd heard Rowan say that often enough to know better.

"I'm sorry," she said, more truth in her voice than she intended. "But I should go."

He nodded and stepped aside with a rueful smile.

Halfway down the curving staircase, Elle paused. A woman moved across the dance floor and the dancers parted like waves, then followed helpless in her wake. Dressed in shining white, her hair a silver river—too beautiful to be human. Her magic sliced through the murky air, sharp and heady as winter.

The woman moved toward Rowan, and Rowan swayed to meet her like a flower turning toward the sun. Red and white circled, came together. Elle's grip on the banister tightened.

A hand closed on her arm as she took a step. The man in the coat. "You shouldn't interfere."

She frowned, trying to shrug away without losing her balance. "That's my sister." Below, Rowan danced in the white woman's arms.

"Even so, it would be better if you didn't get involved."

"What is she?"

"What do you think she is?"

Elle swallowed, tasted predator musk. "Dangerous."

One corner of his mouth curled. Shadows hid his eyes, slid down the sharp hook of his nose. "Very true. She'll take it as a challenge if you interfere."

Her teeth clenched. For an instant she hesitated, then pulled away. He didn't try to stop her again.

She shouldered through the press until she reached the center of the dance floor. People cleared a space for the woman, staring with wide glassy eyes. The desperate *want* of glamourie.

Rowan's eyes shone, her lips parted to catch her breath. She spun to the music, stepped back into the faerie's arms. As the last notes died Elle stepped forward and held out her hand.

"Time to go."

Rowan turned, blinking. The woman glanced at her, lashes sharp and white as icicles; Elle couldn't meet that winter-pale gaze. Her sister's name weighed on her tongue, but she bit it back.

"It's time to go," she said again, voice steady.

Rowan shook her head like she was coming out of a daze. "What?"

"It's late."

The woman chuckled, low and soft. "Do you want to leave so soon?"

Rowan licked her lips. "I—" She looked from Elle to the faerie and back again. "I should."

"That isn't what I asked." She stroked a long white hand down Rowan's cheek.

"Sister." A hint of compulsion and Rowan stumbled as if Elle had tugged a leash. Something dark smeared her face, sparkling as she moved into the light. Only glitter.

"I'm sorry," Rowan whispered to the woman, loud enough for Elle to hear. Then she turned, brushing past her sister as she headed for the door.

Elle hurried after her, away from the faerie woman's mocking laughter. As she paused to retrieve her coat, she caught the man watching her, his expression lost in the darkness.

The night stung her cheeks, snatched her breath away in a shimmering cloud. Her boots sank into frozen slush. "Wait up," she gasped, tugging her coat tighter, trying uselessly to keep out the wind's frigid hands.

Rowan didn't slow. Her hair tangled over her red hood, rust on blood in the glare of the streetlamp. "You could let me have a good time just once."

Elle's lips tightened. "If you want to pick up strangers, do it next week. And not fae—you know better."

Rowan snorted; it steamed like dragon's breath. "Like you don't sell to them every chance you get."

"That's business—" she caught up, nearly jogging to stay even "—and you know it. I deal with exiles, half-breeds. That woman was dangerous, Ro."

"Just because you're a coward—"

"I'm trying to keep you safe!" Her voice carried down the empty street and she winced. "Do you want to end up some glamour-fuddled pet Underhill?"

Rowan stopped abruptly and Elle nearly slipped. "Listen to you!" Her lips pulled back in a sneer, flashing teeth too long for her mouth. "You sound like Mom."

Elle flinched, her cheeks burning hotter. Rowan didn't speak the rest of the way home.

Darkness pressed tight against the windows when Elle's alarm began to shriek. She groaned and slapped it quiet, curling tighter beneath the covers. Hazy city-light snuck around the curtains. Across the room, the space heater glowed like embers, not nearly warm enough. Less than a month till spring, but in their drafty apartment winter seemed to last a hundred years.

Rowan was already awake—if she had slept at all—slouched at the kitchen table. She glanced up, eyes smudged with makeup and not enough sleep. Elle shook yesterday's coffee grounds into the trash and took the can out of the freezer, waiting for her sister to speak, for last night's argument to continue.

But Rowan remained silent. Elle filled the basket with fresh coffee and switched on the battered old machine. A minute later the smell wound through the air, dark and rich, coiling on her tongue, drowning the stuffy heater-scent and the lingering reek of the club on her skin.

"I'm working a double shift today. I'll be home late."

"I know." Rowan picked at the table's peeling varnish, her nail gone black and thick beneath red polish.

Elle hid her frown; her sister's ears were changing too, pointed and tufted with ginger hair. The first full moon wouldn't rise till the afternoon, but the change spilled over sometimes.

She opened the refrigerator, reached behind the orange juice and the milk until her fingers brushed cold glass. The bottle was half-empty, purple fluid separating into clear amethyst and murky silt below.

Rowan glanced away. Glitter still dusted her face, a dark shimmer above one absinthe-green eye. "Can I have a day off, just this once?"

Elle tried not to sigh. "I have to work all week. Next month I'll take some time off. We'll go to the park or something."

"You said that last month."

The sigh slipped out. "I'm sorry. But we need the money."

"I need to get out! You don't have to spend three days a month stuck in here."

No, I have to spend six days a week stuck in a shop smiling at strangers, so we can eat. She kept the words inside, barely. "I'm sorry, Ro." She set the bottle on the table and rubbed cold fingers on her T-shirt.

Rowan rolled her eyes and reached for it, put a thumb on the cork and shook till the dark silt mixed again. Aconite and rue, and a dozen other herbs Elle grew in pots around the house. The poison her sister had taken for six years, to stop the change, or control it.

"It's better here, isn't it?" Elle asked softly. "Better than with Mom?"

"I'm not sure anymore," her sister muttered. She tugged the cork free with a quiet plonk and tilted the bottle. Her pale throat rippled as she swallowed, draining the last of the bitter potion. She gasped when it was done, and a tear slipped free of her coppery lashes. "I'm not so sure."

Rowan scrubbed a hand over her mouth and bolted from the table. The slam of her bedroom door sent a shiver through the apartment.

Elle sighed again and searched for a clean coffee mug.

It snowed on and off all day, heavy wet flakes that turned to gray slush in the gutters and treacherous ice on the sidewalks. The shop was quiet. Elle was grateful, even if it meant no commissions, just twelve hours of folding and refolding and adjusting mannequins, listening to the buzz of fluorescents and the same CD looping over and over.

She missed her job at the little bookstore, but it hadn't paid nearly enough. Most Old Town jobs didn't, unless you knew people, or could do dangerous work. Elle didn't know anyone, and wouldn't take risks that might mean leaving Ro alone if she died. So she caught the bus into Iron Town, to work with blind, deaf, distrustful mortals.

Her back ached by the time she stepped off the bus that night, feet throbbing in her dress boots. The crowds thinned, and people kept their eyes downcast as they hurried past. Cheaper to live here, in this stretch between Iron Town's careful maintenance and Old Town's burgeoning gentrification, though it meant pitted streets and crumbling buildings, uncertain pipes and less certain police. And hungry things that walked the streets at night.

Elle stepped aside for a grocery-laden woman and her boot slipped on a patch of ice. Her ankle wobbled; something cracked loudly. A hand closed on her elbow as she lost her balance, keeping her upright.

"Thanks," she muttered, glancing down. Her boot-heel had snapped, wedged in a chink in the sidewalk. Better than her ankle, but she cursed anyway—her only pair of nice shoes, even if they did pinch.

"Sorry—" She glanced up at the man holding her, and her voice failed. The man from the club.

"Are you all right?" he asked.

"What do you want?"

He smiled, faint and crooked. "At present, not to see you split your head open."

A flush crept up her face. "Sorry." Keeping her eyes on him, she crouched to retrieve the broken heel; maybe she could glue it back. Pedestrians swirled around them without a glance. Safer to mind their own business.

"Thank you," she said again, balancing on one foot as he let go of her arm. "But what do you *really* want?"

"I saw you get off the bus, and I thought—" His ginger-brown skin didn't flush, but he glanced aside, uncertain. "Not a dance, but would you like to get a cup of tea, or something hot?"

Elle's mouth opened, closed again. He wasn't fae, but the smell clung to him. "You're hers, aren't you? The woman at the club."

"Yes." Neither pride nor sorrow, just acceptance.

"My sister—"

"Isn't here. It's you I'm asking."

She couldn't keep standing there like a clumsy stork. "All right. Just a cup of tea."

"Of course." He offered her his arm, and she took it to keep from slipping again.

"Why?" she asked, a cup of hot chocolate steaming between her hands. "Why did you ask me here?" The Gingerbread House was crowded with people escaping the cold, the air warm and thick with chocolate and coffee, spices and sugar.

He gave her another half-smile. "Isn't that how it's done? Asking pretty girls out for drinks?" He glanced at the other couples in the room. "I admit, I don't have much practice."

She waved the compliment aside. "But why me?"

His smile fell away. "You opposed my mistress. Not many people do that."

"I was just looking out for my sister. She's—"

"I know. I smelled her." One hand touched a charm around his neck, a polished bear claw bound with leather and beads.

Elle frowned. "I was going to say, she's young and impressionable." She sipped her chocolate; they served it thick, spiced with cinnamon and pepper. The man dripped honey into his tea and stirred absently, the spoon tiny in his long brown hand.

"What should I call you, anyway?" she asked.

"She calls me Auberon. That will do. And you?"

She paused a moment. "Rose."

His dark eyes crinkled. "Not Snow White?" He glanced down at his tea again. "I'm sorry, I'm not used to this. Dancing, drinks . . . company. I'm no good with people anymore."

"Then why are you here?"

"My mistress will be gone within the week if this weather holds, and her court with her. I thought . . . I thought I could spend my time somewhere warm, while I have the chance."

Elle stared at her own cup. "I'm not good with people either. It's usually just me and my sister." She glanced at her watch. Already after ten. "Speaking of which, I should go. She's alone."

"She's a woman grown, isn't she? Aren't you?"

"I— She needs me. I have to go."

He shook his head. "All right. Good night, Rose."

She almost touched his hand where it rested on the table, but thought better of it. "Good night. I'm sorry I wasn't better company." She turned and hurried home, as fast as her uneven shoes would allow.

Elle shivered as she closed the apartment door, shutting out the sour-spice tang of kimchi that filled the hall—the fox girl next door was cooking again. The apartment was much too cold, and a draft whistled through the balcony door.

The sliding glass door was nudged open as far as its rickety bar would allow, just enough for the icy wind to slip in. Rowan lay with her head on her paws, nose pressed against the crack. Outside, icicles melted slowly, dripping into a puddle on the balcony.

Elle pushed the door shut and bit back a lecture on the heating bill. A brief *otherwise* touch told her that her wards were still intact, and nothing had slipped through the crack. "Sorry I'm late."

Rowan whined softly. The bowl of food in the kitchen was barely touched.

"Are you feeling all right?" She sank into a kitchen chair, tugging her boots off with a sigh. At least the heel had snapped off cleanly—she'd try glue tomorrow.

Rowan heaved herself up, russet fur rippling. A hundred and thirty pounds of leggy girl became the same mass of leggy wolf; her shoulder reached Elle's hip. It had taken months to perfect the dose—enough to allow the physical change, but keep Rowan's human mind intact, to dull the wildness that couldn't endure captivity.

Elle stroked her sister's ears, buried her fingers in winter-thick fur. Rowan *whuffed* softly and leaned against her knee. Then she sniffed and pulled away. Licorice-black lips peeled back from ivory fangs.

"What's wrong?"

The wolf shook her massive head, then slunk into her room, claws clicking on the floorboards.

Elle frowned. Whatever it was would have to wait for morning. As she reached for the refrigerator her neck prickled, like something brushing against her wards. She turned, but there was nothing outside but the gleaming puddle and the wind whistling past the windows.

Elle woke in the predawn darkness to the sound of her sister crying.

Lost behind the steel and concrete forest, the moon was setting. Rowan crouched naked on the living room floor, teeth clamped tight on a rawhide bone, shuddering with the change. Her spine arched and rippled as the last inches of tail retracted. Her nails gouged the floorboards. Ginger fur vanished into white skin.

When it was over, Rowan slumped against the couch, shoulders heaving as she gasped. Elle grabbed a blanket and draped it around her.

"Who was he?" Rowan asked, voice rough.

"What?"

Human lips pulled back in a wolf's snarl. "You were out with someone. I smelled him on you."

Elle's hands clenched. "It wasn't like that."

"What was it like, exactly? It's been so long I can't remember."

"I'm sorry. I didn't mean—"

Rowan barked a laugh. "No, of course you didn't. You never do." Glitter still clung to her eyelid, sparkling as she moved. "Mom never meant any harm either, did she?" She pushed herself up, shrugging off the blanket and shaking back her tangled hair as she disappeared down the hall.

Elle froze, staring after her. She should follow, explain, apologize. But there was nothing to explain. She slumped at the table, the blanket trailing across her lap. When had it gotten this bad? They'd had such plans, when they ran off to the city. They were going to be free. They were going to make a life for themselves.

It was still poison and cages. No one was happy, no one free.

She didn't remember her father, her mother's husband who'd died when she was two. She remembered Rowan's father, though. All bright hair and shining eyes; when he carried her on his shoulders he'd been the tallest man in the world. He smelled of musk and fur, smoke and autumn.

Then one day, when Rowan was just a pink and squalling thing in the cradle, he didn't come back. Or the next day, or the next. The years wore on and Elle still didn't know what had happened.

She wanted to think it was the grief that made their mother cling so, made her stifle and rootbind her daughters, fetter them with chains of guilt and poisoned kisses. It hadn't worked.

Elle had promised Rowan things would be different, but that hadn't worked either. Now she was losing her sister by inches.

She watched for Auberon as she walked home that night, but didn't see him. She cursed the disappointment twisting in her gut.

Until she unlocked the apartment, walked into a frigid draft that whipped her hair around her face and slammed the door behind her. The bottom dropped out of her stomach.

"Rowan?"

No answer, only the sliding door open, blinds rattling in the draft. The balcony and fire escape were empty, but as Elle glanced down she caught a flicker of motion in the ice-melt puddle. A woman's mocking smile.

She bit back a shriek and brought her boot down. Icy water splattered the balcony, soaked her pant-legs. Laughter drifted on the wind.

Her nails gouged her palms. She drew a cold breath, let it out slow. She could deal with this. Not even faerie magic could hide her sister from her. *Just calm down—*

She jumped at a knock on the door, pulse drumming in her throat. Even as she reached for the knob, she knew. "You," she snarled as she yanked open the door. "You did this!"

Auberon nodded and stepped inside. Human, whatever other magics clung to him, and her wards were no proof against him.

"She was here last night, wasn't she? You were only a distraction."

He nodded again. Elle raised her hand, but he caught her wrist easily before she could strike. "I didn't lie," he said softly. "But you didn't ask the right questions."

She nearly kicked him, pulled away instead. The draft tugged at his hair, rattling beads.

"I did warn you."

"What has she done with my sister?"

He shrugged. "Shown her a good time, I expect. She did with me."

"And then you woke up and a hundred years had passed?"

"Not exactly. But she plans to take your sister with us when we leave. The girl is not unwilling."

"What are you doing here?"

"She promised your sister a night of freedom. I'm to keep you here, keep you from interfering."

"Really?" She reached for the door, but he braced one arm against it.

"Don't, Rose. I have no orders to hurt you, but I will stop you."

She folded her arms across her chest. "Is this what you want?" she said after a moment. "To be a pet, a slave?"

He raised one hand, a helpless gesture. "It's what I have."

"Can't you escape her?"

"I tried, and failed." His eyebrows rose. "Why? Would you win me free? Would you hold me fast and have no fear, though I changed shape in your arms?"

Her cheeks stung, and she glanced away. "I have no claim to you."

"No."

Her hands were numb. Auberon tensed as she crossed the room, but she only closed the balcony door against the wind; silence filled the room. Elle rubbed feeling back into her fingers, but the cold in her bones remained.

She'd need it.

They stared at each other while the silence stretched. Elle sighed and let her shoulders slump. "Sit down," she said, waving at the couch. "If you're going to stay, you don't need to hover."

After a moment's hesitation, he sat.

"Why my sister?" She sank onto a kitchen chair.

He shrugged one shoulder, hair whispering against leather. "My mistress likes wild things. Things strong enough to survive her kisses."

"Where will she go? Where will you go?"

"Wherever winter goes."

"When was the last time you saw spring?"

"I don't remember anymore. A long time ago. I'm used to the cold by now."

She let the silence deepen again, then rose and put the kettle on. Her heart beat hard and fast in her throat, but her hands were steady as she sorted through canisters, measured leaves for tea. Steam eddied around her face as she carried the mugs to the table.

"You said you didn't lie last night."

"No." He glanced at her, took the offered honey. Their fingers brushed. "No lies."

"You really wanted to be there with me?"

His throat worked. "I did. I wish it could have been . . . different." He looked down, swirling honey into his tea in slow amber spoonfuls.

"It still could be." She laid a hand on his arm; he stiffened, wary as any wild thing, but didn't move. The smell of his skin filled her nose. "Please, let me go."

"I'm sorry."

He drained half the cup in one swallow, exhaled a steaming breath. His hand tightened on the cup, knuckles blanching, and she thought the ceramic would shatter. "Just a little warmth," he whispered, and took another drink. "There was never anyone to try and win me free."

She reached up and turned his head toward her. The light caught slivers of gold in the depths of his eyes.

"Rose—"

"Elle." Her throat constricted around the words. "My name is Elle." She wished she could blame glamour for the ache in her chest, but it was only loneliness and regret.

His lips tasted of honey and herbs, sweet and bitter, and she made a noise deep in her throat as his tongue moved against hers. As he pulled her closer, she wished things could have been different. Her hands slipped down his rough-seamed coat as she pressed him against the cushions, and his fingers threaded through her hair.

Her lips and tongue began to numb.

Auberon jerked away, teeth scraping her lip. "What did you—"

Elle stumbled back, knocked over the coffee table. Cups shattered, tea and leaves spilling across the floor. "I'm sorry," she whispered, a hand pressed against her mouth.

He tried to stand, failed and fell. "What was it?"

"Aconite."

"Witch . . ."

"Where are they? Tell me and I'll give you an antidote."

He coughed, gasped. "You're as cold as she is. I should have known."

"Where are they?" His chest heaved, face draining sallow. "It was a high dose—you should hurry."

He laughed until he choked. "The Towers, downtown."

"For how much longer?"

"We leave tomorrow, with the first thaw." He coughed again, and saliva trickled from the corner of his mouth.

She grabbed the blanket off the back of the couch and draped it over him. "Lie down, and keep your feet up. You need to stay warm."

"A lie," he whispered, trying to seize her wrist; she evaded him easily. "A distraction—"

She returned to the kitchen, filled a pitcher with warm water and emptied the salt canister into it. In the back of the spice cabinet she found a tiny glass bottle.

"Salt water to cleanse; drink it till you throw up. This is atropine—belladonna—to keep your heart beating." Before she could think better of it, she knelt beside the couch and pressed her lips to his salt-slick brow. His pupils were pinpoints of black amid the brown.

"I never lied. I'm sorry."

"Take my coat," he mumbled as she stood.

"What?"

"My coat, take it. You won't survive her touch without it." He struggled up, tugged off the coat.

The ice in her chest splintered to razor shards. Coarse fur lined the leather; it smelled of him. Too long for her, but she could walk without tripping.

"Thank you."

She left him to live or die.

Sleet rode the wind, biting her face and clotting in her hair, and Elle was grateful of Auberon's coat before she reached the end of the block. The streets were empty, even the predators driven inside.

The buses had stopped for the night, so she walked. The wind stole her breath, her warmth, pricked her with icy needles. Slush crunched under her feet, seeped through the eyelets of her second-best boots.

The wind was against her, the gray curtain of mist that turned buildings into canyons of brick and glass, street signs to trees of ice. Shapes moved in the haze, ghosts of snow and fog, phantoms to lead her astray. She turned too soon, or too late, or in the wrong direction. Time slipped past her as she stumbled on.

A night of freedom, the white woman had promised Rowan. Elle couldn't begrudge her that.

An hour from dawn exhaustion dragged at her limbs, and tears and snot crusted on her face. She'd passed the same newspaper kiosk twice; the old man working shook his head sadly as she stumbled past again. Finally, Elle turned a corner and saw the Towers rising amid the sharp-toothed cluster of buildings. She sobbed against her gloved hands and straightened aching shoulders.

The watchman barely glanced up as she entered the lobby. A wet and bedraggled stray, wrapped in clothes too big for her, but he only nodded and went back to his magazine. No doubt she was expected.

The elevator carried her to the penthouse. The door was unlocked.

It opened into a blizzard.

Not real, she told herself as the wind staggered her and ice bit her face. Only glamour. She forced herself on, one numb step, then another.

On the third step, the illusion died. White on white the room, carpet and upholstery, walls and woodwork. The wide window showed the glittering city, a haze draped pale and shimmering across the rooftops. The air was no warmer than the night outside. Elle shivered in her borrowed fur. A mirror stood beside the bed, black cheval glass as tall as she was.

Rowan sprawled naked—human—across the bed, her clothes a tangle on the pale carpet. The white woman stood by the window.

"Hello, little witch. I wondered if you would best my hunter." She turned, and a slow smile curved her lips as she saw the coat. "Have you come to challenge me?" The woman's face shone bright and blinding, but she didn't look down.

"Yes."

"Which of them do you want—your sister, or the hunter?"

Never anyone to try . . . She banished the echo of his voice. "My sister."

"Do you think I keep her against her wishes? The way you do?"

Elle took a step forward. "You will. You keep Auberon, don't you?"

The woman shrugged. "He made foolish bargains. Your sister and I have yet to come to an arrangement." Her voice was warm, the false warmth that made men lie down to rest in a snowstorm.

"No arrangements. She goes free."

"Freedom like that box of yours? That cage?"

Another step into the thickening chill. "No, I mean free. Wherever she wants to go."

The woman reached out and stroked Elle's cheek; her touch was silk and thorns. "And what if that is with me?"

Elle shuddered, but stood her ground. "Then she can tell me that herself."

Rowan stirred, sheets whispering as she pushed herself up. "Elle?"

"Forgive me," the woman said to Rowan before Elle could speak. "But it can't be this easy." She made a delicate brushing-aside gesture and Rowan gasped and stiffened. Whatever she tried to say became a whine as the change rushed over her.

"The moon sets in an hour," the woman said as Rowan shook off the sheets and leapt to the floor. "If you can find your sister and hold her till then, I will leave her free of bindings and bargains. But that means you must leave her free as well. No spells, no trickery—the choice is hers. Do you agree?"

"Yes."

"Then go." Elle wasn't sure if she spoke to her or to Rowan, but Rowan responded first, turning and leaping at the mirror. She vanished through the glass, nose to tail-tip, without a ripple.

Elle followed.

The mirror stripped the warmth from her flesh as she passed through. Streaks of iridescent black sparkled on her hands as she stumbled over the threshold, flaked off skin and leather. Pulling the coat tighter, she started walking into a dark and winding maze.

The first door she opened showed her a woman tending a room full of plants. Gray streaked her dark hair, and years had etched sorrowful lines into her face. Elle couldn't tell if it was her mother she saw, or herself worn with time. She closed the door against the question. She didn't need to see her future.

The next showed her Auberon, slumped on her living room floor, salt and tea leaves scattered around him in arcane patterns. Whether he breathed or not she couldn't see, and couldn't stop to read the answer. Scrubbing a hand across her mouth, she shut that door as well.

The third door opened into another corner of the maze, where Rowan sat, huddled naked and shivering against the dark glittering walls.

"Elle—" She held out a hand, a smile spreading across her face. "Elle, take me home."

She shut the door.

Tears burned her eyes as she turned away, blurred the glimpse of a rust-colored wolf. Elle scrubbed a hand across her face, smearing mirror shards. "Rowan!"

The wolf turned and ran, and Elle followed.

The halls curved and spiraled inward, toward the heart of the maze. When they reached the innermost whorl, Rowan whirled to face her, teeth bared.

Elle fell to her knees, the burn in her lungs chasing away the terrible cold. "Ro— Rowan, please."

The wolf growled.

"I'm sorry. I'm sorry about everything. Please." She stretched out a trembling hand.

The growl died. For a long moment Rowan watched her with slitted green eyes. Then she moved forward and pressed her cold nose against Elle's cheek.

Sobbing, Elle wrapped her arms around her sister, pulled her close and clenched her hands in thick fur.

Beyond the mirror, the moon began to set.

Rowan shivered, then shuddered, but Elle held on. Spasms wracked her sister as the change came, but she held on. Rowan twisted and writhed, flailing and snapping. Claws scored the side of Elle's face, ripped her hands, and ivory fangs snapped beside her throat, but she held on. Until Rowan slumped in her lap, pale and shaking, their mingled tears slicking her white skin.

The mirror maze dissolved. Elle knelt on soft carpet while the first blush of dawn spread behind soft gray clouds. The white woman watched them silently.

Elle whispered her sister's name, still clinging to her hand. "Rowan, what do you want?"

Rowan wiped her eyes with her free hand. "I want . . . I want to see things, to do things. I know you tried to keep me safe, but I can't grow in a greenhouse, Elle. I want to stay with her."

Elle's shoulders hitched, then sagged. "All right."

Rowan's eyes widened. "You mean it?"

"I promised."

Rowan pulled her tight. "I'll see you again," she murmured into Elle's hair. "We'll come back."

"Yes," the white woman said. "Winter always comes back."

Elle shook back her tangled hair and met the woman's eyes. "No bindings, no bargains. My sister is free to stay with you or go."

"As we agreed."

Rowan uncoiled from her crouch, tugging Elle to her feet. "Thank you." She kissed her cheek, then stepped closer to the woman.

"And I'm free to go in safety?" Elle pressed.

The woman smiled. "That was not agreed, but yes, little witch, you are."

She slid out of Auberon's coat, draped it across the foot of the bed. The cold bit deep, but she could bear it.

"Elle—"

She smiled at Rowan, though it made her face ache. "I'll see you next year."

Her apartment was cold and empty, ice-melt falling in shining streams beyond the window as the sun climbed into the first day of spring. The smell of vomit and sick sweat hung in the air, but Auberon was gone. Her throat was tight, but she didn't cry, only gathered shards of shattered mug and cleaned up the salt and poisoned tea.

Snake Charmer

The dragon is dying.

The city feels it in bones of stone and iron, in scabby concrete skin. The *otherkind* feel it in their blood. Even Simon feels it, mortal as he is. The city waits.

The dragon will die, of age or violence, and another will take its place. Someone will eat the dragon's heart and take its power. A lot of people are interested in the dragon's demise.

Some are less patient than others.

Simon crouches in a narrow alley that smells of blood, piss, and damp brick. Dark clouds, heavy with unshed rain and ash from fires that raged the night before, scrape their bellies across the rooftops overhead. He tastes char with every breath.

A sacrifice. Everyone knows you have to bleed for the dragon, or burn. Simon's already burned; now he sheds blood.

The man at his feet gurgles one last time and falls silent. He's spoken all he needed to. Simon wipes his knife clean on the dead man's shirt. Chance's knife, silver on one side, cold iron on the other—it works on humans, too.

He's going for the dragon tonight, the man said. And, *Mary Snakebones*.

Simon uncoils from his crouch, knife vanishing into his coat. He's not done with blood yet. Maybe not ever.

He still needs to find a costume.

In the Garden of Eden every day is Halloween. Freaks, geeks, and tattooed women.

Tonight isn't much different, except for the costumed crowd and the orange and black streamers hanging from the ceiling, flickering like flames in the draft of the overburdened AC. Dancers writhe in pits and cages, the bass throb of the music drowning a dozen conversations, a dozen propositions and transactions. The air is solid with smoke.

A woman crawls across the main stage, wearing vinyl boots and fingerless lace gloves, a witch's hat balanced on her hair. Not much else. Simon watches her flirt with the crowd and smiles. Chance always loved costumes, fancy dress. She'd have liked his outfit tonight.

His smile falls away. Chance is gone, and the woman he wants tonight won't be onstage.

He slides through the crowd, a colder, cleaner thread twining through the murk of sweat and spilled liquor. Just another costumed schmuck, but elbows and shoulders move aside for him. He rides the current, lets it spit him out in a shadowed back corner where Mary Snakebones holds court.

She's enthroned in a wide, shallow booth, surrounded by pretty hangers-on. Mostly goths and would-be witches. He catches the scent of fae, but it's faint, half-breed at best. Sometimes she runs with a dangerous crowd, but not tonight. Mary's danger enough on her own.

He walks up slow, hands loose at his sides. Sweat trickles down his neck; the holster chafes the small of his back. He should have worn a shirt under the tailcoat. Mary's courtiers barely notice him. They'd all be dead, if that was his business.

Mary notices. She watches him approach, eyes dark as sin under a weight of kohl. Waxy black lips curl. "Hello, Baron."

He tips his top hat, looks down over the tops of his dark round glasses. "Good evening, Mary."

She doesn't wear a costume. She doesn't have to. She's Mary Snakebones, Mojo Mary. The dragon's child. People would dress as her if they could pull it off.

She cocks one eyebrow. "Are you here for me, Baron?"

What would happen if he said yes? He's almost tempted to find out. She looks so soft, so young, all trussed up in velvet and vinyl, but he knows that softness is only an illusion. A trap.

"We need to talk."

Her gaze burns through greasepaint and flesh. She's never seen this face before, but she nods. Maybe she can read his mind, or his soul, or invisible omens spinning around him. She waves a hand and the baby-bats scatter from the booth. "Sit with me."

"I was hoping for a more private conversation."

"Maybe later." She nods toward the stage. "My sister is dancing tonight."

He slides into the booth—easier than arguing. Leather creaks as he settles on her right. He keeps his eyes on the crowd, but the most dangerous thing in the room sits beside him.

"The ghost of Simon Magus." She studies him with a smile. "You're a boogeyman now, the thing waiting in the dark. They say you died too, that night."

He swallows. "I did."

"I like this face."

Whether she means the painted face or the one the surgeons gave him, he doesn't know. Doesn't want to know. "Sal is coming for you tonight."

Her smile widens. "Let him." Under the table she takes his left hand, her flesh warm through the leather of his glove. One sharp nail traces the underside of his ring finger, snags on the metal of his wedding band. "Poor Simon. Still wearing your grief like a brand."

His scars tingle. She moves closer, velvet coat rustling against his shoulder, breath tickling his ear. "You've killed someone tonight."

Their lips nearly brush as he turns to face her, perfume filling his nose—almond and clove and autumn leaves. "Only one." His fingers tighten around hers. "Sal is after the dragon."

Black eyes narrow. "And death comes to tell me this."

"This?" He touches the brim of his hat. "It's just a costume."

"No, it isn't." Her left hand rises, and her thumb trails over his cheekbone. "This face is very real tonight, Simon Magus."

"Don't call me that. I was never the one—"

Her hand trails down his chest, to the slick, ridged scar tissue over his heart. "I know a true name when I hear it, Simon."

He shudders, and wonders what else she knows. If she can read his heart, he's a dead man. She's too close, dizzying him—he could never draw his gun in time.

The music stops, leaving only the ocean-murmur of the crowd and the surf of blood in Simon's ears. Mary shifts her attention to the stage and he fights a sigh of relief.

"And now," The DJ's voice echoes over the speakers, "Eve, and the snake."

A new song starts, slow and deep, and a woman glides onto the stage. Henna-red hair in wild gorgon braids, skin like cream and cinnamon. Her hair matches the python draped over her shoulders.

Someone in the crowd gasps. Simon sucks a breath through his teeth. The snake is longer than she is, its muscle-fat tail wrapped around her waist. Garnet and cinnabar scales shine under the lights, shimmering with dusty yellow-and-black whorls.

Her name isn't Eve, of course, but Helene Dimanche. The dragon's priestess.

Beautiful as her sister, though they don't look like the twins they claim to be. Mary leans forward, her hand still tight around Simon's, eyes trained on the dance.

It's a real dance; Helene doesn't touch the pole, or leave her feet. Muscles play in her arms as she lifts the snake and twirls. Henna swirls across her back and breasts and belly, patterns rippling as she sways to the beat.

I've got something you can never eat.

She doesn't play to the crowd, either. No flirting or winking—she only makes eye contact with the snake. Money flutters onto the stage, but she doesn't touch it.

I've got something you can never eat.

Mary's chest rises and falls, café crème flesh constrained by her tight-laced bodice. Not the woman undulating on stage that affects her so, no matter what the rumors say, but the power Helene raises with her dance. It whispers over Simon's skin like an electric wind. He learned to feel those things around Chance.

"We should go," he says. "It isn't safe here."

"This is my place. They wouldn't dare."

A rueful smile tugs at his mouth. She's young after all, young and cocky. "They came to my place, Chance's place. They dared, and now she's dead."

Her thumb strokes his palm, tingling through the leather to the roots of his teeth. "And you're here to protect me? My white knight."

"I want Sal."

"What else do you want?"

She'll know if he lies. "I want to rest," he says after a moment. Some of the truest words he's ever spoken. "I want to see the dragon." Chance always wanted to see one. He can almost hear her voice, feel her drowsing in his arms—but he can't bear to remember it now, not here, not with this witch.

"Are you willing to pay the price?"

She strikes as the last breath of assent leaves his lips, her fingers tangling in his hair. He stiffens, hand twitching toward his gun, but she's pulling his head toward hers, her lips pressing his till he feels her teeth, till he lets her tongue against his. The rum-sugar taste of her fills his mouth and he can't breathe.

She's strong—he can't break her grip, not without hurting her. Her hand presses against his scars again, against his heart. He hasn't kissed a woman since Chance; he's never kissed a woman like Mary. Her teeth sink into his lower lip and he tastes blood.

He pushes her away and she lets him. His chest and lip sting.

"Damn it, Mary . . ."

She wipes a drop of blood off her mouth, licks her finger clean. "You have to bleed."

His ears are ringing, and the shouts across the room register a heartbeat too late.

The crowd parts, dodging away from men with guns in their hands. Simon draws, but they've already got the drop on him. Muzzles raise, take aim. The look on Mary's face nearly makes him laugh as he grabs her and pulls her over the side of the booth with him.

The world shatters into screams and thunder. Bullets thump into leather and wood, whistle over their heads. The air reeks of fear and bitter gunpowder.

"They are dead men," Mary says. The words are lost in the cacophony, but Simon reads them on her lips and smiles.

"That's the plan, yeah." He leans around the edge of the booth and squeezes the trigger. Bad angle, and a man falls with a hole in his thigh, still alive. Someone else shoots back. The crowd swarms; glass shatters as a waitress drops a tray and lunges for the emergency exit. There's a commotion on the stage.

Then a woman screams Mary's name.

"Helene!" Her coat billows as she runs for the stage. Simon curses and lunges after her, gun kicking in time with his heartbeat as he lays down cover. Patrons shriek and dodge, clogging the front door. Pain stings his left arm like a wasp. Someone behind him screams and chokes.

He tackles Mary, knocking her into the sheltering T-intersection of the stage. Heat soaks his sleeve.

"Mary!" The cry is fainter now, closer to the door.

"They've got her." She struggles against Simon's grip, and he wonders if he'll have to hit her.

He hears the flames first, a crackling rush that floods adrenaline through him. Then the wave rolls over the ceiling, liquid and beautiful. Streamers rain down in sparks and ashes.

Sal's work. Simon's pulse stutters triple-time; a burning scrap of paper brushes his cheek and panic threatens to consume him. He fights it down, prays for the ice to take it away. A woman twitches on the floor, blood bubbling from her mouth and chest. Lung shot. Simon contemplates a mercy kill, but doesn't want to waste a bullet.

"Back door," he shouts at Mary.

"They've got my sister!"

"We can't get her back if we're dead." Already smoke sticks in his throat and his eyes water. Eyeliner bleeds ashen tears down Mary's cheeks. After a second she nods.

He pushes Mary ahead of him and slides along the side of the stage. The shooting's stopped. The woman on the floor lifts a pleading hand toward them. Simon pauses for an instant, then gives her what he can. Blood halos beneath her head.

Something hisses angrily in his ear, a second's warning. His left arm screams as he raises it, screams again as his hand closes around Helene's striking snake. The force jars through him and he barely holds on as its jaws gape in front of his face. Needle teeth glint, dark tongue flickering.

Its body writhes against his arm, looking for a grip to crush. A tube of heavy muscle, covered in oiled leather; his skin crawls at the touch. His hand tightens, glove blood-slippery, thumb squeezing under its jaw.

Mary appears, scooping up the python, cooing as she drapes its massive coils over her shoulders. It flicks its tongue at Simon as he lets go, then settles onto Mary, pacified by a familiar person.

"Follow me." Her heels beat a staccato rhythm as she darts for the door behind the stage.

Smoke billows after them into the raw cement hallway, gray tendrils eddying in their wake. "They'll use Helene to find the dragon," Simon says as they run.

"She won't tell them."

"Then Sal will kill her, and spread her guts out to learn the way."

Mary flinches, and for a second he thinks she'll turn and run back into the inferno. He grabs her arm. "Can you talk to her?"

"Yes," she says after a minute.

"Then tell her to take them to the dragon, and not to fight. We'll meet them there."

She nods, sucks in a deep breath; the python rises with the swell of her chest. Her eyes roll back in her head for a moment and she sways. Simon steadies her, blood dripping off his hand. She's back in a heartbeat and the fear eases around her eyes.

She touches his hand, frowns at the blood. He cranes his neck, sees entrance and exit. The bullet went through the meat of his upper arm; not too serious, though it burns like hell. Blood soaks his sleeve shiny, drips in fat drops off his knuckles.

"That should have been mine," she says. She tastes his blood again, but she's not flirting now.

"Let's go, Mary."

He's afraid the gunmen will have the back covered, but the parking lot and alley are empty. Sal got what he came for. Simon's blood cools in the evening chill. The air still tastes like char. Sirens scream in the distance, getting closer.

Simon holsters his gun, wipes sweat out of his eyes. Somehow he's managed not to lose the hat.

Mary grins, sallow and tear-streaked in the sodium glow. "I told you it was a true face. I'll dress that for you—" she nods toward his arm "—then we'll see the dragon."

Mary drives, her sleek car purring through the crumbling streets. Buildings rise like rotted teeth around them, tearing at the clouds. The city is dying, slow and broken.

The streets are nearly empty tonight—smart residents know when to stay inside and lock their doors. Halloween is dangerous enough, without a dragon's death for *lagniappe*.

The dragon dies tonight, one way or another. Simon feels it in his scars.

The car reeks of blood and rum, both soaking the bandages under Simon's sleeve. It hurts, but he can use the arm. A crust of blood dulls his ring. He slides a fresh clip home, chambers a round.

Mary nearly hums with power, the electric smell of it tingling in his sinuses. They surprised her in the Garden—she won't let it happen again. Streetlights spark and die as they pass; maybe Mary's work, but he doesn't ask. They head for the docks and darkness follows in their wake.

"Is Sal the last?" Mary asks.

They walk now, the car and the snake abandoned in a dark alley. Simon hears water nearby, and the clang of train canisters loading and unloading. Thunder snarls in the distance, but still no rain.

"No," he finally answers. She'll know a lie. Long practice keeps his voice and pulse calm. Tonight will end ugly, one way or another. He touches his tongue to his swollen lip. "Sal's the last of the ones who killed Chance, but he didn't give the orders. His boss dies, too."

"That's a lot of death for one man."

Too much for any man. "I'll manage."

"Sal is trying to break away," she says after a moment. "That's why he's after the dragon. He wants free of his masters."

Simon frowns. "He should have tried sooner."

Sal never set foot in their house that night, never fired a shot. Chance took two bullets, Simon three, but it was the fire that killed her. The fire that brought the ceiling down, costing Simon half his face and very nearly his left arm. Chance died screaming his name.

"What will you do when you're done?"

He sighs. "Rest."

"You don't have to waste yourself on revenge."

"If they die, it's not wasted. I don't have anything left, anyway."

Mary touches his arm, soft enough to make him shiver. "I can give—" She stops, hand tensing. "They're coming. And we're here."

Simon looks up at the building—five stories, cement and brick. A parking garage once, now walled in. Heavy wood-and-iron doors stand where the ticket booth should have been.

Lights cut through the night as three cars pull up to the curb. Simon presses against the alley wall, pushing Mary back. His hand tightens on his gun, and he double-checks the weight of the knife in his pocket.

Mary hums under her breath as she balances on one foot, tugging off her boot. Simon frowns, glances at the broken glass on the ground. She's moved easily enough in heels so far. "Are you sure that's a good idea?"

Her smile makes his shoulder blades prickle; she slips her other foot free. "I walk on pins and needles, I walk on gilded splinters. I want to see what they can do." Her voice is lower, throatier. The air smells of rum and cinnamon. She shrugs free of her coat, vinyl corset shining red as heart's blood.

Car doors open and men emerge. Simon recognizes Sal's scimitar-nosed profile in a brief flicker of light.

Dominic Salieri. Nicky the Salamander, though never to his face. The whisper-stream says he's part ifrit. To Simon, he's just another dead man.

But not yet, because Sal reaches into the car and pulls out Helene. She's wrapped in a man's jacket, doesn't look hurt. Sal handles her gently enough, but Simon can see her tremble. He could shoot past her, but not fast enough to take down the dozen thugs before one of them could kill her.

She doesn't fight. She's waiting for Mary.

Simon's not sure Mary's here anymore.

Two men open the doors, another two rolling in to secure the room. Nothing happens, and Sal escorts Helene into the darkness of the dragon's lair.

Mary turns to Simon, pinning him to the wall. "A kiss for luck, Baron."

His swollen lip throbs and he braces for the pain. But she doesn't bite this time.

Her tongue burns against his, heat rushing through him, drawing out the pain, melting the ice. It hurts like something tearing inside, and he wants to push her away, but somehow his arms are around her, gun hand pressing the small of her back, crushing her to him. He hasn't ached for anyone like this since...

She pulls away, cheeks flushed, eyes shining. The hair on the back of his neck stands up as he realizes he just kissed a goddess. Or something close to one.

"Mary—"

"Not quite."

"Erzulie."

Her smile is fierce and bloodthirsty, flashing bright as the knives in her hands. "Come on, Baron. The dragon wants blood."

She steps out of the alley.

Six of Sal's guards wait by the door and they all turn, guns rising. She's blocking his shot, drawing their fire. He can already imagine the sight of her blood on the pavement.

Then Mary starts to dance.

Simon's jaw drops as he remembers who she is.

She writhes serpent-lithe, daggers like steel fangs. Her sister's dance was just a shadow of this. At first the guards can only stare as she swirls toward them, barefoot on the pitted, glass-strewn street.

Someone breaks the spell and fires.

But Mary isn't there, spinning out of the bullet's path like she could pluck it out of the air if it suited her. Then she's on the man and his throat opens in a crimson spray.

Simon's gun roars and men fall, one, two, three. Mary's heel catches one in the gut as her knife comes down on the other's gun arm. Simon aims, and she slides out of the way, letting him finish the one doubled over retching.

She knows just where to cut as she opens the last man's chest. Simon's guts turn to ice water as she straightens, red to the elbows, blood dripping down her cheek. Her eyes flash like coals in the streetlight.

The smell inside the temple fills Simon's nose, makes his flesh crawl. His stomach cramps with atavistic terror and his balls try to retreat into his torso. Smoke and ash and snake. He blows a long breath out his nose, wrestling the need to flee. He has to see this through.

Mary, or Erzulie, takes his arm, turns him toward her. She traces a wavy line on his forehead with one bloody finger and the fear recedes. He almost misses it.

Dim lamplight spills across the wide room, throws long shadows across the cement floor. Open spaces, wide ramps. Enough room for a bus to maneuver. Or a dragon.

"Which way?" he asks.

Mary's nostrils flare as she scans the room. "Down."

The air warms as they descend, and the smell worsens. Not just the reptile reek, but the smell of age, or illness. Of a dying beast.

A shadow flickers at the edge of his vision and bullets crack against the wall behind them. Simon dodges behind a pillar, but Mary's moving in a blood-streaked blur, bare feet silent on the floor. An instant later he hears a gurgle and a heavy thump.

"Follow me, boy," she calls. "Try to keep up."

Simon's face feels strange; it takes a second to realize he's grinning. Then Mary gasps in pain.

He rounds the corner to find two men bleeding all over the floor and Mary leaning against the wall, a hand pressed against her stomach.

"He had a knife." Her voice is mortal again, and strained.

Vinyl gapes and curls like skin, a wide gash above her navel. Her corset stays took the worst of it, at least, and nothing's punctured. Blood wells dark as pomegranate juice.

"I'm fine," she says, waving him off.

It would be easier without her, but he nods. She keeps up, though sweat slicks her face and her lips are pinched and pale.

Shots echo below them, followed by a sound that curdles Simon's blood. Not a hiss, not a roar, not a volcano's belch, but all of them at once. The screams don't last long. They round the last corner and enter the dragon's chamber.

A blur of fire and ash, smoke and embers. Red and gold and black, cracking, shifting, seething. Winged and scaled and feathered and furred and Simon can't make sense of it. He staggers, goes to one knee.

The dragon.

Chance's voice in his head, soft and resonating. *Beautiful. So beautiful.* For an instant he can feel her beside him, smell her skin. Tears stream down his face.

He climbs to his feet. Sweat slicks his palm, slippery against the hatched gun grip.

Sal stands in front of them, silhouetted against the dragon's glow. He's still got Helene, and Simon won't risk the shot.

"Sal!" His voice cracks, harsh with smoke. "Let her go."

Sal turns, dragging Helene around. He's got a gun in his free hand; the muzzle gleams as he levels it at Simon.

And pauses. His face is in shadow, but Simon feels the weight of his stare. "What's the matter, Sal? Don't you recognize me?" He strips off the torn and bloody coat, one sleeve at a time, tosses hat and glasses aside. Pink and white scars shine in the firelight. "Recognize your work?"

"Simon Marin?" Sal laughs. "So it has been you—the spook story, the thing that's got everyone jumping at shadows. You've done me a lot of favors in the past few months."

"I'll do one more. Let the girl go."

"What is this—revenge? You should know better. It was just a job, Simon."

"It was my wife."

"After tonight, I'll never work for Manny again. Hell, I'll turn him to ash. That was what Chance wanted, wasn't it?"

Simon fights the urge to spit. "Don't worry, that will still happen."

Behind him, Mary's draws a sharp breath. Simon's chest tightens; she's finally read his heart.

He's starting to wonder how long they'll stand here like this, guns pointed, when Helene decides it for them. She slams a foot into Sal's knee and throws herself down.

Simon dodges, pulling the trigger. Both guns flash. Sal falls, but his bullet catches Simon's left shoulder like a hammer. Static washes his vision as he stumbles against a pillar.

His chest heaves, pulse echoing in his ears, louder than the dragon's rasping breath. His left arm hangs nearly useless at his side—pity it's not numb. So tired, but he can't rest, not yet.

He pushes himself up to confirm the kill, but Mary stands in front of him, her eyes hard.

"You came for the dragon."

"I did. I have to."

"Do you even know what he is? Do you understand, or is this just another death?"

"That's what I do, Mary. The dragon is power. I can't take out Manny like this, as a man. I'll kill until there's no one left. If you want to cut my heart out then, I won't stop you."

"That's not how it works. My sister is the priestess, the chosen child. This city has enough killers, Simon. It needs new life."

His eyes sag shut for a heartbeat. "I don't have anything to do with life anymore."

She moves closer and he flinches, but she only lays a hand over his heart. "It's not too late. We can give you something more."

"I just want to rest. But I have to keep going. I promised Chance. . . ." Strength drips out of him in crimson streams. Already his vision is dark around the corners.

He straightens, steps past Mary. "I promised."

She grabs his arm, nails gouging. "Simon, I won't—"

He punches her in the gut, gun still in his hand. She makes a noise like a run-over cat and falls, face blanching.

"Sorry," he whispers as he turns away.

Helene lifts her head from where she kneels naked by the dragon. Tears shine on her cheeks. "It's time. He's dying."

Simon staggers closer, heat washing over him in waves. He can see the beast now, its massive head on the ground beside Helene, body long as a train car sprawled limp. Its chest heaves, dark smoke curling from its nostrils. One lantern eye shines, half-slitted. The other is sunken and swollen shut, leaking blood and clear fluids. Its forked purple tongue flickers amid broken fangs.

Its hide is rough, dark as coal, but as it moves sparks of red and gold writhe like falling embers. Even dying, it's beautiful. Chance always wanted to see a dragon.

Simon brushes its snout with his left hand, hisses as his fingers blister. His blood bubbles as it drips on the dragon's nose. The dragon exhales a steaming sigh and Simon's skin tingles.

Helene looks at him, hazel eyes shining by dragonlight. "I have to eat his heart." Tears drip off her lashes, evaporating before they reach her chin.

Mary staggers closer, limping now, hunched over her bleeding stomach. "You don't have to do it, Simon. You think we won't take care of this? You think you and yours are the only ones Manny's ever hurt? There will be vengeance, all you could ever want, and you don't have to die for it."

"Yes, I do."

He holsters the gun and draws his knife. Silver and steel gleam like a flame in his hand as he stands over the dragon. Mary curses softly; Helene watches him with eerie golden eyes.

The dragon doesn't fight, just rolls, baring the hollow of his breast. The hide is softer here, like oiled leather.

The knife slides home and Helene lets out a strangled scream. Then Simon can't hear anything but the roar of his own heart.

Blood like boiling oil. Clinging. Burning. The pain is worse than anything he's ever imagined, until it simply stops, too much for his body to hold. His vision tunnels. All he can see is the ruin of flesh in front of him, the blackened skin of his arms.

The blade melts as he cuts, barely lasts long enough to sever the great throbbing veins. The gush of blood sears half his face, blinds his right eye. The fluid dripping down his cheek is too thick to be tears.

Then the heart is free, pulsing in his hands. Fire ripples blue-green, washing over him. Consuming him. His own heart is failing.

He turns to see Helene and Mary Dimanche watching him, wide-eyed. Helene has her arm over Mary's shoulder. They really do look like sisters.

He raises the dragon's beating heart. His hands are twisted char and bone. He'll be dead in seconds if he doesn't eat.

He's been dead for a year.

The city needs new life. He can't give it that.

All he wants is rest.

He steps forward, ribbons of melting rubber trailing from his boot soles. He falls to his knees in front of Helene and offers her the burning heart.

Chance. I'm sorry.

As she takes it from him Simon collapses, his wreck of a body giving out at last. Concrete rushes up to meet him, drives the last breath from his lungs.

Simon dies.

Simon burns.

Not the torturous fires of a hell he's never believed in. Not even the fire of his own hell, all too real. This is clean.

No smoke, no soot, just white heat dissolving him. He wishes he could cry for the sheer relief of it.

The dragon is there, inside him, surrounding him. It eats his heart.

He failed, broke his promise, but this isn't so bad. This is a better death than he ever imagined for himself.

Then it's over.

Simon gasps, chest hitching painfully. His face is wet, the taste of blood and tears thick on his tongue. He opens his eyes—both of them—and stares at the soot-scarred ceiling of a parking garage. His gun gouges the small of his back.

He lifts his hands. Whole, clean. He sits up, and nothing hurts, but the skin on his chest pulls oddly as he moves.

His scars are gone.

He touches his chest, his arms, his face. Burn scars, blade scars, bullet wounds, the marks the surgeons' scalpels left. Everything gone.

His breath leaves him on a sob.

"Welcome back, Simon Magus."

Mary sits a few yards away, Helene draped motionless over her lap. No cleansing fire for her—she's still ash-streaked and bruised. The dragon is gone, leaving only pools of blood flickering with green-gold flames.

Sal is gone, too. Bloody footprints lead up the ramp.

Simon pushes himself to his knees and stares at Helene's still form. "Is she—?"

"She's resting."

"She's not . . ."

"A dragon?" She smiles her wicked smile. "She is, just a baby one. These things take time." She strokes her sister's Medusa braids with a gentle hand.

"Why am I still alive?"

"The dragon must like you. My sister will need help, as she grows. She has a lot of work to do."

Simon runs a weary hand over his face. "I just wanted to rest."

"We rarely get what we want." Her smug smile belies the words; Mary is used to getting what she wants. "Besides, a lot of people will need killing before this is over." She shifts her weight and winces. "Help me get her home."

Simon sighs and obeys, crouching to take Helene into his arms. Her skin is feverishly hot.

Mary catches his hand before he can stand, nails piercing skin. "If you ever hit me like that again, I'll have your balls for a gris-gris bag."

He just nods, face carefully flat, and lifts Helene.

Outside it's raining, the sky opened up to wash the city clean. Mary limps beside him as he carries the newborn dragon into the world.

Teeth grinding on teeth

Joshua Hackett

Teeth grinding on teeth
Lips torn, tastes like a crime scene
Kissing the right way

Smoke & Mirrors

The circus was in town.

Not just any circus, either, but Carson & Kindred's Circus Fabulatoris and Menagerie of Mystical Marvels. The circus Jerusalem Morrow ran away to join when she was nineteen years old. Her family for seven years.

She laid the orange flyer on the kitchen table beside a tangle of beads and wire and finished putting away her groceries. Her smile stretched, bitter-sweet. She hadn't seen the troupe in five years, though she still dreamt of them. Another world, another life, before she came back to this quiet house.

Cats drifted through the shadows in the back yard as she put out food. The bottle tree—her grandmother's tree—chimed in the October breeze: no ghosts tonight. Glass gleamed cobalt and emerald, diamond and amber, jewel-bright colors amid autumn-brown leaves. Awfully quiet this year, so close to Halloween.

Salem glanced at the flyer again as she boiled water for tea. Brother Ezra, Madame Aurora, Luna and Sol the trapeze artists—familiar names, and a few she didn't know. She wondered if Jack still has the parrots and that cantankerous monkey. The show was here until the end of the month.

It's the past. Over and done. She buried the paper under a stack of mail until only one orange corner showed.

Salem woke that night to the violent rattle of glass and the sound of wind keening over narrow mouths. The bottle tree had caught another ghost.

She flipped her pillow to the cool side and tried to go back to sleep, but the angry ringing wouldn't let her rest. With a sigh she rolled out of bed and tugged on a pair of jeans. Floorboards creaked a familiar rhythm as she walked to the back door.

Stars were milky pinpricks against the velvet predawn darkness. Grass bent cool and dry beneath her feet. A cat shrieked across the yard—they never came too near when the bottles were full. The shadows smelled of ash. Gooseflesh crawled up her arms, tightened her breasts.

"Stay away, witch."

Salem spun, searching for the voice. Something gleamed pale on her roof. A bird.

"Get away!" White wings flapped furiously.

The wind gusted hot and harsh and glass clashed. Salem turned, reaching for the dancing bottles.

A bottle shattered, and the wind hit her like a sandstorm, like the breath of Hell. Glass stung her outstretched palm and smoke seared her lungs. She staggered back, stumbled and fell, blind against the scouring heat.

Then it was over. Salem gasped, tears trickling down her stinging cheeks. The tree shivered in the stillness, shedding singed leaves.

Cursing, she staggered to her feet. She cursed again as glass bit deep into her heel; blood dripped down her instep. The burning thing was gone, and so was the bird.

Salem limped back to the house as quickly as she could.

For two days she watched and listened, but caught no sign of ghosts or anything else. She picked up the broken glass and replaced the shattered bottle, brushed away the soot and charred leaves. The tree was old and strong; it would survive.

At night she dreamed.

She dreamed of a lake of tears, of fire that ate the moon. She dreamed of ropes that bit her flesh, of shining chains. She dreamed of trains. She dreamed of a snake who gnawed the roots of the world.

On the third day, a bird landed on the kitchen windowsill. It watched her through the screen with one colorless round eye and fluffed its ragged feathers. Salem paused, soapsuds clinging to her hands, and met its gaze. Her shoulder blades prickled.

It held a piece of orange paper crumpled in one pale talon.

"Be careful," she said after a moment. "There are a lot of cats out there."

The bird stared at her and let out a low, chuckling caw. "The circus is in town. Come see the show." White wings unfurled, and it flapped away. The paper fluttered like an orange leaf as it fell.

Salem turned to see her big marmalade tomcat sitting on the kitchen table, fur all on end. He bared his teeth for a long steam-kettle hiss before circling three times and settling down with his head on his paws. She glanced through the screen door, but the bird was gone. The bottles rattled empty in the cool October breeze.

That night she dreamed of thunder, of blood leaking through white cloth, shining in the moonlight. No portent, just an old nightmare. She woke trembling, tears cold on her cheeks.

The next morning, she wove spells and chains. She threaded links of silver and bronze and hung them with shimmering glass, each bead a bottle-snare. They hung cool around her neck, a comforting weight that chimed when she moved.

As the sun vanished behind the ceiling of afternoon clouds, Salem went to see the circus.

The Circus Fabulatoris sprawled across the county fairgrounds, a glittering confusion of lights and tents and spinning rides. The wind smelled of grease and popcorn and sugar. Salem bit her lip to stop her eyes from stinging.

It had been five years; it shouldn't feel like coming home.

She didn't recognize any faces along the midway, smiled and ignored the shouts to *play a game, win a prize, step right up only a dollar*. Ezra would be preaching by now, calling unsuspecting rubes to Heaven. Jack would be in the big top—which wasn't very big at all—announcing the acrobats and sword-swallowers. He'd have a parrot or a monkey on his shoulder. It was Tuesday, so probably the monkey.

She found a little blue tent, painted with shimmering stripes of color like the northern lights. *Madame Aurora*, the sign read, *fortunes told, futures revealed*.

Inside candlelight rippled across the walls, shimmered on beaded curtains and sequined scarves. Incense hung thick in the air, dragon's blood and patchouli.

"Come in, child," a woman's French-accented voice called, hidden behind sheer draperies, "come closer. I see the future and the past. I have the answers you seek."

Salem smiled. "That accent still ain't fooling anyone."

Silence filled the tent.

"Salem?" Shadows shifted behind the curtain, and a blonde head peered around the edge. Blue eyes widened. "Salem!"

Madame Aurora rushed toward her in a flurry of scarves and bangles and crushed Salem in a tea rose-scented hug.

"Oh my god, Jerusalem! Goddamn it, honey, you said you'd write me, you said you'd call." The fake French accent gave way to pure Georgia as Raylene Meadows caught Salem by the shoulders and shook her. She stopped shaking and hugged again, tight enough that her corset stays dug into Salem's ribs.

"Are you back?" Ray asked, letting go. "Are you going on with us?"

Salem's heart sat cold as glass in her chest. "No, sweetie. I'm just visiting. A little bird thought I should stop by." She looked around the tent, glanced at Ray out of the corner of one eye. "Has Jack started using a white crow?"

Ray stilled for an instant. "No. No, that's Jacob's bird."

"Jacob?"

"He's a conjure man. We picked him up outside of Memphis." Her lips curled in that little smile that meant she was sleeping with someone, and still enjoying it.

"Maybe I should meet him."

"Have you come back to steal another man from me?"

Salem cocked an eyebrow. "If I do, will you help me bury the body?"

Ray flinched, like she was the one who had nightmares about it. Maybe she did. Then she met Salem's eyes and smiled. "I will if you need me to."

"Where can I find Jacob?"

"In his trailer, most likely. He's between acts right now. It's the red one on the far end of the row."

"Thanks. And don't tell Jack or Ezra I'm here, okay? Not yet."

"You gonna see them before you disappear again?"

"Yeah. I'll try." Laughing voices approached outside. "Better put that bad accent back on."

The wind shifted as she left the cluster of tents and booths, and she caught the tang of lightning. Magic. The real thing, not the little spells and charms she'd taught Ray so many years ago.

Jack had always wanted a real magician. But what did a carnival conjurer have to do with her dreams, or the angry thing that so easily broke free of a spelled bottle?

She followed the tire-rutted path to a trailer painted in shades of blood and rust. A pale shadow flitted through the clouds and drifted down to perch on the roof. The crow watched Salem approach, but stayed silent.

Careless humming inside broke off as Salem knocked. A second later the door swung open to frame a man's face and shirtless shoulder.

"Hello." He ran a hand through a shock of salt and cinnamon curls. "What can I do for you?" His voice was smoke and whiskey, rocks being worn to sand. But not the crow's voice.

"Are you Jacob?"

"Jacob Grim, magician, conjurer, and prestidigitator, at your service."

"That's an interesting bird you have there."

His face creased in a coyote's smile. "That she is. Why don't you step inside, Miss . . ."

"Jerusalem." He offered his hand and she shook it. His grip was strong, palm dry and rough. She climbed the metal stairs and stepped into the narrow warmth of the trailer.

Jacob turned away and the lamplight fell across his back. Ink covered his skin, greenish with age. A tree rose against his spine, branches spreading across his shoulders and neck, roots disappearing below the waist of his pants.

He caught her staring and grinned. "Excuse my *dishabille*. I'm just getting ready for my next act." He shrugged on a white shirt and did up the buttons with nimble fingers. The hair on his chest was nearly black, spotted with red and gray—calico colors. Ray usually liked them younger and prettier, but Salem could see the appeal.

"How may I help you, Miss Jerusalem?"

She cocked her head, studied him with *otherwise* eyes. His left eye gleamed with witchlight and magic sparked through the swirling dark colors of his aura. The real thing, all right.

"Your bird invited me to see the show."

"See it you certainly should. It's a marvelous display of magic and legerdemain, if I do say so myself." He put on a vest and jacket, slipping cards and scarves into pockets and sleeves.

"Actually, I was hoping you might have an answer or two for me."

He smiled. Not a coyote—something bigger. A wolf's smile. "I have as many answers as you have questions, my dear. Some of them may even be true." He smoothed back his curls and pulled on a black hat with a red feather in the band.

The door swung open on a cold draft before Salem could press. A young girl stood outside, maybe nine or ten. Albino-pale in the gray afternoon light, the hair streaming over her shoulders was nearly as white as her dress. Salem shivered as the breeze rushed past her, much colder than the day had been.

"Time to go," the girl said to Jacob. Her voice was low for a child's. She turned and walked away before he could answer.

"Your daughter?" Salem asked.

"Not mine in blood or flesh, but I look after her. Memory is my assistant." He laid a hand on her arm, steering her gently toward the door. "Come watch the show, Jerusalem, and afterwards perhaps I'll invent some answers for you."

She sat in the front row in the big top and watched Jacob's show. He pulled scarves from his sleeves and birds from his hat—Jack's parrots, not the white crow. He conjured flowers for the ladies, read men's minds. He pulled a blooming rose from behind Salem's ear and presented it with a wink and a flourish. Velvet-soft and fragrant when she took it, but when she looked again it was made of bronze, tight-whorled petals warming slowly to her hand.

He tossed knives at Memory and sawed her in half. She never spoke, never blinked. It was hard to tell in the dizzying lights, but Salem was fairly sure the girl didn't cast a shadow.

She watched the crowd, saw the delight on their faces. Jack had wanted an act like this for years.

But not all the spectators were so amused. A man lingered in the back, face hidden beneath the brim of a battered hat. Salem tried to read his aura, but a rush of heat made her eyes water. The smell of char filled her nose, ashes and hot metal. When her vision cleared, he was gone.

After the show, she caught up with Jacob at his trailer. Ray was with him, giggling and leaning on his arm. She sobered when she saw Salem. The two of them had given up on jealousy a long time ago; Salem wondered what made the other woman's eyes so wary.

"Excuse me, my dear," Jacob said to Ray, detaching himself gently from her grip. "I promised Jerusalem a conversation."

Ray paused to brush a kiss across Salem's cheek before she opened the trailer door. "Try not to shoot this one," she whispered.

"I'm not making any promises," Salem replied with a smile.

She and Jacob walked in silence, away from the lights and noise to the edge of the fairgrounds, where the ground sloped down through a tangle of brush and trees toward the shore of White Bear Lake. The water sprawled toward the horizon, a black mirror in the darkness. She made out a pale spire on the edge of the water—a ruined church, the only building left of the ghost town the lake had covered.

Jacob pulled out a cigarette case and offered Salem one. She took it, though she hadn't smoked in years. Circuses, cigarettes, strange men—she was relearning all sorts of bad habits today. He cupped his hands around a match and she leaned close; he smelled of musk and clean salt sweat. Flickering light traced the bones of his face as he lit his own.

"So, witch, ask your questions."

She took a drag and watched the paper sear. "Who is the burning man?"

"Ah." Smoke shimmered as he exhaled. "An excellent question, and one deserving of an interesting answer." He turned away, broken-nosed profile silhouetted against the glow of the fairground.

"These days he's a train man, conductor and fireman and engineer, all in one. He runs an underground railroad, but not the kind that sets men free." His left eye glinted as he glanced at her. "Have you, perchance, noticed a dearth of spirits in these parts?"

Salem shivered, wished she'd thought to wear a coat. Jacob shrugged his jacket off and handed it to her. "This train man is taking the ghosts? Taking them where?"

"Below. Some he'll use to stoke the furnace, others to quench his thirst. And any that are left when he reaches the station he'll give to his masters."

"What are they?"

"Nothing pleasant, my dear, nothing pleasant at all."

"What do you have to do with this?"

"I've been tracking him. I nearly had him in Mississippi, but our paths parted. He follows the rails, and the Circus keeps to the freeways."

"So it was just bad luck he got caught in my bottle tree?"

"Your good luck that he left you in peace. He hunts ghosts, but I doubt he'd scruple to make one if he could."

"So why the invitation?"

He smiled. "A witch whose spells can trap the Conductor, even for a moment, is a powerful witch indeed. You could be of no little help to me."

"I'm not in the business of hunting demons, or the dead."

"You keep a bottle tree."

"It was my grandmother's. It keeps them away. I like my privacy."

"He'll be going back soon with his load. The end of the month."

"Halloween."

He nodded. "That's all the time those souls have left, before they're lost."

"I'm sorry for them." She dropped her cigarette, crushed the ember beneath her boot. "I really am. And I wish you luck. But it's not my business."

"He takes children."

Salem laughed, short and sharp, and tossed his jacket back to him. "You don't know my buttons to press them."

He grinned and stepped closer, his warmth lapping against her. "I'd like to find them."

"I bet you would. Good night, Jacob. I enjoyed the show." She turned and walked away.

That night Salem drifted in and out of restless sleep. No dreams to keep her up tonight, only the wind through the window, light as a thief, and the hollowness behind her chest. A dog howled somewhere in the distance and she tossed in her cold bed.

Six years ago this winter she'd come back to nurse her grandmother through the illnesses of age that not even their witchery could cure, until Eliza finally died, and left Salem her house, her bottle tree, and all the spells she knew. Years of sleeping alone, selling charms, seeing living folk once a week at best.

We'll always work best alone, her grandmother had said. Salem had been willing to believe it. She'd had her fill of people. The treachery of the living, the pleas and the threats of the dead. Dangerous men and their smiles. Living alone seemed so much easier, if it meant she never had to scrub blood and gunpowder from her hands again, never had to dig a shallow grave at the edge of town.

But she wasn't sure she wanted to spend another six years alone.

October wore on and the leaves of the bottle tree rattled and drifted across the yard. Salem carved pumpkins and set them to guard her porch, though no children ever came this far trick-or-treating. She wove metal and glass and silk to sell in town. She wove spells.

The moon swelled, and by its milk-silver glow she scryed the rain barrel. The water showed her smoke and flames, church bells and her own pale reflection.

A week after she'd visited the circus, someone knocked on her door. Salem looked up from her beads and spools of wire and shook her head.

Jacob stood on her front step, holding his hat in his hands. His boots were dusty, jacket slung over one shoulder. He grinned his wolf's grin. "Good afternoon, ma'am. I wondered if I might trouble you for a drink of water."

Salem fought a smile. "Did you walk all this way?"

"I was in the mood for a stroll, and a little bird told me you lived hereabouts." He raised ginger brows. "Does your privacy preclude hospitality, or are you going to ask me in?"

She sighed. "Come inside."

The bone charm over the door shivered just a little as he stepped inside, but that might have been the wind. She led him to the kitchen, aware of his eyes on her back as they crossed the dim and creaking hall.

The cat stood up on the table as they entered, orange hackles rising. Salem tensed, wondered if she'd made a mistake after all. Jacob held out one hand and the tom walked toward him, pausing at the edge of the table to sniff the outstretched fingers. After a moment his fur settled, and he deigned to let the man scratch his ears.

"What's his name?" Jacob asked.

"Vengeance Is Mine Sayeth the Lord. You can call him Vengeance, though I'm pretty sure he thinks of himself as the Lord."

Jacob smiled, wrinkling the corners of autumn-gray eyes; his smile made her shiver, not unpleasantly.

"Sit down," she said. "Would you like some coffee, or tea?"

"No, thank you. Water is fine."

She filled a glass and set the pitcher on the table amidst all her bottles and beads. Vengeance sniffed it and decided he'd rather have what was in his bowl. Jacob drained half the glass in one swallow.

"Nice tree." He tilted his chin toward the backyard, where glass gleamed in the tarnished light. He picked up a strand of opalite beads from the table; they shimmered like tears between his blunt fingers. "Very pretty. Are you a jeweler, too?"

She shrugged, leaning one hip against the counter. "I like to make things. Pretty things, useful things."

"Things that are pretty and useful are best." He ran a hand down the curve of the sweating pitcher and traced a design on the nicked tabletop. Salem shuddered at a cold touch on the small of her back.

Her lips tightened. Vengeance looked up from his bowl and rumbled like an engine. He leapt back on the table, light for his size, and sauntered toward Jacob. Big orange paws walked right through the damp design and Salem felt the charm break.

"Did you think you could come into my house and 'witch me?"

"I could try."

"You'll have to try harder than that."

"I will, won't I."

He stood and stepped toward her. Salem braced herself, palms tingling, but she didn't move, even when he leaned into her, hands braced against the counter on either side. His lips brushed hers, cold at first but warming fast. The salt-sweet taste of him flooded her mouth and her skin tingled.

After a long moment he pulled away, but Salem still felt his pulse in her lips. Her own blood pounded in her ears.

His scarred hands brushed the bottom of her shirt. "You said something about buttons. . . ."

"Will you help me?" he asked later, in the darkness of her bedroom. The smell of him clung to her skin, her sheets, filled her head till it was hard to think of anything else.

Salem chuckled, her head pillowed on his shoulder. "You think that's all it takes to change my mind?"

"All? You want more?"

She ran her fingers over his stomach; scars spider-webbed across his abdomen, back and front, like something had torn him open. Older, fainter scars crosshatched his arms. Nearly every inch of him was covered in cicatrices and ink.

"Is prestidigitation such dangerous work?"

"It is indeed." He slid a hand down the curve of her hip, tracing idle patterns on her thigh. "But not unrewarding."

"What will you do if you catch this demon of yours?"

He shrugged. "Find another one. The world is full of thieves and predators and dangerous things."

"Things like you?"

"Yes." His arms tightened around her, pressing her close. "And like you, my dear." She stiffened, but his fingers brushed her mouth before she could speak. "Tell me you're not a grifter, Jerusalem."

"I gave it up," she said at last.

"You miss it. You're alone out here, cold and empty as those bottles."

She snorted. "You think you're the one to fill me?"

His chuckle rumbled through her. "I wouldn't presume. Raylene misses you, you know. The others do, too. Wouldn't you be happier if you came back to the show?"

"You don't know what would make me happy," she whispered.

Callused fingers trailed up the inside of her thigh. "I can learn."

He rose from her bed at the first bruise of dawn. "Will you think about it, if nothing else?" Cloth rustled and rasped in the darkness as he dressed.

"I'll think about it." She doubted she'd be able to do anything else.

"We're here through Sunday. The circus and the train." He stamped his boots on and leaned over the bed.

"I know." She stretched up to kiss him, his stubble scratching her already raw lips.

Her bed was cold when he was gone. She lay in the dark, listening to the wind.

Salem spent the day setting the house in order, sweeping and dusting and checking all the wards. Trying not to think about her choices.

She'd promised her grandmother that she'd stay, settle down and look after the house. No more running off chasing midway lights, no more trouble. It had been an easy promise as Eliza lay dying, Salem's heart still sore with guns and graves, with the daughter she'd lost in a rush of blood on a motel bathroom floor.

She didn't want to go through that again. But she didn't want to live alone and empty, either.

The bird came after sundown, drifting silent from the darkening sky. The cat stared and hissed as she settled on the back step, his ears flat against his skull.

"Come with me, witch. We need you."

"Hello, Memory. I thought I had until Sunday."

"We were wrong." The girl lifted a hand, but couldn't cross the threshold. "We're out of time."

Salem stared at the ghost girl. Older than her daughter would have been. Probably a blessing for the lost child anyway—she had a witch's heart, not a mother's.

The child vanished, replaced by a fluttering crow. "There's no time, witch. Please."

Vengeance pressed against her leg, rumbling deep in his chest. Salem leaned down to scratch his ears. "Stay here and watch the house."

As she stepped through the door, the world shivered and slipped sideways. She walked down the steps under a seething black sky. The tree glowed against the shadows, a shining thing of ghostlight and jewels. Beyond the edge of her yard the hills rolled sere and red.

"Where are we going?" she asked Memory.

"Into the Badlands. Follow me, and mind you don't get lost." The bird took to the sky, flying low against heavy clouds. Salem fought the urge to look back, kept her eyes on the white-feathered shape as it led her north.

The wind keened across the hills and Salem shivered through her coat. The trees swayed and clattered, shedding leaves like ashes.

The distended, rust-colored moon rose slowly behind the clouds. Its light was strange tonight, too heavy and almost sharp as it poured over Salem's skin. Then she saw the shadow nibbling at one edge and understood—an eclipse. She lengthened her stride across the dry red rock.

Time passed strangely in the deadlands. They reached the end of the desert well before Salem could ever have walked to town. She paused on the crest of a ridge, the ground sloping away below her. On the far side of the valley she saw the circus, shimmering bright enough to bridge the divide.

"No," Memory cawed as Salem started toward the lights. "We go down."

Salem followed the bird down the steep slope, boots slipping in dust. A third of the moon had been eaten by shadow.

Halfway down, she saw the buildings, whitewashed walls like ivory in the darkness. A church bell tolled the hour as they reached the edge of town. Memory croaked along with the sour notes.

Shutters rattled over blind windows and paint peeled in shriveled strips. The bird led her to a nameless bar beside the train tracks. Jacob waited inside, leaning against the dust-shrouded counter.

Salem crossed her arms below her breasts. "You said Sunday."

"I was wrong. It's the burning moon he wants, not Hallow's Eve." Witch-light burned cold in the lamps, glittering against cobwebbed glass. His eyes were different colors in the unsteady glow.

"Where is he now?"

"On his last hunt. He'll be back soon."

"What do you need me for?"

He touched the chain around her throat; links rattled softly. "Distraction. Bait. Whatever's needed."

"That's what Memory's for, too, isn't she? That's why he was watching your act. You're a real bastard, aren't you?"

"You have no idea."

She reached up and brushed the faint web of scars on his left cheek. "How'd you lose your eye?"

He grinned. "I didn't lose it. I know exactly where it is."

Memory drifted through the door. "He's coming."

Jacob's smile fell away, and he nodded. "Wait by the train station. Be sure he sees you."

"What's the plan?"

"I had a plan, when I thought we had until Sunday. It was a good plan, I'm sure you would have appreciated it. Now I have something more akin to a half-assed idea."

Salem fought a smile and lost. "What's the half-assed idea?"

"Memory distracts him at the train station. We ambush him, tie him up, and set the trapped ghosts free."

"Except for the part where my charms won't hold him for more than a few minutes, that's a great idea."

"We won't mention that part. Come on."

A train sprawled beside the station platform, quiet as a sleeping snake. Its cars were black and tarnished silver, streaked with rust, and the cowcatcher gleamed fang-sharp in the red light.

The platform was empty. Jacob and Salem waited in the shadows. She could barely make out the words White Bear on the cracked and mildewed sign.

"They built this town for the train," she whispered, her face close enough to Jacob's to feel his breath. "But the Texas and Pacific never came, and the town dried up and blew away."

"This is a hard country. Even gods go begging here."

Footsteps echoed through the silent station. A moment later Salem heard a child's sniffling tears. Then the Conductor came into view.

A tall man, dressed like his name, hat pulled low over his face. Even across the platform Salem felt the angry heat of him, smelled ash and coal. He carried a sack over one broad shoulder; his other hand prisoned Memory's tiny wrist. Salem undid the clasp around her neck. The chain slithered cold into her hand. Jacob squeezed her shoulder once. Then he stepped into the moonlight.

"Trading in dead children now?" His growl carried through the still air. "You called yourself a warrior once."

The Conductor whirled, swinging Memory around like a doll. His face was dark in the shadow of his hat, but his eyes blazed.

Jacob took a step closer, boot heels thumping on warped boards. "You fought gods once, and heroes. Now you steal the unworthy dead." He cocked his head. "And didn't you used to be taller?"

"You!" The Conductor's voice was a rasp; Salem shuddered at the sound. "You died! I saw you fall. The wolf ripped you open."

Jacob laughed. "It's harder than that to kill me."

"We'll see about that." He released Memory, dropping the bag as he lunged for Jacob.

Memory crawled away, cradling her wrist to her chest. The chain rattled in Salem's hand as she moved toward them. Jacob and the Conductor grappled near the edge of the platform; she had no clear shot.

Then Jacob fell, sprawling hard on the floor. The Conductor laughed as he stood over him. "I'll take you and the witch as well as the dead. The things below will be more than pleased."

Salem darted in, the chain lashing like a whip. It coiled around his throat and he gasped. His heat engulfed her, but she hung on.

"You can't trap me in a bottle, little witch." His eyes burned like embers. Charcoal skin cracked as he moved, flashing molten gold beneath. A glass bead shattered against his skin; another melted and ran like a tear.

She pulled the chain tighter—it wouldn't hold much longer. The Conductor caught her arm in one huge black hand and she screamed as her flesh seared.

"Didn't the old man tell you, woman? His companions always die. Crows will eat your eyes—if I don't boil them first."

A fury of white feathers struck him, knocking off his hat as talons raked his face. The Conductor cursed, batting the bird aside, and Salem drove a boot into his knee.

He staggered on the edge for one dizzying instant, then fell, taking Salem with him. Breath rushed out of her as they landed, his molten heat burning through her clothes. Her vision blurred and White Bear Valley spun around in a chiaroscuro swirl.

"Jerusalem!" She glanced up, still clinging to the chain. Jacob leapt off the platform, landing lightly in a puff of dust. "Hold your breath!"

She realized what was coming as he stuck his fingers into the ground and pulled the world open.

White Bear Lake crashed in to fill the void.

"Wake up, witch. You're no use to me drowned."

She came to with a shudder, Jacob's mouth pressed over hers, his breath inside her. She gasped, choked, rolled over in time to vomit up a bellyful of lake water. Her vision swam, and she collapsed onto weed-choked mud. Cold saturated her, icy needles tingling through her fingers.

"Did he drown?" she asked, voice cracking.

"His kind don't like to swim." He turned her over, propping her head on his soaking knees. "I could say it destroyed him, if that's how you'd like this to end." Above them the shadow eased, the moon washed clean and white again.

"What could you say if I wanted the truth?"

Jacob's glass eye gleamed as he smiled. "That it weakened him, shattered that shape. He lost the train and its cargo. That's enough for me tonight."

"Not too bad, for a half-assed idea." She tried to sit up and thought better of it. The cold retreated, letting her feel the burns on her arm and hands. "Are you going to thank me?"

He laughed and scooped her into his arms. "I might." He carried her up the hill, toward the circus lights.

Halloween dawned cool and gray. Glass chimed in the breeze as Salem untied the bottles one by one, wrapping them in silk and laying them in boxes. The tree looked naked without them.

The wind gusted over the empty hills, whistled past the eaves of the house. The tree shook, and the only sound was the scrape and rustle of dry leaves.

"Sorry, Grandma," she whispered as she wrapped the last bottle. Light and hollow, glass cold in her hands. "I'll come back to visit."

When she was done, Jerusalem Morrow packed a bag, packed her cat, and ran away to join the circus.

Gingerbread and Time

Snow piles in bone-drifts outside my door, but it's warm beside my oven.

I'm alone in the cottage now. My brother left not long after our stepmother died. Foolish boy—he'd never have found wolfsbane in his tea, but he couldn't trust me. He was little more than sticks bound with skin and rag; I wonder if he'll ever eat without fear again.

Father suffered for months; a little hemlock set us both free.

I'm never hungry now, even this cold winter. I sell cakes and bread in the village, or trade them for things my garden cannot grow. The children love my gingerbread best of all.

Grubby-faced, sticky-fingered creatures—I have no desire to eat them.

Men offer me ribbons to plait in my golden hair, bangles for my white arms. Sometimes they offer me kisses, and sometimes I take them.

But the village is not for me. Neither is this house with its drafty roof and hungry memories.

Deep in the forest, far from any path, lies a ruined cottage. Its walls and windows are gone now, eaten by birds and mice, but no scavengers touch the bones in the hearth.

Her spirit haunts me, moaning in the chimney and rattling icy fingers on the door. She isn't angry anymore, only lonely. I'm lonely, too. Children's laughter and men's kisses cannot sate me.

Spring will come and melt the snow. I will take my baking bowl and favorite spoon, and seeds from the garden. I will take her bones from their bed of ash. We will go into the forest, far from any path, and build a new cottage. It will be built of strong timber, no matter what she says. My garden will bloom rich and fragrant, and the house will smell of gingerbread. Perhaps one day some hungry little girl will smell it and come to me. I have many things to teach.

I will leave no trail of breadcrumbs behind me when I go.

PUBLICATION HISTORY

"Wrack." Originally published in *Strange Horizons*, February 2006.

"Flotsam." Originally published in *Strange Horizons*, August 2006. Reprinted in *Mermaids and Other Mysteries of the Deep*, Paula Guran, ed.

"Ebb." Originally published in *Not One of Us* 37, 2007.

"Dogtown." Originally published in *Strange Horizons*, June 2006.

"The Garden, the Moon, the Wall." Originally published in *Ideomancer*, September 2006. Reprinted in *Running With The Pack*, Ekaterina Sedia, ed.

"The Salvation Game." Originally published in *Fantasy*, Sean Wallace & Paul Tremblay, eds.

"Blue Valentine." Originally published in *End of an Aeon*, 2011. Bridget McKenna & Marti McKenna, eds.

"Snakebit." Originally published in *Strange Horizons*, April 2014.

"The Tenderness of Jackals." Originally published in *Lovecraft Unbound*, 2009. Ellen Datlow, ed.

"Wounded in the Wing." Originally published as "Pinion" in *Not One of Us* 40, 2008.

"Catch." Originally published in *Weird Tales* 347, November-December 2007.

"Ghostlight." Originally published in *Not One of Us* 39, 2008.

"Smoke & Mirrors." Originally published in *Strange Horizons*, November 2006. Reprinted in *Best New Romantic Fantasy 2*, Paula Guran, ed. Reprinted in *Circus: Fantasy Under the Big Top*, Ekaterina Sedia, ed.

"And in the Living Rock, Still She Sings." Originally published in *Aeon Speculative Fiction* 8, August, 2006.

"Snake Charmer." Originally published in *Realms of Fantasy*, October 2006. Reprinted in *Magic City: Recent Spells*, Paula Guran, ed.

"Aconite & Rue." Originally published in *On Spec* 78, Fall 2009.

"Gingerbread and Time." Originally published in *Cabinet des Fees*, May 2006.

"Red." Originally published in *Brave New Love: 15 Dystopian Tales of Desire*, 2012. Paula Guran, ed.

AUTHOR'S NOTE

When I started writing short fiction seriously back in 2005, I had a grand cosmology sketched out—a combination of mythology, Lovecraftian mythos, and plot arcs for several planned novels. Many of these stories were written with that cosmology in mind. Things change, however. Ideas evolve. Novel plots adapt and crumble. So I'm left with a collection of orphaned stories. Mosaic tiles that don't form the picture they were supposed to. They make a nice fossil record, though, and some of them may yet seed larger works. I owe many thanks to Elise Matthesen for her Artist Challenge program. Her jewelry inspired nearly half the contents of this collection. The *They Fight Crime!* generator also gave me several story prompts, even if my characters are more likely to commit crime than fight it.

ABOUT THE AUTHOR

Amanda Downum is the author of the *Necromancer Chronicles—The Drowning City, The Bone Palace*, and *Kingdoms of Dust*—published by Orbit Books, and *Dreams of Shreds & Tatters*, from Solaris. Her short fiction has appeared in *Strange Horizons, Realms of Fantasy, Weird Tales*, and elsewhere. She lives in Austin, TX. Her day job sometimes involves dressing up as a giant worm.